CW01497143

WHAT LIES
BENEATH THE CAIRN

WHAT LIES
BENEATH THE CAIRN

BOOK FIVE OF THE LLANGYNOG MURDERS

JANET NEWTON

KINDLE DIRECT PUBLISHING

This is a work of fiction. Names, characters, organizations, and incidents are either a product of the author's imagination or are used fictionally.

Cover photo of Welsh sheep by Janet Newton

For my first readers:
Lori, Beth, Arlene, Bonnie, & Julie –

You encouraged me more than you know!

NOTE TO READERS:

Unfamiliar Welsh words can be daunting to readers who aren't familiar with the language. Here are some pronunciations for the names I use most often in my books.

Llangynog	Lang-a-nog
Pennant Melangell	Pennant me-LANG-geth
Carnarfon	Ca-NAR-von
Twlwyth Teg	tell-WITH-teg
Pysgotwr	pes-NOT-were

WHAT LIES
BENEATH THE CAIRN

Chapter One

The ferry jolted and began to glide away from its mooring, waves slapping against the sides with a staccato pulse. Almost immediately, the main engines engaged and propelled the ferry into the Irish Sea at speed, trailing a glorious spray that had the passengers on the aft deck lifting cameras. There was no turning back now; she was off to Ireland.

Not that she wanted to turn back. Bronwyn Bagley stood in the lee on the outside deck behind the passenger cabin and watched Wales fade until the faint shoreline disappeared entirely. She knew her fiancé Will Cooper would have watched as long as the ferry was visible, but by now he'd have returned to his car and driven off toward Caernarfon, where he'd work for the next few days until her return. They shared a cottage in her home village of Llangynog, but he kept a flat in Caernarfon for the days he was required to work at the North Wales Major Crimes main station, an hour and a half's commute away. Her being gone was an opportunity for him to catch up with paperwork and to convince his bosses that, after a rocky spring, he could be trusted again to comply with the departmental policies he'd ignored then.

Truth be told, she'd been looking forward to going to Ireland ever since Will had proposed to her. Her childhood friend Margred had married an Irish boy named Michael Byrne and moved to Dublin shortly after they'd finished school. Bronwyn had made the trip over once that first year to visit Margred, but only the once, instead depending on Margred's yearly visits home and occasional phone calls to keep their friendship alive. She never seemed to have the extra money to finance the trip, other priorities sadly taking precedence over their friendship. If she were honest, these days her closest friend was probably Janice Hatcher, the psychologist at St. Melangell's Centre where they both worked, but since she'd served as Margred's maid of honor six years before, she knew it would be expected that Margred would be honored in the same way when Bronwyn's time came.

So now, she'd arranged a few free days off work so that she and Margred could celebrate her engagement by shopping together for Bronwyn's wedding dress. Margred had chatted happily about shops and lunch in the city, and Bronwyn anticipated giggles and a hoped-for renewal of their former closeness. Her parents had sent her with their credit card and instructions to buy whatever struck her fancy, no matter the cost. Bronwyn smiled at that. They knew that her tastes were pretty simple.

The crowd drifted into the cabin as the ferry settled into the journey. Bronwyn thought she should probably do the same, but she lingered for a moment, feeling the August sun on her face. She could hear nothing beyond the roar of the engines, and there was little to see but the wide expanse of water, but the air felt fresh on her face and sunshine sparkled the white caps on the water. She closed her eyes and took deep breaths, drawing in the salty tang of the air and tasting it on her tongue, wanting to experience a different face of nature than she was used to enjoying. She waited for a moment, hoping for more, but the pounding of the engines drowned out any other sounds she might have heard. She opened her eyes and pulled open the door.

Inside, a low rumble of voices filled the silence, with the occasional clamour of a child's voice piercing quiet conversations. A snack bar offered sandwiches and soups, but a slight queasiness in her stomach put her off eating. She chose a seat in an empty row, settled in, and watched the horizon, waiting for Ireland to appear in the distance, finally closing her eyes against the vague nausea and drifting into a light doze.

A shift in the background noise woke her two hours later. Around her, people were setting aside paperback books, gathering trash for the bins, and checking their seats for stray belongings as they prepared to return to their vehicles. She sat up straighter in her seat and looked to the front of the cabin where large windows offered a view of land rapidly approaching. Ireland!

Thank goodness, she thought, although the nap seemed to have dispelled most of the queasiness. She watched the activity for a minute, and then reached for her rucksack, nestled on the floor at her feet. Since she had no vehicle to return to, she could go out onto the outside deck to watch as the ferry docked. Now that they'd nearly arrived, she was excited to get off the ferry and find Margred.

Margred was waving from the waiting area, a grin on her face. "You look great," she enthused, "like a girl in love!"

Bronwyn blushed. "That sounds like blarney. You've been in Ireland too long." She directed her gaze at Margred. "You look beautiful, yourself." She hadn't seen Margred since her last visit home, more than a year ago now. She and Michael usually visited Margred's parents in the summer, most often in July, but this year they'd postponed their visit until September because of Bronwyn's wedding. When she'd last seen Margred, Bronwyn and Will weren't even dating yet. So much had changed in the past year. "How are you feeling?"

Margred was expecting her second child just before Christmas. Her firstborn, a girl named Cara, was two years old. "I'm good now, but it was rough going the first few months. Did I tell you? This one's a boy. We're calling him Conor."

"I love it, a fine Irish name for an Irish lad."

"Yes, we wanted a name that'd fit in." She gestured toward Bronwyn's bag. "Come on, let's get on the road. We've got about an hour's drive to Skerries, and I want to avoid rush-hour when we pass by Dublin. We'll take the train tomorrow when we go into the city to shop." Margred grinned again. "It's going to be such fun!"

Bronwyn followed her to the car park. She dug her mobile out of her bag to phone Will and let him know she'd arrived while Margred unlocked a Toyota Corolla. She knew that Margred and Michael had bought a house in Skerries, which was on the coast north of Dublin, and she was a bit envious of how settled Margred was, with a home of her own, babies, and a decent job as a hematologist in a clinic in the city. She guessed that prices were more affordable in Skerries than in Dublin itself, and Margred had shared that they thought it a nicer place to raise their family, even if it did mean a commute to work.

"I'm sorry we can't have a real hen party," Margred interrupted her thoughts once they were seated. She gestured toward her tummy, which

3

was a bit rounded behind the steering wheel. "I didn't plan my family with you in mind, I'm afraid, so there'll be no drinking for the two of us this weekend."

Bronwyn pulled a face. "I'm sure you thought that I'd never find someone. You couldn't wait forever."

Margred backed out of the parking space. "You're younger than a lot of brides," she said, "and it sounds like the wait was worth it. I can see that you're a happy lady these days. He must be something special."

"I can't wait for you to meet him." Bronwyn watched out the window as they drove through the car park, unused to seeing either the fishing boats on the harbour side or the glass-fronted white-washed buildings across from it. She knew that Dublin wasn't far, but even out here at Dun Laoghaire, civilization dominated the landscape. "It must seem strange to be maid of honor in a wedding where you haven't even met the groom."

"My fault." Margred waited for an oncoming car and then pulled out onto the roadway. "I was the one who moved to another country."

"I miss you," Bronwyn confessed, knowing it was true. She had no girlfriends to meet up with when Will was stuck working in Caernarfon and she was left home alone, no one to talk to about her most intimate problems. She glanced at Margred. "It's not the same just talking on the phone."

Margred returned the look, smiling. "We'll get all caught up this weekend, and it'll be like we were never apart. I want to hear all about this detective of yours. I know how you met, but you haven't really told me how you came to be living together or what happened with that big case of his last spring. I gathered you knew what he was doing?"

"I knew some of it."

"And you probably can't tell me everything. I'm sure a lot of it is still top secret." She made it sound exciting, like a spy movie.

The truth was that Will hadn't told Bronwyn much other than what she'd gathered from the news coverage. He didn't like to talk about it, and she knew he struggled with memories that haunted him. "About all I can say is that I was terrified for him because I knew he was really worried about it. I didn't want to lose him, not after I waited so long to find him." She paused, not wanting to confess that she'd helped him

4

with clues she'd gotten from the Welsh fairies, the Twlwyth Teg. Of course, Margred knew about her past, that she'd innocently announced to her primary school class that she saw the Twlwyth Teg and been relentlessly bullied for it afterwards. Margred had been the only one of her classmates who'd been willing to ignore her peculiarities and be her friend. But Margred didn't know she still saw them, and heard them, too. And Margred didn't know about Pysgotwr, the forest spirit who was her oldest friend, nor about the visions she saw in the pool of water. As close as they'd been as children, some secrets had to be kept from nearly everyone, including Margred …and even Will.

She decided it was time to change the subject. "What colour do you want your bridesmaid dress to be?"

"I get to choose?"

"Yes, I want you to."

Margred mulled it over. "It's an autumn wedding, or late summer anyway, so fall colours would be appropriate. Yellow, maybe? Or a bronzy brown? Not orange!"

"No, not orange," Bronwyn agreed, relieved that they'd moved onto something less personal to talk about. Being with Margred felt more awkward than she'd anticipated. They'd drifted apart through the past few years, and she supposed it'd take some time to get the old ease back into their friendship.

Margred and Michael's home was lovely, smack in the middle of a row of brick-fronted cottages, each with a different colored door. Their door was red, and Margred had amplified the colour with bright red geranium borders around their tiny front garden.

Michael had beaten them home, even with a stop to pick Cara up from her nursery school. He greeted Bronwyn with a hug. "We're so glad you came," he declared, handing his daughter off to her mother. "You have no idea how much Margred has been looking forward to this."

"Well, she's not the only one," Bronwyn told him, with a sideways glance at Margred. She smiled at Cara. "Hello, darling girl. You look like your daddy." She dug into her bag and pulled out a gift bag. "I brought you something from Pennant Melangell." She held it out.

Cara stared at her and then hid her face against her mother's chest. Margred hugged her tightly. "Give her a little while to get used to you. She's at that age when everyone's a stranger."

"Well, I am a stranger," Bronwyn pointed out, holding onto the gift bag because she didn't know what else to do with it. "She was tiny when I saw her last." She felt the awkwardness again the minute the words left her mouth and regretted them.

There was a moment of silence, and then Michael took a breath. "Why don't Margred and Cara show you the spare room while I get us some drinks? There's nothing but tea for Margred, I'm afraid, but I have a nice red wine if you'd like some of that, Bronwyn, or there's whiskey."

"Red wine sounds nice," Bronwyn told him, hefting her bag and following Margred down a hallway. "But don't fuss over me."

"No fuss," Michael called as he headed to the kitchen. "It's rather nice having someone to share a drink with these days."

"I won't let him go to the pub after work," Margred explained as she stopped at a doorway and stood back. "Here's the spare room. It's going to be Conor's nursery when he arrives, so it's good you came while it was still available."

"It's perfect," Bronwyn told her. It was small, with a daybed that might just about be big enough for her to sleep on. It's a good thing Will hadn't wanted to join her on this trip. If they visited in the future, they'd have to find lodging elsewhere.

"I'll let you settle in, then, while I change someone's nappy." Margred grimaced. "I'll meet you in the living room when you're ready. Michael is in charge of dinner tonight, so you and I get to relax."

And relax, they did. The awkwardness Bronwyn had felt earlier finally dissipated with the wine and the easy conversation, and she couldn't help wondering whether she and Will would come across as welcoming when they had visitors in the future. Michael was handsome in the Irish way, dark-haired and fair skinned, with an easy lilt to his voice and an infectious grin that accompanied an acute sense of humor. He carried the conversation, drawing Bronwyn out with queries about Will and about her own job at St. Melangell's Centre, while recounting his own stories and teasing Margred whenever he found the chance. She found herself giggling as she cast glances Margred's way. For her part, Margred only rolled her eyes.

They stayed up until nearly midnight, and when they finally decided to call it a night, Bronwyn realized that she hadn't called Will other than that brief call when she'd first arrived in Ireland. *It's probably too late*, she told herself, but she wondered if he'd waited up for her call. She debated her options while she brushed her teeth and changed into her pyjamas, and then she got into bed and pulled his number up on her phone. He might think it too late, but she felt a need to hear his voice.

"You must be having fun," he observed when he answered, his voice sardonic.

"I am," she told him, feeling guilty. "I'm sorry it's so late. We got busy talking, and time just went by."

He went quiet for a moment. "I'm teasing you. Just enjoy yourself, right? This is your weekend away to have fun with your friend. Don't worry about poor me, back here stuck in the office, working."

Now she definitely felt guilty. "How's it going there? Were you busy today?"

"It was pretty quiet here. I'm on rota with Beth this weekend. We spent most of the day at the office, doing paperwork. The rumours are that we might be getting someone new in by next week."

"A replacement for Notley."

"Yes, and hopefully someone easier to work with. Meanwhile, we're short-staffed here, so I'll be surprised if nothing turns up for us."

"I hope you don't get a big case in the next day or two."

"If we do, I'll still come meet you off the ferry on Saturday. Bowers knows about that."

"But it'd keep you there afterwards, most likely, and I'll be wanting to go home to the cottage with you, not by myself. I miss you already, and I know I'll have lots to tell you." A little nudge wouldn't hurt. It was Will's fault they were short a detective so he tended to take on more than his share to compensate. "If our shopping spree is all Margred promises it to be, I'll have things to show you, too."

"I'm not meant to see your dress until the wedding."

She could hear a smile in his voice now. "Obviously, I'm not going to show you *everything*. There are secrets a girl has with her girlfriends that absolutely have to stay between them." She meant it jokingly, but instantly regretted her words. *Why did I mention secrets?* She kept most of the same secrets from Will as she did from Margred and everyone else, letting him think all the information she got for his cases came from her visions, which she'd been forced to acknowledge when he'd seen her trance as she'd looked into her favorite little pool of water. She'd die if he knew about the Twlwyth Teg and Pysgotwr.

"Secrets, huh? And here, I thought we had no secrets between us these days." His voice faded away. He had to know that some of her information came from other sources than her visions, but he never asked. She thought he didn't really want to know. "Tomorrow you're going into the city?"

"Yes, Margred made plans for us to take the train in and to spend the entire day in the city. Michael is taking care of their little girl, Cara." Relieved that he'd left the subject of secrets behind, she launched into a description of Margred's house and what she'd been able to see of Skerries, and from there they lapsed into easier conversation that left her feeling in synch with him again by the time they'd said goodnight and she'd drifted into sleep.

They decided to walk to the train station the next morning, strolling past a big stone church with a picturesque graveyard up on a hill above it that would have drawn Bronwyn in to explore, had they had more time. They followed a paved walking path over a little stream where swans swam among the reeds, and they stopped on the bridge, Bronwyn closing her eyes to smell the water and the decaying grasses on the shore, and listening for the swish of water as the swans glided by. After that, they continued on past several windmills that Margred told her proudly were on the national historic register. Skerries was a pretty little town, and Bronwyn made a point of telling Margred that she thought so, watching as she beamed with pride.

The train took them into Dublin through lush green countryside, and they emerged from the station ready to shop. Margred had done some research and had a list of shops she wanted to visit, so they set out with a sense of purpose, thinking that they could do some sightseeing afterwards, if they accomplished their task in a timely manner.

They bypassed the first shop entirely when they found it, Bronwyn protesting that the window displays were far too fancy for her tastes. Margred didn't push her, but instead, nodded in a knowing way. "I thought you'd want something simple," she said. "You never were one for dressing up fancy."

"That's just it," Bronwyn agreed, relieved. "I do want a long, white dress, of course, but no lace and no glitter. Will says I'm a jeans and tee shirt type of girl, and he's right."

Margred consulted her list. "I put a star by a couple of the shops," she said, "because they seemed to offer dresses that were more of what I thought you'd want." She smiled at Bronwyn. "There's one just down the street a block or so. Let's go check that one out."

Two hours later, they'd browsed through five shops, they'd bought a bridesmaid dress for Margred in a shimmery bronze, and Bronwyn was debating between two dresses that she thought might serve. It was in the sixth shop, though, that she found the perfect one. Sleeveless, of creamy white crepe, it draped her body softly in an A-line to the floor, with a small train that puddled behind her. She gazed into the mirror, liking what she saw, and then she stepped out for Margred to see.

Margred caught her breath. "It's perfect!" She stared for what seemed a long moment, and then she recovered. "I mean, I love it if you do. Do you like it?"

Bronwyn nodded. "I think it's just what I was looking for." She twirled slowly. "Does it look good from the back?"

"Oh, yeah," Margred murmured, "it looks good. You have to buy it."

"Yes, I think so." Bronwyn tried to reach the price tag, but couldn't see it.

"Don't look," Margred advised her. "This is the dress you want, so you're going to buy it, no matter what it costs."

"But if it's thousands of pounds?" Bronwyn protested.

"It won't be."

And it wasn't, making it perfect in every way.

9

They left the dress to be shipped to Bronwyn at home and wandered away to find someplace for a nice lunch out, Bronwyn's treat. The earlier awkwardness she'd felt with Margred had disappeared and it felt as if they'd never been apart. In the end, she was glad she'd chosen Margred as her maid of honor rather than Janice. It felt right.

The restaurant featured good china and real cloth serviettes on the tables, while oak-paneled walls preserved the elegance of a time long past. Mullioned windows let in just enough light to keep the interior from being too dim, while giving it an ambiance of intimacy. Will would no doubt enjoy the tug of history created by a place that had served Dublin's elite through a couple hundred years, and Bronwyn thought it would be a memory for her and Margred, sharing a hen party lunch in such a place. She pulled out her mobile and snapped selfies of herself and Margred, smiling into the camera.

They ordered elaborate salads and tea and settled in for a good chat. Bronwyn had enjoyed their visit the previous night, but there were topics they'd avoided with Michael present, as nice as he was. Now she hoped that she and Margred could get into more personal subjects.

"Tell me more about Will," Margred demanded as their salads arrived on the table.

"I don't know what to say," Bronwyn protested, but just for show. She wanted to talk about Will. She wanted to brag. "You know how we met, when Glynnis died and I was a suspect in the case."

"You didn't tell me at the time that you were meeting him in secret so you could help solve the case, though." Margred picked up her fork and looked through her salad, mixing the chicken on top into the rest. She took a forkful into her mouth and chewed. "I'd think that'd be the sort of thing you'd tell your best friend."

"At the time, it didn't mean anything." Bronwyn pursed her lips and shook her head. "I mean, I can't say I wasn't hopeful that he wanted to see me for more than just clues in the case, but I didn't want to imagine it being more than it was." She thought for a moment. "If I'd told you that I wanted to keep seeing him and it didn't develop into a real relationship, you'd have pitied me."

"I never would." Margred grinned back at her. "But you liked him right off the start?"

Bronwyn took a sip of her tea. "Yes, I did," she admitted. "There was something about him." She stared off into space, remembering. "He was just that little bit reckless, like he wasn't afraid to go behind his partner's back if he thought he could accomplish more by doing it, the rules be damned. He was really nice to me, and he was always considerate. Maddock liked to say he'd been raised to be a gentleman. Of course," she smiled self-consciously, "he's quite good looking, too."

"Hmm….I suppose he is, at that. From what I can see from pictures you've sent, anyway. Tall, dark, and handsome."

"It's not my fault you haven't met."

"No, it's not, not really. We see my parents four times a year, but they come here every time except summer, and as you said, you and Will weren't together a year ago." Margred's eyes shone with merriment. "But, back to Will, he kept coming around after the case was finished, even though you lived so far away? That's really very romantic."

Bronwyn didn't want to share that he hadn't called again for three months, not until another case brought him back to Llangynog. "We didn't really start dating until fall."

"And then you moved in together in January."

"That was a surprise. We were struggling to try to figure out how to make things work at a distance, and it wasn't going very well. I nearly called you to talk it over." She set down her fork. "There are things you need a girlfriend for when you want to talk, and neither Mum nor Mai would do."

"It had to be awkward, you living at home still."

"That was the biggest issue. I love Mum and Dad, but I didn't think Will wanted to date a child, and that's how I felt. I went to Caernarfon for Christmas Eve and ended up spending the night, but that just made me feel guilty. Things weren't working out." She smiled. "I couldn't afford a place of my own, and I needed advice."

"And I was far away in Ireland with my own life."

"What would you have told me to do?"

Margred considered that while she took a sip of her tea. "I'd have told you to leave Llangynog behind and move to Caernarfon."

"And afford that, how?" She hadn't wanted to leave Llangynog; her role as guardian gave her a responsibility there. But Margred couldn't know that, so she fell back on the obvious: money issues.

"You could have moved in with him."

"I didn't know if he'd want that. We'd never talked about it at all, and Christmas Eve was our first night together, so it was too soon for discussions about living together. At least, I thought it was. And then Will found that cottage. He didn't ask me if I wanted to share it with him until he'd already found it, and I realized afterward that he was afraid I'd say no if I had time to think about it."

"I can just see it. Him, showing you the cottage, all nervous about whether you'd be horrified by the whole idea, and you standing there all agog, with your mouth hanging open." She set her fork down beside her plate. "You didn't need me, after all. It sounds like he handled it for you."

That pretty nearly described it. "He still has his flat in Caernarfon for the days he has to be in the office, and usually he gets three or four nights a week at the cottage, or more if he isn't working late and can come home. Sometimes he stays more often now because his chief super decided it'd be good to have a detective on the eastern side of the district. That's helped a lot. I'm still alone some of the time, though."

"You're okay with that?"

Bronwyn shrugged. "I have my dog, Daisy, and my family is always around if I'm lonely. Work keeps me busy, too."

"You like your job?"

"I do like it, quite a lot." She described the nature meditations she'd been conducting through the summer, feeling proud. "I feel like I've found my purpose there. I was hired as the coordinator, but I've been able to expand my responsibilities to a point where I really feel I'm helping people. I like to think I'm carrying on St. Melangell's mission, if that doesn't sound too corny."

Margred studied her. "You've changed, Bron. You used to be so quiet and self-contained. Now, you've really come into your own. Is it Will who's changed you, or is it your job?"

Bronwyn thought about it. She *had* changed; she knew she had. When she'd first met Will, she'd been so insecure that she'd worried over everything. Now, she knew that Will wasn't going anywhere, and she was confident that she was a valuable member of the team at the St. Melangell's Centre, as well. She used to have to gear herself up to go out on a date or to lead a group at the centre, and now she took it all in stride and enjoyed both. "Maybe I just finally grew up," she admitted, with a wry grin.

"You said it would be a small wedding. Who's coming?" Margred wanted to know.

"Maddock will be there." Bronwyn remembered the crush Margred had on her brother, back in their school days. "With his wife and kids. Maegan is going to be a flower girl."

"Of course Maddock is going to be there. Why wouldn't he be?" Margred shook her head. "I'm over him now, you know. I've been over him for a long time."

"Yes, but there's nothing like a first love," Bronwyn teased her.

"Yeah, well…" Margred's blush told Bronwyn more than her words did.

Bronwyn decided to rescue her. "I've invited Janice from work and her partner Catherine, and the Reverend Wycliff will be conducting the service. He's technically my boss. Will's best man is his friend Edward, who worked with him on that big drug bust in the spring, and he's invited the other detectives from his office and his boss, too. Whether they can come will depend on the workload at the time, so cross your fingers that no one murders anyone around mid-September."

"You've met them all?"

"Yes, everyone but Ian O'Flynn. Will's not as close to him, but he thought he should include him with the others."

"And Will's family?"

Bronwyn grimaced. "They're a bit of a challenge, but his mother and father will be there, and his niece Lark is going to be a bridesmaid, too. I don't think his brother George is willing to come all the way from Canada for us, though."

"I've thought you might be struggling with them a bit, just from the little you've said."

Bronwyn had thought about confiding in Margred, but it hadn't seemed right to complain about her future in-laws over the phone. How

13

could she explain? "Let's just say that I'm not exactly what they had in mind for Will."

Margred's eyebrows went up and her mouth twisted. "What does that mean?"

"It means they'd have liked a daughter-in-law who'd go to the theatre with them, or to fancy charity events, or to, I don't know," she thought wildly, "luncheons out with important people."

"I'm not important?" Margred teased.

"You know what I mean." She'd felt so out of place with Will's mother the first time she'd met her that she'd wanted to scream, or cry, afterwards. He'd said it didn't matter, that he hadn't expected anything different. She'd only seen her twice since she and Will had gotten engaged, and both times she'd had the impression that Mrs. Cooper was trying harder to connect with her. They'd exchanged mobile numbers, out of courtesy, and if Bronwyn still felt uncomfortable around her, she couldn't put the blame entirely on Elizabeth Cooper. It was no one's fault that they came from different worlds, with vastly different interests and lifestyles. Neither had gone so far as to call the other, though, and Bronwyn suspected Mrs. Cooper was as happy about that as she was.

"You still don't know if Lark is going to be living with you and Will?"

Bronwyn shook her head. "Will's mother hired a nanny for the summer, and, after a lot of argument, she's agreed to let Lark have a year at boarding school in Wales to see how it goes before she decides whether to ship her off to George in Canada or whether to let us take her on holidays and weekends instead. Somehow, she's convinced herself that Will's job keeps him from being a fit parent, so she'd rather send her off to live with strangers than let her stay with us, and that's sad because Lark really loves being with us. The thing is, she really can't manage Lark when she's not away at school anymore, not with Will's dad having Alzheimer's. Agreeing to give it a try this year was a big concession for her, but I have to say that Will worked hard for that. She's definitely a control freak, and Will is the one she likes to manipulate most."

"Has Lark visited at all this summer, then?"

"Twice, for a few days each time. Neither of us could get much time off this year since we wanted time away for our wedding and honeymoon, so it's been difficult, and the nanny wanted the work, so that complicated things, too. Will's mother uses our limited time off against us, of course. We were actually surprised when she agreed to let Lark attend St. John's on the Hill this autumn, in Chepstow. Will looked at all the private schools with boarding options, and that one wasn't his mother's first choice, but she agreed to it because it's less than an hour's drive for her when she goes to pick her up. It's closer to us, as well, but still a couple of hours away."

"And you want her with you? I mean, she isn't really your child, and the two of you are just starting off with married life. The last thing you need is a kid right now."

"No, we really want her," Bronwyn protested. Will loved Lark, and she loved Will, so if they could have her, she'd be happy to welcome her into their home. They'd be a family, the three of them, and hopefully it would all work out fine. "She's a real sweetheart, easy to have around," she added defensively. At least, she had been so far, but she suspected that a visiting child was different from one who lived in the household full-time. She couldn't seem to stop herself talking. "Lark will be at school a lot of the time once she gets settled. They have tons of fun activities on the weekends for the boarders. We'll still have time alone." She looked pleadingly at Margred, whose skeptical look said more than words could. "Really, it'll be the best of all worlds." She tried to say it with confidence, but truthfully, she was still trying to convince herself that it was true. With their workloads, she and Will wouldn't have much time together except on the weekends, and that's when Lark would be with them, unless she surprised Bronwyn and really did want to stay weekends at school. It wouldn't be as easy as she tried to convince Margred it would be; she knew that.

By the time the weekend was over, Bronwyn's goodbye hug for Margred was heart-felt. "I'll miss you until the wedding," she blurted. "I had such a great time."

15

"It's only a few weeks," Margred pointed out, "and we'll talk every Friday night on the phone. Friday's good?"

"Yeah, Will usually comes home on a Saturday night when he gets off work, so Friday's great." She suspected that, despite their promises to each other, their weekly calls would taper off again after the wedding, but for the time being, she'd be thankful to have a sounding board for any concerns or last-minute jitters. Margred was easier to talk to about those things than her mother or her sister-in-law Mai.

She waved at Margred from the ferry, her arm arcing high as the ferry shifted away from its docking and out into the water. She'd had a lovely time, truthfully, and she'd found the perfect dress for what she hoped would be a perfect day. Will would be waiting for her on the other side of the sea in a few hours' time. She settled into contentment. The life she'd dreamed of really did seem within reach these days, lingering doubts aside. She was sure that Lark would never be a burden to them, and as for the secrets she still kept from Will, that was how it had to be. There were just some things Will couldn't ever be told.

Chapter 2

Will had watched the ferry disappear into the sea, missing Bronwyn already, but resigned to the idea that he could catch up in the office without regretting the time away from her for a change. He'd miss her, of course. He'd surrendered a year ago to the fact that she needed to be a part of his life. But he'd survived just fine in his little studio flat before he'd moved to the cottage with her, and he wanted her to have a fun weekend away with her friend before the wedding.

He knew she was stressed about the wedding, despite it being a small affair. Bronwyn didn't like being the centre of attention, but her wedding day gave her no choice. He'd happily agreed to the small guest list, and there'd never been a choice about the venue; that little Norman church of St. Melangell's was tightly woven into Bronwyn's life. Truthfully, now that they'd decided to be married, he was ready to have it done and over so they could get on with their lives. The actual ceremony itself was just fluff to please everyone else.

Things had been good between them the past few months. Early in their relationship, she'd often been insecure and tended to worry about little things, some of which he still didn't really understand. After they moved in together, though, all of that disappeared and the easy partnership he craved grew stronger every day. Life was good.

He glanced at the time as he slid into his car and wondered if he could call and talk to Lark. It would pass the time as he drove, and he always enjoyed her lively chatting. The problem was, would the nanny answer the phone, or would it be his mother?

He'd had to walk a tight line these past few months, coddling his mother along to the idea of Lark going to school in Wales rather than moving to Canada to live with his brother George's family. She'd finally agreed reluctantly to St. John's on the Hill in Chepstow, more because it accepted children at age seven and Lark wouldn't be eight until later in the autumn than because it seemed to Will a good compromise for the time being with its location easily accessible to them both.

The nanny would be gone when school started, so he'd have to work hard to prove that he and Bronwyn could provide a steady home for Lark when she wasn't living at school. He'd asked for a day off the first weekend of September so they could get her settled at school, and they planned to have her home at their cottage the first weekend after that, at least. He hoped she'd be settled enough to want to stay the weekend at school after the wedding, so they could have their honeymoon. If not, he'd have to beg his mother to take her, and that wouldn't set well.

Things would be challenging for a while, until they all got used to the new normal. He was sure that Lark would enjoy her weekends at school more than she did at her grandmother's. They had plenty of fun activities for the weekend boarders. The problem was that Lark loved spending time with him and Bronwyn where there was a dog to play with and a pony to ride, so convincing her that school was more fun than that might be a different story.

If things worked out, he thought he could move to the next stage of his plan after the first year. He didn't want to just provide a back-up home for Lark on weekends and holidays; he wanted full custody of her so that decisions affecting her life would be his to make, not his mother's. Yes, his parents had sacrificed a lot taking in their orphan granddaughter three years ago, but now that his father demanded so much time and effort with his illness, her living with them was no longer an option. Lark needed parents of the right age, parents who would commit to attending her sports or musical events and who would be happy to host her friends on weekends from time to time. He and Bronwyn could be those parents far easier than his mother could.

And it would be a huge step forward not having to deal with her manipulating him through Lark.

He decided against the call and settled into the drive. The first part took him along the coast, and he was tempted to stop in some picturesque little village for fish and chips, but now that he'd set his sights on work for a couple of days, he didn't want to make the trip any longer than necessary. Lingering resentments and questions about his venture into unauthorized undercover work in the spring had him trying hard to make amends by doing more than his share and toeing the line. His chief superintendent, Marcus Bowers, had trusted him enough to look the other way during that operation, and in the end, Bowers had taken the action that had saved Will's life. He was more than grateful, would always be. He was determined not to be a thorn in Bowers' side any longer.

He parked his little MGF in the employees' car park, putting up the convertible top and locking it before going inside. He nodded to the duty clerk, stopped by the locker area to throw his kit bag into his bin, and strolled through the open plan room toward his desk.

"All quiet?" he asked Beth Holway as he brushed past her desk. She was his assigned partner for the week; it was their turn to work together on the rotation. Bowers didn't like the idea of permanent partners in his building so their assignments changed weekly, unless they were working a big case.

She nodded and pushed away from her computer, rolling her shoulders and then looking up at him. "Nothing brewing so far. I've been catching up on other stuff."

He knew she had a court case to testify in coming up. "The Clark case?"

"Yes. It's fine. We did it all by the books, but you don't want to look a fool on the stand when you forget some little detail or other."

He flicked on his computer. "I almost hope we get a case this weekend, just to pass the time. Something simple, not too complex."

"Bronwyn's off to Ireland?"

"Yes, off to buy a wedding gown with her maid of honor."

"Dublin's a fun place to celebrate. I hope she behaves herself over there."

"No worries. Margred is pregnant. No drinking other than tea, I'm afraid."

Beth laughed and turned back to her own computer screen, picking up a pen to jot notes on a yellow legal pad. He'd suspected when they'd first worked a big case together that she was interested in him as more than a work partner, so at the time he'd exaggerated his relationship with Bronwyn in order to discourage her. Now they'd become friends, and he was never unhappy when the rotation put them together.

The day passed slowly, with no new cases to call them out. He accepted Beth's invitation to meet her for a drink after shift, but declined her suggestion that they extend it to dinner out somewhere afterwards. He liked Beth, but sometimes she still came too close to crossing the line between them, and he didn't like to encourage her too much. A microwave dinner in his little flat would suffice, and that way he'd be home in case Bronwyn found the time to call him.

He was a little disappointed when she didn't, but he tried not to take it personally. He'd expected that she'd be having fun with her friend, after all. When she finally called after midnight, she woke him from a restless sleep. He shook himself awake and tried to put affection into his voice as they talked, and he thought himself a great success. After, he slept more soundly.

His office time remained uneventful until the next afternoon when Beth's desk phone rang. Will watched her as she answered it, guessing that it would be a case for them to investigate.

She picked up her pen, listened for a minute and then scribbled on a notepad. She gave Will a slight nod to let him know it was a case call before asking a question that he couldn't hear. She scribbled again, listened, and then hung up.

He closed his computer and snatched his warrant card from a drawer. "What is it?" he asked Beth, who'd pulled her own kit from a drawer and stood up.

"Sounds like a domestic," she told him, "in Bangor."

At least it wasn't far away, probably about twenty minutes, if that, unless there was traffic. "Let's take my car," he suggested, thinking of the nice August evening.

She scowled at him. "We'd look silly driving up in that. And what if we need to take someone in?"

"Put them in a panda car with a couple of constables?" he suggested, but he shrugged the idea off. She wasn't wrong. They'd look more professional arriving in one of the department vehicles, and that would give them more authority if they needed it.

They checked out a very conventional black Ford Focus, and Will slid into the driver's seat. "You have an address?"

Beth entered it into the sat nav, her fingers running quickly across the screen. "I didn't get much information from the desk sergeant. A neighbor called it in. 'A fight,' she said, 'between two men,' but I'm guessing there's a woman involved in there somewhere, too."

"At least it shouldn't be too complicated," Will told her as he pulled out into traffic. "We'll arrest them both and then figure out which one is guilty, if not the both of them."

"Easy, peasy," Beth agreed. She glanced out the window, relaxing into the seat. "Gossip says we're getting a new detective later this week."

"I heard. It's about time," he grumbled. "We've been down a man for nearly four months."

"Losing Sean was difficult," Beth murmured, with a sideways look at Will. "Not that I'm blaming you. It was his fault as much as yours."

"I had no choice," Will said, repeating what he'd said over and over in the past months. It was just bad luck that put him on rotation with Notley at a time when the last thing he needed was a partner who hated him. He and Notley had a history. He couldn't trust him not to betray him. He'd had no choice but to go behind Sean's back again, and this time their chief super had sided with Will. Notley had resigned in embarrassment when it was over, and Will still felt guilty about that. He hadn't intended his going rogue to cost anyone else their career. He'd thought he was just risking his own.

The sat nav directed them off the motorway and into a residential neighborhood of 1980s homes. Some had been nicely kept up with neat gardens and fresh paint, while others featured weedy patches alongside the curb and unmown lawns. A herd of panda cars, joined by a fire engine and an ambulance, blocked the roadway ahead of them.

They pulled up to the constable standing beside the roadblock and held up their warrant cards. "What do we know?" Will asked as Beth leaned toward the driver's window to listen.

"It's not good," the constable replied. "Apparently, the homeowner was meant to be away at work, but he came home early and caught the wife in bed with her boyfriend. They took a few swings at each other, and then the boyfriend went out the window. The homeowner called us, and we sent a car out to search for him. They gave it up after an hour or so, figuring he was gone." He straightened and squared his shoulders, glancing back up the street toward the house. "He eventually went back to the house, whether to retrieve his belongings or whether to challenge the homeowner, we don't know. What we do know is that they got into it in the living room, and in the end the boyfriend was taken away in an ambulance." He looked at Will. "He was unresponsive when they carried him out."

Will swallowed, closing his eyes for a minute. This might turn out to be a bigger case than they'd anticipated. "Any updates on his condition?"

"Nothing yet," the constable said. "They're treating the homeowner inside. He'll probably have to go to hospital to be checked out, as well."

"The wife's inside, too?"

"She saw the whole thing, along with their two daughters who were home for it all. Little girls, about seven or eight years old. She's sent the girls to a neighbor's house for the time being."

Will nodded and double tapped the side of the car out the window. "Okay, thanks for the information. We'll just go on in and see what more we can figure out."

The constable nodded, and they drove nearer to the house, parking behind another patrol car. They walked up to the door, where they were handed crime scene suits, hats, and booties.

Inside, broken furniture littered the room, Glass from a smashed decanter speckled the carpet, and there was a fist-sized hole in one wall. Three crime scene technicians bent low, picking up bits of material and squinting at what looked like spatters of blood, while others took photographs, their flashes strobing the dimness of the room. A man sat on a stuffed chair, ignoring the constables who stood on both sides and looking dazed as he watched the activity.

Will led the way over to him. "Sir," he said, but the man didn't look up at him. Will squatted down in front of the man, giving him no where to look but into Will's face. "Sir, I'm DCI Will Cooper. I'd like to ask you a few questions before they take you to hospital."

"I don't need a hospital," the man growled. He tried to look around Will, but couldn't see past Beth, who stood behind him. "I'm not hurt."

He looked hurt, bruises and cuts turning his face into a monstrous apparition. One eye was swollen nearly shut, and blood dripped from his nose into a sparce graying beard. He wasn't a big man, but he looked strong, with tree-trunk arms and hard-muscled thighs.

"Can I get your name, sir?" Will pushed him.

He reached up and rubbed at his swollen eye. "Rhett Vaughan," he mumbled.

"You live here?"

Vaughan nodded.

"Who else lives here?"

"My wife Olwen, and our daughters."

"Where do you work, Mr. Vaughan?"

"I'm a fisherman. A commercial fisherman." He tried again to look past Beth. "What are they picking at out there?"

Will tried to regain eye contact with him. "It's how we do things, sir. They'll pick up tiny bits of everything they find and look to see if it's evidence somehow."

"They know we fought," Vaughan pointed out. He frowned and reached for his eye again, touched it briefly, and then returned his eyes to Will's. "It's pretty obvious, isn't it?"

"Yes, sir, but we have procedures to follow."

"Let's get this over with, then. What do you need to know?"

"Why did you come home early today?" Will's knees hurt from squatting. He thought briefly about moving Vaughan somewhere else, but didn't want to interrupt his currently cooperative attitude.

"The boat had engine trouble, so we came back to harbour early. There wasn't any sense to me hanging around, so I came home."

"Tell me what happened when you got here."

Vaughan's gaze jerked up, and Will looked around to see Beth standing behind him with a kitchen chair in her hands. "I thought you might like to sit," she told him. "I don't think we'll mess the scene up too much if we use the chairs. I'll get one for myself, too."

He straightened and then perched thankfully on the chair. "Thanks," he told her. She'd be sympathetic. Her knees didn't hold up so well these days either. He looked back at Vaughan. "Sir, can you tell me about when you got home?"

"I came in, and the girls were sitting here watching the telly. They know I don't like them doing that during the daytime. It's one of our rules. No daytime telly."

Beth set a chair next to Will's. "Sorry, I didn't mean to interrupt."

Will turned back to Vaughan. "No daytime telly. Did that set you off? Make you angry?"

Vaughan considered the question. Any sign of temper now seemed gone. "It didn't make me happy. I asked them where their mum was, and they said upstairs."

"Did they turn off the telly?" Will wondered if the boyfriend had a warning that all was not right.

"No. I had a feeling then, an idea that Olwen was sneaking around behind my back. Letting the girls watch the telly wouldn't just be a treat for them; it'd give her the freedom to do something out of their sight."

Will nodded. "Did you say anything more to them? Ask them more questions?"

"I could see that Nora, the older one, looked guilty, like she knew mummy was in trouble, but she couldn't see how she could help her. She said she'd get me a beer and I could watch telly with them." He shook his head. "She was trying to help her mum out, but she's not clever enough to make it work."

"What did you do then?"

"I went upstairs." He slumped against the back of the chair and looked toward the ceiling. "They must have heard me, though, because when I opened the door, he already had his pants half on. He grabbed a lamp off the table and threw it at me, and then he pulled his pants up and jumped out the window."

Will could picture it, like a comedy in the movie theatres. "Did you try to follow him?"

"There was no sense in that. I threw Olwen's clothes at her and walked out. Then I called 999 and reported a burglar."

Will glanced at Beth. She hadn't said anything yet, letting Will use the rapport he was building with the man to advantage. She gave him a half-smile and waved her pen at him.

"So, the police came, but they couldn't find the man. Is that right?" Will asked.

"They asked us some questions, got his name and all, and then they drove around to see if they could find him." He shrugged. "I guess you know they didn't. They stopped by again after about an hour and said they were giving it up, but that we should call back if he showed up again."

"And he did," Will surmised.

"I sent the girls to their bedroom, and then Olwen and I had it out. We were going at it hard when he sneaked back in the door. I wouldn't have heard him with all the yelling we were doing, but I saw Olwen's face change, and I knew he was here. I turned around, and he was swinging a walking stick at me." He touched his eye again. "That's where this came from. Fair stunned me for a minute, it did, but I charged right back at him and that was that. Olwen called 999 while we were fighting, and by the time the police got back here, he was down for the count." He seemed a bit proud of his prowess, not worried about what damage he might have done.

Will nodded. "That should do us for right now, sir. I'll let you go in the ambulance to get checked out, and we'll be in touch if we have more questions."

Vaughan licked some blood off his lips. "I'm not sorry. Are you married?"

Will shook his head. "Engaged."

"My advice is, don't go through with it. It's not worth the trouble in the end." Vaughan tried to grin, but it came through as a grimace. "Run away while you still can."

They carried their chairs to the kitchen, where Olwen Vaughan was sitting at a table, waiting for them. She was a pretty enough woman, petite and dark-haired, with smudged mascara and a cut on her lip marring her potential. She wore slim jeans and a glittering tee shirt with a heart painted in sequins.

"Mrs. Vaughan, can we ask some questions?" Beth took over once they were seated across the table from her. "May I call you Olwen?"

She drew a shuddering breath and glanced at Will. It seemed he was destined to carry out their interviews on this case. "Olwen's fine."

He waited, but Beth was silent, so he started the interview. "We understand you had a friend over today while your husband was at work? Is that right."

Her lips twisted. "You'd might as well call him my boyfriend. It's obvious that's what he was."

Will nodded. "Okay. What's his name?"

"Thomas. Thomas Perkins."

"How long have you been seeing Thomas?"

"He goes by Tom." She thought for a minute, and then she smiled. The blood on her lip welled, and she brushed a tissue at it. "We've been together for about three months. It was going fine for us until today. Who would have thought the boat would have trouble, and Rhett would come home early and find us? I worried more that one of the girls would say something, and he'd find out that way."

It took a load of thoughtlessness to carry on an affair with your children right there in the house with you. He thought of Lark, and felt his dislike for this woman curl his gut. "Tell us about what happened when your husband came home."

Her story, when she'd given them the details, matched her husband's almost exactly. "Tom just came back for his things," she insisted when she'd finished. "He didn't come back to fight with Rhett, but when he saw us going at each other, it pushed him over the edge. He wanted to protect me, that's all."

That's unlikely, Will thought, but he didn't say it aloud. A man just retrieving his possessions would hardly swing a walking stick at his girlfriend's husband. He'd try to sneak in and back out without being seen, especially if they were distracted. "How did the fight start?" he asked instead.

She thought about it, obviously trying to find a spin that would make her boyfriend look more innocent than he was. Finally, she mumbled, "Tom hit Rhett with the walking stick."

Bingo. He was sure the children would confirm that detail, making Thomas Perkins the initiator of the incident and probably absolving Rhett Vaughan of any crime.

They got a few more details, thanked her, and then walked across the street to interview the two girls, lookalikes who looked thrilled to be important enough to talk to the police.

"Mummy's friend comes over a lot," said Nora, the older one who told them she was nine. She looked at Beth uncertainly. "I know that wasn't right, but we promised mummy we wouldn't tell on her."

"He hit our daddy," added Tricia, the younger at six. "He hit daddy with the stick, and then daddy fought him and won." She beamed with pride, and Will felt sick.

Will walked away with a profound anger toward both parents. Those little girls shouldn't have had to witness a fight that might well turn out with a man dead, and nor should they have been asked to keep their mum's affair a secret from their dad.

And his mother thought him an unfit parent for Lark. He shook his head. Even with his work schedule and the fact that he was really just her uncle, he'd give Lark a much more stable life than those two little girls had. He wondered what their future would hold. Would the parents stay together after this? He didn't know how they could manage it, but he hoped for the girls' sake, they'd work out some arrangement that'd be more stable.

An hour after they returned to the station, typing their notes into a case file, Beth got another phone call. She waved Will over.

He came around to her side of their adjoined desks and waited.

She mumbled a thank you and hung up the phone. "Thomas Perkins never regained consciousness. He was declared dead about fifteen minutes ago."

Will looked at Beth, who returned his gaze. "What do you want to do?"

He took his time, running it over in his head. "Thomas Perkins initiated the fight. Rhett Vaughan called the police in right away, and it wasn't his fault they couldn't find Perkins before he returned to the house. Could he have stopped beating the man before he killed him? Probably. But I don't see where we have anything that couldn't be construed as self-defense here. Both times, it was Perkins who initiated the fights. Perkins could have stayed away and gotten his stuff back another time."

"So, no charges?" Beth surmised. "It doesn't seem right. He did murder the man, in the end."

"We'll run it all past Bowers tomorrow when he's in, but I don't see how we can make a case that a decent solicitor wouldn't tear apart in a wink. I'd say we recommend no charges, if you agree."

Beth nodded. "I can't see how it can be any different."

"If anyone, we should charge the mother," Will reflected. "Who does that? Carry on an affair with the kids in the next room, and them old enough to figure out what's going on?"

"Swearing them to secrecy," Beth added. "It almost makes Dave look good, that." Beth seldom had anything good to say about her ex-husband, so that was significant.

"I'm sure Dave would like to hear you're softening up on him," Will teased her. "I'll have to let him know what you're saying behind his back."

"You'll never meet him," Beth told him firmly. "I don't want him anywhere near my personal life anymore."

"But there's Liam." Beth and Dave shared a now-sixteen-year-old son.

"You make one mistake, and it haunts you for life." Beth laughed, and then she elaborated. "Liam's never been a mistake. The mistake was Dave." She bit her lip. "You still have time to back out, Will."

Yeah, and maybe you want to move into Bronwyn's place. "Never," he said firmly. "I'm committed now."

The next morning, Chief Superintendent Bowers sat in his chair, listening intently to their summary of the case. He asked questions as they went, and he took some time to look over both the case notes and the autopsy report. "What forensics found backs up the husband's story?" he wanted to know.

"It does," Will admitted.

"Then I think we can close this one." He looked at them each in turn. "Sometimes the wrong person gets away with what they shouldn't, and there's nothing we can do about it."

"Maybe the wife learned something from it," Beth ventured. "She won't repeat that mistake again, I bet."

"If the marriage lasts." Bowers looked at Will. "You have time to write up the last notes on this case before you leave for Fishguard?"

"Yes, sir, I can do that." Bronwyn's ferry wouldn't arrive until evening.

"Enjoy your day off tomorrow, then, and we'll see you on Tuesday."

"Thank you, sir. I hear we're getting someone new in this week?"

Bowers frowned. "Office gossip being what it is, I guess I'd might as well admit that's true. Where did you hear it?"

"Beth told me." Will threw her under the bus.

Bower's eyebrows went up as he turned to Beth. "And you? Where did you get that information?"

"From Betty," she told him, naming one of the duty clerks.

"Well," Bowers said with some satisfaction, "Betty got it wrong."

Beth and Will exchanged looks. "But we really need another detective, sir," Beth blurted.

"That we do. We've been short-handed for longer than we should have been," Bowers complained good-naturedly. "The population's growing, the budget is tight…they're giving us two, not one."

"Two new men?" Beth sounded as astonished as Will felt.

"One new man and one new woman," Bowers clarified.

That should lighten the workload, Will thought. Having two new detectives might free him up for more assignments on the east side of the district. It couldn't hurt. "That's great," he said, meaning it. Maybe Notley's resignation would turn out to be a good thing, even if he did still feel guilty about his part in it.

Will watched for Bronwyn to emerge from the queue inside the ferry terminal.

She saw him waiting and skipped the last few steps to his waiting arms. He hugged her close. "Did you have fun?" he murmured into her hair. "How was Margred?" He pulled away and looked at her.

"It was great," she enthused. "I wish I could show you my dress. It's so perfect."

"I want to wait, to do it right," he told her. "You will look beautiful, though. I already know that." He kissed her and released her, leading her through the little reception room and out the door.

She stumbled and reached for him. "I never can walk right after being on the ferry," she said with a sideways glance. "It feels like the walkway is swaying."

He took her arm. "Then I'll steady you." That's what they did for each other, he thought. She steadied him with her calm peacefulness, and he liked to think he made her more self-assured.

"Are you staying tonight?" she wanted to know. He'd said he could when she'd talked to him that morning, but if a case developed afterwards, he'd have to work.

"I'm totally yours," he told her, and it was true. It had been a hard commitment to make, but he knew it was the right one for him.

Chapter Three

They arrived home late, made slow by the ferry's afternoon arrival time which put them on the roads during rush hour. Clouds darkened ominously as they drove into the Tanat Valley, thunder rumbling over the mountains in the distance. The first raindrops spattered the windscreen when they stopped by Bronwyn's parents' place to get their Labrador Daisy. They had to jog to the car through a sudden squall afterward, thunder now crashing as lightning strobed the sky.

Bronwyn called in an order for takeout from the New Inn from the car and then ran through the drenching rain to fetch it while Will waited in the car for her with Daisy. With the lightning came the threat of a power outage, and she thought it was better to dash through the rain than to skip a decent dinner.

She stopped in the doorway coming out, her hands full of carrier bags. The rain pelted down in buckets, and she prepared to scurry toward the car, hunched down and head ducked low. Just as she tucked her head down against the rain, though, a shadow against the stone wall across the street froze her in place. She lifted her head and stared.

The wolf-like creature stared back at her, nearly invisible against the wet, grey stone wall. The hair on its back created a ragged ridge as it alerted on her presence, and she felt a jolt of terror, squinting back at it through the rain. It was a Cwn Annwn, a mythological dog-like creature whose presence foretold a death. In her experience, it had foretold two that she knew of.

Panic shook her as she watched it. The first time she'd seen one, the old wise woman of the village, Granny Powers, had died, leaving the guardianship of Pennant Melangell to Bronwyn. The second sighting had resulted in the death of her former schoolmate, Glynnis Paisley. Who would it be this time? There was no knowing, but God forbid it might be someone she loved: one of her parents, Maddock, Mai, one of their children – or Will.

The creature stood still, watching her. A flash of lightning lit the sky, giving her a better view of its wiry mottled coat and yellow eyes. She winced at the crash of thunder that followed, and when she looked again, it had gone.

She started across the street, wary of it but wanting to see it more closely, wanting to see if it was still there, but just invisible in the misty darkness.

"Bronwyn! Where are you going?"

Will's concerned voice brought her back to the reality of her situation. From his position in the car, it'd look like she'd lost her mind, wandering across the street away from where he waited for her despite the soaking downpour. How could she explain her actions? He'd surely see the panic on her face and that, alone, would tell him something had happened.

She took a breath, wheeled around, and hurried to the car, pulling the door open and sliding inside. "Sorry," she mumbled, not meeting his eyes. She set the bags by her wet feet and turned her face toward the passenger window. "I thought I saw something out there, a dog. I thought it would be frightened by the storm. If I could have caught it, we could have taken it home until we found whoever it belongs to."

"I didn't see anything," he commented as he put the car in gear. "What kind of dog?"

"A little spaniel," she lied, her mind turning to the first thing she could think of, "over by the wall. It was hard to see through the rain. I was closer than you were." Pysgotwr would forgive her describing his dog Michelangelo rather than the Cyn Annwn. Maybe. *Does he know that I keep secrets from Will?*

32

Will shook his head, but he let it go, steering the car to the left and increasing speed as he drove toward their lane.

She had to regain control of herself before they got to the cottage. She assumed that the Cyn Annwn appeared to her only when the death of someone she knew was imminent. She'd concluded that because she hadn't seen one when Will's cases involved people who were strangers to her. But who could it be? Until she knew that, she'd have to try to mask her worry, or Will would know something was up. *Deep breaths*, she told herself. *Don't think about it.* But how could she not?

As they ate their dinner in the conservatory, Bronwyn pushed herself into tales of her visit to Dublin, knowing that she was being too chatty but hoping that Will would put it down to excitement over her holiday with Margred and the upcoming wedding. When she had exhausted her inventory of stories, she listened with scant attention to Will's summary of the case in Bangor, wondering as she half-listened if she could invent an excuse for calling her parents again. She'd seen them when they'd stopped by for Daisy, and everything had been fine then. Surely, nothing had changed in the past hour. But she worried.

An hour later, Will finally left her alone in the conservatory while he went to take a shower. It was just after nine in the evening, dark except for occasional flashes of distant lightning, which had diminished as the storm passed beyond the valley. She'd managed to push her concern to the back of her mind, at least temporarily, although it wasn't buried deeply enough not to continue gnawing at her. She'd thought she'd take Daisy out for a quick stroll in the garden after she finished cleaning up, and maybe once outside, she could find an excuse to call and check on her family, just to ease her mind.

Daisy's barking alerted her, and her earlier terror came flooding back. She hadn't heard the knock on the door, and nor had she seen the car's headlamps from the kitchen. Shushing the dog, she went to the door and opened it.

Her father and brother stood there, dripping water from their jackets.

Her heart went into overdrive. They wouldn't come that time of night unless something had happened. "What's wrong?" she blurted.

Her dad shuffled his feet on the mat. "It's probably nothing, love. It's just Evan Bennett hasn't come home, and Gwniera's worried. She called us about an hour ago and asked if we'd help search for him."

"We called a few other neighbors and went out to look, but so far we haven't found anything," Maddock added. He looked past her and grinned mischievously. "We thought it might be time to get the local police involved."

Bronwyn glanced over her shoulder to see Will, wearing nothing but his boxer shorts, emerging from the hallway. She felt her face grow hot, but she ignored Maddock's obvious amusement as relief overshadowed her embarrassment. "It's our neighbor, Evan Bennett," she called over to Will. "It looks like he's gone missing." Guilt tempered the relief then as she realized what that meant. She hadn't really liked Evan, but being glad it was him the Cyn Annwn had appeared for and not someone else brought remorse along with the relief. But was he dead, or just missing again? Evan had made a habit of disappearing through the years. Until they knew for sure, she couldn't totally discount it being someone else who was meant to die.

"You'd need to put on your pants," Maddock instructed Will, feigning seriousness, "unless you're willing to face the rest of the neighbors dressed like that."

Will nodded, suppressing his own grin, but he stood his ground. "Come inside and sit down so you can tell us what you know."

Daisy dashed ahead of them as they hung their wet jackets on the wall rack, took off wet boots, walked into the living room, and sat down on the sofa, leaving the two chairs for Bronwyn and Will. Bronwyn patted her knee to call Daisy nearer and grabbed onto her collar, pushing her down to the floor beside her chair. The storm had her agitated, which sometimes made her forget her training.

"When did he go missing?" Will asked as he wandered back into the living room. He'd made a stop in the bedroom and now looked perfectly comfortable as he pulled jeans up over his boxers, zipped them up, and settled into the chair.

"Gwniera says he called just before six. He'd been out working in the field nearest our property line, out near the wooded area where the hillside gets steep. He told her that he went to drive back in the quad, and it wouldn't start up. He was going to walk back.

"She wouldn't go get him?" Will leaned forward, his hands tented together on his lap as he concentrated.

"She says that she didn't want to leave the dinner. It'd have taken her a half hour, more or less, to go pick him up. He said he'd walk back." Bronwyn's dad leaned back on the couch and frowned. "It'd be a stretch of the legs, but if he cut across the pastures, he'd make it in a half hour, most likely. I can see where she'd not want their supper to burn."

Will nodded. "So, he'd have been home around half-six."

"Just before the storm hit, so that wouldn't have been a problem. But he wasn't home by then." Maddock took over. "She says she waited until seven, and then she left the dinner cooling and went out to look for him."

"She walked across the pastures in the storm?"

"She drove to where he was working first. The quad was there, but she didn't see him on the road, so she left the car there and walked back the way she thought he'd go. She had rain gear on, but it would have still been a tough slosh getting home once the storm got going."

"When she didn't find him, she called me," Bronwyn's dad spoke up, "and I called Maddock and a few other neighbors. We thought she might have missed him earlier in the storm, so we searched until it got too dark to see anything, then we went back to get her car and took her home." He looked at Bronwyn. "Your mum is staying with her until we figure out what's happened."

Will thought it over. "I'd think she'd see some sign of him, if he set out for home. Maybe he changed his mind." He looked from Bronwyn to her dad and brother. "Would you consider him reliable? I mean, is it possible that he decided to go into the village for a drink at the pub after he talked to her, or maybe even to a girlfriend's? Isn't it possible that, when his wife wouldn't leave the meal to fetch him, it made him mad so he decided to go drink it off?"

Bronwyn had been watching the conversation in silence, wondering how she could urge them to search further for Evan without them wondering why she was pushing the action. She glanced at her dad. She didn't like to tell tales out of school, but everyone in the village knew

35

about Evan. "He does have a bit of a reputation," she admitted, "but if he's missing and Gwniera is worried, someone needs to keep looking for him. He did tell Gwniera he was walking home."

Will's focus sharpened; she could see it happen. He looked at Maddock. "Did anyone check the pubs?"

"I stopped by. They hadn't seen him."

"He couldn't have gone far without a vehicle," Bronwyn pointed out. She wondered when and where they'd find him. Wherever it was, it wouldn't be in a pub.

"A girlfriend?" Will pushed them.

Bronwyn's dad nodded. "Could be. Like Bronwyn said, he has a past."

"You know who she is? You checked with her?"

"Jenna lives in Bala," Maddock said. "He couldn't get there without a vehicle. I don't think he's seen her for years, anyway, but it might be that there's someone new he's seeing."

"Who might have picked him up. If the wife said no, maybe he called her after, and she was more agreeable." Will glanced at Bronwyn.

She could tell he didn't want to spend the night out looking for someone who might well be cuddled up with a girlfriend. Who would? "Maybe you should talk to Gwniera first," she suggested, "and then decide what to do. She might know if he was having another affair." She couldn't tell them she'd seen the Cyn Annwn and that it was more possible that Evan was dead than with a girlfriend or in a pub. "I think we should look for him, in any case."

Will nodded at the two men. "I'll go with you to the house, if that's okay."

"I'll come, too," Bronwyn offered. "If you do go out searching, I could help, especially if you decide that he might have gone into the forest. I know those woods better than anyone."

"No." Will's voice left no doubt how he felt about it.

"She's right, mate" Maddock argued. "I don't want to get in the middle of things here, but Bronwyn does know every little hidey hole in those woods. If he's out there, she'd have a better chance at finding him than the rest of us would."

If the Twlwyth Teg will help me, I'll find him for sure, Bronwyn thought, *pasture or forest or wherever he went.* "He said he was walking home across the pastureland, not the woods," she pointed out, "but we'll need to search both if Gwniera's sure he's disappeared."

Maddock was watching her. He knew. He knew everything. He was the only one who did, and he knew only because his little daughter, Maegan, was like Bronwyn. "If there's no sign of him between the quad and the house, I say we look in the woods next." He directed his gaze at Will. "I'll stick with Bron if we go out, keep an eye on her. She does really know those woods. Anyway, maybe we won't have to go, depending on what Gwniera has to say."

Will had watched the exchange with more interest than Bronwyn felt comfortable with. "I'll just put some more clothes on, then," he said, "and we'll be on our way. You go on ahead of us," he nodded at Maddock, "and we'll come along as soon as I'm ready." He looked at Bronwyn's dad. "Don't talk to her until I get there. I want to ask the questions."

"Sure," her dad answered easily. "I want to stop by the house first anyway. We'll bring all the torches we can find. Anything else?"

Will shook his head. "Not that I can think of."

To Bronwyn's relief, Will didn't delve into the topic of Maddock's offer to keep track of her in the forest. Logically, of course, Will would be the one to stay near to her if they went out searching. He must wonder why Maddock had blurted out the offer, but maybe he put it down to the fact that he hadn't wanted her to be involved, and Maddock wanted to assure him that he'd watch over her and leave Will free to do what he needed to do. *Not that I need someone to keep an eye on me,* she thought indignantly.

Will did have questions about Evan Bennett, though. He pulled out of their driveway and onto the road, and then he said, eyes firmly on the road, "What weren't you saying back there?"

"We told you Evan had a past." She looked out the passenger window. It was very dark, with thick clouds obscuring any potential moonlight. If Evan was out there in the forest, they'd not find him tonight.

"I saw the looks you and Maddock exchanged. There's more you didn't say. I expect that from other people, but honestly, Bronwyn, how can I help out here if you don't tell me everything you know? It might not be anything more than him off with his girlfriend, but what if it is?"

She pointed out the turn that would take them to the Bennett farm, and then she started talking, determined not to say anything that revealed what she suspected. "Evan is a good-looking man, even now that he's older."

"How old is he?" Will interrupted her train of thought.

"Mid-fifties, I'd think. Near to my dad's age. They were in school together." She gathered her thoughts. "Dad always said that the girls flocked to Evan, and I guess it was true. Evan was spoiled by his parents, from what Dad's said. He had the looks and a fair amount of charm, but he also had a fancy car and nice things. Dad was a bit jealous of him, but at the same time, he didn't approve of him, either. He married Gwniera because she was pregnant, but that didn't stop him for long. He has a son by another woman, Jenna Perry. That's the one in Bala. But there've always been rumors about other women, as well." The porch light from a farmhouse appeared suddenly off to their left, but Bronwyn waved him on. "Not that house. That's his brother's place. The next one is Dylan's, and then it'll be theirs."

"I assume that he and Gwniera have at least one child?" He glanced at the house out his window. It was dark except for the dim light on the porch.

"They have two, Dylan and Meredith. Dylan's older than me, and Merry's a little younger. They're both grown now, but Dylan lives here and helps his dad with the farm. I don't know where Merry ended up. She went away to school and never came back."

"And the son in Bala?" Will watched the next house go by. This one was bright with lights in the downstairs windows.

Bronwyn pondered his question. She'd been young when that one was born. She remembered her parents talking about it in hushed tones so that neither she nor Maddock would hear. "I don't know. He must be a teenager by now."

Will steered around a bend in the road. Ahead, they could see the farmhouse, lights blazing out the windows and on the stoop, looking bright against the darkness. "He'd have kept up a relationship with her, I'd imagine, or the kid, at least."

"Maybe," Bronwyn agreed. She thought probably not, though, knowing Evan.

"Well, we'll find out if we need to." Will pulled to a stop on the circular drive and glanced toward her. "What else do you know that you didn't say?"

Her heart beat a tattoo. "Nothing, Will. There are always rumors about Evan, that he's seeing this or that woman, but who knows if any of that is true?" *Don't push me. I can't tell you the rest.*

"He wouldn't be at the pub?"

"No, he was never much of a drinker. He might stop in a pub to pick up a woman, though."

"Did he have a temper?"

"He never liked Margred and I riding our ponies onto his land, even in the forest where we were doing no harm at all. He used to rage at us if he caught us."

"Okay, I'm going to take that as a yes." Will squinted into his rear-view mirror. "Your dad and Maddock are here. Let's go talk to Mrs. Bennett."

Bronwyn's mum opened the door for them. She must have been watching for someone to come with news. They crowded into the kitchen, Gwniera watching them with fear despite their immediate assurances that they hadn't found anything suspicious. Dressed in blue jeans and a short-sleeved brown blouse, she lifted a hand to push her obviously-bleached hair off one shoulder and tuck it behind her ear. She looked strong and fit, a little heavy in her older years, but still attractive. A cup of tea rested on the table in front of her, and Bronwyn could smell the remains of cooked food in the air.

"Should I call my children?" she asked, looking at Will. "You must be the detective."

Will sat down in a chair across the table from her. "I don't think you need to bother them just yet, Mrs. Bennett. May I call you Gwniera?"

She nodded, although she kept her lips squeezed tightly together as if to prevent a smile coming through. Her eyes were bright. "I don't think he's coming home tonight."

Will nodded. "What makes you think that?"

"He'd probably be here by now if he was coming." She glanced up at Bronwyn's dad. "He was probably mad when I said I couldn't leave the supper to come get him, so he's taken off somewhere. He won't be home until tomorrow. I shouldn't have made such a fuss, calling everyone out like this."

"He's done this before?"

She took a deep breath that shuddered a bit, shaking her shoulders. "He used to do it a lot, when we were first married. After Jenna, I thought he'd behave himself. That should have taught him a lesson, if nothing else." She looked across at Will. "She was his girlfriend a few years back. They have a son together. Awstin. He's eighteen."

"Did you check with Jenna to see if he'd gone there?"

She nodded. "I called her when I couldn't find him. She said she hadn't heard from him, but I don't know if I'd believe her. Evan didn't want much to do with her after Awstin came along, but maybe he's gone back to her again behind my back."

"Did you try to call him?"

She nodded again. "He doesn't answer. It goes right to voicemail, like he's turned it off."

Will hesitated, and Bronwyn thought he was trying to be delicate with his wording. "Would Evan have any other friends he might have called to come get him?"

"Another girlfriend, you mean?" Gwniera spat back, a sudden flare of temper. "He's always got someone, so I suppose the answer is yes."

"You don't know if there's anyone specific, though?"

Gwniera glared at him, her eyes fierce. "He's been late home quite a few times in the past year or so, and lots of times he says he's going to town to buy something for the farm, but he's gone too long and he doesn't bring anything home. I know what to watch for, after all these years." She hesitated. "He hasn't stayed away overnight in a long time, though."

"Is it possible he's just with a girlfriend, then, and that time got away from him and he'll be home soon?" Will's voice was gentle, soothing.

Gwniera reached a hand up to her cheek and dapped at a spot beneath her left eye. "I suppose he could be."

"Do you have any idea of who it might be?"

She shook her head, a quick negation. "I don't know." Suddenly, she sounded tired.

"Why did you call for help, if Evan has a habit of coming home late?"

"He called me and said he'd walk back. Usually, he wouldn't bother calling if he wasn't actually headed home." She hesitated again. "I had a bad feeling about it when he didn't show up." She looked around at them all. "Maybe it was just the storm making me feel anxious tonight, but somehow, I think this is more serious than him just being out with a girlfriend."

Will nodded. "There's not much we can do until morning. If he's out in the woods, he might have taken shelter from the storm somewhere. If he's gone somewhere else, he'll turn up sooner or later, I'd think. Do you need someone to stay here with you tonight?"

Bronwyn didn't see the necessity for that. After all, in Gwniera's mind it was probably only a false alarm, and she would feel foolish if Evan turned up after she'd made a fuss over nothing. No one here knew what she knew, and she didn't see a way to push them into a search at the moment unless they thought it necessary themselves. She'd have to let it go.

Gwniera obviously agreed. "No, I'm fine here on my own." She looked at Bronwyn's mum, sitting at the end of the table and sighed. "Really, just this once, I'd like to make Evan feel ashamed of himself, more than anything."

Will stood up, pushing his chair back into place at the table. "We'll check with you in the morning. If he isn't back by then, we'll organize another search and try to look into other possibilities. Meanwhile, try to call him once in a while. Maybe he'll turn the phone back on and you'll get through."

"Thank you," Gwniera said, pushing her own chair back from the table. "I appreciate your help." She sighed. "It's probably just Evan being Evan, and all this was for nothing."

They regrouped on the driveway, the rain having finally cleared. Overhead, a bright moon peeked through a haze of cloud passing over it, and Bronwyn thought the sky would clear quickly. The air smelled fresh, cleared of the dust of late summer. She wondered if she could talk Will into going out when the others left to search on their own, if only she could think of a way to do it without raising his suspicions.

"What do you think?" Maddock asked, leaning against his truck's fender. It was still wet from the rain, but he had his rain jacket on and didn't appear to notice.

"It can't have been easy for Gwniera all these years," Bronwyn's mum said. "She's had to put up with a lot."

"But why call us out to search tonight in the rain, when it's obvious he does things like this on a regular basis?" Maddock insisted. "Why this time?"

"Perhaps she's finally had her fill of it," Bronwyn's mum suggested. "She was more angry than worried when we came over. Maybe she thought she'd embarrass him if she called out a search party, and, as she said, he'd be ashamed to have created such a fuss. Maybe after that, he'd at least be considerate enough to let her know when he's coming home in the future."

"I'd doubt that," Bronwyn's dad mumbled. He'd made it clear through the years that he never really approved of Evan. "The only one who'll end up embarrassed is her."

"And here, I thought everyone who lived here was morally upright and trustworthy," Will said, with a wink at Bronwyn.

"We are," she told him, "most of us, anyway."

"What do you think, Will?" Maddock wanted to know. "You're the expert on these things. Do we need to worry?"

Bronwyn could tell that Will was reluctant to venture an opinion without further evidence. "Let's see what the morning brings," he suggested noncommittally. "We get called out more often than you'd guess for nothing important."

"I'm tired," Bronwyn said. "It's been a long night." She wasn't so much tired as looking forward to it being just her and Will, alone together without all the fuss of family around. She'd suggest that they search on their own, but if Will didn't want to, she couldn't keep pushing without telling him why. If it was Evan the Cyn Annwn was there for, it was too late to save him anyway.

"We'll talk in the morning, then," Bronwyn's dad said. He reached out to touch Will's arm. "Thanks for coming out tonight, Will."

"It's no problem," Will assured him. "My chief super wants me handling more cases on this side of the district anyway. I might write up a report, just to show him I've done something here tonight, impress him, more or less."

Maddock laughed. "If only all your cases could be solved so easily," he said.

Chapter Four

The next morning, Bronwyn wasn't surprised when no sign of Evan Bennett had turned up. Gwniera called Bronwyn's mum at eight o'clock to let her know, and Bronwyn's dad came by the cottage as they were eating their breakfast and discussing a day's hike to Llyn Geirionydd, a hidden lake near Betws-y-Coed. Will had seemed enthusiastic about the hike, and she hadn't wanted to dampen his interest, so she'd gone along with his plans even while suspecting that they'd have to be cancelled before they could get out the door.

Disappointment bit at her. She'd looked forward to getting outdoors with Will after being in a city all weekend, and he'd only have the one day before he'd have to go back to Caernarfon for his turn in the rotation. She'd heard there was a good chance of seeing both peregrine falcons and buzzards in that area, and they hadn't managed a good, long hike in several weeks, between work, wedding planning, and trying to impress Will's mother by seeing Lark more often. The warm days of August were dwindling fast into fall. By the time their wedding was over, autumn rains would have arrived, with winter looming.

Her dad knocked and then let himself in the door, calling out to them as he walked through the house.

"In here," Bronwyn answered, wrinkling her nose at Will. "Bugger," she mouthed, and he smiled.

Her dad stopped in the doorway to the conservatory, his face serious. "There's been no sign of Evan overnight," he informed them.

"Gwniera's tried to call him?" Bronwyn asked. *Of course, she'd try to call him,* she thought. *Silly question.*

"His phone still goes straight to voicemail," her dad said. "She says she's really worried now. He's never been away like this before, not since Jenna, not without letting her know when he'd be back."

"Maybe he's not coming back," Bronwyn suggested without thought. She tried to recover. "Maybe he's finally decided he's done with the marriage and he's gone for good."

"He wouldn't just leave the farm," her dad insisted. "I know he's not always worked as hard as he might have, but he'd not leave it all to Dylan to do, not this time of year." He looked at Will. "I heard what you said last night. Most of us are morally upright and trustworthy, and that includes Evan in his own way. He might have a hard time being faithful to Gwniera, but in the end, he'd take care of things at home."

"Did Gwniera check with Dylan and – what's the daughter's name? Meredith? - to see if they'd heard from him?"

"She did. She says she called them both this morning. Dylan's there with her now, but she told Merry not to come just yet until she knows more about what's keeping him away."

That made sense. She'd remembered that Meredith lived in Bangor, so it'd be quite a drive for her to rush over when they didn't know if anything was wrong.

"We usually wait a minimum of twenty-four hours before we investigate a missing person, if that person is an adult," Will spoke up. "Evan hasn't been missing that long."

"I just thought we could go back out to the pasture," Bronwyn's dad told him. "It'd be neighbors coming out, nothing official at this point."

"But it'd embarrass Evan if we did have an official search going on," Bronwyn pointed out, wanting them to find him so her mind could be at peace, "if that's Gwniera's purpose with all this. Imagine if he came home and found out the police had been called out."

Will set down his fork. "My chief super wouldn't sanction a police inquiry at this point, but we'll help search, if that's what you want. If we haven't found him by tonight, then I'll see if I can get something more going."

"You'll know what to do," Bronwyn's dad conceded.

Bronwyn eyed him. "Do you want some tea, Dad, while we get ready?"

"No, I'll just get back to the place. Gwniera's going to show us where the quad is, and then we'll spread out from there."

"The storm will have erased any footprints," Will told him.

"It can't hurt to walk back across the pastures and have a look."

"We'll follow you there," Will decided. He looked at Bronwyn and shrugged. "It's not the hike we had planned, but I guess it'll have to do."

She wished she could go off on her own for few minutes. Maybe if Will wasn't with her, the Twlwyth Teg would tell her what had happened to Evan Bennett and where to find him. But there was no chance of that, not without telling Will what she was up to. She couldn't think of an excuse that wouldn't alert him to the fact that she kept secrets, even from him.

They took Bronwyn's Land Rover, Will driving it slowly down the summer road and then off into a pasture where a muddy red quad sat abandoned in the drying grass of late summer.

Will shifted into park and looked around. "It's pretty here," he remarked. He pointed at a distant farmhouse. Made of golden-brown stone with a red front stoop, it was set back against the forest land behind it. Even from a distance, the overgrown grass and weeds that surrounded it were clearly visible. "Who lives there?"

"That's Lloyd and Carys' old place," she said, "Evan's parents. It was the family home that was passed down through a few generations."

"Who lives there now?"

"No one. Evan and Gwniera built the newer house, and Dylan lives just beyond in the other newer house we passed by. I guess they're just letting it go." It seemed a shame. The farmhouse wasn't in bad shape and had been updated through the years when Lloyd and Carys lived in it. Obviously, it wasn't the fancy home that Evan had wanted, though, and he and Gwniera had needed a place of their own years ago when they

46

married anyway. Maybe they'd sell it one of these days. She wouldn't mind owning it, if she and Will could afford it. The property bordered the woods where her pool of water was. She filed that thought away for later.

They walked over to the small group of people who stood by the quad. "This is my fiancé, Will Cooper," Bronwyn told them, taking Will's hand. She introduced Dylan Bennett, a bluff man with rugged good looks, dark hair curling just a bit at the edges, and Dylan's wife Lisa, a slender brunette who, like Bronwyn herself, looked capable of long hikes in rough terrain. Dylan had a little boy in a backpack who peered around at them curiously.

Dylan saw her looking. "My son, Aeron," he said, looking over his shoulder at the little boy.

Besides the two of them, both of Bronwyn's parents were there, along with Maddock.

"Will's a detective," her dad explained when she didn't mention it, "but he's here in an unofficial capacity today."

Dylan studied Will. "What's the plan, then?" He seemed willing to let Will run the search.

"We'll take a look at the quad first," Will told t hem, "and then we'll spread out and walk back toward the house. We'll have to guess how Evan would have done it."

"I looked in the old house," Dylan said. "I thought he might have gone in there because of the storm, but it's empty. The door was still locked."

"Your dad would have had a key," Maddock pointed out. He was wearing jeans and a plaid shirt, despite the warmth of the day.

"Not with him," Dylan said. "We kept the key on the peg in the hallway. It was still there."

"How's your mum doing?" Bronwyn's mum wanted to know.

Dylan shrugged. "It's not like he hasn't done this before. I think she's just really mad at him for starting it up again. I just hope we haven't called you all out here for nothing." He turned around and reached out to open the box fastened to the back of the quad.

"Let me do that." Will spoke quickly. He pulled a pair of latex gloves out of his jeans pocket and pulled them on while the others watched in shocked silence. No one said a word, but Bronwyn could tell they were startled by Will's actions.

She watched with the others as Will opened the box and sorted through the objects inside. "It's tools mostly," he announced, "and a tarp and some bungee cords." He nodded toward Bronwyn. "Go get me a bag out of the car," he said. "I put some in there this morning, in case we needed them, in the back seat behind the driver's seat. Bring a few, just in case."

She heard them talking as she walked away.

"Is this what he'd typically have in the quad?" Will wanted to know.

She heard Dylan's answer. "I doubt he looked in the box much. Stuff accumulates, and you don't think to empty it out."

She brought the bags back, handing them to Will. They were thin evidence bags, another shock to the small group. They were quiet as Will pushed the tarp and bungees into a bag, then set that bag on the ground and stuffed the other bags into his jeans pocket as best he could.

He nodded at Dylan then. "Maybe we should try the quad, to see if it starts."

Dylan stared at him. "You think he lied about that?"

"I'm just saying that it'd be a good idea to check it," Will said.

"You're thinking he lied about the quad as an excuse, that he had someone else picking him up and didn't want my mum watching out the window to see who drove up the lane," Dylan surmised. He seemed about to refuse, and then he jerked around and reached for the key, turned it, and pushed the starter. The quad rumbled into life, startling a flock of crows from a nearby tree.

"So, it does run," Will said after a minute of startled silence.

Bronwyn could tell he was running that over in his mind, working out various possible scenarios. "Sometimes they're touchy," she offered. "It won't start for anything, then you wait a few minutes, and it starts right up."

"She's not wrong," Maddock agreed. "That happens. The engine cuts out and needs to cool down." He pointed toward the forested area. "You can see he was riding out there."

They all looked toward the forest. The rain hadn't erased the deep tire marks in the dirt.

"Maybe we should start out there," Bronwyn's dad spoke up. "Gwniera already walked toward home, and we went that way last night."

Will thought it over. "No, I think we should go toward the house. He said he was walking home, so logically that's the direction we need to check out first," he said after a minute. "There's no reason right now to think that he went back into the woods, is there? He was working out there yesterday?"

"He'd call it working. He'll have lied to her again," Dylan growled bitterly. "We never could trust anything he said. He'll be with some woman. Probably not Jenna, but some new slag he's taken up with now. I knew he was cheating on her again."

"Still," Will urged them, "he did call home and say he was walking that way, so we'll need to look in that direction, just in case."

He organized them into a ragged line, spacing them out about ten feet apart. "Look for anything out of the ordinary: broken grass, muddy prints, litter," he instructed them. The sun shown hot on them as they followed his orders, and Bronwyn felt a tug of pride, watching him take charge. This was what he did, day after day, and when it came time for someone to take the lead, there was no hesitation. His voice took on authority, and everyone there listened.

Almost everyone. "Couldn't I just go through the woods?" Bronwyn begged, thinking it the chance she needed to be out on her own. She wanted answers, wanted the peace of mind that would bring.

"No." Again, Will's voice left no room for argument. "Until we know what's happened to Evan, you can't be wandering around in the trees by yourself, and I need to be with the group here."

"I could go with her," Maddock offered again.

Will looked at him, frowning. "The more of us there are searching together, the better our chance of finding something. Bronwyn and I can go out there later, when we're done here."

And so, they began the long, slow walk across the pastureland, spread out at the distance Will demanded and eyes on the ground. Occasionally, someone would call out, and then Will would stride over

49

to see what they'd found. He bagged several items, and other times he just shook his head and continued on his way.

Then Maddock called out, his voice excited, and they all jogged over to see what he'd found.

Will put his gloves back on and reached for an object lying in the grass.

Bronwyn leaned closer with the others.

When Will straightened, he was holding a black mobile phone in his hand. He held it up and looked at it. "Powered down," he commented. He looked at Dylan. "Is it his?"

"I don't know," Dylan said. "I wouldn't know what his mobile looked like, but if it's here, it must be his."

"Odd, that it's lying out here in the field," Bronwyn's dad said.

"Definitely odd," Will agreed. He looked back the way they'd walked. The quad was still nearby; they hadn't covered much ground.

He dropped the phone into a bag and looked around at them all. Bronwyn could tell he thought the finding of the phone disturbing, but that he was being careful not to raise more alarm than the others already felt. "It probably fell out of his pocket while he was walking home. It doesn't mean anything by itself."

But they knew it probably did. Despite his reassurances, they'd know the evidence was mounting that something was very wrong. At least, that's how it felt to Bronwyn.

Will walked beside Bronwyn for a few minutes after that. "I probably should have let you go to your pool of water in the woods," he grumbled. "I thought we'd get a hike in today, but not like this."

She knew it was too late to change tactics at that point, but he wasn't wrong. If he'd have let her, she'd have walked out there before they started out, just in case. "I'll go after we're done," she said, hoping he wouldn't want to accompany her. It embarrassed her for Will to see her having a vision. It had only happened the once, but he'd obviously seen a trance and known it for what it was. She didn't want him thinking her odd, although he seemed to accept her scrying as the blessing it was.

If she went alone, though, she might run into the Twlwyth Teg or Pysgotwr, and that's how she got most of the information she shared with him. She just didn't know how to manage time alone, without Will tagging along. If Evan didn't turn up soon, she'd have to think of a way to do it, if she could. She sighed under her breath. Sometimes Will was too protective for his own good.

Gwniera must have been watching for them to finish their walk because she came out to meet them as they opened the pasture gate and straggled onto the driveway.

"You didn't find him," she cried out, and Bronwyn saw a change in her from the night before. Then, she'd been vindictive, she'd thought, and now, she seemed nervous.

They went into the living room, dragging chairs in from the dining room so they could all sit down. Bronwyn's mum went into the kitchen and made tea, which she brought into the room with a plate of packaged chocolate biscuits.

"What do we do now?" Dylan demanded when they were settled, looking at Will.

Will shook his head. "We wait, I think," he said, "and see if he gets in contact by this evening. If not, then we can start a proper investigation."

"He wouldn't leave his mobile behind," Gwniera insisted. She'd seemed to freeze when Will showed it to her, and Bronwyn felt bad for her. What had probably started as a way to embarrass Evan had turned into something more ominous. "Isn't that enough evidence to start an investigation?"

"No," Will told her. "He could well have just dropped it and not realized." He sighed. "I can do some more checking around in the meantime. I don't mind, even if it's unofficial."

"Someone should talk to Jenna," Bronwyn's mother suggested, looking at Gwniera. "She might know something to put your mind at ease."

"I don't want her brought into this." Gwniera's voice rose. "He wasn't seeing her anymore."

"But surely, he was seeing Awstin," Maddock reminded her. "Maybe he knows something about where his dad is."

Gwniera glared at him. "Evan was never a part of Awstin's life. She wanted that boy well away from us, and that was fine with me. The only thing she wanted from Evan was money, and more money. He wouldn't be sharing his plans with her, if he made any." She looked toward the ceiling and blinked hard. When she looked at them again, tears glittered her eyes. "Something's happened to him."

Bronwyn watched Will. He'd know Evan's disappearance was suspicious, but he wouldn't want the family involved in the investigation.

"We'll put Jenna off for now," he conceded, "but if there's a police investigation, we'll have to talk to her. Is there anyone else that might know where he's gone?"

He waited, but no one spoke up.

After a long silence, he went on. "I know you have chores that need doing, animals to tend to. Let's go our separate ways for a while. If you find you have free time," he addressed Dylan, "you might ask around after him at the pubs. They might talk to you, seeing as you're his son."

"What are you going to do?" Dylan's voice was aggressive. Clearly, he wasn't happy.

"I can get someone to check for CCTV in the area, see if there are any cameras that might have picked him up. Then I think I'll have a stroll through the woods. Bronwyn can come with me."

"How about the rest of us coming with you?" Dylan still sounded quarrelsome.

"We'll get more accomplished if we split up," Will said firmly. "If you check at the pubs, maybe ask around to see if there's someone he's been seeing lately, that'd help more than you stumbling around in the woods, which is probably a dead end anyway."

There was a silence that stretched too long, but finally Bronwyn's dad stood up. "That's us done for now then," he said, with a meaningful look at the rest of them. "Dylan, can you drive us back to the field so we can get our cars?"

"Sure, I can fit at least a few of you in Dad's truck." Despite his words, he still sounded grudging.

Will handed around cards with his contact information on them. "Call me with anything," he instructed them, "if something turns up or even if you just think of something. I'll have my mobile with me."

"What do you think?" Will asked Bronwyn as they pulled back onto the main road through the village.

She was flattered that he asked. "I don't think he's disappeared on purpose. Between the phone and the quad that runs when he said it didn't, things don't add up."

"I agree. But what's happened? An accident, or something more in my line of work?"

She shivered, despite the sunshine. "Let me walk out to my pool of water, Will. Maybe I'll see something."

"I thought we'd go together, like I told the others," he suggested, his voice firm. "I don't want you wandering around on your own if someone's murdered the neighbor."

She tried to think. She really didn't want him with her, but how could she tell him that without him taking offense? *Maybe the truth.* "I'm embarrassed if you're with me when I'm scrying," she told him. "I concentrate better if I'm alone." She tried a smile. "You distract me."

He wasn't fooled. "You just don't want me around when you're off in another world."

"No, I don't. I probably look weird."

He studied her, and she wondered if he was thinking about how she heard things, as well as saw them. Surely, he knew there was more to it than she'd let him know.

"I was proud of you today, Will," she told him, wanting to distract him. "I don't often get to see you working. People respect you and listen to you when you take charge like that."

He capitulated. "It is my job. I don't do it consciously; instinct just kicks in. I'm sure Maddock wanted to butt in, but this time he let me run with it."

"Maddock likes you. You're like the brother he never had."

"Yeah," Will confessed. "I like him, too."

They went to the cottage to eat lunch and get Daisy, and Will rooted around in the garage for a few tools and other items he thought he might need, depending on whether they found anything. Ready then, they drove back to where the forlorn red quad sat in the field, and Will took a few minutes to cover it with a blue tarp, which they weighed down with rocks from the field. "Just in case," he told her. "It might end up being evidence."

Daisy romped happily ahead of them, ranging from side to side in true hunting dog form.

"Which direction?" Will asked, looking at her knowingly.

She pointed. "We should follow the quad tracks. There used to be a trail, but I'd imagine it's overgrown to non-existence by now." She'd given up hope of scrying in the pool of water without Will. He'd made it clear that he wasn't going to leave her alone in the forest, so any chance of getting information from other sources was hopeless. She'd have to try scrying with him watching her and, while she knew his presence wouldn't stop her visions, she also knew she'd be embarrassed if it worked.

She relaxed into the walk, though, as the forest welcomed her. She'd always loved nature, but this little piece of forestland bordering the home farm's pastures was special. This was where her father had taken her walking as a child, where she learned the names of trees, bushes, wildflowers, birds, and other forest creatures. He'd taught her to recognize the calls of the various birds, as well, and to listen to the buzz of insects and to watch for the tiniest of things: mushrooms, lichen, seeds. She'd learned not only to listen to and see the forest around her, but to experience it with all of her senses, and that early training had led to what she now did at Pennant Melangell when she led people in nature meditation.

Will distracted her just with his presence; she didn't expect to see anything that might help them find Evan Bennett. But, as they walked, she kept her eyes and ears open, just in case.

After a bit, they detoured off the quad tracks and walked toward where Bronwyn thought her family's land began. It took them twenty minutes to get to the pool of water beneath the oak tree. The pathway she found had been rough, and she'd strayed off it several times before realizing her mistake. Tangled weeds and bushes littered with inedible berries grabbed at their feet and forced detours. Finally, though, she found the stepping stones that crossed the little brook and, once on the other side, she found her way easily to her rock, which wasn't far from that point.

She settled onto the rock where she always sat, encouraging Daisy to jump up and lie down beside her, with Will watching from a few feet away. "You can come sit here, too," she told him, but he'd obviously taken her earlier words into consideration and was trying to give her some distance. He leaned against a tree and waited.

She settled herself, calmed her breathing, and looked down into the water. A trio of leaves floated there, lapping up against a rock, one of them orange with brown edges, another creamy pale, and the third dried mud brown. She wondered if they were a sign of some sort and put the image to the back of her mind for thinking about later. Maybe they represented her, Will, and Lark?

She shook her head and tried to clear her thoughts, watching the water. It was a still day, and the surrounding rocks and shrubbery were reflected in the quiet water. It made her want her sketching materials, another distraction. Again, she tried to clear her mind, leaving it open to whatever might appear.

She waited. A dragonfly flitted over the water, its iridescent blue body glimmering in the rays of sun that broke through the branches above. She focused on it, enjoying the brighter colors against the dark water.

Beside her, Daisy lifted her head and stared at the water. Bronwyn touched the dog's back, distracted and hoping to still her, but to no avail. Scrambling to her feet, Daisy knocked her hand away and leapt into the pool of water, where she swam in circles, head high, looking for whatever had inspired her swim. The splash of her landing both soaked Bronwyn's clothes and disrupted any hope of her seeing anything meaningful in the water.

Bronwyn brushed water from her jeans and tried to wring out the ends of her tee shirt, watching Daisy with amusement. She was obviously hunting whatever had caused her dive into the pool and not finding it. Maybe Daisy had seen something she had not, but, if so, it was long gone.

Will strode over. "I guess you won't be seeing anything today, love." She could see laughter in his eyes.

She slid off the rock and pulled him close against her wet tee shirt. "Want to snuggle?" she asked, grinning.

"Only if you take that wet shirt off," he suggested, pulling away, and then he reached out and pulled the shirt up and over her head.

"Will!" she protested. "What if Dylan came out to search the woods, too?" She reached for her shirt. "Or worse, my dad or Maddock?"

He held it up high above her head with one hand. "Daisy would let us know if someone else was around," he told her. He bent forward and kissed her, whispering into the kiss, "What do you think? Is that flat rock big enough for the two of us?"

Oh, God, what if the Twlwyth Teg or Pysgotwr are out here? But she didn't want to say no. She was having too much fun. "I think it is," she murmured back.

Later, Will sent her on a short walk with Daisy up the roadway that passed their cottage while he started the grill for their dinner.

She wandered the roadway past the other cottages, watching Daisy frolic ahead of her. Late summer grasses had turned the edges of the road golden, and she could smell ripe weeds in the air. The sun warmed her arms and puffs of dust rose from beneath Daisy's feet as she dashed off the road to explore the scents that drew her.

She hadn't realized they were there until they emerged from the tall grasses alongside the road, nearly invisible as they blended with their surroundings. Dressed in gold and brown and palest green and yellow, they at first appeared to be a scattering of fall leaves that swirled beside her. She stopped short. Beautiful and grotesque, delicate, yet sturdy, with wizened faces still innocent and youthful, and filmy wings that fluttered in the still air, they were the Twlwyth Teg, the Welsh fairies, come to give Bronwyn the message she craved.

She stood shock still, hoping that Daisy wouldn't run back into the middle of them and disrupt their words. Sometimes, the dog was more nuisance than she was worth with her undaunted exuberance.

"Greed from accidie," intoned one melodious voice, and Bronwyn turned her eyes to see a creature no taller than one of Lark's Legos glaring at her with angry eyes.

"Arquebus burns at Vespertine," whispered another, a tiny creature that fluttered near Bronwyn's ear like an insect. She turned her head to see it better, but it buzzed away quickly.

"Gnoff beneath the cairn." She jerked her head back as the last voice whispered its message, but she was too slow to see which of the creatures had spoken.

"Once, twice, thrice," they chanted in unison, as she'd known they would, and then they disappeared even more quickly than they'd appeared, leaving nothing in their wake, not even the tiny mushrooms she'd come to expect.

Excited, she pulled out her mobile and pulled up the medieval word dictionary she liked to use to interpret their words to her. *A cairn is a pile of stones that makes a grave.* She knew that from local history. Was there something like that in the woods? She didn't remember seeing one, and she'd spent a lot of time out there through the years.

Her fingers tangled as she typed "gnoff" into the search bar. At first, she spelled it without a "g," but then she puzzled over the sound of it, wondering. Giving up, she scanned the list of words and, after too much time had passed, she landed on the correct spelling. "A rascally, foolish, and rich old man," she read on the screen. Well, that described Evan Bennett, for sure. He must be dead, then. She paused, a wave of sadness bringing tears to her eyes. She hadn't really liked Evan, but any death came unwelcome to those who knew a person and cared about those he left behind.

She'd concentrated on remembering the unfamiliar words, so she had to think for a moment before recalling the rest. "Arquebus." She typed several spellings before she found one that seemed pertinent: "a portable gun supported by a tripod or other type of rest." Suddenly, she felt chilled. Of course, if Evan was buried in a cairn, he'd been murdered. Logically, she knew that. But the very specific message about the means of his death disturbed her, nevertheless.

Almost reluctant now, she thought about the second message before typing it onto her screen. "Accedie," she found quickly. "Laziness, both physical and spiritual, leading to indifference." Was Evan lazy? He'd worked the farm and made it profitable through the years, so she wouldn't necessarily call him lazy. Still, maybe he'd gotten to a point where he was tired of the farm, tired of Gwniera, tired of it all and wanting to try something else in his elder years?

But there was the matter of the cairn. She put aside the other messages to focus on that one. She'd need to tell Will, but how? How could she have had a vision without water? She couldn't pretend to have experienced one earlier when they'd walked out to her pool of water. She'd have told him then, even as distracted she was by the time he'd lured her onto that flat rock with him. She smiled at the memory.

The answer came as she watched Daisy stop to lap water from a puddle left from the previous day's storm. Would Will believe she'd seen the cairn in a puddle of water? And the arquebus? Both would be easily visible in the pool of water. He'd believe that easily enough. She thought she could ignore the rest. They'd know soon enough from interviews that both accidie and gnoff applied to Evan.

She ran home, Daisy loping beside her, both excited and daunted by what she knew. Poor Evan. He wasn't a very reliable man, and he'd made Gwniera's life a torment, but if a cairn and a gun were involved, that surely meant that he was dead, that someone had killed him, and in her forest. The Cyn Annwn had come for him.

Will looked up when she came through the house to where he was waiting to put the meat on the grill. It'd be salmon for her because she didn't eat meat, and a steak for him, she thought irrationally when she saw him.

"You saw something," he said immediately. He stepped toward her and grabbed her arms to steady her.

She looked up at him. "It was a puddle of water," she lied, "just a puddle left from the storm."

He nodded. "You couldn't see it in the pool of water because of Daisy, so you saw it somewhere else."

That gave her pause. Was he right? Was the message so important that she'd get it, no matter what? "Do you know what a cairn is, Will?"

"It's a pile of rocks. A grave. Or sometimes a cache of treasure."

"It has to be a grave this time, Will. Evan's grave."

He nodded again, trusting her. "Where?"

Now she hesitated. They hadn't said where, had they? Just that it belonged to a gnoff, a foolish, rich old man, and that he'd been made careless by his indifference to things. "I don't know where, but I think it must be in the woods, Will. It's the only place that makes sense." She swallowed. "There's more, Will. I saw a gun, too."

"What kind of gun?"

She thought fast. It'd have to be bigger than a pistol to be supported on a rest. "A long gun, Will. A rifle, I guess. It was propped on a support. I think it means that Evan was shot."

"Did you see the shooter?"

"No, only the gun and the grave."

"And you couldn't tell where they were?"

She shook her head. "They have to be out there near to the quad."

He took a breath. "Well, that's enough, isn't it? It's a murder then," he concluded. He looked down at her and gave her a quick kiss. "Well done, sweetheart. Well done."

Chapter Five

They abandoned their dinner and followed the tracks left from the quad into the forest, back-tracking at times when the tracks circled around and taking false leads on narrower trails probably left by Gwniera's horseback riding excursions. The ground had been dry before the rain, so the quad hadn't sunk into mud, but just flattened grass, bushes, and seedling trees as it traveled, making it harder to find a trail. Bronwyn hadn't spent much time in the Bennetts' part of the woods, just sneaking in occasionally when she and Margred were playing at Robin Hood or some such thing. It wouldn't have made a difference anyway. There was no way to know where their destination lay.

Finally, they discovered the cairn at the furthest reaches of the forest where the hillside rose in a rocky overhang that allowed no tree to thrive and provided plenty of stones to pile atop a makeshift grave.

Will examined it carefully from a distance. The stones might have been there a day, or they might have been there for hundreds of years. Haphazardly piled, they made a coffin-sized jumble that bore little moss and less debris than he might have expected, if it wasn't newly done. The rain and wind would have weathered it just a bit overnight, and it looked to him like that's exactly what had happened. He doubted that it was old.

Still…"What if it's hundreds of years old, and there's a Viking cache down there full of ancient swords and helmets and jeweled cups?"

he mused, pulling his mobile from his pocket. He raised it and snapped some pictures, walking around for various angles. "Do we open it to see what's underneath, or leave it for the experts?"

"What experts would you call?" Bronwyn wondered. She'd kept a distance from it, probably wondering if they'd be disturbing forensic evidence if they got too close. He wondered that, too.

"I'd call it in, and probably they'd send a team of SOCOs over. They'd look at it and decide if they needed to call an archeological team before digging into it."

Bronwyn stared at the pile of rocks. "It looks newly-built to me. I think I'd have noticed if it had been here back when I used to sneak onto the Bennett land with Margred on our ponies. You know how it is when you're a kid. If we'd seen it then, we'd have been sure that we'd found a treasure hoard."

"You're sure you don't remember it?"

She shook her head. "I'm pretty sure nothing like that was here before."

"I'll call Bowers and ask him what he wants me to do," Will decided. *Bowers will love me putting my questionable actions off on him again.* If his chief superintendent told Will to go ahead and see what was beneath the stones, he'd take any flack that resulted, just as he had the previous spring when Will had gone off on his own investigation without anyone's approval. "He'll probably send someone to investigate, and we'll get to watch from a distance." He grinned at Bronwyn. "It'd be better that way, anyway. I don't know about you, but I don't fancy dismantling that rock pile by hand."

He glanced at the sky as he scrolled to Bowers' number. It'd be dark before someone got there, and surely with Evan Bennett missing now for over twenty-four hours, there'd be some urgency to see what lay beneath those stones. *But it's not my decision,* he told himself firmly. He'd gotten in enough trouble in the past for doing things without following protocols, and now was not the time to try it again.

"Don't touch it," Bowers said when Will had explained. "Don't even get near it. I'll send a crew out there as soon as one can be called in, and they'll set up lights so they can get it done tonight." It wouldn't be ideal; even with the bright lights they'd bring, it'd take more time than usual for them to dismantle the cairn while they checked for bits of forensic evidence to show up. "It's remote, is it? Give me directions for them, and you'll have to meet them and show them the way. I'll call some locals out to block the road in and keep spectators out."

Will didn't mention the gun. There'd be no logical reason to search for a gun until they had a body and knew the cause of death, and he didn't want Bowers questioning how he'd come by the information in advance of opening the cairn. It'd be better to just let things evolve on their own.

His duty done, Will gestured to Bronwyn and filled her in as they made their way back through the woods to where they'd left the Land Rover. "We probably should tell Gwniera and Dylan something," he decided. "They'll notice all the traffic up the road and wonder what's going on."

"I want to call my parents and Madd, too," she told him. "Bowers believed you when you told him we'd followed the quad tracks and found it that way?"

"It's the truth," Will defended himself. "That's what we did. Your family will keep it quiet?"

"I'll ask them to, and they will. They'll keep an eye out from their end, that way. You don't want people sneaking through the woods from the other side to see what's happening."

That made sense. "Just don't tell them about a gun yet. I'm keeping that just between us until we know more." He reached out to caress her hair. "You should go home now. Let me handle this."

"I've come this far with you. I want to see what's under those rocks." She looked up at him. "You won't have time to take me home by the time you go talk to Gwniera and Dylan. Please? I won't get in the way."

He didn't think he wanted her seeing what was beneath those rocks, but he supposed he could ask her to keep a distance away, if it came to that. He nodded. "Okay, but if they find Evan under there, you'll have to go. I can catch a ride home with someone later." He reached out to brush a smudge of dirt off her cheek. "Bowers wouldn't like it if I let you stay at a crime scene."

He pondered what to tell Gwniera and Dylan as they drove to the house. It'd be better to keep it vague at this point, but surely, they'd jump to conclusions as soon as they saw the emergency vehicles coming by. *Some form of the truth, then.*

He left Bronwyn in the car, suspecting that she'd give away more than he wanted to say, not intentionally, but just by the look on her face. When Gwniera opened the door, he asked to go inside, sat them down at the kitchen table, and told them as much as he thought he needed to. "We've found something that looks suspicious, but we have no real idea if it relates to Evan's disappearance at this point. It very well might be a false alarm, so there's no need to jump to conclusions at this point. I'll ask you to please be patient. I'll tell you more when we know more." He thought he'd sounded reasonable.

Dylan asked what they'd found, of course, and Will successfully evaded the question by explaining that he really couldn't say while the investigation was ongoing. He didn't like the angry look Dylan tossed his way afterward, but there was nothing he could do about that.

Both Gwniera and Dylan assumed they could follow Will back to where the quad had been left, and neither was happy when he told them they couldn't. "It's our land," Dylan pointed out. "We can go where we want."

He tried to sound authoritative when he told them that no, they couldn't, even if the land belonged to them. It was a potential crime scene. They'd have to stay away from the site until the police could do their work. He left them unhappily watching him walk back to the Land Rover and hoped they wouldn't make things difficult by challenging his authority.

The local constables turned up first, within a half hour of Will's call, which he considered fast. He stationed two of them on the roadway, blocking access to it beyond the Bennett's house, left one to guard the quad, and led the remaining four through the woods to the place where they'd found the cairn.

"Who's this, then?" one of them asked, nodding toward Bronwyn.

Will had introduced himself, but had purposely ignored her when greeting them. She'd walked with them through the woods, and he'd pretended not to see their curious looks. Technically, she shouldn't be allowed near the cairn at all, but irrationally, he wanted her there to see what they uncovered. True, they'd have found the cairn without her information if they'd just followed the quad's track through the forest, but having the information from her sped things up since they wouldn't have gotten to it until the next day. He felt she'd earned the right to be there.

"Her name's Bronwyn Bagley," he told the man, after a hesitation. "Her parents own the adjoining property, and she grew up wandering these woods. She's the one who told me the cairn hadn't been here before, and I thought she'd be handy if we had other questions about the locale."

The constable, a short, compact man with a roguish grin and burly arms, snorted. "And how is it that you came to have her with you when you were out searching?"

Will gave up the pretense. "She's my fiancé. And that's enough cheek from you." He took note of the man's name, though, for future reference in case of a complaint. Robert Thomas, he was, although the others called him Robbie.

He took Bronwyn with him after leaving them at the cairn and walked back to where the quad waited to be examined. They'd have to walk the forensic people out to the cairn when they arrived, as well, although a path was now more visible, thanks to all the trampling feet making their way that direction. They were getting their exercise, just walking back and forth.

They waited, making small talk with the constable there. Will's stomach rumbled, and he thought of the steak still waiting to be cooked. It had been a long time since lunch, and they'd gone light on that as they'd anticipated a nice meal later. The way things were going, they'd be out there all night. Maybe he should send Bronwyn for something to eat, but then she'd be noticed more when she had to pass by all the constables guarding the site, and he didn't want that.

Dusk had darkened the forest when, at last, the forensic crew arrived, three men and a woman. They bypassed the quad; after all, if no body awaited in the cairn and Evan Bennett turned up alive, time spent on it would be wasted. Will and Bronwyn showed them the way through the woods to the site, helping to carry the equipment they felt they might need: tarps, battery-powered lights, rolls of crime scene tape, a fold-up table, protective suits, a camera, and tools like pry-bars in case the rocks had been jammed too tightly together. "We'll be able to tell you right away if this is an archeological site or something recently made," one of the men informed Will.

He and Bronwyn stood at a distance with the constables, watching the group set up lights and then kneel down to look closely at the cairn, touching a rock here and there with gloved hands and taking close-up pictures of the rocks. After what seemed a long time, they slowly began to disassemble the rocks, one by one, laying them on a tarp for further examination once they'd finished the main work of discovering what, if anything, lay beneath them.

After a while, tired of standing, he took Bronwyn's hand and led her to a larger shelf of rock he'd thought they might sit on. The surface was hard beneath them, and there was nothing to rest their backs against, but it was better than standing for hours on end. She leaned against him, and he put his arm around her, holding her there.

It was quiet in the forest in the darkness, the pool of light from the lamps reflecting off the tarps they'd propped over the area making the surrounding trees look blacked out. The techs moving around in their puffy white suits gave it a surreal feel, like a group of aliens examining a selected segment of Earth. They moved quietly on bootie-covered shoes, murmurs and occasional grunts their only sounds.

Finally, there was a stir of excitement at the hole that had shortly before been a cairn, and one of the technicians called Will to come over. He slid off the rock, cautioning Bronwyn to stay. If a body had been buried there for the past two days, he really didn't want her seeing it.

He crept up to them, his own shoes covered, as well, and leaned over the hole to watch while they continued to pull rocks away from what was now pretty obviously a body. Will felt his stomach sour as a face slowly appeared, bruised and partially collapsed from the weight of the rocks that had covered it. He clenched his muscles, determined not to let his sudden nausea turn into something that would embarrass him. It was a man's face, late middle-aged, with dark hair liberally streaked with gray and a neatly-trimmed gray beard. Bronwyn would recognize him if it was Evan Bennett, but he didn't want to call her over to identify him. They'd do it some other way.

"He's been shot," one of the men said suddenly, and they all stopped working and stared at the man's freshly-uncovered chest, where a small, neat hole had stained the man's tee shirt a rusty brown. There was movement there, and for a moment Will thought the man's chest was rising with breaths. Then he realized. Maggots had already found the body, and what he saw was their movements beneath the tee shirt as they fed on the flesh exposed by the wound. Thankfully, they hadn't traveled as far as the man's face yet. Will suppressed an urge to gag and knelt down, took a pair of gloves from the female technician, and touched the man's chest, probing lightly. "God," he murmured, "the wound's small." He pulled his hand away and looked up at the woman. "Do you think he was dead when he was buried?"

She bent over and looked at the body for a long minute.

"I'd doubt it," one of the men spoke up beside her. "That wound doesn't look very big, so he might have taken a while to die. It's plenty big enough to be fatal, though. They usually look smaller than they really are."

She nodded in agreement. "It looks like he might have been buried alive, but that's for the doctor to say, isn't it? The maggots make it more likely he was dead before he was buried. We'll know either way once the doctor does his examination."

Will stood up and backed away from the hole. He glanced toward Bronwyn, and decided that he should talk to her before calling for a pathologist. He wished now that he'd told her to go home when he'd wanted to earlier, back to the cottage and away from the ugliness that was his job. *If I'm going to be called out for local cases, she can't get used to coming along with me.* Bowers would never approve of that, and he'd find himself living more full-time back in Caernarfon in the blink of an eye.

He glanced back at the grave, and a sudden memory flashed in his brain. He fought against the despair that washed over him. *That could have been me,* he thought. He wondered if the men who'd threatened his life just a few months past would have bothered to try to hide his body afterwards. *Probably not*, he decided, trying to push the memory away. His time with the department psychologist had left him feeling that he could cope with the demands of his job again, but every now and then, something would trigger the memories that brought it all back, and he'd feel as if he teetered on the edge. He wondered if he'd ever be able to fully put it behind him.

"It looks like we've found Evan," he managed to say when he was near enough, concentrating on Bronwyn and trying to dispel the images that shook him.

"He's been murdered, then," she responded, trying to look over his shoulder at the scene. "Do you want me to identify him? I know what he looks like."

"I don't want you anywhere near him," Will told her firmly. "In fact, as soon as I put a call in for a pathologist, you and I are leaving. I've seen what I needed to see for now. I'll take you home and come back later." He wanted her well-away now that they knew what lay beneath that cairn.

He called Bowers, who said he'd call for a pathologist and gave him permission to leave the scene to the forensic people. "Check in with them later to find out what they know," Bowers told him. "It may be a long night. You'll want to hear what Francis has to say, too."

Francis Ruark was their usual pathologist. It seemed a long way for him to drive that late at night. "You're asking him to come tonight?"

"If he will," Bowers told him. "Who's on the rota with you this next week?"

"It must be Jay," he said, hoping he was right. He liked working with Jay Mehta more than with anyone else. "I was with Beth last week." He hadn't worked with the other detective inspector, Ian, for several weeks. Ian was fine, if that's the way it turned out, but Jay was better.

"I'll send him your way in the morning," Bowers told him. "You think this one will take some time?"

"No suspects stand out as obvious right now," Will noted. He thought of Gwniera and Dylan, but he was sure there were others who'd be considered suspicious, especially if Evan Bennett had been the womanizer local gossip made him out to be.

"Can you book Mehta a room locally, then?"

"Yes, sir, that's no problem," Will assured him. They could probably put him in Lark's room and he'd not complain, but he'd be more comfortable in the local B&B. The department would pay for it.

"Good, then," Bowers concluded. "You should probably stay there until Francis does a preliminary exam, and then maybe you could get a couple hours' sleep. Keep me informed, will you?"

Will assured him that he'd share anything that seemed important and rang off. He intended to take Bronwyn home and then to return to the scene to watch the SOCOs work. He could just ask for a summary in the morning, but Francis Ruark would be there in less than two hours, so by the time he took Bronwyn home and, if lights were on in the Bennett house, stopped by to deliver the news, he'd might as well just stay on site and get the news as it developed.

To his relief, the Bennett house was dark when he passed by. He'd rather have more definite news for them before he made what had now become a death notification. They'd have to do the identification with dental records or DNA; either one could be rushed and results available quickly.

To his further relief, Bronwyn didn't argue when he told her he'd return the Land Rover in the morning so that she could drive to work. He could see the defiance in her eyes, just a brief flash of annoyance, but she knew he'd want her careful for a few days until whoever'd murdered Evan Bennett was caught, so walking to work would not be an option.

Time passed slowly then as he waited by the quad for the pathologist to arrive. The moon was nearly full, lighting the pasture with a soft glow. He chatted with the constable he'd left to guard the quad, a burly man named Lew Griffiths, who told him he lived just outside Llangynog and worked out of the local station in Llanfyllin. He'd known Evan Bennett, having been at school with Dylan. "I was a year older, but we all hung around together back then," he explained.

If he'd known that, he'd have left a different constable to guard the quad and taken Griffiths with him, in the hope that he could identify the body they'd found. Maybe it wasn't too late for that. Will picked up his torch. "Come on, then," he said, "let's see if you can identify the body for us."

Griffiths seemed happier at the prospect of being in the centre of things. "What about the quad?"

Will waved at it. "It's not going anywhere. I'll bring someone else back here after I hear what you have to say."

What he had to say was useful. "Yeah, that's Mr. Bennett," he told them when he looked down at the body in the hole a half hour later. He turned his head away and twisted his lips, seeming to try to regain control, and Will suspected he'd suffered the same reaction to the body that Will had. "I recognize that little beard of his, even though his face is pretty beat up. Is that from the rocks?" He straightened and backed away, right into the rocks that had been piled on the nearby tarp. Slipping backward, he fell awkwardly onto his back and yelped in pain.

The others hurried to help him, but he brushed them away. "I'm fine. I didn't hit my hard head, at least." He scrambled off the rock pile and got to his feet, looking sheepish. "Got a little distracted, there."

"You're sure it's him?" Will wanted to make certain before he said anything to the Bennetts.

"He looks a little different with his face smashed up like that, but yeah, it's him."

It was nearly two in the morning when Will's partner, Jay Mehta, drove up the lane, followed less than five minutes later by Francis Ruark, the pathologist. Will had been sitting in the Land Rover with the constable who'd replaced Griffiths at the quad. They'd tried some casual conversation, but after a few minutes it seemed more work than it was worth, as tired as they both were. Will was dozing, thoughts of the upcoming wedding running through his brain, when headlamps swept the pasture and he saw Jay's little green Subaru Impreza pull up beside them.

He shook himself into wakefulness and got out to greet him.

"Bowers says you've got a murder here," Jay called out as he got out of his car. "Handy, that. Did you do it so you could stay locally? I mean, the wedding's only a couple of weeks away, not that it matters, things being the way they are with you sharing that little cottage with her already."

Will snorted. "Don't be cheeky. Yes, it's definitely a murder, and at this point I've no idea who to suspect." He filled Mehta in on what he knew. "Bennett was a bit of a ladies' man, if local gossip is to be believed, so that might figure into the investigation. I've only met the wife and son, but I suppose either of them could be a suspect, given that someone will inherit the farm and neither seemed overly fond of our victim. There's another son, as well, the product of an affair some years ago."

"I like a good puzzle," Mehta said. He didn't seem bothered by the lateness of the hour. He'd let his dark, curly hair grow out longer in the past month or so, and a neatly-trimmed beard echoed Will's own.

"Just so you know, if this puzzle turns out complicated, you'll be working it alone on Saturday. I've booked that day off to take my niece to boarding school. She checks in that day, and I want to get her settled." His mother would have Lark on the first flight to Canada if he bailed on the very first obligation he'd promised to take on where she was concerned.

"I'll carry on alone, if I need to," Mehta assured him, and then he smirked. "Hey, maybe there'll be a beautiful suspect I could get tips from. I hear this area is known for that sort of thing."

Will glared at him. "I've told you to do what I say, not what I do. You're not to go looking for trouble."

"Why not? I heard from one of the best DCIs in the area that it's a great way to solve a case."

Their conversation was interrupted by Francis Ruark's arrival, so Will went over the facts a second time, and then they turned on their torches and set out through the woods. Their footfalls padded lightly on the forest floor as they walked slowly, not wanting to trip over bushes that had been smashed flat by the quad earlier. Ruark had called for an ambulance, instructing the crew to give him two hours with the body before they needed to be there.

He didn't need that long. He knelt beside the hole and took snapshots with a camera, the flash strobing the dark forest and overhanging rocks nearby. When he was satisfied with the first of these, he set the camera down on the tarp and leaned further down into the hole, seeming agile despite his gray hair and bifocal eyeglasses. He touched the man's face, probing smashed bones and gashes, frowning as he did his initial examination. He took more photos, and then he moved down the man's torso, examining it minutely despite the fact that the hole in the chest seemed the most likely cause of death. He spent more time on that, his finger in the hole probing, and he took note of the maggots, brushing them away from the wound as he encountered their grub-like little bodies and bagging a few of them to take back to the lab.

When he'd finished with the initial examination, he nodded to the forensic technicians, who came over to help lift the body out of its resting place. This, they did cautiously, wary of disturbing any forensic evidence in the cavity. They had straps which they slowly worked beneath the body and, when five of these supported the head, shoulders, waist, thighs, and legs, they stood on both sides of the hole and, with Will's and Mehta's help, lifted the body carefully up and set it on a newly-laid, sterile tarp covering a stretcher.

Ruark again hovered over the body, looking more closely now that the body was more accessible. He opened the eyes and gazed at them, looked into the mouth, nose, and ears, and turned the head from side to side. He used a sharp instrument to probe inside the chest wound, tutting to himself, and took a temperature reading. When the techs turned the body over for him, he did a similar examination from the back.

Finally, he straightened, grasped his hands behind his back and groaned, and then waved the technicians away with instructions to carry the body on the stretcher out to the road, where they were to stay with it until the ambulance arrived to take it back to his lab in Caernarfon. "I'd say the gunshot wound to the chest is probably the cause of death," he told Will and Mehta. "It wasn't a perfect shot. It missed his heart, but my feeling at this point is that it nicked the inferior vena cava and did enough damage that he'd have bled to death within a few minutes."

"Would he have been conscious?" Will asked.

"For a minute, most probably." Ruark pulled his gloves off inside-out and threw them in a wad into a plastic bag. "It looks like a rifle to me, something they'd have around for hunting or sport. I'll know what it was when I get the bullet out of him. It was a lucky shot because, even though it missed the heart, it hit a major artery that caused massive internal bleeding."

"Any guess as to time of death?"

Ruark considered the question with a wry look at Will. "You know I can't say until I get him in the lab, but from the looks of things, I'd guess somewhere between twenty-four and forty-eight hours ago."

"So, it fits with our timeline," Will concluded. He did some quick calculations in his head. "Evan Bennett's been missing about thirty-two hours," he glanced at the sky, where puffy clouds were beginning to lighten in the east, "or call it thirty-four hours now." The time had passed quickly while Ruark was doing his examination. "Along with Constable Griffiths' visual identification, I think we can be pretty sure who our victim is."

"We'll notify the family now?" Mehta wanted to know.

Will glanced again at the sky. "It'll still be early by the time we walk out of here and get to their place. I'd rather not get them out of bed, if we can delay it a bit."

"I doubt they're getting much sleep, what with the wondering," Ruark observed. "They'll have seen the vehicles coming and going." He didn't mention that one of those was an ambulance.

Will nodded. He'd rather not disturb Bronwyn's sleep, considering how little of it she would have gotten that night. Maybe he and Mehta could hang around a bit and help the technicians carry their equipment out, if they finished up in the next hour or so. He'd need to call Bowers, as well, and fill him in. He thought they could stall for another hour, and then stop by the Bennett's around six, putting them back to the cottage by seven or so. Bronwyn would be awake by then, and they could have breakfast together before he and Mehta settled into the investigation. "Let's hang around here for a bit, then," he suggested, "and we'll stop by the Bennett's and give them the news around six." He wondered if Dylan would be around, or if they'd have a second notification to make. "We can drop Bronwyn's car at the cottage afterwards."

It looked like it might become a long, involved investigation, with their victim not being found for more than a day after the death and no suspect or murder weapon readily identifiable. *Maybe I will be staying in Llangynog until the wedding, Jay's taunting be damned.* Their mid-September date was only three weeks away. The idea kind of pleased him.

Chapter Six

The SOCOs were still crawling over the burial site at six. The sun was well-up by then, adding brilliant sunlight beaming through the trees to the artificial lights they still used. During the night, they'd found bloody drag marks from a spot several feet away to the cairn, creating speculation that Bennett had been transported on the quad after he'd been shot and then dragged to his grave. "It makes me think premeditation," Will told Mehta. "Time would have been a concern, so it's likely he had the grave ready before he shot Bennett."

"He'd have taken the quad back as fast as he could so it'd be there if anyone came looking," Mehta agreed, "and then he could return and finish covering him with the stones afterwards." Mehta looked at the bloody track and frowned. "Or there were two of them, one to stay and bury Bennett, and the other to return the quad and stand watch."

Little blood was found on the rocks that had covered the body, indicating that Bennett had probably stopped bleeding by the time he was buried. There'd been smears on the rocks nearest the bullet wound, but those that had crushed his face were relatively clean, supporting Ruark's initial theory that Bennett was already dead when he was buried.

Two of the technicians tagged along with Will and Mehta as they walked back through the woods to where the tarp-covered quad waited. They pulled the tarp off the quad and set to work dissecting it for evidence. They'd probably take it back to Caernarfon in the end, but a preliminary examination might provide clues faster for Will and Mehta to follow. Once the SOCOs had finished with both the quad and the cairn, they'd spend hours following the quad tracks to look for more evidence, and then they'd comb through the nearby pastureland looking for the gun and any other evidence that turned up there. It would be an all-day exercise, with such a large area to cover. Will pointed out the approximate spot where the mobile phone had been found, but otherwise, he felt that he and Mehta had no reason to stay.

It was nearing half-six when Will and Mehta parked in front of the Bennett house. Gwniera, wearing blue jeans and a sleeveless blue blouse, opened the door at their knock. Her hair was neat, and small silver hoops dangled from her ears. She looked at them apprehensively. "You'd better come in." She stood back to let them pass and then led them to the living room, talking over her shoulder to them. "I sat up all night and watched the vehicles coming and going, so I know you've found him. I saw the ambulance." She stopped just inside the room and turned. "Is he dead?"

Will stepped toward her and took her arm, steering her toward a chair. "Please, you should sit down, Mrs. Bennett. It's better…"

She dropped hard into the chair and raised her chin. "Just tell me."

Will backed off and joined Mehta on a couch. He leaned forward, wanting her to feel engaged with him. "We found Evan late last night, Gwniera. He was dead." He paused to let her take that in, but she seemed impatient rather than grief-stricken, so he went on. "It appears that Evan was murdered. Cause of death was a gunshot wound to the chest."

"He couldn't have done it himself?"

"He'd been buried, Gwniera. It wasn't a suicide. Someone killed him."

She seemed unusually calm to Will. He glanced at Mehta, who returned the look with lifted eyebrows. "Can we ask you some questions, Gwniera? I know it's a difficult time, but the sooner we start an investigation, the better chance we have of finding Evan's killer."

She blinked at him, and then she put both hands to her face, covering her eyes. She held them there for a minute, and Will could see them trembling. When she finally took them away, tears glittered in her eyes and she looked more shaken than she had before. The reaction looked forced to him; he'd get Mehta's take on it later.

"You know he called here and said that the quad wouldn't start," Gwniera said. "He said he was walking home."

"Did he say what was wrong with the quad?" Will kept his voice gentle. Everyone reacted differently when there was a death, but he always liked to take it easy with the survivors, no matter what.

"No, he didn't say, just that it wouldn't start so he was walking home."

"Can you check your mobile to see exactly when he called?"

She put a hand to her cheek and her face scrunched. "It was around six."

"I'd like the exact time, please." Will made it a firm request.

She glared at him, but grabbed her mobile from the side table and scrolled to the call. She held it out to him. "5:48." Her earlier display of grief had disappeared. She seemed restless now.

"Thanks for that. Would he have called someone else to come get him, do you think? Maybe Dylan?"

Her answer was immediate. "Dylan was busy with the sheep in the east pasture. He'd have been finishing up for the day. Evan wouldn't have wanted to interrupt his work."

Interesting, that. She hadn't even paused to think it over. It was almost as if she thought Dylan might need an alibi. "No one else?"

"You're thinking of a woman, and I'll say there's probably been one again lately. I said before. He's been home late a lot in the past few months."

"You wouldn't know who it might be?"

She shook her head and reached again to wipe tears from her cheeks. This time, they looked genuine.

"I know this is hard for you," Will sympathized. "We won't keep you much longer. Can you tell me about the family?" He hoped she'd include the former girlfriend Jenna and her son without him having to specifically ask. "Does Evan have siblings?"

"He has a brother, Conway, who farms the land joining ours on the south. It was all one estate originally, but they divided it when Evan and Conway reached their majority. Their father, his name was Lloyd, kept half for himself and gave each of his sons a quarter."

"Is that still the case? They each have a quarter of the original farm?" From the corner of his eye, he saw Mehta taking notes, and he was thankful.

Gwniera froze for a second, and then recovered, as if realizing that the information would be readily available. "Lloyd was killed in an automobile accident twenty years ago."

Will took that in. Farmland could be valuable. Farmers barely scratched a living, and the more land they owned, the easier it was. No one wanted to lease land. Profits were small enough as it was. "Who owns his half of the estate now?"

Gwniera seemed lost in whatever thought had startled her with his earlier question. "He left it to Evan," she said finally, bringing her focus back to him. "He was the eldest, and he was also the only one with a son to farm it after. Dylan would have gotten it all eventually, or at least, our three-quarters, anyway." She blinked. "I guess that time has come."

"How did Conway react to the fact that his brother got all the rest of the farm when they lost their father?"

She hesitated. "He wasn't happy. Truthfully, it left him struggling for a living, while we were better off. He and Evan argued over it. Conway felt that Evan should have shared it with him, despite their father's wishes. Evan didn't agree. There's been a rift between them ever since." She lifted her head as a thought came to her. "You know the Bagleys, of course. They'll tell you about it, I'm sure. Evan and Conway haven't spoken in twenty years."

Would that be a motive for murder? Will didn't see how. Surely, if Conway wanted to kill his brother, he'd have done it long before now. And there was Dylan to consider, as well. Dylan would inherit the farm, so killing Evan would be no benefit to Conway, in the end. Why risk killing his brother when there was nothing to gain from it?

Gwniera was watching him, her earlier tears gone again. "Conway has a son now, too," she told him. "He had the two girls with his first wife Rhosyn, but she died of cancer. He married again, and Mabyn gave him a son."

Will glanced at Mehta, who was frantically scribbling now. "Let's get all the names, please. Can you tell me again? Conway's first wife was Rhosyn? What are his daughters' names?

"Evie and Eiriana."

"They're grown now, I'd imagine?"

"Yes." Gwniera thought about it. "Evie was born the year before Dylan, so she must be twenty-nine. She's married now and lives in Wrexham, I think. Eiriana is a year younger than Dylan, so she'd be twenty-seven. As far as I know, she isn't married, and I know she doesn't live here, but I'm not sure where she is now. I used to try to keep track of them, but it's been too long. It's difficult with our families being estranged."

"Dylan is twenty-eight, then?"

"Yes, that's right."

"And you said Conway had a son now? How old is he?"

She did some calculations. "He married Mabyn about a year after Rhosyn passed. That was the same year Lloyd died in the accident. Terrwyn came along the next year, so he must be about nineteen."

"And that's it for Conway's family?" Will glanced at Mehta, who gave him a subtle thumbs-up to show he'd gotten it all.

"Yes, that's them." She looked away. "I missed Rhosyn after the men argued, and I did manage to see her from time to time, when the men were busy. I understood that Lloyd thought he was doing right giving Evan the land, but it was hard for Conway and Rhosyn, and she couldn't work, being sick, so they only had the farm income. Then, when Conway finally had a son after he married Mabyn, I thought Evan might soften a little and give Evan his share, after all."

"But he didn't," Will concluded for her.

She shook her head. "Evan wasn't an easy man, Inspector. He liked to flaunt what he had, and he thought himself an important man about town, if you can call this village a town."

"What was your relationship with him like, if I may ask?" Will ventured, hoping she'd say more.

"Well, I stayed, so you have to give me that," she told them. "You'll know about his affair with Jenna. I nearly left him then, but he didn't want to give up the money I'd be owed. Evan was always interested in the money. He talked me into staying, and, truth be told, I didn't want to give up what I had here, either. Maybe Evan wasn't the best of husbands, but I grew up in the village, and I liked being near to my parents." She paused. "They've moved now, to Shrewsbury." She hesitated again. "I guess, in the end, I just didn't want to admit defeat where Evan was concerned. I like living here, and I have my horses, as well. If I left, I couldn't take them with me. And I didn't want Evan to think he'd finally driven me off, after all these years."

Will wanted to ask if she loved her husband at all, but it felt too obtrusive. "Can you give me Jenna's last name?"

"She's Jenna Perry, and her son's name is Awstin. He'd be about eighteen now."

"He still lives with her?"

"Yes. She never married, so I suppose she learned something from the affair with Evan, even if he didn't. She's spoiled the lad, but I hear he's not a bad kid, all in all. Evan wasn't interested in him, so we never knew him."

"Is there anyone else Evan had relationships with through the years that I should know about?"

"I'm sure there were lots of women, some I knew about and some I didn't, but I don't know names, Inspector. I tried not to know."

"Did he have enemies?"

She spat out a rough laugh. "I'm sure there were husbands all over who'd have liked to do him in. Maybe some of the women wanted that, too." She thought for a minute. "There'd probably be other people, as well. Evan liked to drive a hard bargain sometimes, and not everyone was happy when all his deals were said and done." She looked him over, and her eyes drifted to Mehta. "You two have your work cut out for you if you're going to find whoever killed Evan."

"Yes, I think we do," Will agreed. He couldn't think what more she could tell them. He glanced at Mehta, who shook his head slightly. "Can we look around inside the house, Gwniera? We sometimes find something that leads us to our killer when we do that. There will be crime scene technicians here soon, but we'd like to have a quick look before they arrive, if that's okay with you."

She looked shocked. "Is that really necessary? Evan didn't die here. He was out in the forested area."

Will assured her that, yes, it was necessary. "We need to know as much as we can about Evan's life if we're to sort out his death."

She stayed in the kitchen while they wandered around, looking the house over. This was no stone farmhouse, but a modern structure with stone accents and lots of large windows looking out over the fields and a horse paddock. It was clean, which didn't surprise them since the two of them lived here alone with no children to clutter things up. Family photos of Dylan, some of them with his wife and son, competed for space on a fireplace mantel with photos of a pretty, brown-haired young woman who they supposed to be Dylan's sister Meredith.

Upstairs, they found three bedrooms. The largest, they explored thoroughly, putting on gloves and poking through a walk-in closet full of clothes, his and her chests full of more clothes, and nightstands containing books, lotions, and the other detritus of nighttime needs. A hunting print decorated the wall, and brown and cream-colored bedding looked inviting. On a top shelf in the closet, they found a tin full of coins and a box containing a pistol.

Evan's laptop computer lay charging on a desk in a small study. Will put on fresh gloves and bagged it, sealing the bag and telling Gwniera that the crime scene technicians would take it with them when they arrived shortly.

They asked about other firearms and were shown a collection of rifles that would also be confiscated. They had no way to bag them, so they sealed the gun case with crime scene tape and hoped it wouldn't be disturbed. Gwniera assured them that she knew how to shoot the guns as well as Evan did. "We used to hunt together," she told them, "but now it's just skeet once in a while."

When they'd finished, they sat in Mehta's car. "You want to give me your take on that?" Will asked. Mehta had remained silent through the interview, taking his notes in the background, but not interrupting.

"The way I saw it," Mehta said after a moment's thought, "she tried to fake a little grief in the beginning, but when you gave her the chance to lash out at her husband by reminiscing about family history, that distracted her and she forgot about pretending to care about the man."

"I got the idea it was a pretty miserable marriage. It began with her pregnant and Evan forced to do right by her. She got her horses and a bit of prestige in the village, and what did he get?"

"I bet he resented her for most of their married life," Mehta said. "It's a wonder it wasn't her who was murdered, if you think about it."

"She admits that she knows how to handle a gun."

"Yes, and she has no alibi other than that she was cooking their dinner at the time. Unless Dylan stopped by and saw her, there'd be no one else to verify that." He paused, thinking. "Maybe the two of them did it together."

"Mummy and son murdering the cheating husband and father?"

"It's possible. You met the son. What did you think?"

Will considered the question. "I didn't really get to know him while we were searching the pasture, but he lashed out at me when I said we couldn't open an investigation until his dad had been missing twenty-four hours. I'd say he has a bit of a temper." He looked at Mehta and then rubbed at tired eyes. "Gwniera was angry when we first came over. I got the impression that she was at the end of her rope with Evan. If he was having another affair, maybe she saw that as the last straw. As for Dylan, I'd guess he'd not want to share his inheritance with a number of half-siblings, and letting Evan go on with woman after woman risked the number of those rising. I don't know whether Evan would have left some of the land to his illegitimate children, or not. Maybe if he fancied himself in love with this new woman and she produced a son, that might see him turning his back on Dylan when it comes to who gets the estate."

Mehta expelled a heavy sigh. "If we're looking at means, motive, and opportunity, so far we have a fair number of potential suspects."

"Here comes another," Will observed, nodding toward the side window through which they could see a newer black Ford pickup pulling up beside them. "I'd like to get back to the cottage so Bronwyn has the Land Rover to drive. Let's do that and come back to talk to Dylan later."

They waved at Dylan and drove off, probably to his total bafflement. *I should have at least done a death notification,* Will chided himself, but at the moment he was too tired and run-down to think straight. They'd let Gwniera tell her son about his father's death and come back later to interview him. Will needed a shower, a meal, and maybe a short nap if he was going to function efficiently. He suspected that Mehta needed the same.

Bronwyn had been sitting in the conservatory eating her toast when they drove up. She saw them and waved from the window, and Will wished they'd been earlier so they might have shared a breakfast together, the three of them, while they told her about the case.

She fussed over them, greeting Mehta with a hug that made Will feel just the little bit jealous. The kid looked good with his short beard and thick curls. Mehta grinned at her, chatting happily, and Will's early wish that they'd have more time together turned into a slight grumpiness that had him wanting her out the door and off to work.

He gave her a very abbreviated summary of what they'd discovered while she pulled bacon, sausage, and eggs out of the fridge, and then shooed her out the door, telling her she'd be late for work.

He followed her out, opening the back door for Daisy to jump into the Land Rover. Then, he turned and caught her hand before she could slide into the driver's seat. "Are you okay with all of this?"

She cocked her head to one side quizzically. "You mean Evan being murdered, or you making sure I wasn't there when they uncovered his body?"

He smiled. "Both, I guess. It wasn't that I didn't want you with me last night, you know. It wouldn't have been professional to let you stay, and right now I owe Bowers a huge debt. I don't want to do anything that puts him in a bad light with his superiors again."

She nodded. "I know that."

"It's not only that, though." He hesitated, thinking about how to say what was in his mind. "I see a lot of ugliness when I'm working. It's what my job is all about. You don't belong in that world, any more than you belong in my parents' world." He dropped her hand and waved toward the roadway, which wasn't the right image he wanted to create, but it'd have to do. "You're my peace at the end of the day. That's your side of things, when there's a crime I'm working. That's how you can help me most."

"That, and giving you clues," she reminded him with a smile.

"You'll call your parents and let them know what's happened?"

"Yes, I suppose I should." Her smile faded. "It does bother me to know that a neighbor has been murdered, right in our shared woods. I never really liked Evan, but you don't want that to happen to anyone you know."

"No, you don't," he agreed, "and you like to think you're safe on your own property. Any ideas who might have murdered him?"

She shook her head. "No, sorry. You'll have to figure that out for yourself this time."

"I can probably do that." He kissed her. "You'd better be off, or you'll be late. No walking on the footpath today, right? I want you safe until whoever did this is caught."

"I'll be careful," she promised.

He stood watching as Bronwyn drove away. The thought made him feel rotten, but in a way, he was relieved to know that not everyone in Llangynog was as warm and upright as Bronwyn's family was. He'd tiptoed around her family at first, not sure if he'd be up to their standards, not sure how to fit in. He'd grown more comfortable with them as time passed, of course, but sometimes even now he felt overwhelmed by them. It was a relief to know that even in a tiny village in rural Wales, there were people whose moral compasses weren't quite as high.

When he went back inside, Mehta grinned at him. "If I didn't know better, I'd think you don't want me around Bronwyn," he teased. "Your face turned surly and you pushed her out the door fast and went right out behind her. You couldn't say goodbye right here, with me watching?"

Will shook his head and punched Mehta's arm. "You're too full of yourself. She'd never fancy you, even if she didn't have me outshining you at every turn."

Mehta laughed. "Okay, now we've settled that fuss. Breakfast first, or showers?"

"Showers," Will decided, "and then it's a full English for us to pump up our blood sugar again."

They went their separate ways, Will taking the bathroom off the master bedroom and Mehta the guest bath. When Will emerged twenty minutes later, the scent of frying bacon and sausage had his stomach rumbling with anticipation.

"I didn't know you could cook," he told Mehta, watching him flip the bacon over expertly.

"I live alone." Mehta nudged the sausage to see how brown it was on the bottom. He nodded toward the fridge. "Do you have any eggs in there?"

Will walked over and opened the door. "Yep, and they'll be fresh, too. Bronwyn's mum and sister-in-law are delving into organic fruits and veggies, but eggs are on the list, too. There's a tomato and some mushrooms, as well."

"I'm not much for the veggies," Mehta confessed, to Will's relief. He wasn't crazy about them, either. The more he worked with Mehta, the more he liked him.

Although they'd have liked a nap after breakfast, they decided to tackle Dylan Bennett's interview first, and then decide from there what to do next.

His truck was still parked at his mother's house when they drove up, so they left the Subaru parked next to it and wandered toward the pens and barns behind the main house.

Dylan saw them coming and strode toward them from a small pen where he'd been watching some ewes mill around.

He closed the gate behind him and scratched his head absently as they approached. "I can't figure out how I'll do the shearing by myself," he confessed. "It takes two strong men, at least, to manage it."

"What did you do yesterday?" Will wondered. "Your dad was out by the woods all day, wasn't he?"

"We're not shearing now." Dylan said, glancing at the sheep. "I'm just trying to think toward the future. Guess I'll have to hire someone."

"What was your dad doing out there yesterday? Do you know? It must have been some sort of chore he could do by himself," Mehta observed.

Dylan eyed him. "He was set on having that forested area logged and plowed up. He had it in mind to maybe build some houses there, a little neighborhood, make some big, easy money. I told him over and over there's no market for that here, but he'd already talked to some logging company. and he was determined to get it done." His eyebrows went up as he rolled his eyes. "He was out measuring and marking, deciding on lot sizes and so on. I wasn't about to help him with that, so I left him to it and went to work on the other side of the farm."

"Surely, if you objected, he wouldn't have gone ahead with it," Will said, frowning.

"My opinion didn't count so much once he got that idea in his head." Dylan's voice was bitter.

"What did your mother think about it?" Mehta wanted to know.

"She liked to ride through those woods, so of course, she'd want them left as they are. Besides, she could see it was a stupid idea, just like I could."

"And the rest of the family?" Mehta persisted.

Dylan looked at him again. "You weren't here with him yesterday," he nodded toward Will, "were you?"

"I was here unofficially yesterday," Will reminded him. "It was just neighbors looking for your dad at that point. Now it's a murder, so my partner came over from Caernarfon. This is DI Jay Mehta."

"Yeah, that'd be right." He paused. "No one else wanted him to do it. Bunch of environmentalists, the lot of us, other than him."

Mehta had his list out from their earlier interview with Gwniera. "That'd be your uncle Conway, right? And maybe your sister?"

"My uncle was putting words in my grandmother's ears, and she has a lot of say in what happens." Dylan looked from one to the other of them. "Family, right? What a nuisance."

Will had a sudden thought. "Who inherits the farm, now that your dad's gone?" He remembered Gwniera saying that the grandfather had left it to Evan because he had a son to inherit after, but obviously there were other male children in Dylan's generation now that had come along after the grandfather's death.

"It'll be mine." Dylan smirked, "so I guess I can do whatever I want with it from now on." He went silent as he realized that his words might not be taken as innocently as he intended and then he blurted quickly, "I didn't murder him, though. Why would I, him being my own dad? I need help to run this place. What we do with the woods was a minor disagreement."

"Is there anyone you think *would* have murdered him?" Will asked.

"Lots of people might have." Dylan leaned back against the gate. "I'd start with the husband of my dad's latest girlfriend, if she has one."

"Do you know who that might be?"

"No idea. I'm sure he had one, though. He always had someone on the side." The bitterness made his voice clipped and tense.

"Anyone else?"

"If Conway was going to do it, he'd have done it a long time ago."

They'd heard the same from Gwniera, but maybe something had recently changed. "How about your half-brother?"

Dylan snorted. "What reason would he have? He wasn't going to inherit anything." He blinked as he realized the import of his words again, and then shrugged. "Guess I'd better watch what I say, hadn't I? You'll be fingering me for the main suspect if I'm not careful."

"Should we be looking at you?" Will glanced at Mehta, who was watching the man intently.

"Well, you'll find my fingerprints all over that quad, and I don't have an alibi that you can check since I was working alone that afternoon. My mother will have seen me when I came back to the farm to feed. But, again, I didn't do it."

"Can you run us through some details? Did you work alone all day, or just for the afternoon?"

"Just the afternoon. We mended some fences in the morning." He barked out a laugh. "We've got a couple of lambs, we call them the devil and the demon, and they seem determined to break through any barrier in their way. They're always out on the roadway or stuck in a ravine. One time we found them in the feed trough. Thanks to them, there are always fences to mend."

"What time did you split up, then?" Will could see Mehta had his pen out, taking notes again.

"After our noon meal. We had a bit of an argument about it while we were finishing up with the fence. I went home to my place to eat, and Dad came here, and then I didn't see him again." He reflected on that. "I feel bad about it, truth be told. Our last words were said in anger."

"When did you get home that evening?"

He shrugged again. "It'll have been about six. I came by here and did a few chores, figuring to save Dad the time and maybe make it up to him a little after our argument, and then I went home."

"Your wife will verify that?" They nearly always did, no matter whether it was true or not.

"Yes, she will." He sighed. "You met her. Lisa."

"Does Lisa work outside the home?"

"No. She worked for a while before we were married. She's a nurse."

"You have just the one child?" It made no difference that he could see, but Will was curious. Dylan had brought the little boy in a backpack while they'd gone out searching, but maybe there was a baby being watched by a neighbor while they were out there.

"I have a son, Aeron. You saw him. He's just two and a half, but he already likes to help us out here when I'm willing to put up with him." It was said with some pride. "That's why I brought him along when we were searching for my dad."

Like his mother, Dylan admitted to shooting as a hobby, but he was also an avid hunter, at least for birds. They asked if they could stop by his house and pick up the guns he owned, but he shook his head at that. "Lisa won't have them in the house with Aeron around," he explained, "so whatever I own is here at my dad's place." They would already have taken those, and they'd already be on their way to the lab in Caernarfon for the techs to check them over.

After the interview, Will and Mehta drove back to the crime scene area and watched the technicians comb through weeds, bushes, and even dirt for anything that might give them a clue as to how the crime was carried out and who to suspect. Most of them were still sifting through debris alongside the track the quad had made through the woods, but two had been given the task of examining each of the rocks that had formed the cairn.

Will watched for a few minutes, and then he gave Mehta a sideways glance. "Glad it's them and not me."

Mehta nodded. "I've never really liked getting my hands dirty."

That done, they stopped at the cottage for lunch, hungry again despite their big breakfast. They'd debated taking an afternoon break, but now that their noses were on the scent, they both just wanted to get on with the investigation. They felt able to ignore their exhaustion from the sleepless night as they both caught a second wind.

Will pulled two local craft beers from the fridge and handed one to Mehta, who twisted the lid off and drank. "Dylan didn't try very hard to eliminate himself from our suspect list, did he?" he asked, setting plates of egg mayonnaise sandwiches on the little table in the conservatory.

"I think he likes to talk," Mehta agreed, "and he doesn't always think out his words before he says them." He took a crisp from his plate and popped it into his mouth. "I didn't get any sense of grief at all."

Mehta had a university degree in psychology, so Will respected his observations. "Bronwyn's dad can probably give us some idea of what their relationship was like."

"From what we saw today, I'm guessing they weren't close. You said you saw a bit of a temper on him. I didn't see that at all this time."

"No," Will agreed, "he was in a much better mood. I might ask him about that later." He chewed thoughtfully on a bite of his sandwich. "Get that notepad of yours out, and we'll make a list for this afternoon." He waved his sandwich toward Mehta. "Put down Bronwyn's dad. He'll be out working, but we'll catch him without too much trouble. Maddock'll probably be there, too, so we can talk to the both of them and get a feel for things."

Mehta set his sandwich down and ran his finger down his list. "Conway has the next farm over, so we can see him this afternoon, as well." He glanced at Will. "I wonder if anyone's bothered to tell him about his brother's death?"

Will shrugged. "Gwniera sounded sympathetic toward him, so she might have." He took an apple from the bowl on the table and began to slice it with his knife, putting the pieces on a plate and pushing it toward Mehta. "Have some apple. You need something nutritious."

Mehta shook his head, but he picked up a slice. "I don't remember Bala being far. Could we visit Jenna Perry this evening?"

"I think that's reasonable," Will agreed. "We can save the rest of the family for tomorrow."

"I think we should check with Evan's mother. What was her name?" He looked at his list. "Carys. She might have something to say about who inherits. Dylan did say she had some influence over it."

"It might not be as cut and dried as Dylan made it out to be? That's an interesting point. We'll put Quigley onto finding out who the solicitor is and see if we can get any information about that, and he can tell us where Carys Bennett is living now, as well. We'll need to try to track down the girlfriend, too, if there is one."

"I'd want to talk to the other family members," Mehta said. "Dylan has a cousin who's older than he is. Maybe she thinks she should inherit, or that she would if her dad got part of the farm. It might be Conway who is in line to inherit after Evan, and not Dylan."

"There's Conway's son, too," Mehta pointed out. "And the illegitimate son. They're both late teens, so it could be that one of them reached an age where he decided to deal with Evan."

"Maybe they teamed up together and did it?" As far-fetched as it sounded, it wasn't impossible, was it?

"We should call Bowers and fill him in," Mehta concluded, "and hopefully we'll get some reports back this afternoon from the SOCOs and Ruark. Do you want me to call Quigley and get him onto phone numbers and addresses for the other family members?"

Will grabbed the last two apple slices and popped them in his mouth, one at a time, thinking as he chewed. "I'll call Bowers and you call Quigley. Tell him to get contact information for everyone we know about, and if he could find out where they're working, that'd help, too. We don't want to waste a drive to Bala or Shrewsbury, only to find out whoever we're looking for is gone to work. Tell him to check their criminal records. I'd like to see Evan's phone records, see if there are calls to a girlfriend there we don't know about yet. Computer, too. They'll have picked that up with the guns, I'm sure. Let's get moving, then. I'd like an evening at home later, if we can manage it."

Chapter Seven

Maddock and Bronwyn's dad were busily dipping the sheep, a process that was not just messy and smelly, but also physically difficult. It involved prodding the unwilling sheep through troughs filled with insecticide-laced water. Both wore boots and rubber aprons and were splattered with filth when Will and Mehta wandered around behind the farmhouse to find them.

"That looks like so much fun," Will shouted to them when they were close enough. The bleating of the sheep made his words hard to hear. He dodged the sheepdogs that circled the two of them happily, apparently excited that they'd arrived to watch the commotion with the sheep

"Come join us," Maddock invited them. He pushed a last ewe through the trough and straightened, leaning his crook against the fence and pulling his gloves off. "It's more fun than it looks."

Will waved a hand down the front of his body, pointing at his collared shirt and tie. "Thanks for the invitation, but we're just not dressed for the occasion. Maybe another time?"

"I'll hold you to that," Maddock said with a short laugh. He shoved a wet ewe out of the way and opened the gate. "I'm Maddock," he told Mehta, reaching out a hand that was mostly dry, although not too clean.

"Jay Mehta." Mehta looked as if he was trying to suppress an urge to hold his breath. It did stink.

Bronwyn's dad came up beside Maddock. "This is Rees Bagley," Will introduced him to Mehta. He felt a nudge of surprise that they hadn't previously met, but of course, his professional life and his personal life rarely collided. He nodded at his future father-in-law. "Can we ask you some questions about the Bennetts?"

"Sure, of course you can. Do you mind if we stay outside here? It's just that we'd have to change our clothes if we walk into Gwawr's kitchen just now, and we'll have to get right back to our work after we talk to you."

"That's fine," Will assured him. One of the sheepdogs brushed past him and squeezed through the fence, dashing at the wet ewe still blocking the gate, chasing her off. "What can you tell us about Evan? We know there were rumors about him, but beyond that, what was he like? I assume you've known him a long time?"

"Their land was passed down in the family like ours was, and Evan and I were in school together. He always had an eye for the girls, even then, and they liked him, too, most of them. He was flashy, a good-looking man with money to spend on them." Rees Bagley reflected for a moment. His voice, as always, was quiet. "I'd say that he didn't take things too seriously, for the most part. His school grades were mediocre, as I remember, and you couldn't depend on him to show up if you made plans with him. He helped his dad out on the farm, of course, and he must have been fine with that because he inherited the lot." He shook his head. "I don't know much more. After Lloyd was killed, the farm wasn't as prosperous as I thought it might have been. He liked owning it, but maybe he didn't like working it so much."

That jived with what Dylan had told them. "Did you know he was thinking of logging his part of the forested area that adjoins yours?"

"I heard he had some hairbrained scheme idea that he could build homes there." Maddock shook his head. "Evan liked to take the easy way if he could find one. Dylan was against the idea."

"Did you talk to him about it?"

"Dylan or Evan?" Maddock asked. "I was there in the Tanat when Dylan was venting his frustrations about his dad one night. That's where I heard it."

"We wouldn't have asked Evan about it," Rees Bagley put in. "It was his land; he could do with it what he wanted. It was his money to lose, I guess."

"He wasn't going to get rich on it?"

Maddock glanced at his dad. "If he put up the money to clear the land and to build the houses, I'm guessing that he'd lose a bundle. There's no market here for that sort of thing."

"He wouldn't have listened to anyone," Rees Bagley went on. "Once he made his mind up to something, he was bull-headed about it."

"It doesn't sound as if you liked him much," Mehta commented.

'I'd have said hello if I met him in the pub or drove by where he was working, but did I approve of his life choices? No, I wouldn't say that I did. He cheated Gwniera out of a life where she could go out and about and hold her head up high. It wasn't fair to her, what he did."

"I can tell you that his kids were ashamed of him, too," Maddock joined in. "He was always a topic of village gossip, and what kid likes to think his dad is being talked about, and not in a good way?"

Will hesitated. "Would either of them get to the point where they'd murder him, do you think?"

They looked at each other, each waiting for the other to answer. Finally, Maddock shrugged. "I wouldn't think so, not after all these years, but you never really know, do you, what the breaking point will be?"

"You're saying it's this land development idea of his that might be a breaking point?"

"That," Maddock said, "or the rumor of another woman in his life, again."

They asked about Dylan, then, and Maddock revealed that, as far as he knew, Dylan hadn't followed in his father's footsteps. "He's good-looking, too, but he's always had his feet more planted on the earth than his father did. He and Lisa seem to have a good marriage, and he's besotted with that little boy of his." When they asked about a temper, though, he nodded. "He's been known to get into a fight now and then.

I could see him having it out with his dad if he had a mind to. Now that he's grown, he might not have been reluctant to let him know exactly how he felt about things."

"I'm getting a definite picture of our victim," Mehta confessed as they drove toward the other Bennett's house. They'd gotten directions from Maddock before leaving him and Bronwyn's dad to get back to their chores. "I don't want to see him as deserving what he got. Maybe we need to get a more objective viewpoint."

"I doubt you'll get more objective than the Bagley men." Will signaled and turned off the main road and onto another, narrower one. Summer grasses leaned over into the roadway on both sides, making it feel even narrower. "They probably made him out to be a lot better man than he actually was, if I know them. They'd not want to speak out of turn."

Mehta frowned. "If that was a flattering viewpoint, I'd hate to hear from someone who really didn't like him."

"I think it's more a matter of not respecting him than not liking him," Will said, thinking it out. "He didn't share their values, and that's what they talked about."

"And Dylan? As Maddock said, he's a man grown now. Maybe he decided it was time to take over before his dad did any more damage."

Will thought about that as he watched for the house out his side window. "We won't be taking him off the list just now," he agreed.

Conway's house, in contrast to his brother's, was an older slate farmhouse that had been given some remodeling through the years, but could use more. A brightly-painted red front stoop drew them up stone steps that were crumbling on the edges. Will was reminded of Carys' and Lloyd's abandoned farmhouse with the same red-painted entrance. The oak door, though solid, was scratched deeply down at the bottom where something, probably a dog, had scored it while asking to come inside.

Will knocked, although it was still early afternoon and the likelihood of Conway being at home was slim. He was almost startled when the door opened to reveal a woman in her mid-forties with a round face and softly-waved hair. Behind her, a dog yipped, and she used her foot to block it from escaping, nudging it back away from the door.

"Mrs. Bennett?" Will asked, holding up his warrant card. "Is your husband in?"

"You'll be here about Evan," she answered. She reached down and grasped the dog's collar. "Gwniera called us this morning to tell us what happened."

She didn't seem very distraught over the news. "Is your husband home?" he repeated. "We'll need to talk to him."

Her lips twisted. "I suppose we're all suspects. Everyone knows that Evan and Conway didn't get along." Her arm jerked as the dog tried to tug away from her. "Conway's out dipping the sheep." She pointed. "The trough is back behind the house."

It must be the season; everyone seems to be dipping sheep today, Will thought. "Thanks, Mrs. Bennett. We'll just go around and find him."

She watched them descend back down the steps and wander around to the back of the house. There, pens and troughs bordered a larger barn, reminiscent of the Bagley's barn and from about the same era. A chemical smell nearly overpowered the reek of the sheep, and Will was, again, glad he wasn't a farmer.

A middle-aged man in rubber pants and apron stood just outside the pens, leaning on the fence, waiting for them. His light brown hair framed a weather-roughened face; he looked older than the early fifties they knew him to be. "I saw you drive up," he told them, his voice quiet. "I figured you were police. You'll be wanting to talk about Evan."

Will held out his warrant card. "Thank you for cooperating, sir. I understand you already know what happened to Evan."

"Yes, Gwniera called this morning. She said he was shot, and that he was buried after. Is that right?"

Conway was well-informed. "Yes, sir, that's right. We think it happened around six last evening."

The man shook his head, his face downcast. After a moment, he brought his hands up to his face and rubbed hard at his cheeks. "I don't know what to say." He looked at Will and then sideways at Mehta. "It's such a shock."

"Would you like to sit down somewhere?" Will asked. "This may take a few minutes."

"No, I'm fine here." He waved a hand. "There's not much to sit on unless we go into the house, and I've got my work clothes on. Unless this doesn't work for you?"

"We're fine," Will assured him. A soft noise behind him startled him, and he jerked around to see that Mabyn Bennett had come up behind them.

She nodded at them and walked around them, standing beside her husband and taking his hand. "Terrwyn's on his way," she told him. She looked back at Will and Mehta. "That's our son. He works part-time at an auto-repair shop in Llanfyllin and then he comes home to help out here."

Beside Will, Mehta addressed Conway. He tended to take over when they interviewed women, who typically responded favorably to his soft brown eyes and dark good looks. Will was happy to let him run this interview. "We understand you and your brother had a somewhat contentious relationship. Is that right?"

"If you mean we haven't spoken to each other much in the past twenty years, then yes, that'd be right." Conway's voice was steady, almost devoid of emotion.

"That'd be because Evan inherited all of your father's land, and you got nothing?" Mehta was direct, if a little intrusive.

Conway considered the question, exchanging a look with Mabyn. "That had something to do with it, yes, but it wasn't the major issue between us. We're just two very different men."

"You got along as children?"

"As much as two brothers usually would. Evan was the elder of the two of us, and he got his way more often than not if there was a disagreement." He shrugged. "Now, looking back, I'd say our parents spoiled him. He was charming, and he could wheedle his way to whatever took his fancy."

95

"Nice cars?"

Again, Conway and Mabyn looked at each other. She seemed to encourage him with a slight nod. "Cars, women, whatever he wanted," Conway elaborated. "He grew up with the expectation that he could have anything that caught his eye, and that gave him the confidence to make it happen. You'll know about his women, then?"

Mehta nodded. "We've been told he had an eye for the ladies."

"They returned the interest," Mabyn spoke up. She looked at Mehta and smiled sadly. "Poor Gwniera couldn't keep him at home."

"Do you have a relationship with Gwniera?" Mehta asked her.

"We see each other once in a while, but I can't say that we're best of friends. I do like Gwniera. She's easy to talk to, and she has no illusions where Evan is concerned." She looked at Conway. "We were still newlyweds when Lloyd died and left the land to Evan. I hardly knew the family then." She hesitated. "It was hard on our girls. They were close to their cousins and missed seeing them. They still saw Dylan at school, of course, but Merry was quite a bit younger."

"You said his inheriting your father's land wasn't the major issue between you. What was?" Will spoke up, trying to redirect the focus of the conversation.

Conway seemed to flinch. "I shouldn't have said that." He took a deep breath and let it out. "As I said, we were very different. I can't say I approved of Evan's affairs with other women, of the lifestyle he chose to live." He eyed them. "I lost my first wife Rhosyn to cancer. She was young, only in her twenties, and her death changed me. It brought home the fact that life is short, and our time with people we love should be treasured. I was devastated by her loss; it took me a long time to get over it. In the end, it was my girls who did it because I had to move on for them. They didn't need to grow up with a father so lost in grief that he couldn't raise them the way they deserved to be raised." He glanced at Mabyn affectionately. "When I married Mabyn, I devoted myself to her and the girls. I'd say that's when Evan's affairs with other women really started to disgust me. Maybe it was because Gwniera was pregnant when they married, maybe it was because women were always going to be easy for him to charm – I don't know why he did it, but I couldn't approve."

He stopped talking, his voice trailing off, and tears began to trickle down his cheeks. He swiped at them with his free hand.

"And then Lloyd died and left the land to Evan," Mabyn took over. "I know he said he did it because Evan had a son. He had Dylan, who could farm it after Evan was finished, and Conway only had the two girls then. But Lloyd always favored Evan over Conway, and we realized that, too. We always believed that Dylan was just an excuse that Lloyd used to do what he wanted to do anyway."

"We actually thought that Evan would do the right thing, once our son Terrwyn was born," Conway mumbled.

Mabyn gave him a sharp, concerned look. "We thought he'd deed some of the land to us," she clarified, "but that was never Evan's plan. We realized that later. We actually asked him to do it, and he laughed at us."

"That must have been difficult." Mehta's psychology degree took over. He waited for them to elaborate.

"It certainly cemented the rift between us," Conway said. "We had nothing to do with them after that." He looked past Will and Mehta as the sound of an approaching motorcycle had two sheepdogs racing toward the house. "That'll be Terrwyn."

"How old is your son?" Will asked, assuming that Mehta would take notes if he started asking questions.

"He's nineteen," Mabyn answered. She smiled as the motorcycle rumbled around the house and toward them, rolling to a stop beside the sheep pens. A young man dismounted, removed his helmet, and hurried over, shooing the dogs out of his way.

"DCI Will Cooper," Will reached out a hand for the boy to shake. He waved at Mehta. "This is DI Jay Mehta."

Terrwyn Bennett looked like his mother with short brown hair and restless brown eyes. He was shorter than Will, about Mehta's height, but heavier than Mehta. He looked strong and fit. "I'm Terrwyn," he introduced himself. "We thought we should all be here when you asked about Evan."

All? Will wondered about Conway's two daughters from his first marriage. "Do your sisters live locally?"

Terrwyn looked abashed. "I meant all of us who still live here on the farm," he tried to correct his earlier statement. "My sisters are kind of out of the picture."

"Evie lives in Wrexham," Conway clarified, as Mehta scribbled notes. "She and her husband are trying to establish themselves as photographers. It's a tough business, but they have an online studio that allows them to work from home unless they're out on a job, so that keeps expenses down." He paused. "Eriana lives in Cardiff. She has a job with Aer Lingus, so she's able to travel. She seems to enjoy it."

"You live here on the farm?" Will addressed Terrwyn. "You help your dad?"

The young man flicked a brief smile at his father. "I want to farm it someday when Dad's not able to manage anymore, but right now there's not enough income from what we have to support all of us, so I work part-time in Llanfyllin, too. I'll probably go to full-time at the shop pretty soon, but I want to keep my hand in the farm work so I know how to keep it going when it's time to take it over."

"We've talked of him going to university, getting a degree in agriculture," Mabyn added. "He wants to save up a bit first, is all."

"I'll go next year," he assured her. "I'm saving all my extra money to finance it, but I'll still probably be living in a squat." His grin was self-deprecating.

"Did you have a relationship with your uncle?" Will asked.

Terrwyn gave a quick shake of his head. "I saw him once in a while. The village is small, so you're bound to run into each other from time to time. But we didn't speak." From the tone of his voice, Will gathered that the feud between his father and his uncle mattered to Terrwyn. Maybe it'd be down to his youth, but perhaps he found the idea of vengeance toward his uncle exciting. Was it possible that it would it extend to murder, though?

Will glanced at Mehta, wondering if he had any more questions before they asked for alibis.

"Can you tell us how your father's will was set up, Conway? How about your mother? Were provisions made for her support?" Mehta caught a topic Will had forgotten.

Conway took a breath. "It was set up as a trust. Mother got an income from the investment fund to support her for the rest of her life. She lives in a retirement community in Shrewsbury now, quite comfortably."

"Can she change the terms of the trust, if she wants to?"

"I'm not sure. Maybe, with Evan's agreement, she could have. I don't know. It might be up to Dylan now, I suppose."

"Do you maintain a relationship with her?" Mehta pushed him.

"We do," Conway told them. "We see her often, take her out to lunch or to go shopping."

"How did she feel about Evan inheriting their portion of the farm? Did she ever talk about it?"

"You have to understand, Inspector, my mother was a practical woman. She grew up on a farm and understood what a farmer's wife's role should be. She let my father make all the major decisions and supported him fully, so when he decided to give his part of the farm to Evan, she wouldn't have opposed him. In her mind, I'm sure she thought that I already had a portion of the farm, and since Evan had a son to farm with him, it was right that he should have all the rest." He hesitated. "You're probably aware that there are abandoned farms in the area. I might have bought more land, but I'd have had to mortgage what I had to manage it. I do lease extra land, but it's expensive and I don't make much off it after expenses." He paused thoughtfully. "I love my mother, Inspector. The last thing I'd want to do is to make her feel she cheated me out of my inheritance. When I'm with her, I make her feel that we're doing well here, that the farm is very profitable so she doesn't worry over it."

"Did Evan visit her, as well?"

"Yes, of course, he did. Neither of us had a quarrel with her. We called ahead to make sure our paths wouldn't cross, but we both visited her as often as we could manage."

Now it was Mehta who looked to Will for the next question. It was time. Will took a breath. "Can I ask you all where you were around six in the evening on Monday?"

"We were all here," Conway told him. "Terrwyn had finished for the day in Llanfyllin. He got here around – what time, Terrwyn?"

"It was around two," Terrwyn supplied the answer. "I worked the morning at the shop, and then I had some lunch and came here to work through the afternoon. I said hello to Mum in the house, and then we got to work. We were finishing up the shearing, and it takes two of us to manage that chore."

"You finished that, when?"

Terrwyn looked at his father, then shrugged. "Dad had done some of it earlier. We finished around half four, I guess."

"Did you stay here afterwards, maybe relax with your parents after a day's work?"

"No, I wanted to get myself cleaned up and out of here." Will didn't miss that his words contradicted what Conway had just said. "I was headed off to Chirk for some farm supplies, and then I thought I'd get some dinner there, treat myself."

"I'd forgotten that," Conway interrupted. He looked sheepish. "I wasn't lying to you, Inspectors. I just forgot."

"What, specifically, were you after?" Will addressed Terrwyn again, watching him closely.

He didn't hesitate. "We'd left some shears to be sharpened. I needed to pick them up."

Will glanced at Mehta and saw that he, too, had picked up that going after the shears wasn't exactly the same as going for farm supplies. "What time did you get back here, then?"

Terrwyn took a breath, looking skyward, thinking. "It must have been near eight."

Plenty of time to do the deed. "Can you give me the name of the restaurant where you ate?"

"Lord Moreton. It's a pub."

Will grinned at him, trying to make it sound jokey. "I don't suppose you used a credit card?"

Terrwyn responded in kind. "Cash. It was a busy place, but maybe they'll remember me."

Again, they asked about guns, and again, they were told that both Terrwyn and Conway liked to shoot recreationally. Terrwyn belonged to a club in Llanfyllin, where he target-shot regularly, and occasionally Conway joined him, a father and son activity they could enjoy together.

Conway took Will into the house and showed him the gun safe, agreeing to allow him to take the guns for examination in a lab. It took nearly an hour to carefully bag each gun in separate black plastic bin bags and load them into the boot of the car.

It was a short drive back to Evan's house, where the crime scene technicians were still at work. They transferred Conway's gun collection to their van, glad not to have to deliver them to the lab in Caernarfon themselves.

"Of course, if one of them shot Evan, that gun wouldn't be back in the safe with the others," Will pointed out as they drove down the road toward Llangynog and the cottage. "It's out in the woods somewhere, is my guess."

"That's left us a lot of territory to search," Mehta observed. "Terrwyn didn't have much of an alibi, did he?"

"You caught the slip about the shears, too. Going for farm supplies isn't quite what he was doing, if he was just picking up resharpened shears."

"But does it mean anything?"

Will shrugged. "Probably not." He slowed as they drove through the village. "We should get you booked into the B&B. Not that it's likely to fill up, but it'd be nice to have that done." He turned into the car park and glanced at Mehta. "Unless you want to stay with us? You can have Lark's room."

"The B&B will be fine for me." Mehta assured him. "I know the department will pay for it, and I won't feel like I'm in the way in case you feel like some romance."

Will reached over and punched him lightly. "I've told you before. I won't tolerate that sort of cheekiness from you." He smiled and pulled into the car park beside the New Inn. "Come on, let's get you a room. You can have a nice night of imagining what I'm up to while you try to get some sleep."

Once the booking was accomplished, they drove to Llanfyllin for groceries and, with nothing else on the day's agenda, arrived back at the cottage in time for a drink before they expected Bronwyn home.

Will put the groceries away and got two beers out of the fridge, handing one to Mehta. "I don't suppose you brought a white board with you in the car?"

"I think the assumption is that we'd use the local station to set up a room." Mehta took a sip of his beer. He looked at the label. "Local brew?"

"Buckskin from Wild Horse," Will told him, "over on the coast. I bought some to leave here the last time I saw it on the shelf in the off-license." He settled into his chair. "I don't want us driving to Llanfyllin every day to update a board."

"It's not far, only twenty minutes. They'll have other resources we might need."

"You're thinking of computers and techs to use them." Will pondered the idea, and then rejected it. He'd rather spend his time at the cottage, at the place he now thought of as home, than enclosed by the walls of a station. He gestured toward the largest of the living room walls. "We'll make our own board here in the living room. We can tape up a picture of Evan Bennett and then use sticky notes for the others."

Mehta grinned. "Bronwyn doesn't mind a murder board on her living room wall?"

"She won't care." They'd grown comfortable living together the past half year, and he knew she'd enjoy being as involved in the investigation as he'd allow her to be. His task would be to try to keep her involvement limited, and that would be harder with it right there in front of her. "We can get Quigley to send a picture of Bennett and some of our suspects, too; he can collect them from the driving licenses, if nothing else."

"We'll want to print them. Could Bronwyn do that at the centre?"

"She could," Will allowed, "but I wouldn't like to ask her to. The centre struggles financially, and color ink is expensive when you're printing a bunch of photos. I wish we'd thought of it sooner. We could have done that when we went to Llanfyllin for groceries."

"Here's an idea," Mehta said. "How about we take Bronwyn into Llanfyllin for dinner when she gets off work? That way we could print the pictures and get other things we need, like sticky notes, string, tacks, like that. We'll make a list." His dark eyes were alight with happiness.

"Call Quigley and ask for the pictures. He must have other information for us by now, too. We can have a nice evening, and then when we get back here, we can drink some of your whiskey and set up our board."

"That sounds perfect to me," Will agreed. He hoped Bowers would think so, too. Maybe it'd be better if they just didn't tell him they were doing it that way.

Chapter Eight

Bronwyn had anticipated a quiet day at work. They had no groups scheduled in that day, so all she'd need to do was catch up on paperwork and be available in case of a wandering pilgrim who needed attention. There were days, and this was one of them, when she felt she didn't earn the salary they paid her.

Janice had some counselling sessions scheduled that would keep her busier than Bronwyn, but the two of them could doubtless find common free time to enjoy lunch out in the sensory garden, and Bronwyn looked forward to that. Not that she had any worries at the moment. It was just nice to relax and chat with a friend.

And that was exactly how the morning went. Bronwyn logged onto her computer and answered three emails, took two phone calls, and sorted through the mail when it arrived, throwing most of it away. She looked over the calendar, making sure she had lunches prearranged for the days that groups would require them while she was away, and she made a list of supplies they'd need when the next order was requested.

When she could think of nothing more that needed to be done, she took Daisy out into the sensory garden and sat on the bench, relaxing. She'd made some improvements to the garden the past spring, paying for some of them out of her own pocket. She'd bought some new plants that would create different textures to be explored: ferns, grasses, Dusty Miller. She'd also added a bird feeder that needed filling again, and – her favorite item – a solar-powered pump for the birdbath that kept water splashing merrily as long as enough sun came through the clouds to make it work. It had been a success through most of the summer, but autumn rain would put an end to the music of the water until the next season. Thanks largely to this garden, her nature therapies had been well-received, even if she didn't get as many bookings as she'd like. She'd have to change it up when the cold weather arrived, but nature didn't disappear in winter, and she'd find a way to continue despite the cold.

She wondered how the investigation was going, whether the SOCOs had found the gun yet and what Will and Jay had learned from their interviews. She knew they'd talked to her dad and Maddock, who really couldn't give them any more information that she, herself, could. She was eager to talk to Will, to see if he had a suspect yet. It was still a little unnerving that a neighbor had been murdered nearly in her own backyard.

Janice joined her in the garden at lunchtime, opening her own container of salad that nearly matched Bronwyn's own. She'd been eating salads all summer, partly to assure that she'd look good on her wedding day, but mostly because she enjoyed them. She varied the ingredients, today's salad being spinach-based with chopped figs, goat cheese, and walnuts.

"Mmmm…that looks good," Janice commented, peeking at Bronwyn's lunch. "I've run out of ideas."

"I got lots of ideas from my workshop last spring," Bronwyn told her. "I want to say thank you every time I think of that, by the way. I'd never have gone without your encouragement, and I got so much out of it, I'm still using something new nearly every time I take a group out."

"I'm glad it was useful." Janice leaned back on the bench and looked up at the trees. "I love this time of year." She mixed her salad with her fork. "Wedding plans all in place now? Any jitters?"

"There isn't much to do," Bronwyn told her. "I've got my dress now, and the bridesmaid dresses are taken care of. Margred picked out her own, and then we bought a similar one for Lark. I had it sent to her to make sure it fits, and she tells me it does." She watched Daisy sniffing around the garden, poking her nose into a cluster of asters. "Truthfully, I'll just be glad when it's over," she confessed, thinking that Janice would understand. "We already feel married. The ceremony is just for our families, not really something we need to feel committed to each other." Making it official was important to her, though, despite her words. She'd thought of a registry office wedding, but she knew she could never get married without her family there, so St. Melangell's it was.

"I get that," Janice told her. "Catherine and I have talked about getting married, but so far we haven't really felt the need. We've been together now for six years, and I don't see either of us wanting out of the relationship. What difference does a piece of paper or a blessing in a church make, in the long run?"

"There are legal considerations," Bronwyn pointed out, wondering how they'd gotten into this conversation. "Being able to make medical decisions for each other, inheritance, things like that."

"And it's the same in your situation," Janice agreed. She sighed and ate a forkful of salad, watching Daisy. "Maybe I'll be next, then."

With nothing else to occupy her time after lunch, Bronwyn escaped the centre and walked up the lane toward the village. She thought that, if she walked up to where she had a signal for her mobile, there might be a message from Will, giving her an update. He didn't like to call her office phone unless it was an emergency. A bank of clouds in the west threatened rain later in the day. Summer was nearly over and autumn tended to be damp in the Tanat Valley. She hoped their wedding day would be one of the rare dry ones, but if not, rainy days made the best pictures, didn't they?

Daisy ran ahead of her, chasing the pheasants that fluttered between the hedgerows and ran up the road, seeming not to understand that they could fly. Daisy dashed from side to side, breaking through the openings in the shrubbery and racing past grazing sheep who jumped away from her, startled.

When her mobile rang, Bronwyn snatched it up quickly, sure that it would be Will. It wasn't. "Hello, Mrs. Cooper," she said when she saw the caller ID. Why would Will's mother be calling her now?

"Why don't you call me Elizabeth?" Mrs. Cooper suggested. There was a moment of silence. "Is this a good time for a call?"

Bronwyn grimaced. What had prompted her to walk up the lane just then? "Yes, it's fine, Elizabeth." It felt strange calling her by her first name. "I'm just on a break and, luckily, I've walked up the lane to where there's a mobile signal." Why did she say that? Now Will's mother would be even more certain that Bronwyn lived in the wild backcountry with sheep and quarries and not much else.

"I just wondered if you might be free the weekend before your wedding? I've been thinking that it would be nice to have an engagement tea for you in the garden, if the weather's nice enough. I know it's rather last-minute, but I had to wait to see what I could arrange for Charles."

Bronwyn's heart raced. *Oh, God, I can't. I just can't. I'd die, not having Will there to run interference for me. This is not happening.* Just having dinner with Will's parents had been a horror. A garden party? "That sounds nice," she replied, trying to keep the panic out of her voice. "I might have to work that Saturday, though."

"I was thinking of the Sunday afternoon. I believe William said that you usually have Sundays and Mondays off work. You could drive down on that morning, pick Lark up from school, and then stay the night in Chepstow, after you take her back."

"That might work," Bronwyn hedged, "but I'd have to check the schedule to make sure I have the Monday free." *Please, God, let there be a booking for that day.*

"I didn't realize that your schedule was as unpredictable as William's is." Bronwyn heard the criticism and frowned. "Still, it wouldn't be unreasonable for you to drive back Sunday evening. I'm thinking that it might last from one until three. Even if you left at four, you'd be home by eight."

"Yes, of course," Bronwyn said.

"Lark would love having a party for you. If you'd like, you could bring your mother along. I'd like to meet her, and I'd like my friends to meet you. With the wedding being so small, they'll not have that chance otherwise."

Bronwyn rolled her eyes. She shouldn't be surprised that Mrs. Cooper thought to mention that the small size of the wedding guest list had left her friends out, an implied insult, at the least. Will always said she was difficult. "Yes," she said again. She couldn't seem to come up with any words beyond that. She knew that she was making the conversation awkward, but she couldn't think what to say. She'd have to think of a nice way to refuse the invitation, and do it soon before Mrs. Cooper had it all set up. Panic clogged her brain.

"We'll talk on Saturday, when you come to get Lark to take her to school. We can firm up the details then, before I call my friends."

"Yes," Bronwyn said again, for the last time, and then the phone went silent in her hand.

She fretted about it that afternoon, suppressing the desire to race home and talk it over with Will. *He'll have an idea how I can avoid going*, she told herself. Really, she couldn't go. A garden party with all of Elizabeth Cooper's wealthy, cultured friends? There was no possibility of her managing that, even with her mother at her side. She'd end up looking a fool and embarrass not only herself, but Will's mother, too. And she'd fret about her own mother being there with her, feeling she'd have to be a buffer against any insults, intended or not, that were thrown her way. It was impossible. She just couldn't do it.

She left early, poking her head into Janice's office to mouth, "I'm off home," before she gathered Daisy and climbed into the Land Rover. She drove blindly, in a hurry to talk to Will, to let him solve the dilemma caused by his mother. She'd been handling the wedding well until this came up, almost looking forward to it. Now, though…

She was relieved to see Will's car in the driveway when she got to the cottage, but disappointed to see Jay's, as well. Their discussion would have to wait until they had time alone.

Inside, she found them in the conservatory, enjoying a beer and chatting, which made her smile. Jay was proving to be a real asset to the department, and Will seemed more excited about the cases the two of them worked together.

Will leaned down from the chair to ruffle Daisy's ears, and then he grinned up at Bronwyn. "We've a surprise for you," he announced. "We're taking you into Bala for dinner."

"At first, it was going to be Llanfyllin," Mehta elaborated, "but then we decided to drive past the house of one of our suspects, in the hope of catching her at home."

"You wouldn't mind, would you? It wouldn't take us long to talk to her, and it'd save a trip tomorrow."

"You couldn't have done that earlier?" she asked, a little irritated at their evident good humor when her own thoughts were racing, on the edge of panic.

"We didn't have an address for her until just a few minutes ago when Quigley called. She works at the Acme Market. We aren't sure what shift she has, so if we catch her at home, great. If not, it'll be a trip for tomorrow."

"You've both got to be tired," she pointed out, knowing that she couldn't relax until the issue of the garden party was resolved. "I can just fix you something here."

"We need some supplies," Mehta informed her. "Sticky notes, string, stuff like that. We need to make a board so we can visualize what we know and what we need to do."

"It can't really wait until tomorrow," Will added. "Would you mind if we stopped in at the centre and printed a picture of Evan? I know it uses ink, but I promise to make a donation to cover it."

The both of them seemed too cheerful, considering that they were working on a murder, but maybe it was just that she was feeling stressed. She wondered if they'd gotten into Will's Famous Grouse before she'd arrived home.

Seeing no other choice, she agreed to their plan. She fumed about it as she changed her clothes, wishing that Will would at least come into the bedroom to give her a kiss in private so she could talk to him. But that didn't happen, so she finally stormed out of the bedroom and they shut Daisy in the cottage, got into her Land Rover, and drove off.

She was quiet as she sat in the back seat, listening to Will and Jay talk over the case. Although she thought she could have supplied them with all the information they'd gotten so far because she knew everyone they'd talked to, she found she was interested in what they were saying, despite her mood.

"Someone sabotaged the quad," Jay insisted at one point, "so it had to be someone living nearby."

That would mean Gwniera, Dylan, or maybe Conway, she surmised, not speaking, but thinking grumpily. Of course, they would have already had those names tagged as main suspects. They didn't need her input.

"No," Will argued then, "they say quads are quirky, that they sometimes just won't run. It doesn't mean anything."

But it does, she thought. It's suspicious, at the least.

The two of them kept talking, while she fumed silently behind them. Finally, Will seemed to notice her silence. "How was your day?" he asked her, looking at her in the rear-view mirror. "Were you busy?"

"It was quiet," she responded shortly. "I didn't have much to do."

"No pilgrims dropping in?" he asked.

She guessed that he wasn't really interested, but just making conversation, trying to figure out why she was so quiet. *Well, he'll just have to keep guessing.* "Just Janice's appointments. I told you, it was quiet." She knew that she was being short with him, that he'd realize something was wrong, but she couldn't help herself.

She was afraid he'd push her further, but just then his mobile rang. He reached into the centre console for it and tossed it to Mehta. "Put it on speaker, will you?"

It was Delwyn Jenner, one of the scene of crime technicians, with news for them. "We found where the gun was fired." His voice came through the speaker louder than Bronwyn would have thought. "It was nearer the quad than the mobile phone, in a place where the forest juts out toward the pasture. That's how we found it so fast. The place looked likely to us. Our shooter would have stood behind a tree at the edge of the field. There were marks on the ground indicating that he used some sort of brace for the gun, which would make his shot more accurate. We found casings, just two shells. One hit the victim, and the other must have gone wild."

"Any idea what type of gun it was?"

"Yes, it looks like a Lee-Enfield Mark 4, .303 caliber. It'd be an older gun. They were produced for the U.K. and Canada for use during the Second World War. Most of them ended up coming home with the soldiers who used them, so this would have probably been in the family

110

for a couple of generations." There was silence for a moment. "After we found that, we fanned out toward the field, and we found blood, quite a lot of it. The rain had diluted it, but enough was left for us to know it was where Mr. Bennett died. There were quad tracks right up to that spot. We could see more clearly once we knew what we were looking for, although the field is so dry this time of year, even the rain wouldn't make mud. It was just flattened grass, mostly. He was almost definitely transported on the quad after he was killed. He'd have died there in the field. That's why there wasn't so much blood at the cairn."

Will looked over at Mehta. None of this was a surprise.

"We've also finished with the quad," Jenner went on. "When we got it up on the rack, we could see right away why it didn't start for Mr. Bennett. There was a nail-sized hole in the bottom of the gas tank."

"Why did it start later, then?" Mehta asked.

"The hole was plugged and more gas put in. He used a bit of clay, like modeling clay, to plug the hole. We're sure your victim was carried to the cairn on the quad, so the shooter would have brought what he needed to repair the hole to the scene with him. If he hadn't driven the quad out to the cairn, there wouldn't have been tracks to follow unless Bennett went out there earlier."

"That fits with what we've speculated," Will said. "We think the cairn was prepared ahead of time, as well. Bennett would have had no reason to ride out there before he was killed. What he was doing didn't involve him being in that area. It'd be too rocky to be included in the clearing of the forest."

"Lots of premeditation on this one," Jenner commented.

"Yes. Anything else?" Will asked.

"No identifiable prints on the quad yet. I'd say it was wiped, but I'm betting we'll find some prints somewhere, when it's all said and done. It won't mean much. It's a farm vehicle. I'm sure most of your suspects would have been expected to touch it at some time or another. The shell casings were clean. No help there."

"Okay, thanks," Will told him, and Mehta cut off the call. They exchanged looks. "It makes our job harder, not having prints," said Will. "I guess you'll be working this case on Saturday by yourself."

111

Bronwyn blinked at that. At least Will was still planning to go with her to take Lark to school. Then she shook herself mentally. Of course, he'd do it. Nothing could stop him. After all, he'd told Maddock once that he was an honorable man, and that meant dependable, too. He'd not back out on something as important as settling Lark in a new boarding school.

They drove past the house belonging to Jenna Thomas, Evan's former girlfriend. They eyed it from the street, a nondescript cottage that looked empty. Will parked, and he and Mehta got out. Bronwyn watched them walk up to the door and knock. They waited, knocked a second time, and then came back to the car. "We'll catch her tomorrow," Will told her as they clambered back in. "It was worth a shot."

It was at the bistro they'd chosen for dinner that Bronwyn finally got a chance to tell Will about his mother's call. They'd perused the menus and sent Mehta up to put in an order. There'd been a queue at the bar, so she decided that sooner was better than later, just to get the conversation done and over with so she could relax and try to enjoy the evening.

She glanced sideways at Will. He was watching her, his eyes wary, and she could tell he knew something was wrong. He leaned closer and started to speak.

She interrupted him, keeping her eyes on Mehta at the bar as she blurted out a summary of her phone conversation with his mother as fast as she could get it out. "She didn't really give me a chance to say what I thought," she complained when she'd finished. She looked at him, sitting beside her, and she picked up her napkin and twisted it in her hands. "I can't do it, Will. Mum and I couldn't cope with what she has in mind; we just couldn't."

"That's why you've been so quiet," he concluded, his voice hushed. He reached an arm around her and hugged her to him. He held her for a long moment, and then he said, carefully, "You'll have to do it, though, love. You do know that, don't you?"

She pulled away and stared at him in horror, ignoring the fact that Mehta had reached the front of the queue and would soon return to the table. "I can't. I thought you'd understand. You know how awkward I am around her."

"I do understand," he said, his voice grim, "and you will, too, once you think about it." He took a breath. "This is typical of what my mother does. She likes to think she's in control and she'll be thinking that, until the issue with Lark is settled for good, we'll both try to appease her by doing whatever she asks us to. She's unhappy that our wedding isn't going to be a big social event she can impress all her friends with, and she was already unhappy that Father's illness keeps her social life in check. She's probably trying to regain some control of her life by seeing if she can manipulate you like she does me, by holding Lark over both our heads. She's done it with me for years, and at least now she realizes it's the two of us, I'd guess. That's something. We're in this together now, for better or worse." He slung his arm around her shoulders again and squeezed her to him. "And we'll have to do what she wants, at least until I can talk her into giving me full custody of Lark. Otherwise, she'll make good on her threats to send Lark to Canada. I know she will. She had it all arranged before I found out about it, and it was all I could do to talk her into waiting."

A flood of emotion crushed her: anger, anxiety, and disappointment, but also empathy for what Will had gone through to maintain his relationship with Lark. She knew his mother manipulated him, and she knew he allowed it. She just hadn't thought about it much. Now, she felt ashamed for not realizing that she'd have to become a part of that struggle with his mother, even though reluctance still had her mind scrambling for a way out of her current dilemma. What he'd said, though, was right. They were a team now. She'd let her panic prevent her from seeing what that meant.

So now, she'd have to gear herself up for another ordeal with Elizabeth Cooper. She'd be the centerpiece of a fancy societal event, meant to be lovely and charming and self-assured. She'd be completely out of her element, a disaster.

Janet Newton

Later, she tried to relax on the couch while Will and Mehta created their murder board on the living room wall. They taped the picture of Evan Bennett in the centre, and then wrote the names of all his relatives on sticky notes and arranged them in a circle around the photo. They'd get photos of the others, too, when they had a chance to print them without using precious resources at the centre. They tacked string from one note to another where there were further connections, like from Gwniera to her children, and they used smaller notes to add details about possible motives, access to the type of weapon that had been used, and alibis, or the lack of them.

When they'd finished with what they had, they poured shots of Will's Famous Grouse and sat down to look at their creation.

"The problem is, we have too many suspects," Will commented, "and all of them seem to have a motive of some sort or another."

"The ones we've talked to so far also have weak or no alibis," Mehta added, "and they all seem comfortable with a gun in their hands."

"Maybe it'll come clearer once you've talked to the others." Bronwyn tried to encourage them. She patted the couch, and Daisy jumped up beside her, snuggling into Bronwyn's lap.

"Our main problem is that Evan Bennett, for all his charm with the ladies, wasn't a very likeable man in the end." Will sipped his drink. "Beyond that, there's the issue of the land. It seems to be a valuable asset. If for some reason Dylan felt that Evan would change his will to favor someone else, or even to split the land up, that would be a strong motive for him to murder his dad."

"We don't know if that's the case yet," Mehta pointed out, "but there's also the issue of Evan planning to invest in developing the land. Everyone we've mentioned that to thinks it was a bad idea, that he would lose money on it, and not just a little bit of money. Dylan or Gwniera might have done it to protect their own financial interests. And Conway mentioned investment money, too. We didn't pursue it then, but we'll need to clarify what he meant by it. Maybe that's something else that one of the family would gain access to after Evan's death."

"We need to talk to Evan's mother, Carys," Mehta said. "I'd like to know how that trust is set up, and whether she can change the terms of it if she wants to. Both Conway and Evan apparently spent time with her

114

through the years. Maybe Conway intends to persuade her to give him the half of the land he feels he's entitled to, now that Evan's out of the picture."

"Quigley's slow with information this time."

"Maybe they're slammed with cases. When do you want to visit Carys?"

"Tomorrow," Will decided as he emptied his glass. "I think she's more important than the daughters in the family." He sighed. "Why can't they all live nearby? It's going to take a lot of our time driving from Shrewsbury to Cardiff to…" he stood up and squinted at the wall, "Bangor. Anyway, I'm all done in right now. Let's get some sleep and regroup tomorrow, here, at nine. That's early enough, considering."

Bronwyn would be gone to work by then. She'd have liked to have been there, to know what their day would entail. But, she reminded herself, she wasn't meant to be involved. Will's boss, Chief Superintendent Bowers, had made that very clear, and she knew that Will was still trying to make up for going off on his own in the spring with his old partner. Never mind that they'd exposed several high-ranking officials in the department as the criminals they were. Now it was time to conform to expectations, to prove that he could follow rules and still get results. If Will was going to be allowed to work from Llangynog, even part-time, she had to stay far away from his cases, or at least appear to. She wondered if she'd get a clue from the Twlwyth Teg that'd help solve this case. She usually only saw and heard things that related to the local area. Evan Bennett had certainly been local. No one could argue with that.

Chapter Nine

Will whimpered in his sleep, tossing his head restlessly on the pillow, breathing hard. Images flashed through his mind, a rapid succession of blood, guns, and the leering face of Chief Superintendent Mathews. Panic came with the images, growing more and more vivid, threatening to stop his breath. He gasped aloud, unaware, and pushed the quilt away from his sweating body.

Something nudged his hand once, and then twice, and he opened his eyes to see Daisy, face-to-face with him in the dim light of the moonlight shining in the window.

He turned over to look at Bronwyn and was relieved to see her still asleep, breathing softly but regularly. He hadn't awakened her, then.

He tried to keep his nightmares to himself, not wanting to worry her. He didn't have them often, but once in a while something triggered them, he didn't always know what. His therapist had told him that stress might bring them back and that they'd fade in time. She'd cleared him for regular duty rather than the easy investigations he'd been assigned when he'd first returned to work, and he'd been relieved when he hadn't had one for the past six weeks. He didn't want to remember the moments when he'd thought he was going to die in that barn in mid-Wales, but it seemed his subconscious mind wasn't ready to let the memories go completely yet.

Thankful that Daisy had wakened him before he woke Bronwyn, he pushed away the sheet and sat up on the edge of the bed, trying to do it carefully. He eased up off the bed and tiptoed out the bedroom door, Daisy trailing behind him. She'd been getting her training as a therapy dog. He didn't know what all that entailed, but obviously waking a distressed sleeper was one of her accomplishments, whether intentional or not.

He went out the French door into the front yard, not caring that he was wearing only his boxer shorts. No one would be awake in the night to see him, he reasoned, and he needed to relax his mind before he dared try to sleep again.

He watched Daisy poke around the garden, her yellow coat visible in the light of the half-moon in a clear sky. He looked up at the stars and wished he knew some constellations to look for. *That's something Lark would like*, he told himself. He suspected that the issue with his mother had brought on the nightmare; as unrelated as it was, it was still stress. He wished he hadn't had to insist that Bronwyn attend his mother's garden tea. He knew how much she'd dread it, but there was nothing he could do about it. Once his mother set her mind to something, he couldn't oppose her or she'd take vengeance one way or another, always involving Lark. He'd worked hard to get her to the point of letting Lark attend school in Wales on a trial basis. He couldn't screw it up now.

The night was quiet, but if he concentrated, he could hear crickets chirping at a distance, probably behind the house where a steep ditch led to fields behind the houses. He felt groggy and cotton-mouthed from the whiskey he'd shared with Jay; it had been more than his usual one shot. He'd have to ration it in the future or both of them would become raging alcoholics. He shut his eyes, trying to relax. He felt chilled now. It was time to try to sleep more.

He called to Daisy, and she trotted into the house ahead of him. He grabbed her collar and pulled her back, not wanting her to disturb Bronwyn. Daisy knew the routine. She obediently sat by the door and watched him walk back into the bedroom. Usually, she'd wait for one of them to tell her, "Okay," and then she'd romp in to join them. Tonight, though, he didn't want any romping, so she'd have to just wait and wait until she decided for herself it was long enough, and then she'd slink into the room quietly so as not to be in trouble.

Despite the interruption of his sleep, Will felt rested in the morning as he padded into the kitchen early. Bronwyn hadn't said much when she'd gotten up, so he thought he'd pamper her with breakfast, and hopefully that would bring some forgiveness. He set to work caramelizing mushrooms and sweet onions in the pan, and when he heard her emerge from her shower, he added eggs and cheese. He popped the toaster down, poured orange juice, and set it all on the table in the conservatory.

She rewarded him with a smile when she saw it. "You don't need to spoil me, Will. I didn't think through the situation when your mother called me. You're right. Keeping her happy is our priority right now, until we get the whole problem of Lark settled."

"She's struggling to keep her life together right now," he said, thinking it was true. "Maybe she really did intend the engagement tea to be a treat for you. I've given up on trying to figure her out. The timing isn't great, with it being the weekend before the wedding, but she probably just now thought of it and there isn't any other time. You'll be okay?"

"I'll have Mum and Lark to keep me company," she said. "I'll do my best to impress her for you, Will."

He smiled, but didn't respond. He wanted to tell her that, if she got him a clue to solve the case in time, he'd go with them to Gloustershire. He couldn't go to the tea, of course, but he'd be there to ease her mind and help her cope afterward. He didn't like to pressure her for clues, though; she did enough of that just by herself. It was probably better to say nothing for now.

He made more omelets when Mehta arrived, and they ate them in the living room as they studied their work from the previous night and made a plan for the day. They agreed that learning the terms of the trust was a priority, so they called Quigley to see if he could find out how they might access that information. He promised to call them back within the hour. They'd also want to talk to Carys Bennett to get information about the trust and anything she might know about Evan's will. Beyond that, they still had family members to interview, some of them living far from

Llangynog. They decided that Jenna Perry would be their afternoon goal, and they'd leave the others for the time being. Cardiff and Bangor were long drives, in opposite directions, but Will might be able to detour toward Cardiff on the Saturday after they delivered Lark to her school, and Mehta could head the other direction to Bangor that same day, which would also allow him to check in at the station and spend a night in his own bed.

"It must be hard to concentrate on the case when your wedding is only a few weeks away," Mehta commented as they drove toward Shrewsbury in Mehta's Subaru. There was no direct route there, so they took the little B4396 toward Oswestry, where they could catch the A5 South, and he watched the narrow road carefully for both wandering sheep and oncoming cars.

"I'm still a little shocked that I'm getting married," Will confessed. "I tried hard to talk myself out of it, even though I always knew that Bronwyn wasn't the sort of girl who was a casual relationship." He hesitated, not liking to confess more. Jay was a good listener, though, almost like a therapist; he'd understand. "Then I almost died last spring," he continued slowly, "and all I could think of was that I'd never get to see whether the two of us would end up together. After it was over, I wanted to make sure that happened." He tossed a grin at Mehta, trying to diffuse the solemnity of his confession. "It'll happen to you one day, too."

"My family would like that."

"Not dating anyone right now, though?"

"It's hard to find the right one." Mehta slowed for a blind corner.

"Tell me about it," Will commiserated. His lips twisted. "Bowers didn't approve of my relationship with Bronwyn for a long time."

"I know. You were dating a suspect in a case. He had no choice but to disapprove."

"I mean, after that. He isn't stupid. He knows that she gives me tips about my cases when they're near to Llangynog. He doesn't like that she's involved."

"But he does like that you solve them," Mehta pointed out. "Did he tell you not to see her?" He pulled over and stopped at a wider spot in the road to allow an oncoming car to pass.

"No, he told me 'no pillow talk.' That was before we moved in together." Will paused, embarrassed, watching Mehta grin as he steered through the last of the lane and merged onto the motorway. "But he also told me that I was entitled to a personal life."

"No pillow talk?" Mehta chuckled. "I'll have to remember that for future reference."

"You aren't to tell anyone in the department." He trusted Mehta not to. "I wouldn't want the others to know." *Especially Beth.* He'd never hear the end of it.

Quigley called just as they were following the sat nav directions to the Riverside Retirement Community, on the east side of Shrewsbury. Will put it on speaker. "Success?" he queried.

"Williams and Williams Solicitors handled it," Quigley informed them, "but they won't release any information about it without a warrant."

"We figured that," Will said as Mehta took a turn across traffic. "Can you get one?"

"Not without more information from you about why you need it."

Will nodded. "Let's wait on it, then. We'll see what we can find out without a warrant first. It may not be important to our case anyway." But he suspected that it was.

"I've checked on that list of suspects for you, and no one has any real criminal past. There are some speeding issues, and Evan Bennett was done for drink driving three times. He's also the major violator when it comes to fast driving with three citations for that."

"Can you text that list to me?"

"Sure, I'll do that. I have current employment for them, as well. Should I text that, too?"

"That'd be helpful. We'd like hours they work, too, if you have that information."

"I don't have shift information, but you can probably figure out most of it from their jobs. I'll send along what I have, and if you need it more specific, let me know and I'll dig deeper."

They drove through the gates of the retirement complex and followed signs toward a modern building of luxury flats, each with its own balcony and plenty of windows. Gardens abounded between buildings, with fountains flowing and August roses still blooming. Many residents were outdoors, sitting on benches, playing at bowls or croquet, or sipping coffee drinks from disposable containers.

We should have called ahead, Will chided himself, seeing this. If Carys Bennett was outdoors, they wouldn't be finding her easily.

Surprisingly, though, she answered the door at their knock. She looked at them inquiringly with fading blue eyes. She wore a flowered blouse in reds and pinks with gray slacks and held onto a zimmer frame, despite looking healthy and spry.

She must be in her eighties, Will thought. He held up his warrant card and introduced himself and Mehta.

"You must be here about Evan," she said, and sudden tears filled her eyes. She dabbed at them with a tissue and then stood back to let them pass by her into the flat. "Please, come in and sit down. I'll make a pot of tea."

The flat was spotlessly clean and nicely furnished. A collection of Staffordshire figurines lined the mantel of an electric fireplace, while vintage china plates, cups, and teapots sparkled in a china hutch. An oil painting of a riverside scene held pride of place over a comfortable sofa, and twin recliners faced the sofa across a coffee table.

Will sat on the sofa, leaving the recliners for Mehta and Mrs. Bennett. Mehta rolled his eyes, indicating the room, and Will nodded. There was money here.

Mrs. Bennett returned quickly from a small kitchen with a tray containing a pot of tea, three mugs, milk and sugar, and a plate of shortbread resting on the seat of the zimmer frame. She pushed it across the floor, paused to set the tray on the coffee table, and then sank gratefully into the empty recliner, pushing the zimmer frame to one side.

"Would you mind doing the honors?" she asked Will, gesturing toward the tray.

"Of course," he said, and he poured three mugs of tea, added sugar and milk to Mrs. Bennett's mug, sugar only to Mehta's, and leaving his own dark. He handed out serviettes and passed the shortbread from one to another of them, helping himself to a piece afterwards. He sipped the tea. Good quality Earl Grey, he thought to himself.

"We're sorry for your loss," Mehta started, once they were settled. Will would let him take the lead again. "We just have a few questions. We won't take much of your time."

"I have all the time in the world, Inspector," she said. "There's not much to keep me occupied unless it's meals or a program of some sort."

"We're curious about your husband's will, Mrs. Bennett. May I call you Carys?"

She nodded.

"We've been told you have an income off it. Is that right?"

"Yes, that's right. Evan was to have the land and the income from that, but I was to have as much of the investment money as I needed." She looked from Mehta to Will. "You're thinking I'm living well now, for a farmer's wife. It's true. I went from an old stone farmhouse to this." She smiled. "I've only been here two years, Inspectors. I stayed in our farmhouse until it got to be difficult." She reached out and touched the zimmer frame.

"Investment money?" Will interrupted, to his shame. He'd meant to stay quiet and take notes while Mehta asked the questions. But Conway had mentioned investments, too, and now was the time to find out what that meant to the investigation. "We were led to believe that the inheritance was primarily about the family land."

"Oh, no," she corrected him with a sad shake of her head, "the land was only part of it. Lloyd's family had the farm, but my family had property that eventually became a quarry. Slate made money for them, and they invested that money in other properties and business opportunities. Lloyd held onto those investments after our marriage for the most part, but Evan has been selling them off as needed to finance this." She waved a hand in the air. "My husband had a rather complicated will; he set it up so that I could live comfortably off the profits of what was, after all, my money."

"The terms of the trust were that the proceeds from the investments could only be used for your support?"

She shook her head. "No, it could be used for other purposes. We had sold off some of the properties before Lloyd's death. Evan built his new house with the money he received, and Conway bought the farmhouse he and Mabyn live in, with the few acres surrounding it." She directed her gaze at Mehta. "That might seem foolish to you, selling it off, but we couldn't all live in our old farmhouse so we had to do something. Once the boys were grown, they needed homes of their own."

"Did Evan make all the financial decisions once Lloyd had passed, or did you retain some voice in it?" Mehta's voice was soft, inviting confidences she might not ordinarily have wanted to share. He was doing a good job with her.

"I let Evan take charge, for the most part. The terms of the trust gave me some control over the investments if I wanted it, but not the land, of course."

That's interesting. So, the farmland might not be the most important part of the inheritance. Will watched them sip their tea, trying not to catch Mehta's eye. Carys might notice their growing interest and stop confiding in them.

"Do you mind me asking, does Dylan inherit both the land and the investments now? Or are there other beneficiaries?" Mehta kept his voice calm.

She rocked back in her chair, resting against the cushions. "Evan wanted to use much of the investment money for a project he had in mind. We'd talked about cashing most of it in and were in the process of doing that."

"So, you're saying there wouldn't have been any investment money left? Just the land?"

"Evan would have used most of it, yes. There'd have been enough left to continue my support, of course. Now," she said reflectively, "the investments will be left as they are, I suppose. Dylan was opposed to his father's scheme. He won't want to cash it all out." She stirred, remembering. "You asked if Dylan would inherit that money, in addition to the farm. The answer is yes. I'd had it in my mind to change the terms of the trust so that Meredith and Conway's children would get a share." She paused. "It's something I've been thinking of since moving here, and I made it a condition for Evan's using the money to develop that forestland that he give them all an income from what he made on that estate, but we hadn't made it official and no one other than Evan and myself knew what I wanted him to do. Now I suppose it'll be up to Dylan to decide how to use the money, other than what I'm entitled to. The circumstances have changed."

"If I may ask," Mehta said softly, "Why was Lloyd set on leaving the farm to Evan? Did he not think Conway a competent farmer?"

"Oh, no, that's not it at all," Carys protested. "It was only that Lloyd was set on keeping the farm intact, and at that time Conway had no sons. He saw the future in Dylan, so he left it to Evan so it could be passed on in the family. He thought Conway's girls would only sell their share, if they inherited it at some future time. He couldn't have foreseen that Conway would someday have a son, too. Even at that, though, dividing the land wouldn't make sense. Farming's a poor man's occupation, and the less land, the less profit you make. Conway had a share of our original land, and we thought he'd eventually sell it back to Evan and find something else to do. Dividing it further would have made no sense."

Not to her, nor to Lloyd, but almost certainly it would have made sense to Conway, who was forced to watch his brother flaunt his inheritance, Will thought. Conway hadn't wanted a different occupation. He'd wanted to be a farmer, too. Carys would realize that now.

They finished their tea with idle chat, and then made their farewells.

"Wow," Mehta summarized their findings as they drove back through the gates of the complex. "Things just got a lot more complicated."

"That about sums it up," Will agreed. "What idiot would set up a will like that? I'm surprised it wasn't Carys in the crosshairs."

"I've got the definite impression that Evan was always the favored son. It makes me wonder why?"

"From everything we've heard, he was the one with the good looks and the charm. Maybe that's all he needed."

"It sounds like Carys and Lloyd thought they'd done enough for Conway by giving him money to buy the nearby farmhouse when it came for sale." Mehta signaled and merged onto the A5.

"I wonder how much that investment money is worth? Carys implied that it was quite a lot of money, if there was plenty to support her in that place and to finance Evan's development."

"Now we have a bigger motive. Dylan would have known that he'd have the land, but he might have been worried that his dad would agree to his grandmother's scheme to divide the money among his sister and cousins and then blow the rest on a venture no one thought would succeed."

"It's something to think about, anyway. Do we need to reopen an investigation into Lloyd's death? Now that we know about the money, too, it might not be a bad idea."

"Let's have Quigley do a quick look at the file, and then if anything looks off, we'll investigate it more." Will hoped it wouldn't come to that. Tracking down witnesses, investigators, doctors and others after twenty years was a time-consuming and probably fruitless effort.

They stopped in Oswestry and shared a ploughman's lunch in a small pub, running the case over and over between them. Working with Mehta always reminded Will of working with his old partner Edward Smythe, and he enjoyed bantering back and forth with him. In the end, they decided interviews with the other family members would be important to their investigation, now that they knew about the investments.

"Can't you get Bronwyn to give you a tip?" Mehta joked. "It'd be easier if she could just describe the car the murderer drives or give us a physical description of him."

Will's lips twisted. "She can't always come up with what we need."

"She seems to do it more often than not."

Will couldn't argue. "We'll just hope this is one of those times. Otherwise, I'll probably have to cancel my honeymoon, and I definitely don't want to do that."

They programmed Jenna Perry's address into the sat nav again. Having driven past it the previous evening, they had a good idea where it was, but neither of them was sure enough to try it without technological help. Twenty minutes later they parked in front of her house, a small stone cottage in an older neighborhood, as nondescript as it had appeared to them before in the dwindling light of the previous day's dusk. They walked up to the door.

A young man opened the door to their knock. He looked at them, startled, his blue eyes wide. He brushed a shock of too-long dark hair away from his face and said, "Who're you?"

My turn, Will thought. *This one might take a firmer hand.* He held up his warrant card. "DCI Will Cooper and DI Jay Mehta," he said as he stepped forward to place a foot in the doorway to block its being shut on him. "We're looking for Jenna Perry. Is she home?"

"She's not off-shift until three," the boy said, giving the door a little push. He frowned at Will's foot. He was a good-looking kid, despite the hair and a shadow of beard on his cheeks.

"We'd like to talk with you, then," Will said firmly. "It's not long until she'll be home, so that'll pass the time while we wait." He glared into the boy's eyes, and the boy backed down. "You're Awstin Perry?"

The boy considered the question for a moment and then nodded. "Okay, then, come on in. What's this about?" He backed away to let them pass into a living room furnished with inexpensive, but well-kept furniture. A large television on the wall had cords running from it to several game consoles, and remotes littered the couch opposite. They hadn't heard from Quigley yet about records on this extension of Evan Bennett's family, but he'd bet this kid had some things in his past he'd not want them knowing about.

Will didn't wait for an invitation to sit, choosing a wingback chair to the left of the couch. Mehta sat on the edge of the couch, and with a sigh, the boy shoved the remotes into a pile and sat beside him.

"We're investigating the death of your natural father, Evan Bennett," Will told him, keeping his voice as calming as he could. "Did you know he'd died?"

"Yeah, Gwniera called us yesterday," Awstin said. "You don't have to call him my natural father. He's my only father. She said he was murdered?" He made it a question.

"We believe so," Will replied, hoping to keep the details to himself. "When did you see him last?"

"On Saturday. He came to watch my rugby match."

Will tried to keep his face from registering his surprise. "Did he do that often?"

"Yeah, he came to most of my matches." Awstin's cheeks reddened in a blush, giving them a glimpse of the obvious charm he'd inherited from his father. "Just in the past few months."

"We were under the impression that you and your father were estranged."

"He wasn't around when I was growing up," Awstin admitted, "but this past year or so, we've gotten to know each other."

"How did that come about?" Will tried to wrap his head around the fact that Evan had a closer relationship with this son than they'd been told.

Awstin shrugged. "I'd only seen him a couple of times, and then after my sixteenth birthday, he called and asked if he could see me. We went out for lunch, just the two of us, and we talked." He glanced at Mehta, obviously embarrassed. "It was awkward at first, but he kept calling me, and after a while it felt okay to be with him."

"How did your mother feel about it?" Will was grasping for connections, trying to put it together. Gwniera thought Evan was having another affair. Maybe he was just seeing his son on those occasions when there were unexplained absences.

"She was fine with it. Mum was never selfish with me. She'd have liked him to come around sooner, is all."

Will nodded, giving himself time to think. "Are you still in school, Awstin?"

"Yeah, I'm finishing up my A levels this year. I'm seventeen." He grinned, suddenly at ease. "University next year."

Thoughts spun in Will's head, but he couldn't form another question. The silence stretched awkwardly.

"What are your future plans?" Mehta came to his rescue.

Awstin ducked his head again. "I like microbiology."

Will blinked. He risked a glance at Mehta, who looked impressed. *That's what I get for stereotyping someone.* Maybe this kid didn't have form, after all. Just because he'd been raised by a single mum and his hair was a little overlong, it didn't follow that he'd be trouble.

"That's impressive," Mehta complimented him. "Do you have a university picked out?"

"I've applied to Oxford, but we'll see. My teachers think I have a chance. I have Liverpool University as a backup plan. It's nearer to Mum, so that'd be okay with me."

"Why microbiology?" Mehta asked. "It seems a strange goal for a rugby player."

"Rugby's just for fun," Awstin elaborated. "I'm good enough, but it's not a career path. I like the idea of microbiology because of the medical applications. Maybe I'll have a hand in developing a cure for some horrible virus or a disease that's been around too long, but never cured. I'd like to think I've helped people."

After that announcement, there didn't seem to be much more to ask, so Will let Mehta guide the conversation toward the merits of the two universities and then to rugby, when they ran out of school questions. Despite his longish hair and single-parent background, they discovered that Awstin Perry was a young man with a lot of potential, and he seemed to have his life figured out.

Jenna Perry arrived home shortly after four, coming in through the back and into the kitchen and then poking her head into the living room, her surprise at having visitors obvious. They stood and introduced themselves and bade Awstin farewell. He was late to rugby practice. Will wanted to ask him for an alibi, but it seemed an awkward start to their conversation with Jenna, so he put it off for the time being. They could ask Jenna about it when they'd finished up her interview instead.

She made tea for them all and then perched in Awstin's spot on the couch, sitting up straight on the edge as if prepared to flee if their questions became too intrusive. She was a pretty woman, if just a bit on the heavy side, with honey-colored hair and soft brown eyes. "I don't know how I can help you, Inspectors. Evan and I haven't had a relationship for a long time."

"Awstin says he's been seeing Evan, though," Will pointed out.

"Awstin's an adult, or near enough to it," she retorted. "He wanted to meet Evan, so I agreed."

"Whose idea was that?" Will wanted to know.

She eyed him. "Evan contacted me nearly a year ago and asked if he could see Awstin. Awstin and I talked it over, and he was in favor of the idea, so they met for lunch. It apparently went well, because after that, they started seeing each other more often."

"How often, would you say?" Will was curious.

She frowned. "Once or twice a month. At first, they went out for meals, and then he learned that Awstin plays rugby, so he started going to the matches and it became a regular thing. He seldom missed a match."

"So, you saw Evan, too?" Will asked, thinking it was logical. "At the matches?"

"I have to work most weekends," she told him. "I work at Spar here in Bala, and my shift doesn't often allow for rugby matches. Occasionally, both Evan and I would be in attendance, but we didn't sit together."

"What caused the rift between you?"

She settled back onto the couch, letting her mouth turn down into a frown. "Evan wasn't happy when I became pregnant. He wanted me to have a termination, and I refused." She glared at Will, and turned her gaze to Mehta, where it softened a little. "I never asked him for anything, no money, no support of any kind. I chose to have my baby, and if he didn't want to be a part of that, then great, I'd manage on my own. And I did." Her chin went up defiantly. "Awstin and I did just fine together."

"He seems a fine young man," Mehta commented.

She smiled at him. "I am very proud of him."

"Can we ask, when did you last see Evan?"

She closed her eyes and thought. "It'd be at one of Awstin's matches during spring season. We met and chatted for a moment after they finished, but I couldn't give you a date." She looked at them. "As I said, Awstin is an adult now. He and Evan met on their own. I didn't keep track of the two of them."

"You didn't mind them seeing each other?"

"I was happy for Awstin to know his dad. Even though Evan and I didn't keep up a relationship, it was important for Awstin to think his dad was someone good, someone he might even look up to. I wanted him to think he came of good parents on both sides."

"Did Awstin know his siblings? Dylan or Meredith?" The thought suddenly occurred to Will and he wanted to ask before it disappeared.

"Neither of them wanted much to do with him," Jenna admitted. "He tried to connect with them on social media, but that's as far as it went."

"Neither you nor Awstin would benefit in any way from Evan's death, would you? Life insurance? An inheritance?" The investment money was still on Will's mind.

She shook her head. "Not that we knew of." She smiled. "Maybe Evan mentioned Awstin in his will? If so, we'll be informed. It wouldn't surprise me if he left him something, now that I think of it. They had been getting on well lately."

Mehta spoke up again. "You never married?" Jenna would be in her late thirties, and she was a pretty woman. Surely, Evan Bennett wasn't the only man to pass through her life.

She blushed. "After Evan, I wasn't keen on getting involved with anyone for a long time. That little affair was pretty disastrous for me, but I lived through it." She smiled. "I've had a long-term boyfriend now for about five years, but we maintain our own homes. I didn't want Awstin to have to deal with a step-father. He knows Phylip and they get on well, but I thought things might change if we all lived in the same household, especially since Phylip has younger children who live with him part-time." She looked at Mehta, doubtless seeing a young man who'd made a success of himself. "Awstin and I always got along fine by ourselves. He never was a lick of trouble. I just didn't want to rock the boat."

"Phylip is happy with that arrangement?"

"He knows that, once Awstin is able to support himself, I'll probably agree to marry him and take on his children. That day will come soon, Inspector. Awstin will be attending university next year."

"Can we have Phylip's full name?" This time, Will was taking the notes.

Her gaze wasn't happy. "I don't want you harassing Phylip over this. He never even met Evan and would have had no quarrel with him."

That's a possibility, Will thought, *but then again, if Evan's death had been expected to bring Awstin some financial support of his own, Phylip might see it as the opportunity to move on with their lives. He might not be as patient as Jenna thinks him to be.* "His name?" he insisted.

"Phylip Thomas." Her voice had turned clipped, and Will thought the interview might be coming to an end.

"Do you or Awstin own any guns, Jenna?"

"No guns here, Inspector," she answered, with a wry twist to her mouth.

"And where were you on Monday evening?"

Now she gave a little laugh. It sounded forced. "I was home, here, alone, so I don't have a good alibi to give you. Did you ask Awstin?"

"We didn't quite get around to that."

She nodded. "He was out with friends, playing video games at his friend Owen's house. They got a pizza ordered in for dinner. He came home around nine in the evening."

"He seemed normal to you?" It wasn't impossible that he'd made up that alibi, or that his friends hadn't helped him murder his father.

"Perfectly normal, Inspector. I can give you his friends' names so you can check with them. Their parents should have been home, as well."

That was that. They thanked her and climbed back into the car for the return trip to Llangynog.

Mehta wrote on the sticky notes that evening as they sipped on Will's Famous Grouse, while Will stuck them up on the wall. Bronwyn watched, curled on the side of the couch with Daisy lying at her feet.

131

"We're getting more motives than we can handle," he commented as he stuck an orange note beside Carys Bennett's name. "The terms of that trust make it possible that any of the family could benefit from Evan's death."

"I'd think none of them would have wanted him wasting the money on a project that they didn't think would be profitable," Mehta agreed.

"Carys reinforced the idea that Conway would have resented being left out when the land was being divided up, at least in my mind." Will reached for another note, this one also orange. They'd decided to assign each suspect a different color, as far as they went. It looked like they'd have far more suspects than they had colors.

"Well, Carys didn't kill Evan at least," Mehta concluded. "She could have hired it done, but what motive did she have? She's the only one we've spoken with so far who seemed to like Evan."

"The favored son," Bronwyn murmured.

"He might not have approved of her living arrangements," Will speculated. "That place has to be expensive. Maybe he'd rather have seen her in a cheaper place so more of the investment money would be available for his project, and she objected."

"I never saw her as a fancy person," Bronwyn said, "but maybe the reason she lives in an expensive place is that she thinks spending the money is better than leaving it behind for the family to argue over."

They thought about that in silence as Will and Mehta sipped their drinks.

"I was surprised by Awstin," Will admitted. "When I first saw him, I thought he'd taken after his dad. I mean, a good-looking kid, raised by a single mum who'd struggle to keep him in line – that's the stereotype, isn't it?"

"Single parents often do a great job raising their kids," Mehta told him. "Statistically, there's no more likelihood of a kid like Awstin having troubles than there is a kid with two parents who might not be any good at the job. Still, there are genetics at play here, too."

"It doesn't look like Dylan took after his dad, either," Will pointed out. "Maybe the both of them are smart enough to see that their dad made mistakes that they don't want to repeat."

"So, we put Phylip Thomas down as a possible suspect?" Mehta's hand hovered over the pile of sticky notes.

"I think we have to," Will said, with an inward groan. Their suspect list was growing, not shrinking. "He could want to hurry things along before the money's gone. It sounds like Awstin had established a good relationship with his dad so maybe he'd be one of his beneficiaries, after all."

Mehta wrote on a yellow note and handed it to Will. "Jenna might not have been opposed to hurrying things along, either. She's been waiting a long time."

"It's true. They might have done it together." He waited while Mehta wrote another pink note to put next to Jenna's name on the wall. "She didn't have an alibi, and we have no real idea whether she has a gun in the house, or whether Phylip does."

There was a quiet moment while they thought. "We haven't heard back from Quigley about Evan's phone and computer," Mehta commented. "I'll talk to him while I'm there, see if he's got anything."

"That'll be helpful," Will told him, stretching his arms up over his head and groaning.

"You're not going to figure it all out tonight," Bronwyn told them. She sat up and reached down to pet Daisy's head, catching Will's attention in more ways than one.

"Let's call it a night," he told Mehta. "We'll decide on tomorrow's plan over breakfast. Eight okay for you?"

Mehta grinned. "I can see I'm not wanted here." He wouldn't have missed the nuances of Bronwyn's words. "Eight works for me. I'll let myself out." He popped the pen closed, stood up, and walked to the door, tossing a look over his shoulder. "Have a nice evening, you two. I'll call Bowers and update him. I can tell you have other things on your mind."

Will laughed. He stood up and gathered the dirty glasses from the tables. "Jay doesn't miss much, does he?"

Bronwyn pushed Daisy away from her feet and got up. "I'll just let Daisy out for a minute."

"Don't be too long," Will told her with a meaningful look. "I do plan to have a nice evening so as not to disappoint Jay. After all…"

"It's nice when you can stay here and work your cases," she grinned as she opened the door for Daisy. She walked out behind her, leaving the door open and watching from the front stoop.

He could see her in the porchlight. Her hair gleamed in the light, surrounded by the darkness, and she looked insubstantial, like an apparition from Welsh mythology. *I'm a lucky man.* Who would have thought so much might change just because he defied the rules and dated a suspect in a case? He'd never regretted it, not then and certainly not now.

Chapter Ten

Bronwyn looked away from her computer toward the window in her office, rolling her shoulders. She'd welcomed in a group of primary school teachers from Dolgellau that morning. They were mid-level teachers, with students Lark's age, and as was often the case with teachers, they were a lively, largely self-sufficient group. They'd had several teacher groups booking conferences in the past month, but with school back in session the next week, that would dwindle off for a while. It was too bad. She enjoyed teacher groups. They were unfailingly cheerful and undemanding.

The sun was blazing in, making the room stuffy, and she longed to be outside, preferably hiking somewhere. It had been a few weeks since she'd had time for a good sketching session, and both the little gift shop at the church and the bigger one at Bodnant Gardens needed restocking of her work. If she could ditch work for a while, she could at least sketch the churchyard, a subject she'd done over and over, and if she got out, she might encounter the Twlwyth Teg and get a clue for Will to help solve his case, as well. But with a group in the conference room, she had to be available, so escaping at the moment was not going to happen.

She took a deep breath and let it out. Her mind wasn't on work these days. Between the wedding and now Evan's murder, she had too many other things to think about. She needed a pilgrim to come in who wanted her advice or a festival to organize, something to make her feel needed and useful. It was probably the wedding on her mind, but somehow her work there at Pennant Melangell felt less important lately than it usually did. She needed to regain her sense of purpose.

It had been four days since Evan Bennett's body had been discovered, but from what she understood by watching Will and Mehta organize their thoughts in the evenings at the cottage, it didn't seem that they were getting anywhere fast as far as figuring out who had killed him. With the wedding only just over two weeks away, she suspected Will was putting more pressure on himself than usual to get it solved quickly. She and Will had both asked for the coming weekend off in order to take Lark to her school, and then they'd, of course, planned to have their wedding weekend off, as well as the week following that. Her schedule could be easily arranged; she simply didn't book anything in for the days she'd asked for off. But Will was a different story. If the case hadn't been solved by then, she wondered what would happen. Surely, Jay couldn't work it alone, so maybe another detective would be assigned to help him, coming in the middle of the case.

She returned her attention to the computer screen. She'd only been answering email inquiries for a half hour, and she still had a couple to deal with before she could get to the major task she'd set herself for the day: updating the website. Sitting in front of a screen wasn't her favorite activity, and she was tired from the late nights spent with Will and Jay. She loved watching them work, but it did disrupt her and Will's normal routine.

She was thinking of taking Daisy out for a quick walk when a tap came at her door and the Reverend Wicklyff peeked in. "Do you have a minute, Bronwyn?"

"Yes, of course." She pushed away from her desk and stood up, wondering what he had on his mind. Maybe he just wanted to go over some of the details for the wedding? "Do you want to talk here, or in your office?"

He glanced around. "I have more room and tea made."

"You don't have to ask me twice," she told him with a grin. "Can Daisy come, or should I have her stay here?"

Daisy was watching him with bright eyes. She was used to him coming and going at the centre, but not so often being in Bronwyn's office. "Of course, she can come, too."

She followed him down a short hallway and into the office he kept in the centre, Daisy padding along behind. He had a desk, of course, with two big bookcases lining the walls, each crammed with books. He sat down at the desk and indicated an easy chair across from it. "Please, have a seat. You take your tea with milk, right?"

Daisy sat beside Bronwyn, watched him for a moment, and then laid down with her head on Bronwyn's foot.

He poured and handed her a cup, and then he sipped and relaxed, closing his eyes for a moment, and then opening them to focus on her. "Are you all ready for your big day?"

She'd been right. "I think so. It's not going to be a fancy wedding, just families and a few friends like we talked about. I have the dresses ready and the flowers are ordered."

"How are you feeling? A bit nervous?"

She wrinkled her nose at him. "Just about the ceremony, not about marrying Will."

"That's good, then. It's going to be very nice." He leaned back and sipped his tea. "I know you have reservations about his family. All okay there now?"

"We'll get through it." She didn't like to confide too much. "Will's mother is having a wedding tea for me on the Sunday before the wedding. I can't say I'm thrilled, but I do think she's trying to get to know me better."

"And the little girl?"

"Lark will be boarding at school this year. We plan to have her most weekends and holidays. It's hard for Will's parents. You know his father has Alzheimer's?"

"Yes, I do. I'm sure his mother is overwhelmed between his care and worrying about her granddaughter. It must be a great comfort to her to know you two are willing to help out as much as possible."

That wasn't quite correct, but Bronwyn didn't like to complain about her future mother-in-law. "We'd like to get full custody of Lark someday, if we can manage it. This year is a sort of trial run, to see how it goes." That was an understatement, for sure. Lark was, Bronwyn thought, the biggest stress she and Will had in their lives, even more than the distance between Llangynog and Caernarfon. Will would be very disappointed if things didn't work out the way he wanted them to.

The reverend set his cup on his desk. "I actually wanted to talk to you about something else."

Bronwyn kept her breathing steady. "What is that?"

"I've thought that our congregation, as small as it is, might enjoy being introduced to the nature therapy you do. We could arrange some small groups after services for a couple of weeks, to see how it goes. After your honeymoon week, of course. I thought I could mention it and then people could sign up, if they want to try it."

"Every service?" It'd be a lot. There were nine services weekly at the church.

"Not the evening service, of course. I'd thought the morning and noon ones, when you're here already. We could schedule them for the days when you don't have a group to attend to."

She did end up with a lot of free time that could be filled by doing this, and she could see how it would enhance the spiritual feeling of Pennant Melangell. "Not after every service, then?"

"No, that would be overdoing it," he admitted, "with as few people as we generally see. Perhaps we could try one morning and one noon, and see how it goes."

"I like the idea." Despite that she still was nervous about leading a group in the exercises, she did like the feeling of helping people find connections to the natural world that brought them a sense of peace. "I know they do this sort of thing in parks and forest areas, but Pennant Melangell is a special place. For me, the mysticism present here is important to the experience. It doesn't just lead to a connection to nature, but also to a place with a long history of sanctuary. I don't think I could convey that sense of both peace and history as well in another place."

He nodded. "I was hoping you'd like the idea, but we'll put it on hold right now. I don't want you thinking of anything else in these next two weeks, just about your beautiful wedding." He reached across the desk and touched her hand. "We're all very happy for you, Bronwyn." He took a breath. "I don't suppose you can say, but do they have any leads on Evan's murder yet?"

"It looks complicated right now. They don't have a lot of clues to go on yet, so they're just doing interviews, getting alibis, that sort of thing."

"Yes, well, I hope they solve it soon."

"So do I." She didn't envy Will and Mehta the work of sorting it all out.

Janice had clients all afternoon, so Bronwyn brought her school group outdoors to the sensory garden for a picnic lunch. Daisy loped happily around the garden, woofing at a bird high in one of the yews, entertaining the strangers in her garden. They sat on chairs she'd brought out for them, eating their sandwiches and crisps and coaxing Daisy over to sample bits while Bronwyn pretended not to see.

She noticed they lingered past their allotted lunch time, and she didn't blame them. The day was brilliant with sunshine and warmth, a perfect early-September day. It might mean they'd end by staying later than they were supposed to, but she didn't mind too much. She had the car, so she'd still most likely beat Will and Mehta home, and she liked being outdoors, too.

She stayed outside when their headmaster finally called them back to their workshop indoors. She'd hurried over to ask if he needed anything from her and was told that they were all set for the afternoon. They even carried their own chairs back inside.

Sitting on the bench afterwards, she closed her eyes against the sun, seeing the red glow that lit her eyelids like a sunset. A breeze stirred her hair onto her cheek, a portent of a change in the weather, and she hoped it would either rain now and get it over with or hold off until after their wedding day.

She took a deep breath and concentrated on her sense of smell. It was early September now, and September smelled of autumn, of ripe grasses and overripe fruits. An ancient apple tree of unknown variety grew at the edge of the garden. No one seemed inclined to chop it down, but nor did they care for the tiny green apples, so they dropped to the ground to rot and scent the air. Bronwyn's mind wandered to apple tart and applesauce and sweet cider as she breathed in their aroma.

She listened next, and she heard Daisy as she explored the garden. A car rumbled in the distance, probably Janice's next appointment, and she opened her eyes to call out to Daisy, to keep her close as they drove up. No one expected to be greeted by an overenthusiastic Labrador when they came for counselling.

She relaxed into the afternoon after that, finishing with the web update and making a couple of phone calls, scheduling a few sessions for Janice. At two-thirty, she checked on the group who were then playing a game that had them running from one corner of the room to the other with stickers in their hands, put a note on her door and called Daisy for a walk down the first part of the footpath toward Pwll Iago, the farm that marked the first mile toward home.

As she wandered, she pondered Evan's murder. Someone had known he would be working out in the woods that day. It was possible that the cairn had been prepared days or weeks ahead of time, waiting for when the chance to murder him came, but the killer would have had to know that Evan was working there or he'd not have been in place to shoot him. He'd sabotaged the quad, waited and watched for Evan to set out for home, and then shot him as he walked. The shell casings and mobile phone hadn't been found far from the quad, but he'd have wanted the cover of the nearby forest to conceal him. The rumbling of thunder might have disguised the sound of the gun, if anyone was near enough to hear it.

She didn't like to think it, but those facts seemed to point to Dylan. Anyone else would have had to take a day off work in order to accomplish all of that. Dylan would have known that Evan would be working in the forested area that day, and he could have easily done it all without worrying about someone seeing him. After all, it was his land to farm, too. If someone saw him poking around the quad, he could say they'd had trouble with it and he was looking it over. If someone saw him out in the woods, so what? He could have been out there for any number of reasons. There were no houses along the lane that led to that part of the farm, so there was no one to report that he'd driven that way after Evan's murder. Would Gwniera give him an alibi? She probably paid little attention to his comings and goings. It was routine for him to help with chores at various times during the day. She couldn't be bothered to greet him every time he drove up or to watch him drive away afterwards. Dylan looked very suspicious. The question now was, should she share her conclusions with Will? *Probably not.* He and Mehta would have their own ideas, and she didn't like to taint the investigation with conjecture that might not be valid at all.

She turned her mind to the engagement tea her future mother-in-law had planned. Will was right, and she still felt ashamed that she hadn't thought it out before complaining to him. If they wanted to stay on Elizabeth Cooper's good side, they both had to work at it, not just Will. By marrying him, she was taking on his family, too. She hadn't told her mum about it yet, but she thought she'd better do it tonight so she could make plans to come along. That's if she wanted to, and Bronwyn wouldn't blame her if she didn't. In fact, she half-hoped that would be the case.

Daisy woofed, a soft bark of greeting, not alarm. Bronwyn stopped walking and smiled as the thoughts fled from her mind. Ahead of her on the side of the path stood Pysgotwr, towering like a stout sapling tree against the hedgerow. His rough brown skin nearly blended with the tunic of overlapping bark pieces he wore, and the leafy crown on his head had begun the change to autumn, green leaves turning rusty on the edges with orange berries gleaming like jewels hanging from tendrils of pale golden grass. She hadn't seen him for several months, and she'd wondered at his absence.

"What are you doing here, so far from the river?" she asked. Nearly always, he'd be fishing with his spaniel when she encountered him.

"I've come to see you, of course," he answered, his voice a growl that could be mistaken for a rumble of distant thunder or a clatter of stones dislodged by a footfall. He bowed his head, shutting his eyes for a moment, and then opened them to look at her. "You are to be wed soon."

"Yes, that's right," she agreed, "in just a little more than a week."

"Here, at Pennant Melangell?"

She was surprised he didn't already know. "Yes, I couldn't have done it anywhere else. This is where I belong, where my heart is."

"You haven't told him, your lover, about us." His voice boomed, and it was hard to determine if there was criticism or even hurt in it. Had her predecessors told their loved ones about their contact with the Twlwyth Teg? With Pysgotwr? Were they proud of their ability to cross the thin lines between worlds, rather than embarrassed like she was?

"Should I?" She wouldn't, no matter what he said, she thought stubbornly. They were her secret, to be kept from almost everyone, but especially from Will. Would the Twlwyth Teg disappear if they felt slighted by her not acknowledging them? Would Pysgotwr? She couldn't imagine her world without them. If it came to a choice between telling him or losing them, what would she choose?

"Secrets are best not kept from the one who is heart-matched with you," Pysgotwr warned her, watching her. "Love cannot live where there is no trust."

"The world is different now," she protested. "Will would think less of me if he knew about you. You know it's true."

He regarded her solemnly. "I do know that your world is changing, but ours is not, except in the ways the two must co-exist."

"I feel honored to call you a friend, and to talk to the Twlwyth Teg, too," she said carefully. "I'm doing my best to continue St. Melangell's mission, as I know you want me to. It's just that it's best if I keep some of what happens to myself, if you don't mind too much."

Brittle, drying leaves crackled as his mouth twisted in a smile. "I came to give you my blessing, not to urge you to do now what you know in your heart you must someday do. We know of the sacrifices you've made to remain here, to protect this place, and for that we honor you. I've come to give you the blessings of your predecessors, of St. Melangell whose spirit still resides here, and my own. I think you will be happy in this marriage."

She drew a breath of shaky relief. "Thank you."

The school group finished early, to her surprise. A few of them lingered behind, chatting together, and a couple of them wandered toward the church. It made her glad. This group hadn't requested a nature meditation, but if they at least took time to look inside the church, they'd feel a little of the benefit of being there.

The suds swished in the sink as Bronwyn eased the five mugs into the water and began to wash them. She took her time, pulling the washcloth around each mug's rim and then pushing it down into the mug and turning it before rinsing it in the hottest water she could tolerate.

She heard Daisy's tail thumping and twisted quickly to see why. She was still nervous alone in the centre after being threatened there nearly two years earlier, but she'd locked the door after the group left and she thought she'd feel safe, despite the silence of the empty building.

A young woman stooped at the kitchen doorway, patting Daisy's head. She hadn't heard her approach, being occupied with the washing up. The woman glanced up at Bronwyn before turning her gaze back to Daisy. "She's beautiful. Friendly, too." With a final rub of Daisy's ears, she straightened and smiled. "I'm Alwena Rosser, the new cleaner." The woman was about Bronwyn's height, but bone thin, with dark hair pulled back and fastened with a band at the back of her neck. She wore denims and a rainbow-colored tee shirt that bagged on her thin frame.

Bronwyn hastily grabbed a tea towel and dried her hands. "Bronwyn Bagley. Call me Bronwyn." She remembered now that the church board had decided to hire a cleaner rather than depending on volunteers, which had been the case for several years past.

The woman peered around the kitchen. "I'm glad to meet you, Bronwyn. You're the coordinator, aren't you? You shouldn't be doing the washing up. That's my job."

"I'd forgotten, that's all," Bronwyn protested. She waved a hand at the counter. "There isn't much to clean up this time anyway. It was only a small group, and I already did the lunch washing up. I rather liked doing it."

"It's okay, then, if I clean the conference room now? They're finished?"

"Sure, yeah, we're done for the day." Bronwyn looked at her curiously. "You must be about my age. Alwyn, is it?"

"Alwena."

"Did you grow up here? Only, I don't think I know you."

Alwena shook her head. "I grew up south of here, in Mallwyd. Do you know it? It's near to the sea coast."

Bronwyn hadn't heard of it. *It must be a tiny village, like Llangynog*, she surmised. "What's brought you here, then?"

"My husband is an accountant, and he does the books for some of the churches in the area, including Pennant Melangell and St. Cynog's. He ran across an ad for properties for sale near to the churches, and we found a bargain on a cottage just down near St. Cynog's. It's nice for me, just having to walk a short way when I clean the church there, and it's not far to walk here, either, in good weather like this."

Bronwyn thought. "Not Granny Powers' old cottage, is it? It's been empty for a few years now."

Alwena blushed. "It was a little run-down, but the price was right. We might fix it up some."

Bronwyn had wondered about buying that cottage, too, but it was more than a little run-down, barely habitable, she thought. Where were her manners? "Would you have time for a cup of tea, Alwena? I've done the kitchen work for you, so you can mark that off your list for tonight. It'd be nice if we could get to know each other a little, don't you think?"

"I wouldn't want to take advantage…"

"Just this once," Bronwyn insisted. "I can find some biscuits in the freezer, I'm sure. Shortbread?"

"Ummm…my favorite." Alwena's face brightened. She wasn't what anyone would call pretty with her thin face and sharp nose, but she seemed nice enough. Bronwyn thought she might become a friend, like Janice, a co-worker to chat with in her free time.

She nodded toward a chair. "Then sit, and I'll just put the kettle on. I can help you if you get behind on things."

"Don't you need to get home, to get dinner? Or are you still single?"

"I'm getting married in a couple of weeks," Bronwyn told her as she filled the kettle and turned it on, "but my fiancée will probably be working late tonight. He's a detective, a DCI, and he works out of Caernarfon major crimes." She was proud of Will and didn't mind bragging a bit. "He stays here on his free days or when there's a local case he's working, which is the case right now."

Alwena blinked. "Why don't you live in Caernarfon, then, if that's where he's based?" She looked at Bronwyn shyly. "I mean, does your job pay so much that you couldn't find something else nearer to him?"

Bronwyn opened a tin and pulled out a tea bag. "I love my job here, and I love living here in Llangynog, so we make it work for us. Do you know what 'hireath' means?"

"Welsh was my first language as a child, and I went to a Welsh school."

"Then you understand why I want to stay here. Will understands, as well." She poured the hot water into the tea pot and hesitated. "I feel called to carry on the work of St. Melangell. Do you know about her?"

"Not much." Alwena watched Bronwyn put shortbread on a plate and microwave it warm. "I think it's something to do with rabbits."

Bronwyn laughed. "She came here in the late eighth century, about twelve hundred years ago, and she established a sanctuary to protect women and also the wildlife in the Tanat Valley." She tossed Alwena a grin. "Including rabbits. That's what this centre is all about: helping individuals to find peace, to restore them mentally and spiritually, to hopefully help them cope with whatever problems they are facing. I like to think I help to enable that healing." She sat down across the little table from Alwena and poured two mugs of tea. "I don't actually do the counselling, at least not much. We have a psychologist for that, and I wouldn't be qualified. But sometimes we get a pilgrim in – that's what we call our drop-ins – and if Janice is busy, I try to help them with whatever they need, which is mostly just a listening ear. I feel good about what little help I can give them. My job doesn't pay very much, but I love what I do, and that's important, too." Her lips drooped in a little pout. "That's why I didn't want to leave the village, and Will respects that so he's the one who does the long commute."

Alwena nibbled on a piece of shortbread. "Cas would never do that." She glanced at Bronwyn. "That's my husband, Cassian. He likes to keep me close by."

"Have you been married long?"

"Three years. It'll be four in the spring." Her voice was soft, almost hushed. "We have a daughter, Nia, who's two and a half." She peeked at Bronwyn over her tea mug. "Her name means 'brightness.'"

"That's beautiful," Bronwyn told her.

"Soon you'll be a newlywed. Will it seem strange to be married?"

"In some ways," Bronwyn conceded, "but we've been sharing the cottage since January, so there's that."

"Working here, with the church board in charge, I wouldn't think that'd go over very well." Alwena was frowning a little.

"Modern times," Bronwyn offered as an excuse.

"Which church do you attend?"

"I don't usually go at all," Bronwyn admitted, "but I guess if I had to choose one or the other, it'd be St. Melangell's. It has a spiritual feel, if you're open to it. I feel connected to all the souls who've come here for sanctuary for the past twelve hundred years." She blushed.

"That's God, working in your life." Alwena said it with the fervor of a true believer.

Bronwyn wondered what she'd say if she knew the truth, that she saw visions in pools of water, chatted with fairies, and counted the Green Man of mythology as one of her most trusted friends. *Time to change the subject.*

But Alwena beat her to it. "I need to get my work done now. I only have an hour before Cas comes to pick me up."

"No staying after hours, then?" Bronwyn tried to tease her.

"I'm to stick with the schedule," she said, her voice serious. "I need to be home for Nia's bedtime, and Cas expects me to be finished on time."

She was the first to arrive home, so she changed into her jeans and called her mum. She explained about the engagement tea. "I'm sorry to do this to you, Mum. It's not my idea of fun, either. But I think I have to do it, to make Elizabeth happy. You don't have to come unless you want to."

"It's a nice gesture," her mum said. "It'll be a nice chance for me to meet her."

"She's not like us," Bronwyn warned her.

"I gathered that. But the world would be a boring place if we were all just alike, wouldn't it? And I'll get to see Lark and spend a weekend with you just before your wedding. I'll look forward to that."

It wasn't long ago that Bronwyn lived at home, that she saw her parents every day. Things had changed fast, good changes, but her relationship with her family was different now already. "We'll come to Monday dinner," she offered on impulse. Her family generally ate together on Mondays, but she and Will had drifted away from that tradition, wanting time alone together since he had to be in Caernarfon so much of the time.

"Bring his partner," her mum suggested.

That was nice of her. "He'll like that." She rang off, and went into the kitchen to start on dinner.

That evening, she sat relaxed in the corner of the couch and watched Will and Mehta as they talked over the case and stuck their notes to the wall. It was beginning to look tattered, with bits of all colors stuck willy-nilly in a widening circle, not the décor she'd imagined for their living room. They'd enjoyed a barbeque, with two bottles of wine, and she was feeling more mellow about... *well, about everything, the engagement tea, Evan's death, life in general,* she thought. The time she'd spent in the sensory garden had calmed her, as she'd known it would, and she'd enjoyed the group that had booked in the conference room that day. Meeting Alwena was a bonus; she'd had a nice time chatting with her. On some days, life was sweet.

Will and Jay had interviewed Dylan's wife Lisa, who verified his alibi, not that it meant much. Wives nearly always provided an alibi for their husbands, even in cases where it was obvious that they despised them. She'd said she'd been home with their son, Aeron, so that was her alibi, as well.

"What's she like" she wanted to know. While she knew Evan's family, Dylan and his sister Merry, she'd only met Lisa in passing.

"She seems nice enough. She says they met through Dylan's sister Meredith, that they were friends at university in Bangor. She and Dylan started dating, and eventually he married her and brought her home to the farm." Will stopped, thinking. "We asked her if she missed the city, and she admitted that she did. But, watching her with their little boy, I'd say she wasn't missing it too much. She seemed happy staying home and being a mum."

"It must get lonely for her, though," Mehta said. "She'd not know any other women her age, and there's no real chance to get out away from the house for a bit."

"There's the playground in the village," Will pointed out. "She can take the little boy there and maybe she'd meet another young mum to chat with."

Bronwyn smiled, watching them, thinking that Alwena might be a friend to Lisa, with her own little daughter not much older than Aeron. Will and Jay worked well together, tossing ideas around, both of them scribbling notes, not arguing, but sometimes disagreeing about things. She wondered what Will's boss would think about her being with them as they worked the case. Surely, Will had mentioned that they were working out of his house, so he must not have raised any major objections.

She noticed that neither of them narrowed their focus on one suspect or another. While she was focused on Dylan, they didn't emphasize him more than anyone else. She wondered if that was usual, or if it was because she was present. Maybe they saved their guesses for when they were away from the cottage.

After a while, they ran out of speculation about the case and chatted about more personal things. She learned that Mehta's family had a bakery in London, and that he had five younger siblings. One of these, a brother next to him in age, had shown an interest in police work and was now a constable in London. "He took after you," she complimented him, and he nodded, pleased.

When Mehta left for the B&B, Will and Bronwyn turned out the lights and took Daisy out behind the cottage for her evening romp. They stood in the growing dusk, watching the sun dip behind the horizon, and then Will took her hand and led her across the lawn toward the sunset. They stopped at the edge of the lawn and listened to Daisy rustling around in the ditch that ran beyond it, dry this time of year, but often swampy otherwise.

A medium-sized oak tree had been planted in the back garden, and she looked up at it now, seeing the limbs stretching like skeleton arms toward the sky. The leaves had thinned, the squirrels having chewed off clusters of them as they harvested the tiny acorns for winter, and she could see the shape of the branches, twisting skyward.

Will pulled her around to face him. "I'm loving this case," he said, "because I can be at home working it."

"And Jay is a good partner."

"He is."

"It's okay for you to take tomorrow off?" Settling Lark in at school would be a big event in her life and one they dared not miss.

"Jay is going to Caernarfon tomorrow. There's a lot that needs to be done – giving Bowers an update, talking to the crime scene techs to push them for details, giving Quigley a "to do" list to save us the time of researching everything ourselves. We need to know more about our suspects' employment situations and relationships, other background stuff, like that, and he's been slow getting back to us about what's on Evan's phone and computer. There's more we're behind on, so he'll get it all caught up again. If he has time, he wants to go to Bangor to talk to Meredith, too."

"She couldn't do it. She lives too far away."

"You can't eliminate anyone at this stage," Will warned her. "Even if she isn't guilty, she might say something that puts us onto someone else."

Bronwyn went quiet for a minute. She turned as Daisy ran up and nuzzled her hand. "I'm worried for Lark. I hope she likes school."

He squeezed her hand. "I know you don't think boarding school is a good option at her age, but trust me, Lark is going to thrive there. Homesickness won't be a problem for her, and she gets along with everyone. We'll probably have to beg to get her to spend a weekend with us once in a while."

"You got her present?"

"Yeah, I picked it up when we were in Shrewsbury."

They were ready, then. *We'll feel like a family tomorrow, she thought, dropping our daughter at school.* It was a strange feeling, not one she was sure she was ready for.

"Bron?" His voice was soft. "I don't say it enough, but thank you for Lark, for letting her be so much a part of our lives." She turned toward him and he smiled down at her, but his face was anxious. "I didn't propose to you just to keep Lark from going to Canada. You know that, right?"

He hadn't told her that his mother disapproved of their living arrangements enough to balk at letting Lark stay with them, even on weekends, but she'd been suspicious. Who wouldn't be? Mrs. Cooper had been happy enough to push Lark off on Will before they'd moved in together. "I believe you, Will; of course, I do." She smiled at him, hoping to ease the worry in his eyes. He wouldn't have proposed simply to keep Lark in his life. "And you had to take on my family, too. I know they're too involved, that they're always in the way, and I still can't believe you kept seeing me when I had to go home to mummy and daddy after every date. That had to be hard."

"Well, I won't say I enjoyed staying in the spare room when I knew you were right upstairs." He looked happier now.

She laughed. "Well, you took care of that problem, all right." She turned again to look at the sky, still holding his hand. The earlier promise of change had brought clouds in the distance, pink and charcoal against a pale blue sky. Just above the horizon the sky blazed red-orange beneath a bank of dark cloud. "Mum called. She wants us to come to family dinner on Monday and to bring Jay. I told her we'd come."

"We should. I know they miss you since you moved out."

She smiled, happy. "I love this life, Will. You and I and Lark, we'll be just fine together."

He pulled her around again and kissed her. It was all the answer she needed.

Chapter Eleven

Bronwyn and Will arrived at Will's parents' house at ten in the morning, having left Llangynog just after six and taken the main motorways south. They'd dropped Daisy off at her parents' house as they passed through the village; there'd have been no room for her with Lark's baggage taking up the cargo area.

Bronwyn smiled broadly as Lark ran out to greet them when they emerged from the car, her short reddish curls bouncing on her shoulders. Excitement lit her face, which was a good sign. Will was probably right; she'd adjust nicely to school life. She was wearing the subdued blue checked gingham dress and blue blazer that comprised the school uniform, but her glittery shoes sparked in the sun that had emerged after a night of rain. The day had turned sunny, fresh and clean after the rain, and that seemed to portend a promising start to Lark's new life as a public-school student.

Will reached out to tousle her hair. "All ready?" he asked, smiling at her with a fondness that shook Bronwyn's heart. She realized that she wasn't the only woman in his life and, despite her assurance to Will the night before, she wasn't so sure she wanted to share him so soon into their married life.

"I have a big suitcase and a small one," she informed him, "mostly full of my uniforms and other clothes. I brought the rabbit you bought me at Pennant Melangell." Her smile drifted to Bronwyn.

"What are you going to do with that? It belongs in the garden." Bronwyn could tell, though, that Will was pleased that she'd liked it enough to bring it along.

"Grandmother said I should pack some things to remind me of home," Lark told him. She glanced back at her grandparents, who had both come out onto the porch.

Will left Lark and walked over to greet them, holding his hand out to shake his father's and nodding at his mother.

"I think we're ready to go, aren't we, Elizabeth?" Will's father said, looking to his wife for agreement.

Bronwyn was confused. She and Will hadn't planned on them coming along. If they did, she and Will would have to drive them all the way back to Gloustershire after. She looked at him sharply. Maybe he'd gotten it mixed up?

"We aren't going with them, Charles," Will's mother said quickly, grabbing his arm. "Remember? William and Bronwyn are taking Lark to stay at school today."

"That's right," he agreed easily. "We have to stay here and keep the house going." He looked at Will. "Is she going to you for holidays, then? Or coming here?"

"We hope she'll come to us," Will exchanged a look with Bronwyn, "but sometimes she'll want to come to see you instead. I'm sure you'll miss her."

"Well, I hope you don't put her in danger," he said, frowning. "I remember now when she was threatened by that woman you were trying to catch. Bad business, that."

"We'll keep her safe," Will assured him. He glanced at his mother, who looked tired.

"He's having a bad day," she said. "It's all the fuss about Lark leaving us. Things that are not part of our usual routine confuse him."

"Did you get someone booked for respite care?" He hadn't mentioned that to Bronwyn. She wondered if the two of them had discussed it, or if he'd just now thought of it.

"Yes, there's a man who's starting next week. He'll be in on Tuesday and Thursday afternoons, as well as on Sundays. That'll free me up some. I can arrange emergency care at other times if I need to. It isn't always like this. Usually, he's more self-sufficient."

Bronwyn still wasn't used to the more formal atmosphere of Will's childhood home. She felt awkward, as if the conversation was forced, too polite.

Will must feel it, too, because he said, "Well, I think we should be on our way. We'll want to be there to get her stuff put away before the welcoming ceremonies at noon."

"You might have come early enough for breakfast with us," his mother complained, "and then you'd have had plenty of time to get there from here."

"It's a long drive, Mother," Will said shortly, "and I'm working a case, so I couldn't get off until late last night."

"Of course," his mother said sourly, "it's always a case."

Will and Bronwyn went up the grand staircase inside and carried Lark's luggage back down the stairs, hefting the bags into the cargo area. Will's father hovered, watching them, and his mother stood on the porch, holding Lark's hand. At the last minute, she turned and hugged her. "You be good at school. Make us proud."

"I will," Lark promised, looking over her shoulder at the car and then back at her grandmother. "It's going to be fun. Uncle Will told me so."

In Chepstow, they drove through the gates to the enclosed campus and followed the drive to the car park nearest to Wye House, the residence hall to which Lark had been assigned. She'd been quiet during the drive, playing her video game sporadically, but as they neared their destination, the sounds of play ended, and Bronwyn glanced back to see her watching out the window.

She's nervous, Bronwyn thought, *and who wouldn't be?* "What are you looking forward to most, Lark?" she asked. Will shot her a grateful look.

"I want to try sports," she answered after a moment's pause. "I thought it would be fun. Grandmother never wanted me to try them before. She said it wasn't ladylike."

"Girls play sports as much as boys do these days," Bronwyn assured her. "Which ones did you have in mind?"

"Um…netball? Hockey? I don't know."

"I think they let you try them all. You can see what you like best."

"I'll wait to see what my friends play," Lark said wisely, "and then I'll play the same thing."

Will parked the car, and they got out. Other families were unloading cars, and a couple in their thirties greeted people as they approached the door.

Will took a breath and grinned at Lark. "Let's go meet your house parents first," he suggested, "and see what the dormitory looks like. Then we'll come back for your kit."

They each took hold of one of Lark's hands and led her through a throng of busy people to the doors of the building. They waited for a family ahead of them to talk to the house parents, and then it was their turn.

"Hello, I'm Will Cooper," Will said, "and this is Bronwyn," he nodded toward her, "and Lark."

"I'm Stacy Bowen," the house mother introduced herself, "and this is William. We're the house parents for Wye House, which is the best house of them all." She grinned at Lark. 'You can call us Stacy and William."

"He has the same name as my Uncle Will," Lark observed solemnly.

"That'll make it easy for you to remember," William told her, bending down and taking her hand. "Welcome to Wye House, Lark. We've been looking forward to meeting you. Can you tell us just one thing?"

She nodded.

"What's your favorite animal?"

It was a question they probably used to break the ice with all the new students. Lark loved animals, so for her, it was a good one. "I like horses best. Or dogs. Does it have to be just one? I love them both."

"I couldn't choose just one, either," Stacy told her. "I'm like you; horses and dogs are both the best. Do you have a horse or a dog?"

Lark looked at Will. "I have a black pony named Hobbs and a Labrador named Daisy." She looked uneasy, as if she was unsure about claiming them. Bronwyn saw Will squeeze her hand and nod.

"That's wonderful," Stacy said. She watched Lark smile. "Just now, we have to say hello to everyone else, but later, we'll chat more and get to know you better, okay, Lark? I love your name, by the way."

"A lark is a bird."

"Or something you do just for the fun of it," Will added. He was probably thinking of his sister Julia, of her getting pregnant with Lark on a whim, or whatever it was. No one would ever know.

"You're her guardians?" William wanted to know, checking a list in his hand.

"We share custody with my parents, Elizabeth and Charles Cooper," Will said, straining to read the list upside down, "but our names should be on your list. We plan for her to be with us for holidays and weekends, unless she wants to stay here."

"We have some wonderful activities for those who stay. I hope she'll want to join us, at least some of the time."

They were waved off to an older student, who led them up to the girls' dormitory. Lark found her little area, with a bed, a wardrobe, and a nightstand, and they retrieved her luggage and helped her unpack.

Lark stayed close to them through the welcoming ceremonies, watching carefully, but quietly sitting between them on the bleachers. At the barbeque lunch, she dutifully filled a plate and sat beside Will. Within minutes, though, she was chatting with another girl who'd sat down beside her, a little girl about her age with short, dark hair and blue eyes.

Lark had barely finished half of the food she'd taken before she asked Will if she could run off with her new friend. He smiled at her indulgently. "Run away! Play!" He gave Bronwyn an embarrassed smile. "I've been through it. Anything that gets her away from our sides and off with a new friend is a big step forward. We don't want any tears when we leave."

Will would be such a good dad, even if Lark wasn't really his. "I admire her. I never would have been that outgoing," she told him.

The pride came off him in waves. "She's something, isn't she? I don't know how she turned out the way she did, but I'm very proud of her."

He'd briefly described his sister and Lark's early life with her, and Bronwyn suspected life with her grandparents hadn't encouraged Lark's obvious independence and joy for life, either. She'd gotten it somehow, though, despite it all. Suddenly, she caught a glimpse of the future. Lark would flourish here where she'd be encouraged to take risks, to experiment with new ideas and activities, to make lifelong friendships. Perhaps it would be a good place for her, after all.

There was a tense moment when the time came for goodbyes on the lawn in front of Wye House. Lark looked around at the other children, and suddenly, tears filled her eyes. She looked at Will, but she didn't say anything.

He squatted down to her level. "Hey, sweetheart, what's this?"

She shook her head, squeezing her eyes shut.

He reached out to tilt her head up so she'd have to look at him. "Bronwyn is coming for you next weekend. You're going to the tea party, remember?"

She nodded reluctantly, glancing at Bronwyn. Tears ran in trails down her cheeks.

"And the weekend after that is our wedding, so you'll be with us then, too. You're the bridesmaid; you have to come." Will smiled at her. "We're a family now, you and Bronwyn and I. We'll be together every weekend, if that's what you want."

She drew in a shuddering breath. "Stacy says I can call you anytime I want to on the house phone."

"Yes, that's right." Will extended his hand toward Bronwyn, and she handed him the little bag she'd retrieved from the car. "Look. We've bought you a present. Want to open it?"

She nodded, so he handed it to her and she peeked inside. There was a moment of silence as she stared at what she saw, and then she looked up in shock. "You got me a mobile of my own!"

He stood up. His knees were probably killing him after all that squatting. "This way you can call us whenever you want to chat about anything, sweetheart, okay? I put my number in it, Bronwyn's, and grandmother's. You can put friends' numbers in it, too. I'll show you how."

"I already know how," she told him. "I'll take good care of it, I promise. I'll put it in my rucksack during the day while we're in class." She had pulled it out and powered it on. "It's pink, Uncle Will!" The earlier tears had disappeared.

"I know your favorite colour."

"Grandmother said I couldn't have one until I'm twelve."

"I talked her into it." Will tried to impress her. Truthfully, it hadn't been much of a challenge. Elizabeth Cooper had seen the wisdom of Lark's being able to call them whenever she felt the need, and the residence phone, while adequate, wasn't like having one of her own. Will suspected that nearly all the other students would have their own mobiles, so now Lark wouldn't be left behind. It was important to have all the coolest stuff, after all.

"I'll call you every day," she cooed to them, glancing over her shoulder at her new friend, whose name, they'd discovered, was Aderyn.

"I'll see you next Sunday," Bronwyn reminded her again, "for the tea party."

"And then the wedding. After that, can I choose if I want to come home or stay here?"

"You can," Will answered her. "I think it'll be fun here on weekends and we won't mind if you decide you want to stay, but we'll love to have you with us whenever you want to. Like I said, the three of us are a family now."

"Grandmother said so?" she asked doubtfully.

"Yes, she did." Will exaggerated his mother's approval, but Bronwyn hoped it would work out the way he wanted it to.

157

Will bent down and kissed Lark's cheek, Bronwyn did the same. Lark blinked at tears that threatened again, and then she took a breath and straightened. "Can I go show Aderyn my new mobile?"

"I think that's exactly what you should do," Will told her. They watched her for a minute, but there didn't seem to be any point to their staying longer, so they took advantage of the moment and left for home.

Will was quiet as they wound around the smaller road that ran alongside the River Wye until they reached the motorway, and then he relaxed. He reached over and patted Bronwyn's knee. "All right?"

"That was hard," she told him, "but you were brilliant. You handled it just the right way, giving her the mobile just at the moment when she needed a distraction."

"I told you. I've been through it. The first time you're left behind is rough, no matter how prepared you think you are. She's going to thrive there, though. You can see that now?"

"I can. We'll have her for weekends, it sounds like."

"The first few, and then it'll probably taper off. They'll have fun weekends planned for the boarders, and she'll want to stay and play with her friends."

She didn't want to ask, but she couldn't stop herself. "And if she ends up not liking it?"

"We'll figure it out if that happens." Will was non-committal. He'd want Lark to stay with them, and she was fine with that, but his mother would probably balk again if she wanted to stay with them full-time.

He signaled and passed a slow-moving lorry in the right-hand lane. "I wonder if Jay is back from Caernarfon?"

Work was never far from his mind, especially when he had a big case going. "Should we call him?"

"No, I don't think so. If he's driving, he can't answer. I'm guessing he was kept busy at the station all morning and then went up to Bangor in the afternoon. We'll get in touch later."

They rode in silence for a minute. Bronwyn watched the scenery go by, but thick shrubbery along the verge obscured most of the view. She wondered what Will was thinking, whether his mind was still on Lark, or on the case, or even on the wedding coming up now so quickly. "Who do you think killed Evan?" she finally blurted, wanting to fill the silence so she wouldn't keep picturing Lark with tears overflowing her eyes.

He was quiet, concentrating on his driving, probably thinking it over.

"You and Jay never talk about who you suspect in the evenings," she pointed out. "You write down their motives, their alibis, their relationships, stuff like that, but you don't try to figure it out. Is that how it always works?"

"No, it's not always like that," Will said. "We do spend a lot of time planning strategy and making notes so we don't forget things. It helps to have it all up in front of us, like we've done on the wall at home." He shrugged. "We have a lot of suspects this time, love, and you're there, so that puts a damper on speculation. Not that we don't appreciate your input, but you haven't been trained in police procedure and all. You'd be going more on gut feeling than evidence, and that might colour the way we see the case."

"Do you talk about it when you're away from the cottage?" She wouldn't care, either way, but she was curious.

"Not this time, not so far."

"Do you want to know what I think?"

He grinned. "Okay, what do you think?"

"Dylan has the best motive. He inherits the lot, and he gets it before Evan could spend all the money on a poorly thought-out investment. He has the access. No one would take notice of him going up there on their own property to make the cairn and to stalk his dad, if that's what it was. He'd know that Evan was up there that day." She looked out the passenger window, seeing nothing. "I don't like to think it's him. I know him, and I think he's a good man. But everything kind of points to him, doesn't it?"

"I agree with you," Will told her, making her happy. "Dylan looks guilty. But everyone so far that we've talked to has a motive of one sort or another. None of them have much of an alibi. They all seem comfortable with guns and shooting. I *do* like Dylan for it. I agree that he's got the most to gain from it, at least financially. That's not to say that, for example, Gwniera didn't take things into her own hands, though.

159

She admits that she's done with Evan's girlfriends, and she says she wants to stay on the farm. If they'd divorced instead, Evan would have gotten that nice house and the land; he was the farmer. Or maybe she'd have done it for Dylan, so he could prosper." He glanced at her. "See what I mean? That's just Gwniera. I can take you through all the family, and I bet every one of them has a strong motive for killing Evan."

She felt chastened. "It must be hard to sort out."

He nodded. "We just keep at it until something turns up that proves which one of them is guilty. It usually happens, if we're diligent."

His mobile startled them, vibrating in the centre console and then ringing loudly in the car. Will grabbed it with his free hand and touched the green button. "Jay," he mouthed to Bronwyn. He set it back down and touched the speaker button. "Hey, we're on our way home, just passing Hereford. Where are you?"

"I just went through Bala. I stopped and got takeout for the three of us for dinner. It's pasta; we can warm it up when we're ready."

"Did you have a productive day?"

"It was good to stop in the office and catch up. Bowers approved of our methods so far, but he'll want you in next week for a day unless we're really busy here. He doesn't like you to get too used to living in Llangynog."

"Your words, or his?" Will was grinning.

"You caught me," Mehta admitted. "He does think we should try harder to find out if Evan was having another affair and, if so, with whom."

"He's thinking angry husband?"

"It is a possibility. Gwniera said he was coming home late, gone for unexplained periods of time."

"And now we know he was spending time with Awstin, so maybe that's all it was," Will pointed out.

"Quigley checked out all the family members, so we now have work information for them all." There was a pause, and Bronwyn assumed Mehta was consulting notes, which he shouldn't do while driving. "We already know that Evan, Dylan, and Conway are farmers. Neither Gwniera nor Lisa work outside the home now, but Mabyn, Conway's

160

wife, works part time at a knitting shop in Llanfyllin. Quigley wasn't able to get her hours, but it wouldn't be hard to check."

"She didn't mention that, did she?" Will mused, exchanging a look with Bronwyn. "They probably need her income."

"As for the others, Meredith Bennett works as an independent graphic designer, sets her own hours. I did get to interview her today."

"You got to Bangor?"

"Why not? It's a beautiful day for a drive around North Wales."

"How was she?"

"She looks like a younger version of her mother, except a lot cuter."

Bronwyn suppressed a smile. Mehta was a good-looking kid, and Merry would be the right age to attract him. It probably gave him an advantage, talking to her alone.

"She says she was working from home all day on Monday. She had a project deadline this week, so she didn't have time to go skipping around the country. There's no way to verify that, but I did get the name of her client, who did agree that it was a big project with a Thursday deadline. She says she hasn't been home to visit her parents since midsummer. Her flat isn't anything to brag about, but she seems to be surviving on her own."

"Any motive?"

"The same as the others, money. She seemed to think that Dylan would share the investment portion of his inheritance, at least with her, if Grandmother Carys agreed to it. She told me that it'd only be fair."

"I'm surprised she'd admit that. Add her to the list, then. What about the others?"

"Conway's daughter Evie is married and lives in Wrexham, which is nearer if we're looking for someone who could get to the murder site easily. She and her husband have a photography business that they run out of their home, so again, it'll be hard to pin them down to an alibi, I'm guessing. Their hours would be flexible."

"We'll have to talk to them."

"Yes, we'll have to. Her sister Eriana is a flight attendant for Aer Lingus. She's the one working out of Cardiff."

"That'll be easier. She'll have a definite work schedule. Is she married?"

"No, but that doesn't mean there isn't a boyfriend. You never know what might motivate someone."

"Yeah, we'll have to see her, too."

"Quigley couldn't get a schedule for her so I don't know if she was around when Evan was killed."

"It won't matter if she has a boyfriend. He could do it while she was away. I can't see a woman digging that big hole and piling all those rocks on top anyway, can you?"

"Not really," Mehta conceded, "but we still need to talk to her."

Will and Mehta would be doing a lot of traveling, Bronwyn realized. She wondered if all their cases were as far-flung as this one.

"Jenna Perry works at Spar, in Bala, which we knew. Quigley called, and her shift is seven a.m. to three, Tuesday through Saturday. Her boyfriend, Phylip Thomas, works at Barclay's Bank, banker's hours, Monday through Friday, nine to five. I find that interesting, Will. I'm wondering if Barclay's handles the Bennetts' investments, and if so, what department at the bank Thomas works in."

"That's a good question," Will complimented him. "Quigley couldn't get that information?"

"Apparently not."

"Did you find out about Evan's mobile and computer?"

"There's some sort of big case going on that's got them all busy. He says he'll get around to it as soon as he can find a few minutes. He'll let us know. And by the way, Jenna Perry did grow up with a step-dad, so maybe that explains her reluctance to hook up with Thomas as long as her son's at home. I'm not sure if that's relevant to our case. I wonder now if she was rebelling against him when she hooked up with Evan and got pregnant."

"Could be," Will mumbled as his attention was grabbed by slow traffic ahead. "I've got to go. It looks like an accident ahead of us. Traffic's backed up." He rang off and hit the brakes.

Bronwyn's mind wandered as they waited in a long queue of traffic, inching ahead a few feet at a time. If Jenna's boyfriend handled the investments, maybe he was cheating them somehow, and Evan's wanting to cash them out would uncover whatever he'd been doing. She knew that Will would be thinking the same thing. Suddenly, she wasn't so sure

162

that it was Dylan who was the murderer. When she really thought about it, any of them could still be guilty.

Chapter Twelve

"Bronwyn thinks Dylan is our murderer," Will confided what had rolled around in his mind at some point during the night. He hadn't slept well again, whether due to a feeling of abandoning Lark at school or to more nightmares, he didn't know. He'd tossed and turned, lying there in the dark with a circus of thoughts racing through his mind, finally focusing on the case in lieu of the other, more worrisome thoughts.

He wondered if Bronwyn had seen something, if she knew more than she was saying. Sometimes, she was reluctant to share the visions she saw in the pool of water, especially if she worried about trying to explain where they'd come from to someone like Jay, who didn't know. He'd promised to keep the secrets she was desperate not to reveal, but he'd broken that promise when he'd told Edward the truth. He'd been backed into a corner and felt he had no choice, but he regretted it now. He hated to think it, but maybe she didn't totally trust him anymore.

Beside him, Jay took a breath. "Do you agree with her?" He steered the car down the narrow lane, slowing for the turn that would take them into Llangynog. After a lazy morning that had seen Mehta not arriving at the cottage until noon, they planned to try to discover whether Evan Bennett had a girlfriend and, if so, who she might be. Will had appreciated Mehta's consideration in giving him and Bronwyn time alone together that morning. He was a good kid, all around.

"I think it could be him," Will ventured. He'd thought it out in the night. "We'll have a devil of a time proving it, though. The SOCOs didn't find anything incriminating?"

Mehta had spent time going over their report with them while he'd been at the office in Caernarfon. "There are fingerprints, but we can't match them to anyone unless we print every suspect we have. Unless there's a strange one there, though, it wouldn't help anyway. Dylan would have used that quad, too, and probably Meredith did when she visited. Gwniera, as well. Farm people ride around on those things all the time, don't they?"

"I guess they do," Will said. He thought of the Bagley men. They owned quads, too. He hadn't seen Bronwyn ride one, but she probably did from time to time. "No matches on the guns?"

"There's no Lee-Enfield among them. You didn't expect there to be, did you?" Mehta glanced at Will. "Meredith told me that she used to shoot, too, when she was at home." He slowed and turned into the little car park near the pubs.

"They all shoot for sport," Will observed. "How was Meredith? You sounded as if you fancied her a bit."

Mehta backed into an empty space and parked. He turned toward Will. "She likes to be called Merry, spelled like Christmas. I did like her. She went to university in Bangor on her dad's money and now she's been out for a couple of years. She says she'd prefer to live in a bigger city, but all her friends were in Bangor, so she stayed there. There's not much going on there as far as jobs in her field – she's a graphic designer – but she figured out that she could work remotely, from home, so that's what she does."

"How's her relationship with her family?"

"She says fine. She visits for Christmas every year, and she tries to get home for birthdays, but that doesn't always work out. She was last there for her mum's birthday in early June. Her parents visited her, as well, but that was mostly during the winter months when there wasn't so much work on the farm."

"Did you venture into her financial situation at all?" Will watched a mother pushing a baby in a pram on the roadway as she passed by. *It's a good thing there isn't a lot of traffic this time of day.*

"From what I saw, she could use an infusion of cash. The flat was small, and she had a roommate who'd moved out recently, so she's looking for someone else to move in. One of her university friends says she'll do it as soon as the lease runs out on her current flat." Mehta pulled the key from the ignition, palming it as he turned toward the door. "That's not unusual. Lots of kids share a place to save money."

"I wouldn't think Bangor is an expansive place to live, though," Will said, opening his own door and sliding out of the car. "She doesn't have a man in her life?"

"Not yet." Mehta grinned.

They walked past the New Inn, and Will glanced up at the fairy lights dangling from the roof. "You like staying here?" He checked the road that ran through the village for traffic and started across the street toward the Tanat Inn.

Mehta shrugged, following him. "It's fine. It's clean, and I have my own bath. Breakfast this morning was pretty good."

"Was it odd to ask them about Evan?" Mehta had approached the pub man the night before when he checked into his room.

"I should have done it sooner. I didn't need a picture to show around; everyone knows everyone else in this little village." His lips twisted down in a frown. "He says he hasn't seen much of Evan lately, and he's sure he wasn't showing any interest in the ladies last time he stopped in."

"Well, it's a long shot, isn't it, thinking we'll get onto someone right here. He'd be a fool to be seeing someone this near to home."

They pulled open the door to the Tanat and stepped inside. Three women polishing glasses and wiping counters near the bar looked at them curiously. It was early for customers.

Will showed them his warrant card. "Okay if we ask you a few questions?"

One of the women, a stout woman wearing blue jeans and a printed blouse, answered. "I know you, don't I? You're marrying our Bronwyn Bagley, isn't that right?"

Will felt a blush, which didn't happen often. "That's right, two weeks from now, at Pennant Melangell."

"You're the detective," she concluded unnecessarily. "This'll be about Evan?"

"Yes." He and Bronwyn ate at the pubs frequently. He'd expected to be recognized. "We're wondering if Evan's been in lately?"

"He stops in once in a while." She seemed to be the spokeswoman, but she looked to the other two women for confirmation. "I'd say the last time we saw him was a couple of weeks ago, maybe a week before the murder."

"What we'd like to know is whether he was with anyone. He might have come in alone and left with someone, or maybe they'd have come in together."

"Well, you'll not be talking about Gwniera, I'd guess," the woman laughed shortly. "You're wondering if Evan had a girlfriend he met here." She wasn't stupid. "The answer is no. He'd have been a stupid git to pick someone up right here under Gwniera's nose."

"Besides," another of the women finally spoke up, "he's tried it on with all the women around here long ago. No one's interested anymore."

Beside him, Mehta chuckled, and Will felt a wide smile growing. "That's what we expected, but we had to ask."

"Just being thorough," the second woman concluded wisely, with a teasing smile. "I'd try Bala or Llanfyllin, or maybe even Welshpool."

"We'll do that," Will assured them. He snuck a peek at Mehta as they walked back out into the sunshine. "You're sure Bowers said we had to do this? I think he's been spending time with Awstin, and Gwniera just assumed he was seeing someone."

"That's probably true," Mehta skipped a step up onto the pavement, "but Bowers wants it done, just to make sure we've covered all the bases."

They decided to try Bala next, reasoning that it was larger and located on a major crossroads, whereas Llanfyllin, although nearer, was still on the little B4391 that ran through Llangynog.

Clouds gathered in the distance as they traveled west, and Will guessed that it would be raining by mid-afternoon. *I hope it doesn't rain on our wedding.* But hadn't someone said rain on a wedding day was good luck?

Quigley would have the Sunday off, so he wouldn't be getting back to them with Evan's phone records until the next day, if that. That meant that the only possible way they'd find out if Evan had a girlfriend was to ask people who might have run into him with her, and their best bet was to visit the pubs and ask if he'd been seen with a woman recently. It was a long shot that anyone would remember him outside of Llangynog, but neither Bala nor Llanfyllin was very big, so maybe they'd get lucky.

Bala ended up a waste of time. They made a circle of it when they finished there, realizing at the last minute that other towns were just as logical and not far away, so they drove north through Corwen and then the short distance to Llangollen before turning south through Oswestry. Will wished he'd invited Bronwyn along for the ride. It was a pretty day, with blue sky edged with the dark clouds he'd seen earlier. They thickened as the day went on, but still the sun beamed through a break in the cloud at times, edging them in brilliant light. The fields beside the road were crispy dry from the unusually warm August weather, green at the roots, but brown and golden above.

They parked in each of the towns and walked from pub to pub, showing Evan's picture and asking if anyone recognized him. A few knew him.

"He's been around for years," commented a ruddy-cheeked young man in Corwen as he wiped glasses clean and filled an occasional order. Sunday afternoon was not a busy time in the local pubs, and tourist season had ended, for the most part. "It's Evan Bennett, isn't it? His family's been here for generations. I heard he'd been murdered."

"Yes, that's right," Will agreed easily. "You haven't seen him in here with a woman, have you? Or maybe he came in alone and picked someone up?"

"I might have noticed that," the young man observed. "We're not so busy that we don't see what's going on. Lew, he's the evening manager, or Helen, she's a barmaid, they've been around for years. If they saw Evan chatting up a woman who wasn't his wife, they'd have spread that gossip around, if you know what I mean. Not much gets past them."

Llangollen and Oswestry featured more pubs, and they were far enough from Llangynog that none of the employees knew who Evan was. They showed his picture around, and people gathered close to peer at it. *Morbid curiosity*, Will thought, but at least it made them look. No one remembered seeing him, alone or with anyone else. They came up empty.

Raindrops splatted on the windscreen as they detoured to Llanfyllin on their way back to Llangynog. Will watched glumly. He'd thought that he could send Mehta on some sort of errand for a while so that he and Bronwyn could go for a little hike before dinner, maybe out to her rock above the pool of water. It was starting to look like they'd need something more from her if they were going to sort out the mystery of Evan Bennett's death, and getting her away from Mehta was key to that goal.

Not that they didn't have suspects. They had suspects galore. But evidence was proving hard to come by, and anything she came up with would probably help.

Llanfyllin was the nearest little town to Llangynog, about three times as large and with more shops and places to grab a bite to eat or a drink if you were thirsty. It featured a cross marker that established it as an important market town in days gone by, and even a picnic table in a little square off the roadway that might have drawn people to linger, had it not been spitting rain.

Will and Mehta sat in the parked car with the rain pelting down in rivulets on the windows and debated whether to check in at the local constabulary, in the end deciding that stopping in, even for a few minutes, would give an appearance of cooperation that they'd be expected to encourage. Will wanted a chance to print the pictures of the suspects. It'd be easier to keep them all straight on the wall if they had photos to look at rather than just sticky notes, and it'd give them a good reason to stop in at the station.

169

"How fast do you think Quigley could text us photos of more of the suspects?" Mehta wondered. "We only have the family. We need to add Jenna and Awstin Perry, and if he can get Phylip Thomas, that'd be nice, too."

"Quigley isn't working today," Will told him. "But someone would answer the phone who could do it for us."

Mehta made the call while Will sat beside him watching the rain. To his surprise, Quigley did pick up. "Working on a Sunday?" Mehta asked him.

Will couldn't hear the answer. The rain had turned into a downpour. A sudden clap of thunder boomed just seconds after lightning lit the sky.

Mehta was listening, his face intent. "We can do without the pictures if you're busy," he said after a minute. "Can you text me anything you find from the numbers?"

Will took off his seatbelt and watched people dash to take cover from the weather beneath awnings and in doorways. The rain bounced on the pavement as it pelted the ground.

Mehta ended the call. "Lucky for us Quigley's working from home today, trying to catch up. He says the pictures won't take long, and he'll text them within a few minutes." He looked at Will.

Will nodded. They could just pop in and give the chief constable a report on their progress while they waited.

"He was going to call us later. The techs got into Evan's computer, but they didn't find anything they thought suspicious. He didn't do social media, just email, and nothing caught their eye. It all seemed to be business-related stuff for the farm and the project he was taking on in the woods. He'll send a copy of all the correspondence related to the project to us, in case we find something there that looks suspicious."

Quigley was, as always, the most efficient of techs.

"He has the phone records from Evan's mobile. There aren't a ton of calls and even fewer texts. He back-traced the numbers. Most of the calls were to Gwniera. There were quite a number going to Barclay's Bank, and then a few other, scattered ones that he'll check further. I have a feeling none of those will lead anywhere. The only other one that came up more frequently traces back to Awstin Perry. Evan paid the fees on that phone, so it was attached to his account. If Evan had a girlfriend, he didn't call her on his mobile."

Will nodded again. "That's no surprise. If we come up empty at the pubs here and nothing else looks suspicious from the mobile, I say we call it good on that line of thought."

"Agreed." Mehta looked at him. "What's the plan?"

A crack of thunder drowned his words. "Let's sit here for a minute and wait to see if this stops. The station is just across the street. If we get a break, we can dash over there fast, and by the time we're finished printing the pictures, maybe the storm will be over and we can walk around to the pubs."

"Sounds like a plan," Mehta agreed.

A few minutes later, the rain did, indeed, slow to a steady drizzle. They ran across the street and into the station, where they showed their warrant cards and were shown into an office.

"Chief Constable Owen Bach," a balding man with a bristling brown mustache shot with grey greeted them, shaking their hands. "I'm glad of an update. Thanks for stopping in." The building was old, with whitewashed stucco walls and windows foggy from the rain. Dark wainscoting probably hid wiring that would be necessary to run the technology they'd need to function.

They didn't tell him it had been a last-minute idea. Will lounged in a hard-backed wooden chair while Mehta detailed their investigation. The kid had a great memory, remembering every name with details about motives, alibis, and relationships.

"You think it was a family member, then?" Bach wanted to know. His eyes were keen, interested, and Will could see that he was running it all through his mind as Mehta spoke. He'd probably like to solve the crime himself, make it a local triumph rather than the credit going to detectives from far-away Caernarfon.

"It's all we have so far," Mehta confessed. "It was definitely premeditated, so that points to someone close to him. The road in there is a farm lane. Someone else driving in would probably have been noticed."

When they'd finished with him, they printed the pictures of the family members and other suspects, interested spectators watching as they worked. It was a local crime, Will reflected, and some of them probably knew Evan Bennett. And, he guessed, things were slow in that little constabulary, so a local murder would draw more attention than it would in a city.

Afterward, feeling proud of their performance at the station, they wandered to the pubs in town, pausing at other cafes and restaurants as they went. They tried to accomplish the task more quickly now. They had wasted time in Oswestry and Llangollen; it was getting late, and they both wanted to call it a day. They watched as barmen, waitresses, and patrons poured over the picture of Evan Bennett and shook their heads, feeling discouraged.

"We accomplished exactly nothing today," Will summarized as they sat looking at the living room wall that evening. The storm had knocked the power out, so Bronwyn had made sandwiches for their dinner. They sat with plates on their laps and drinks beside them on tables, squinting to see the wall in the light of the fading day. Daisy hovered, nervous from the thunder.

"We did what Bowers asked us to," Mehta contradicted him, "so now we can cross that off our list and get back to work." He set his sandwich on his plate and shook a crisp from the packet.

"It doesn't mean that Evan wasn't having an affair," Bronwyn said, her voice tentative. She usually watched, but didn't often volunteer ideas with Mehta there. Will was glad she felt comfortable enough to speak up. "If he's seeing someone, he wouldn't like to take her somewhere in Bala, with Jenna still living there. She'd notice. Same thing goes for Llanfyllin. It's too near us. Gwniera would hear. Things are more anonymous in Oswestry and Llangollen, even Corwen, where it's not likely anyone would recognize either of them, unless the woman is from there. Just because they didn't remember Evan, that doesn't mean he's in the clear."

"So, you're saying we not only accomplished nothing today, but we should keep looking?" Will's voice was more critical than he intended.

"I mean, of course we'd keep the possibility in mind, but I don't like to waste time doing what we did today unless we have something more definite saying there was an affair going on. Gwniera's suspicions were pretty vague, and no one else mentioned it."

"You should talk to Dylan again. Maybe he knows something he's not saying."

Will took a breath and let it out. "We'll ask him about it when we have time." He decided to be conciliatory. "You're right. He might know something and not want to say, for whatever reason. Maybe he's protecting his dad's reputation or would rather his mother not know." He was tired from lack of sleep and discouraged after spending the entire Sunday accomplishing nothing. *It even rained so we couldn't go for an evening walk*, he thought, grumpy with the realization. *Wedding nerves*, he realized suddenly, wondering if he was right. He'd never pictured himself married until he'd met Bronwyn, and then only after he'd thought he'd been going to die. He tried not to think about it now, truth be told. That way he wouldn't have to suppress the urge to run away while he still could.

"I think we should talk to Jenna Perry's boyfriend tomorrow, the banker," Mehta interrupted his thoughts. "I think that merits looking into. He really could be embezzling money, skimming – what do you call it? If Evan wanted to cash out, he might be panicked enough to murder him."

Will nodded, glad his frantic thoughts had been cut short. "Back to Bala, then," he said. He looked at Bronwyn, and smiled, hoping she hadn't seen the panic he'd felt for the moment. "Want to ride along?"

She smiled back. "I'd just be a third wheel," she said, "and there are things I want to do here, if the weather is nice."

He looked at her inquiringly. She wouldn't say it, but he'd bet she intended to try the pool of water for clues.

She shook her head slightly. "I'm behind with my art projects," she told them. "I'm busier now, as you can imagine, and I need to get some sketches done for both Pennant Melangell and Bodnant Gardens. If I don't get to it now, I won't have time until later this fall, with the tea party next weekend and then the wedding right after."

Will's mobile vibrated on the table and then rang out. He snatched it up and looked. "It's Lark." He was happy she'd called, hoping it wasn't bad news.

"I'll be off, then." Mehta stood up and obediently carried his empty plate and glass to the kitchen. He came back into the room and walked to the door, pausing to wave at Will, who was busy listening to Lark.

"So, you did what?" he asked her, listening to her excited chatter. He nodded to Bronwyn and put the phone on speaker. It sounded like Lark was settling in just fine.

Chapter Thirteen

They had another call from her on Monday morning, early, while they were eating their breakfast in the conservatory. The day had dawned bright with sunshine, the rain of the night before creating a freshness in the air. Gone was the summer haze, made of dust and smoke and exhaust, and the sky dazzled. Will's phone rang, and he put it on speaker. As often as Lark was calling, maybe she wasn't settling in as well as they'd hoped.

"Hi, Lark. I thought you'd be getting ready for classes."

"We had our breakfast, and I finished fast so I could call you before I go find my classroom."

"You have to do that by yourself?" He tried not to sound critical. She'd be lost on that campus.

"No, someone is coming to collect the new students. That's Aderyn, Eleri, and some boys and me. I don't remember the boys' names yet."

"That's good, then." He didn't know why she'd called or what to say. He looked at Bronwyn, hoping she'd come up with something.

She got the message. "Hi, Lark. Last night it sounded like you were having fun."

"We got to watch Harry Potter last night, with popcorn and butterbeer. William and Stacy are really nice. Everyone is."

"Who's your best friend so far?" Will asked. Bronwyn had a talent for connecting with her, but he wanted to be a part of the conversation, too.

"Aderyn," she replied without thought, "but Eleri is nice, too."

"Maybe you'll be like the three musketeers," Bronwyn suggested, "taking on the world together."

"I've got to go." Lark sounded rushed. "I just wanted to call and say good morning."

"We love to hear from you," Will assured her. "Call us tonight again and tell us how classes went, right?"

"I will."

"Do you have your rucksack ready to go?" Bronwyn hurried to ask.

"It's all packed. I remembered everything."

"Okay, then," Will said, "off you go. Have fun!" He loved that she'd thought to call. It was probably just an excuse to use her new mobile, but he'd take it. He wondered if she'd called her grandmother, as well. He rather hoped not. It was nicer to think that he was the priority now, but they couldn't let her make her grandmother mad, or she'd never agree to give Will full custody, not while she had Canada to hold over their heads.

He kissed Bronwyn goodbye when Mehta arrived and climbed into the green Subaru's passenger seat. It was Mehta's turn to drive, and they were off to Bala again, to Barclay's Bank in the hope of finding Phylip Thomas at work. After the previous wasted day driving from town to town and walking from pub to pub with no result, he was hopeful. Maybe it was just an odd coincidence that Thomas was a banker with a connection to Evan Bennett through Jenna Perry, but he thought that connection ripe with possibilities. He'd bet money that Thomas wasn't just a banker, but an investment banker.

Mehta read his thoughts. "You're thinking that Phylip Thomas was skimming money from Evan's accounts? When he decided to cash them in, Thomas knew he'd be caught out, so he murdered Evan to cover his crime?"

"That's one possibility," Will hedged. There were others, though. "Maybe he thought that Awstin would inherit some money when Evan died, especially if they were spending time together, developing a relationship. Better for Awstin to know his dad late than not at all, right?

If they were close enough that Evan wrote him into his will, Awstin would be out from under Jenna's wing sooner rather than later, and she'd finally be free to marry him, if that's what he wants. Maybe Thomas saw that happening and decided to hurry things along, while Awstin and Evan were still friendly. Who knows? Maybe he really likes Awstin and wanted to help him through uni and into a financially successful future. There are lots of possibilities."

Mehta slowed for a trio of sheep, their bare rumps painted with stripes of orange paint, standing in the road. He sounded his horn, hooting loudly in the quiet of the morning, and the sheep jolted into action, running off the road and into the adjoining pastureland.

Will laughed. "They'll send ahead a warning, 'watch out for the green car,' and the others will scurry away before we can catch them unawares."

"I can't believe you want to live here," Mehta grumbled, with a grin. "It's uncivilized."

"I think you'll find it's more civilized here, as a general rule, than it is in a city." He'd gotten used to the quiet, to the dearth of people.

"There are other possibilities, too, that you didn't mention." Mehta was back on topic. "Maybe someone paid Thomas to somehow prevent the sale of the investments. If he confesses to that, we'll have a better idea who else might have killed Evan." Mehta rounded a bend in the road and slammed on the brakes. "I thought you said they'd send word ahead to get off the road?" A fat ewe stood on the verge, blocking the roadway with her rump as she bent to crop the grass growing there. He slammed his hand on the horn again, and watched with satisfaction as she hopped to her feet and fled.

Barclay's Bank in Bala was a white stucco building with the name written in blue lettering. Located on the main street through town, it featured a working ATM, wide windows overlooking the street, and a sign informing the public that it was permanently closed.

"Bugger," Will swore. "You didn't think to ask which Barclay's Bank he works at?"

"Sorry," Mehta shrugged, "I just assumed it was Bala. I should have asked."

"Quigley should have said," Will corrected him. "Ring him and find out where we're headed from here."

He fumed, tapping his foot on the floorboards impatiently while Mehta made the call. He hated wasted time. For all they knew, Thomas probably worked in Welshpool or Oswestry, somewhere in the opposite direction. No one had said that he lived in Bala either; they'd just assumed it all.

"He works at the branch in Dolgellau," Mehta said as he shut down his mobile. "Quigley sends his apologies."

"At least it's the same direction," Will grumbled. They'd have had to pass through Bala to get to Dolgellau, so it wasn't really wasted time, in the end.

Mehta looked back over his shoulder for traffic and pulled out onto the road, picking up speed as he merged onto the A494 toward Dolgellau. "That'll be a bigger branch. Should we call ahead for an appointment?"

"No, let's surprise him. If he's done something illegal, he's probably already taken steps to hide it, but maybe he doesn't think we'll be onto him yet."

"How hard is it to hide money stolen from a client's account?" Mehta wondered. "I don't know how it works."

"Neither do I," Will admitted, "but we have people who can figure it all out. We'll get a search warrant and get the paperwork. We should have done that already. I'm calling Quigley; we'll see how fast he can get that done for us."

The Barclay's Bank in Dolgellau was a solid brick building, missing the big windows they'd seen at the closed branch in Bala, but still featuring an ATM on the outside.

They walked inside and approached a woman behind a desk who greeted them with a smile. "How can I help you gentlemen?"

They held up their warrant cards in unison. "We'd like to talk to Phylip Thomas," Will said.

Her eyes had gone bigger. "I'll just see if he's available." She picked up a phone and pushed a button, murmuring into the receiver.

Will fidgeted. He wished they'd arranged to meet Thomas away from his place of employment, where they'd have the upper hand. He glanced at Mehta and leaned toward him. "Want to lead the interview on this one?"

"I think you should do it," Mehta whispered back. "It seems the sort of place where your public-school education would put you on a more solid footing than my own inner city London education would."

"Phylip will be right out for you," the woman interrupted them. She looked at them curiously, her thin eyebrows and pulled back hair emphasizing a long forehead. "He wanted me to ask what this is in reference to?"

"I'm afraid we'll have to talk to him personally about that," Will told her firmly. Ghoul. He probably hadn't asked at all; she'd just want to satisfy her own curiosity and that of her colleagues, when they met up in the breakroom later.

Phylip Thomas appeared from a hallway and reached his hand out to shake theirs, introducing himself. Will guessed him to be in his early forties, a solid-looking man with thick dark hair neatly combed and gray eyes behind black-framed eyeglasses. Will wondered if he needed the glasses or whether he thought they'd make him look more professional. His face was smooth and pale.

He must not spend much time outdoors, Will thought to himself. "Sir, we're investigating the Evan Bennett murder in Llangynog," he said quietly so as not to be overheard by the woman at the desk. "We'd like to ask you a few questions, if that's okay."

Thomas looked startled, and then his face turned thoughtful. "Come with me," he said with a glance around, and he opened a door and let them pass by him into a small office. He waved at a padded chair in front of his desk and hurried to pull another one away from the wall and put it next to the first. "Please, sit," he said. He closed the office door.

He sat down in his office chair and put his hands on the desk in front of him, leaning toward them. "Evan was Awstin Perry's natural father," he said. "I know Awstin and his mother, but I didn't know him."

Will took his time, looking around the office. Small pictures on the desk showed two children, probably two or three years older than Lark. There was a picture of Jenna Perry, too, smiling into the camera at what looked like the seaside. "We understand that you've been seeing Jenna Perry for some years."

Thomas nodded. "We've been together for four or five years. Just a casual thing."

"Why is that?"

Thomas looked confused. "Why is what?"

"Why keep it casual? I'd think that, after five years, you'd have decided whether you really like each other or not. You've never talked of marriage with her, or at least, of moving in together?"

Thomas picked up a pen and turned it around and around in his fingers. "That's private, Inspector," he told Will, with a glance at Mehta. "I can't see where it's any of your business why we haven't taken our relationship to the next level."

Will thought about conceding the point, but he didn't want to set a precedent for the conversation where Thomas controlled what he wanted to answer. "Just talk to us, sir. I'm sure you have perfectly logical reasons for keeping it casual."

Thomas paused, manipulating the pen in his hand. He looked at Will. "Jenna doesn't want Awstin dealing with a blended family," he said at last, his voice resigned. "She grew up with a stepdad she didn't get along with, and she was determined that Awstin not have the same experience. Not that he would." He took a breath. "I'd have been a good stepdad, if given the chance. I have two kids of my own, and they're happy and well-adjusted. My wife and I share custody."

"Tell us about Jenna," Mehta interrupted.

Will thought it a good request.

Thomas seemed to want to think things through before speaking. Again, he paused before he started to talk. "Jenna is beautiful, as you've no doubt seen." He glanced from one to the other of them, and they both nodded. "She's also very independent. From a young age, she wanted

180

to be able to support herself and not have to depend on anyone else for anything. She never asked Evan for anything, not once through the years. She's been a great mum to Awstin, always putting his needs before her own. That's why she wanted to wait with me." He looked at them again, and they saw him surrender. "I've wanted to marry her ever since I first saw her. I spend my nights dreaming of our life together; how perfect it will be." He paused again. "Jenna wanted to wait, though, until Awstin was out on his own, so I had no choice but to agree. She made it clear that pushing her wasn't an option. Awstin will be at university next year, and we're talking of a wedding in the summer."

"Won't she still have to support him?" Will wanted to know.

"Yes, of course, she will, financially. But he won't be living at home full-time, just when he comes for visits, and that's good enough for the two of us. She's as eager to make it official as I am."

Interesting, that. Will abruptly switched gears. "What do you do here at the bank, Mr. Thomas?"

After his speech about Jenna, he didn't seem thrown by the abrupt change of subject. "I handle people's investments."

"Did you handle Evan Bennett's investments?"

Thomas' face took on a wary look. "I don't believe so."

"You don't believe so?" Will made his voice incredulous. "I'd think that, if you had a client with whom you had a connection, however tenuous, you'd be aware of it if he came up murdered."

"Yes, well, we have quite a few clients." He turned toward his computer screen and tapped on the keyboard. He reached up to adjust his eyeglasses, and then tapped again, scrolled, and tapped another time. "Evan Bennett's investment portfolio is handled by our branch in Welshpool," he said, his relief obvious.

Did he really not know whether he'd handled it or not? Will was disappointed. "Is there a name we can check with there?"

Thomas looked at his screen, tapped again. "It's Cassadee Richards." He looked up at them. "I trained Cassadee when she first started out." He sounded astonished.

"Do you still see her, maybe in a professional way?"

"Yes," Thomas sputtered, "well, of course we meet occasionally for regional meetings and such. She's a nice woman, always ready to chat with me a bit." He stared at the computer screen.

"Would you have access to Evan's portfolio through the banking system?" Will asked.

"Well, yes, I suppose I could have, if I had a reason to," Thomas said. "I really didn't even know that he had an investment account, Inspectors."

"We're expecting a warrant to come through at any moment for Evan's investment portfolio," Mehta informed him. "We'll request copies of his statements for a year back, at least."

"I could look through it for any irregularities," Thomas offered.

"Thank you, but we have to have our own people do it," Mehta informed him with a smile.

"Of course," Thomas said. He was still staring at the screen.

"Unless you're seeing something off right now," Mehta wondered.

He blinked and looked up at them. "No, it's nothing. I was just startled to see that Cassadee was handling this portfolio, is all."

Will wondered what he wasn't saying. "Can you tell us where you were on Monday evening, around six?"

He stiffened. "I was home, alone. I'd had my children over the weekend, and I was just relaxing after all the chaos, happy to sit with a glass of wine and watch the telly. That'd be the time of night I'd be making my dinner, just a bit of pasta with jarred sauce."

"You weren't seeing Jenna that night?"

"No, she came over on the weekend when I had the kids. Not overnight, of course, but we took the kids to the lake, had a picnic on Sunday. I called her on Monday evening. We talked for nearly an hour as I remember." They could check that in her phone records.

"I think that's all for now, Mr. Thomas, unless you want to add anything?" Will was ready to wrap it up.

"No." He was adamant, wanting them gone. "I'll call you if I think of anything that might help."

They left him with their cards and wandered back toward the car.

"Lunch?" Mehta asked hopefully.

"It's a little late now, but sure, why not? Just don't eat too much. We're going to have dinner with Bronwyn's family tonight, remember?"

They found a pub and ordered toasties and beer. *A bachelor's lunch if I ever saw one,* Will thought as he carried his glass to an empty table. He'd have to sneak a lunch like this when he was away working these days. Bronwyn's idea of meals comprised something healthier.

"He was nervous," Will commented through a bite of his sandwich.

"Can you blame him?" Mehta said, setting his own sandwich down. He reached for his beer. "He thinks he's found the ideal woman, he's waited years for her to have a real relationship with him, and now all of a sudden we're talking to him about the murder of her ex-boyfriend. He knows he's a suspect, and he knows she probably is, too. It's freaking him out."

"You're sure that's all it is?" Will chewed thoughtfully.

"He was surprised that his colleague, Cassadee Richards, handled Evan's investments. I don't know what that was all about."

"My guess is that he fancied her back when she was training with him, and he was startled to find her drawn into our investigation, too."

"We're seeing her this afternoon?"

"I think so." Will reached for his beer. "As soon as we serve the warrant and get the locals started collecting the investment materials, we can take off. Welshpool's the opposite direction. It'll take a while."

"We can't be late for dinner," Mehta warned him. "You'll want to keep a good reputation with her family, at least until after the wedding's over."

Will punched his arm across the table, sloshing his beer. Mehta laughed.

The drive to Welshpool took an hour. They had to park up the one-way street a block away from the bank which, like its counterpart in Llanfyllin, was white stucco with big arched windows and the name in bright blue.

They went inside, showed their warrant cards to the receptionist, and were told to wait in a lounge area until Ms. Richards could see them.

She came out ten minutes later, an attractive strawberry blonde whose dark roots hinted at a dye job, but not much of one, Will thought. She had the pale, creamy complexion that went with the red hair. She batted blue eyes at them, and they followed her into her office, a bigger space than Phylip Thomas had worked in. She smoothed her navy skirt and sat down opposite them.

"We're investigating Evan Bennett's murder," Will started again, feeling as if he were repeating the same words over and over and over. "We understand that you managed his investment portfolio."

"That's right," she said in a rich alto voice. "We were very sad to hear of Evan's death."

"We understand that he was in the process of selling off some of the investments to finance a project on his property."

Her smile faded a little. "Of course, Evan's money was his to spend however he wished, but we hated to see him sell it all off, considering how strong the market is right now."

Will noticed the plural pronoun. It was always *we*, not *I*. Distancing herself from Evan for some reason? "Had he begun the process of cashing out some of his portfolio?"

"We'd met to talk over which were the best to drop at this time," she explained, "but he hadn't actually sold anything yet."

"We've gotten a copy of his statements from the past year to look at," Will informed her, watching her face. "We wanted to make sure there were no irregularities."

"You won't find anything like that," she assured him. She bit at her lip. "I would have noticed if anything was off."

"Did he tell you what he planned to do with the money?"

She hesitated. "I know he planned to develop some of his farm, a wooded area, into a housing estate, possibly for retirees who wish to spend their time away where it's quieter."

"You discussed that with him?"

"We talked about it, here in the office."

Will watched her. She was hiding something, he could tell. He risked a glance at Mehta.

184

"How well did you know Mr. Bennett?" Mehta asked.

Her cheeks colored. "What are you implying, Inspector?"

She hadn't answered. "Just, we'd like to get an impression of him, that's all. I thought if you were friendly, maybe you could give us some insight." Will tried to put her at ease.

She shifted in her chair, and her hand went to a locket on a chain around her neck. She was wearing a wedding ring on her finger. She touched the locket and then said, "I thought of Evan as a friend, even though he was just a client. We do get close to some of our investors, working with them as we do." She tugged on the necklace and then let it go. "Evan was charming, for a man of his age. He was fun to talk to and made me laugh. I liked him."

Will nodded. "When did you last see Evan, Ms. Richards?"

She blushed again. "I'd have to think about that. He came in a few weeks ago to talk about selling off his investments. I'll have to check my records to see when that was."

"Will you do that, please?"

She straightened in her chair and turned to her computer screen. She tapped the keyboard and leaned close to look at the results. "It looks like he came in on August 14th, at nine in the morning."

"That's your last contact with him? He didn't call with questions or concerns?"

"He did call me here, quite often the past few months," she admitted after a moment's thought. "He sometimes had questions about how his investments were performing on any given day. He was very interested in them, given that he intended to sell some of them off."

"Some, not all?"

"No, of course not. His mother was still entitled to her maintenance money. That's in the terms of the trust. He'd have to leave enough here to fulfill that obligation."

They gave her their cards and asked her to call if anyone else called or came in to inquire about the investment portfolio.

"I think we stumbled onto something," Mehta said once they were seated in the car. He reached out to turn the key and the car rumbled into life.

"She's the girlfriend?" Will surmised, pretty sure of the answer.

"I'd say so. Did you see her body language?" Mehta glanced at the traffic and waited for a car to pass.

"I noticed that she said "we" rather than "I" when she talked about managing his account, at least at first. She didn't want us to think their relationship was personal."

"The phone calls wouldn't have been to check up on his accounts."

"No, that was him, setting up dates with her. No one would think anything was off if he was just calling the bank." Will pulled his mobile out of his pocket and scrolled to Quigley's number.

"I sent the warrant," Quigley answered the call.

"I know. That's all done. What I need now is some information on a woman. Name of Cassadee Richards." He spelled it for him. "She works at Barclay's Bank in Welshpool. Find out if she's married, will you?"

"Got it," Quigley said. "That's all?"

"That'll do for now. If she has a husband, you might find out if he has a record. We'd be interested in anything that suggests a temper, maybe a history of violence."

"I'll call you back," Quigley promised.

With a little free time left in the day, they decided that a visit to Evie Lewis was in order. They'd driven to the far corners of Wales to interview the other Bennet family members, but, somehow, they'd overlooked Evie, despite Welshpool being almost local. Now, they were in the area, so a quick interview wouldn't be an inconvenience to them, and she'd be another person they could possibly cross off their list of suspects.

The door to the garden flat was opened by a tall man with short dark hair and a friendly demeanor. "Hugh Lewis," he introduced himself, looking at them expectantly.

They held up their warrant cards and introduced themselves, watching his expression change from welcoming to alarmed. "Can we come in?" Will asked.

"Yes, of course." He stood back and let them pass by him into the room. "I'll just get Evie. She's working in our office."

They looked around the room while they waited. Comfortable, if inexpensive, furniture invited them to sit, but they wandered instead, looking at the collection of framed photographs that filled the walls of the room. Portraits competed for attention with landscapes and close-ups of wildlife and flowers, each arranged in groupings in different parts of the room. The collection was a reflection of a life's passion.

Evie and her husband Hugh walked into the room and saw them looking.

"Did you take all of these?" Will asked, putting admiration into his voice.

"We did," Evie answered for them both, with a smile for her husband. "We have a photography business, and we often meet clients here, so it's our display room, if you will."

Will sat down, and Mehta followed suit. "We're investigating the death of your uncle Evan Bennett, Evie."

"We assumed you'd show up sooner or later," she answered. "We were both working when he was killed, inspectors. A wedding in Shrewsbury. I can give you contact details if you want them."

"We'll take the information and verify it, just so we can cross you off our list," Will told her. "What we're really here for, though, is to talk to you about your family. The more we get a feel for them all, the faster we'll be able to solve our case."

She frowned. "I don't know what I can tell you that'd be of help. We haven't had any real contact with Evan since I was a child."

"We understand that," Will assured her. "But you knew about him. What did you think of him?"

She settled back into her chair. "Mum and Dad always disapproved of Evan, not just because of the inheritance, but because of his lifestyle. We all grew up thinking that he was the black sheep of the family." She gave him a direct look. "But none of us hated him enough to kill him. Why now, after all these years?"

Indeed, why now? Will thought. "Did you stay in touch with your cousins, with Dylan and Merry?"

"We couldn't, thanks to our fathers being estranged. We'd been close as children, playing together all the time. I missed them, and I know that Eriana did, too. Terrywn never really knew them at all."

This was getting them nowhere. "Who do you think killed your uncle?" Will pressed her, thinking it was time to end the interview and get on the road back to Llangynog.

She thought for a moment, reaching out for her husband's hand. "We've been talking about that, but we really have no idea. I'd hate to think that a family member did it. Dylan…" she started to say and then stopped.

Her husband Hugh came to her rescue. "From what we've heard, Dylan wasn't as close to his dad as he might have been, but he'd not have killed him over the money. That would have come to him anyway, sooner or later, in some form. He'd have had no reason, and we can't imagine him doing it."

"It had to be a stranger," Evie said, "someone mad at him over a woman or a business deal. Not the family."

Chapter Fourteen

Bronwyn watched Will and Mehta drive away, feeling content. She enjoyed having a day to herself, a day to catch up with things at home or to wander off with Daisy somewhere quiet to catch up on her sketching before the weather turned. She loved that Will stayed in Llangynog nearly full-time now, but with him there, her alone time was virtually non-existent and, truthfully, she sometimes missed it. Not that she didn't love Will. She did. She wouldn't change things with him for all the alone time in the world.

She called to Daisy and went inside, intending to do some housework before the outdoors called to her. It was a brilliant, clear day, perfect for sketching or hiking, and later she'd do both, but first, there were dishes to wash and put away, laundry to wash and hang out on the line in the back garden, and the floors could use a good hoovering. She'd been seeing clumps of Daisy's hair where the wood floor met the wall in every room, and that wouldn't do.

She put a load of laundry in to wash, and then tackled the dishes. They had an automatic washer, but sometimes it was just easier to fill the sink with water and wash them by hand. That had been her job as a child at home, and she'd always loved the feel of the soap bubbles and the warm water running across her hands. Sometimes when she was very young, her mother had helped her onto a stool in front of the sink with a handful of toys, and she'd played for hours, pretending her little animals and people were swimming or boating or just floating.

The laundry kept her at home through the morning. She hung the first load on the clothesline, enjoying the scent of it in the sunshine, and went back inside to clean the floors, Then, with time remaining on the automatic washer, she went back outdoors and surveyed the little garden she'd planted in the spring. The fence Will had struggled to construct had mostly kept the rabbits out, although they'd had to reinforce it a few times over the summer. She pulled some of the weeds that never seemed to stop appearing and checked to see what needed picking. Too many ripe tomatoes would have to be either eaten or chopped and frozen for winter, and the rocket was overgrown now and probably inedible. The winter squash were growing nicely, though, and there would be carrots and potatoes enough for a few months.

Finally, chores done, Bronwyn had free time to do whatever struck her fancy. She loaded her rucksack with her sketch pad and pencils, adding an apple and a carton of yoghurt for her lunch and a handful of treats for Daisy.

She set off down the road toward the village, stopping for a moment to chat with her neighbor Maeve, who was watching her children play outdoors, and waving to Cecil Lumley as he was unlocking the doors to the Tanet. Otherwise, the village was quiet at that time of day, with no traffic at all.

As she passed by Granny Powers' old cottage, her thoughts drifted to the new cleaner, Alwena. She'd seemed friendly, devoted to her husband and little daughter, but she'd seemed overly nervous about getting her work done properly. Perhaps it was her first job? She was a little old for that, but it might explain her determination to finish her chores in the allotted time frame, proving that she was a reliable worker. Maybe as time went on, she'd relax a little and not be quite so single-minded. It seemed odd that her husband had come to pick her up after work rather than let her walk home on a fine late-summer evening, but maybe it was just because it was her first day, and he was eager to hear how it had gone. Whatever, she liked the idea of another young newly-married woman in the village. Truth be told, she'd like a friend to chat with when Will or Janice wasn't available.

She hesitated at the turn to Pennant Melangell, but after a moment's reflection, she resisted the lure it posed. She sketched on her lunch breaks there, so what she needed today was to go somewhere else, somewhere she hadn't sketched for a while. She thought for a minute about Pistyll Blaen-y-Cwm, the waterfall a couple of miles past Pennant Melangell, but walking there would take more time than she had, and again, she could hike up there any afternoon after she finished with work. No, today she needed to walk to her parents' farm and through the pasture into the woods, where she could sit on her rock beside the pool of water and sketch and, maybe, see something that would help Will end his investigation before their wedding day.

She stopped by the garden her mum and her sister-in-law Mai had created in the spring. They'd had an idea to grow and market organic fruits and vegetables to local shops and restaurants, and, although this was only their first year with it, it had been surprisingly successful. They were both there, wearing jeans and old tee shirts against the heat, pulling weeds with gloved hands.

"Come join us!" Mai called, straightening and placing both hands on her back, stretching.

"No, thanks," Bronwyn called back. She leaned on the fence. "Griffyn started back to school today?"

"Yes," Mai wandered toward her, "and Maegan is at primary school this morning. I have to pick her up soon, and then she'll be here, distracting us from our work."

Bronwyn's mum came to stand beside Mai. "She's never a bother. She'll help us a bit and then go out and help her dad, or at least watch what he's doing." She smiled at Bronwyn. "What are you up to on this fine Monday?"

"Will and Jay are off to Bala to interview a suspect there. They invited me to ride along, but I thought I'd rather stay here and catch up with other things. I'm headed out to the forest now to do some sketches."

"It's too bad it's not a little later," Mai said. "I'd send Maegan out there with you. She could take her own crayons and paper, and the two of you could have some nice auntie/niece time together."

Bronwyn wondered if Mai had an ulterior motive in her suggestion. Maegan appeared to have the same gift of sight as Bronwyn did, and her parents were struggling to understand and deal with it. Maddock had hinted more and more strongly that they'd like Bronwyn to talk to Maegan, to help guide her as she learned that such things had to be kept private while assuring her that she wasn't different or odd, and that others, like Bronwyn, had the same gift. Bronwyn had resisted them so far. She didn't want Maegan knowing that she shared her ability to see the Twlwyth Teg, fearing she'd say something in Will's presence to give her secret away. Besides, she wouldn't be able to concentrate on her own work with Maegan needing attention. "I may be out there for a while," she told them. "I'm way behind on my sketching. Don't worry over me if I don't come back for a few hours."

She called to Daisy, pushed through the gate, and strolled across the pasture toward the stile and into the forest.

Despite the late summer warmth, she could see signs of approaching autumn. The bright orange of the rowan tree berries turned darker day by day; they'd be nearly red by the time the trees' leaves dropped. She could hear the crackle of dry brush as Daisy foraged off the path. The grasses had been green just a short time before, and now they were pale ivory and brown. Bracken and ferns lay rusty brown beneath the trees. The birds were busy with their own harvest. Wrens rustled in the higher shrubs and low trees, and a magpie perched on a hornbeam branch and watched her progress.

She watched for the Twlwyth Teg and for Pysgotwr, but neither seemed inclined to put in an appearance. She wondered if they'd continue to appear to her once she and Will were married, especially since she denied their existence to others. They'd named her guardian, the last in a line stretching from St. Melangell's time, but as long as she filled that role as best she could with her job at the counselling centre and her nature meditation sessions, perhaps they'd see no need to interact with her more openly. As she'd told Pysgotwr, the world was changing. They were as aware of that as she was. Perhaps their time was dwindling away as the modern world encroached on the few remaining thin places in the world. The thought saddened her.

When she got to her pool of water, she sat cross-legged on the flat rock and opened her rucksack. She ate the carton of yoghurt while she studied the surrounding rocks and trees, deciding on a subject for her first sketch. Daisy sat at the base of the rock and watched her with eager eyes, wanting to lick out the carton when Bronwyn had finished. She ate the last spoonful and then invited the Lab up onto the rock, where she eagerly cleaned it of any remaining custard.

She settled into her work, sketching the oak tree overhanging the pool of water, creating swirling eddies with her pencils that weren't really there, but that added interest to the sketch. She drew quickly and then went back to add detail to the work, frowning at it in concentration. She finished the first sketch, knowing she'd polish it later, and took some time to gaze down into the pool.

The water was still in the warm air. Tiny insects flitted just above it, swarming near the bank where green moss grew year around. She breathed quietly, deeply, and focused on the tiny details, watching for something to appear.

And it did. Suddenly, she could see an image forming in the water. At first, she thought it might have been a shadow, but as it took shape, it looked like a man. He wasn't floating in the water, but rather the water made a sort of background against which he stood, almost like a movie. As the details took shape, she could see that it was Dylan, his face grim, and he was talking to someone she couldn't quite see. A young man's silhouette, she thought, or a woman dressed in jeans. She bent forward to see more of the vision, unconscious of Daisy lying on the rock beside her, and that was all it took. Daisy sprang to her feet and hurled herself into the water, splashing away any lingering vestige of what Bronwyn had seen.

"Daisy!" she shouted, irritated. "Come here!" This was the second time Daisy had disrupted one of her visions in just the past few days. She had to be taught not to swim in this particular pool of water.

Daisy swam to where rocks jutted out into the water and dragged herself out, dripping. She shook, further angering Bronwyn as the water splatted onto her sketching pad. Now furious, she slid off the rock and grabbed Daisy by the ruff on the back of her neck. "Bad dog! You sit and stay." She shoved her down onto the path beside the rock, glaring at her. "Do not move."

Daisy's head drooped between her front paws. She rolled her eyes up to look at Bronwyn, shameful and repentant, and then she rolled over, lying on her back and looked at Bronwyn mournfully.

Bronwyn sighed. She bent down and rubbed Daisy's belly, but when the dog tried to get up, she pushed her back down. "No, you're staying there for a while. I want to get some work done."

She'd done two more preliminary sketches when Daisy sat up, ears cocked. Bronwyn looked down at her and then she heard it: a quad, still some distance away, the rumble of its engine just discernable in the quiet of the forest. She was suddenly alert, her heart thumping.

The sound was coming from the Bennett's part of the woods, so it would probably be Dylan. She wondered what she should do. The quad was still quite a distance away, and if he came close enough to see her, she knew that she'd hear him coming long before he arrived. If the quad came closer, she decided, she'd just walk back to her parents' house. Dylan would have no idea she was out there, so he'd not come after her. She was perfectly safe.

Convinced, she started another sketch, listening to the noise of the quad in the distance. It didn't seem to come any nearer and, after a few minutes, she lost the sound entirely. She relaxed and sketched some pale grasses with a brown pencil, thinking that the rocks behind them would be a pale grey with darker accents. Daisy still sat up, listening just as Bronwyn was.

Then Daisy gave a little woof, just a quiet warning, and she stood up, staring into the trees.

Bronwyn's head jerked up and she caught her breath.

Dylan stood a few feet away, watching her. He'd obviously walked; there was no quad nearby. "I didn't mean to startle you," he said.

She pushed her pencils into the rucksack and slid off the rock to stand beside Daisy. "What are you doing here?" she asked. Sure, she'd trespassed onto their part of the forest in the past, but she wasn't aware that any of the Bennetts did the same on her parents' land.

194

"I was trying to figure out what happened to my dad," he said. "I thought maybe someone came from this direction, and that's why no one saw another vehicle going down our lane."

She wondered if he was telling the truth. "We'd have said if we'd noticed anyone."

He walked closer and then leaned against a tree. "What are the police saying? Do they think I did it?"

She shook her head. "They aren't far enough along in the investigation yet to come to any conclusions."

He studied her. "Is that the truth? I know I'm a suspect, and I know that I probably have the best motive of any of us."

She nodded and smiled self-consciously. "As far as I know, it's the truth. Will can't talk to me about his cases while he's working them."

He took a breath. "Where did you meet him? I mean, it isn't like he's from here, is he?"

"We met when I was a suspect in one of his cases. Remember when Glynnis Paisley was killed in the churchyard at Pennant Melangell? I was the main suspect in that murder for a while."

"So, you know a little about how I'm feeling," he said. He eyed her. "I do remember that. I didn't know you were a suspect, though." His eyes drifted to her rucksack. "Were you drawing?"

She nodded. "I do some sketches that I sell in gift shops."

"And you're getting married next week."

"Week after next." First, she had to survive the wedding tea with Will's mother.

"You know, I didn't really get along with my dad," he blurted suddenly, surprising her. "When I was little, I didn't know what he was up to, but once I was a teenager, I realized he was cheating on my mum, and I hated him for making her feel like she did."

"Did you know about Awstin?"

"I was eleven when he was born. I remember my parents having a huge fight, yelling at each other and slamming doors. My dad left and didn't come back for nearly two weeks. I didn't know what he'd done, but I was mad at him because Mum was crying all the time." He looked at Bronwyn. "I promised myself that I'd never be like him when I grew up."

"You have nice things, Dylan," she pointed out cautiously.

He looked startled. "Well, yes. That's not what I meant, though. I'd never want to hurt Lisa like he did Mum."

She wanted to ask if he'd killed Evan, but she knew it wouldn't be smart to do so when she was alone in the forest with him. "Do you ever see Awstin?"

"No," he was adamant. "He's never been a part of our lives, not even Dad's."

She didn't know what to say. She didn't know Dylan very well. He was older, more Maddock's age, but he'd gone to a private school rather than the local comprehensive, so they hadn't had much contact.

He seemed to notice her discomfort. "I'll just go and leave you to your artwork. I'm sorry I disturbed you." He gave her a twisted smile. "I'm not a murderer, just so you know."

"I believe you," she told him softly. She wasn't sure if it was the truth, but he took it with a nod of acceptance before he turned and started to pick his way back through the woods.

She watched him until he disappeared. A robin lit on a branch of the oak tree and looked down at her with its head bent to one side. She'd might as well go now, too. She'd be nervous about staying alone in the woods, and it was time to get back home and get ready for dinner with her family.

They surrounded her as she trod the pathway through the dark forest, early-fallen leaves softening her footsteps. She saw movement and froze, afraid that Dylan had somehow cut around through the trees and waited for her. Then she saw them, their footsteps also silent as they always were. Wizened, breathtakingly beautiful, grotesque, and miniscule: they were the Twlwyth Teg, come with a message. Her heart fluttered in anticipation. Will would be grateful for any clue right now.

But the clues were not for Will, at least she didn't think so.

"The charwoman seeks a frend," stated the first, her head cocked to one side as if she were considering Bronwyn as a candidate. The way she pronounced the word made 'friend' sound different.

"Be hoful," chimed a second voice, high-pitched and somehow too shrill in the quiet forest, like the whine of a mosquito too close to an ear.

"He has a nose of wax," a third voice informed her. She turned her head to look, but that figure flew off too quickly, dipping beneath a branch and disappearing.

"Once, twice, thrice," they chanted, and then they were all gone, leaving Bronwyn and Daisy standing alone on the path.

She'd be seeing Will in a short time. If the words she'd been given were to be of any help to him, she'd have to use her mobile to figure them out quickly.

She sat down beside the path, cross-legged, and Daisy looked at her as if she might be crazy, then laid down beside her. Quickly, she typed.

"Charwoman' gave her what she expected: "a woman employed to clean." She frowned. None of Will's suspects fit that definition, but Alwena did. She sighed. She'd made the mistake before of assuming the words the Twlwyth Teg gave her referred to her, and not to the cases Will worked. But what else could she think this time? They had to be telling her that Alwena was looking for a friend. She checked the medieval dictionary to be sure. "Friend" was spelled "frend," but it was the same thing.

"Be holful," quickly gave her "be careful," but what did that mean? Did Alwena pose a threat? She couldn't imagine it.

She typed quickly. "Nose of wax," was a medieval term meaning "fickle personality." They'd said "he," not "she." What on earth?

Whatever they'd meant to convey to her, she liked Alwena, and she intended to be a friend. She wondered why they were interested?

They were the last to arrive at Bronwyn's parents' farm, Will and Mehta being held up by the unexpected trip to Welshpool. They chattered excitedly about Cassadee Richards as they drove to the farm, sure they'd stumbled on Evan's last fling. She'd been reluctant to tell Will about her own meeting with Dylan in the forest, but he'd uncharacteristically dismissed it, not seeming worried about her coming across suspects in their investigation alone and far from rescue, if it had been needed.

She didn't know whether to feel insulted or glad.

Her mother directed traffic in the dining room while she and Mai carried dishes across the flagstone floor to the scarred oak table. "Jay, you sit there next to Will," she instructed him, "and Bronwyn, you can move over next to Maegan." They submitted meekly, tossing greetings back and forth.

"It must be a challenge," Maddock started right in, "working beside this waster day after day." He grinned at Will.

Mehta glared at him. "You, I have heard much about," he announced, his tone a good imitation of a lowlife suspect they'd once encountered, Sunny Salahudin. He held the look for a long minute while everyone went silent, and then his face crinkled in a laugh. "All of it good."

Maddock laughed. "You, I like." He nodded toward Will. 'I'm still making my mind up about him."

Mehta took it in stride. "I have to work hard to keep him focused on work rather than on his love life, I'll admit. Maybe after the wedding, he'll settle."

"We can only hope," Maddock carried on. He held out a bottle of wine. "Can I fill your glass?"

"Better give Bronwyn some first," Mehta retorted. "She looks like she could strangle you right now."

She laughed with them.

"You must have a big family, too," Bronwyn's dad observed, drawing attention away from the bantering. "You've settled right into this group."

"I do have," Mehta said. "I have three brothers and two sisters, all younger than me. One of my brothers is a constable in London, and my eldest sister is engaged to be married in the spring."

"Not until spring," Maddock jumped right in again. "She's not in as big a hurry, then, as our Bronwyn and Will."

"Why wait?" Will defended himself. "We know it's what we want for ourselves. I never saw the point in putting it off once you've decided."

"And when you've already moved in together, you'd might as well make it official." Maddock looked at Bronwyn.

She could feel her face grow hot. She couldn't think what to say.

Her mother was watching. She shot a quelling look at Maddock, shaking her head in warning. "Can you tell us anything about the investigation?" She looked at Will.

"I would if I had anything to tell," he said. "We've talked to most of the family now, and no one stands out more than the others. We're assuming a financial motive, but that might not be the case, taking Evan's reputation into account. We're looking for evidence that he was having another affair. If so, there might be an angry husband out there."

"Gwniera thought he might be seeing someone again." Gwniera had obviously confided in Bronwyn's mum.

"We've found someone we think is a possibility," Mehta said, with a glance at Will, "but we also think it possible that what Gwniera thought was an affair was just Evan finally spending time with his illegitimate son, Awstin."

"Evan was seeing Awstin?" Mai asked, looking incredulous.

"Both Jenna and Awstin say he was," Will said.

"Well, that's a surprise." Mai leaned across the table to wipe up a bit of Gryffin's juice that had spilled. "I didn't think he'd ever come around to that. He spent years ignoring the boy."

And then it happened.

"The fairies were brown and orange and yellow today," Maegan announced in her clear, little girl voice, looking across the table at Maddock.

Seated beside her, Bronwyn froze.

"I'm sure they were lovely," Mai said quickly as other banter continued around her. "Did you play fairies at school?"

Maddock gave Maegan a stern look, and she retreated. "No, it was here, after school. They're just make believe," she said, but obviously only to appease her father. "I pretend."

Bronwyn didn't look at Will. He was seated on the same side of the table as she was; she hoped he hadn't seen her reaction to Maegan's words. Other conversation had continued, overlaying Maegan's announcement, so perhaps he hadn't noticed anything untoward.

"I used to play at fairies, too," she told Maegan quietly, "when I was little like you, but I liked horses more."

"My daddy says I can have a pony like Hobbs when I'm bigger." Maegan was successfully distracted.

That there'd be more moments like this, Bronwyn had no doubt. But for now, at least, she thought her secrets were still safely hers. *Someday I might have to tell him*, she thought. *Someday.*

Chapter Fifteen

"You're sure that's all he said?" Will questioned Bronwyn more aggressively as they ate their breakfast in the conservatory on Tuesday morning.

The previous afternoon, he'd been excited about Cassadee Richards, his mind filled with speculation about her. He'd all but dismissed Bronwyn's tale about meeting Dylan in the woods, but in the night, he'd woken and fixated on visions of her being attacked, of Dylan hiding out and shooting her, as Evan had been shot.

Dylan was a primary suspect, he reminded himself, maybe even their best suspect. He freely admitted not getting along with his father, he'd opposed his father's obsession with building a housing estate with what he probably hoped would someday be his money, he had every reason to be in the vicinity when the murder occurred, and he was an experienced shooter. What that added up to was that Bronwyn should not be going out to the woods, alone or even with others, until the case was solved.

Did he need a clue from her? Of course, he'd welcome one. But not at the cost of risking her life to get it. He'd have to solve this case on his own.

"He told me that he'd come over to our part of the forest to look for evidence that someone had gone to the cairn from our direction, rather than theirs," she repeated for the third time.

"You believed him?"

She let out a little exasperated breath. "Maybe. Not really."

"Why not?"

"It didn't totally make sense to me. What could he have found? There'd be nothing there to tell him if someone had come from that way, would there?"

"No, there wouldn't." He wished that she'd asked Dylan what, specifically, he'd been looking for, but she couldn't know how to conduct a proper interview. "What else?"

"He said he hated how his dad treated his mum. He realized from the time he was little that his mum was sad a lot of the time, and he remembered a big fight when Awstin was born. He said that he didn't want to be like his dad."

"As far as we know, he isn't." Will thought of that long-term anger, simmering through the years. It was more than possible that Dylan had come to the end of his patience with his dad.

"We talked a little about being suspects," Bronwyn went on. "I told him about us meeting when I was a suspect in Glynnis' murder. He seemed glad to have someone around who could understand what he's feeling."

It's too bad Bronwyn isn't police. Dylan might trust her with the truth, if she was able to establish a connection with him. "We're going to talk to him today. I have a lot more questions for him now than when we last spoke." He looked into her eyes. "Don't go out to the woods again until this case is over, right? You know how I feel about putting you at risk."

She did know. This wasn't the first time it had come up. He was probably being over-protective again, but things Maddock had said in the past made him feel that he was right to be. He was soon to be a part of their family. Maddock and his dad had watched over Bronwyn as she'd grown up, and now that responsibility was his, and he knew it.

He'd seen Bronwyn off to work and cleaned up the breakfast things before Mehta arrived in his little green Subaru. He invited him in, and they drank coffee as they made a plan for the day. Their primary focus was on Dylan, but if there was time, they'd try to find out more about Cassadee Richards, as well.

They drove through the village in Will's little convertible and up the tiny lane toward Dylan's house. Summer seemed to be lingering, with two days of sunshine alternating with a day of rain, or at least a storm. He hoped their wedding day would be one of the sunny ones.

Lark hadn't called the night before, nor that morning. He wasn't sure what to make of her silence. He hoped it meant she was too busy and settled to bother calling so often. Once a week was probably often enough, after all. She was pretty independent; no doubt a result of her somewhat chaotic upbringing. She'd be fine.

His mobile did ring as he turned into Dylan's drive. He parked and snatched it up, hitting the green button to accept the call. *Quigley.*

"Hey, what's up?"

"I checked into Cassadee Richards for you." Quigley was, as usual, all business. *No time for chit-chat in his day.* "She's thirty-nine, married to a Steffan Richards for eight years. No kids, but her husband has two children ages thirteen and eleven from a previous marriage. She's been employed at Barclay's Bank for nine years, starting as a teller and working up to what she does now."

"You got Evan Bennett's investment statements?"

"Yes. Our financial expert is going through them now. I'll let you know if there are any irregularities."

"Do we know anything about Steffan Richards?"

"I checked him out." Quigley was always efficient. "He works on a roads crew, when they're doing road repairs."

"Manual labour, then?"

"Yeah, I'd say so. Some of it would be night work, when the roads aren't so busy."

Interesting. "Any previous trouble with the law?"

"Not for a while. When he was a kid, he had a few run-ins with the police in Liverpool, where he grew up. There are a couple of possession convictions, underage drinking, vandalism, that sort of thing. The one that stands out is an assault when he was twenty-one. He and two friends ambushed another guy who apparently was from a different social group."

"A gang?"

"Yep. They did some major damage, but the guy recovered in the end, after a few weeks in hospital and some intense physical therapy. Our Staffan did some time for that one, but it looks like it paid off. His record's been clean since."

Will and Mehta exchanged looks. Maybe Steffan Richards needed looking into. "Anything else?"

"I had a quick look at the investigation into Lloyd Bennett's death. From what I could see, it was pretty straightforward. He was coming home from Welshpool late, driving too fast for that road. He rounded a bend and hit a sheep, and it tossed his car off the road onto some rocks. He wasn't wearing a seatbelt. He was thrown out, hit his head on the rocks, and died. I've got a couple of people looking into it further, talking to the investigating officers and that, but I don't think you're going to find anything suspicious there."

"He was alone in the car?"

"Yes, coming home after a sheep co-op meeting that ran later than usual. After the meeting, he went for a drink with a couple of other men, and that turned into a late meal before he headed for home."

Will ran that over in his mind. It did sound like just a tragic accident, but maybe something would still turn up. "Thanks, Quig."

"Whatever I can do, sir," Quigley quipped and the phone went dead.

Dylan wasn't at home, his wife Lisa informed them when they arrived. Like his parents' house, Dylan's was newer, built probably within the past ten years. Not as large as theirs, Dylan's looked more traditional, a white-washed house with stone accents and a lot of windows. A wooden playset with a swing and a metal slide sat in the front garden, with a fort atop the frame that would allow their son to play at castles and Vikings when he grew a little older. For now, the swing had been replaced with a baby version, and Lisa was playing with him there when they walked up.

"He'll either be at his mum's working or out in the fields. I don't know his plans for today," Lisa told them, pushing her son on his swing.

He had a chubby face and light hair, looking nothing like either of his parents.

They'd might as well take advantage of her being alone and ask a few more questions. "Can you walk us through the Monday again, Lisa?" Will asked. Beside him, Mehta took out a notepad.

"I don't know what more I can tell you," Lisa said. "We had breakfast around half-seven, and then Dylan went to the barns, you know, behind his mum's house. He came back by about an hour later, saying that he and his dad had an argument about the housing estate plan, and he'd stormed off away. He thought he'd repair some fencing and do some work here, mowing the lawn and the like."

That was new. "So, he was back here by ten or so, and then again in the afternoon?"

"It must have been around two. He did a few chores and then went off to do the feeding around five or so."

"He didn't mention trying to see his dad then?"

She reflected on that. "He'd had some time to think and cool off by then. He didn't say, but I had the feeling that he'd have been happier if the two of them could have talked it out."

"You're sure he didn't go out to that pasture by the forest to talk to his dad when he left here?"

She saw what he was getting at. "Dylan didn't kill his dad. I know him. He was like his mum, ready to forgive and forget." That wasn't reallly true. From what they understood, Gwniera hadn't forgiven nor forgotten. "Besides, Gwniera said he was there at her place, so he obviously didn't go out to see his dad by the woods."

"And nothing else seemed strange that day, or even in the days leading up to it? Nothing unusual or odd? No one hanging about that shouldn't be here?"

"Everything was just like always." The little boy, Aeron, started to grumble, trying to get out of the baby swing. "I can ring Dylan if you like, and he'll come back here to talk to you, or you can meet at the main house."

"We'll be happy to go out to the field, if that's where he is," Will told her. They'd prefer to interview him away from his mother, if possible.

She nodded, and they waited while she made her call, looking at the well-kept yard and the flowers, now fading, that edged the house. It was a cheerful place, and Will would bet that Dylan loved coming home to it at night. He wondered if Lisa kept the garden neat, or if Dylan did it in addition to his farm work.

Lisa finished her call and directed them further down the lane. "You'll see his truck when you get there," she told them. "It's those lambs again, the devil and the demon. I think those two will make someone a fine meal sooner rather than later."

They thanked them and climbed back into the MGF, bumping further down the lane until they found Dylan's truck, the flashy black Ford. *He'll probably manipulate things so that he can buy whatever he wants now that he has a say in what happens with the investment fund: a new truck every year, maybe even a bigger house*, Will thought. *He must think he's won the lottery.*

Dylan was sitting on the tailgate, drinking from a plastic bottle of water. He waved it at them. "Want one? I have a cooler full."

They declined. They stood in front of him, a bit awkwardly.

It was Mehta's turn to ask the questions; they'd agreed on that earlier. "We have a few more questions for you, if that's okay, Dylan."

"I don't know what more you can ask." He echoed his wife. "I've told you everything I know."

Mehta made him wait a minute, hoping that he'd volunteer something more to fill the silence. Will could hear the cry of a hunting hawk somewhere in the distance. When the silence stretched to awkwardness, Mehta said, "Tell us about the argument with your dad that morning."

"It wasn't exactly an argument," Dylan defended himself immediately. "I told you we'd been disagreeing about him building the housing estate. All of us thought he was wasting the investment money, throwing it away. He didn't want to hear that. He had in his mind he was going to build all these houses back there in the forest, and people would be snatching them up like crazy, wanting them for holiday homes in the country. He thought he'd make a paddock and stable so they could keep horses, and I don't know what all else. I guess there'd be hiking and mountain biking."

"Did he say why he thought it would be so successful despite your reservations? He must have defended his plan to you."

"He said it was beautiful here. People would want to come and relax away from cities."

"It is beautiful here," Mehta told him.

Dylan shot him a derisive look. "People want shops and restaurants. They're not going to pay big money for a cottage in the back of nowhere, are they?"

"So, you argued." Mehta looked him in the eye. "Did you shout at each other?"

Dylan thought it over. Someone might have overheard, after all. "Okay, we shouted at each other, said things we shouldn't. All families do that from time to time."

"Is it possible that you were already angry with him because your mum thought he was having another affair?" Mehta said, his voice reasonable.

"He had no right," Dylan spat. He rolled his shoulders and put his hands to his temples, rubbing them. "You'd think he'd have learned after Jenna, but he kept right on doing it, one after another."

"It was a constant parade of women?"

"No, but it might as well have been. He'd be all loving with Mum for a few months, and then someone would catch his fancy and off he'd go again. Mum could always tell. He was an old man now, but he still had no trouble finding someone to be with."

Mehta let him stew about that for a minute in silence.

"It's the money," Dylan finally said. "Don't you see? He had flash cars and money in the bank. His women were stupid. They always thought he'd end up with them and then they'd have money, too."

Money in the bank, Will thought. Cassadee Richards was looking better all the time, if they were right about her being the newest girlfriend in Evan's life. Maybe she wasn't skimming money from the accounts. Maybe she looked at those statements and thought she'd get at that money in a different way.

207

"What will you do with the money now, Dylan?" Mehta asked. "You'll leave it in the investment accounts?"

Dylan reached up and scratched at his shoulder. He stared off toward the pasture, seeming deep in thought. "My grandmother needs her share." He hesitated. "Dad had to sell some of it off from time to time to finance her care placement."

Mehta nodded. "I gather it's quite a lot of money?"

"It was my grandmother's money from her family. They made money from the quarry a long time ago." He hadn't answered the question. "I thought…" he hesitated, "that I might give Merry a share." He looked from one to the other of them, seeking understanding. "She never got anything from the estate, other than her education, and she could use the money. I'll inherit the land, free and clear, and I'll make a good living off it, like my dad did, even giving Mum a share. Merry should get something, too."

Mehta considered that. Will watched him think it out and knew that he'd ask the right question to follow up. "It sounds like you have your immediate family taken care of. I'm sure they'll be thankful. How about your cousins, though? Evie and Eriana and Terrwyn? Your uncle Conway? Don't they deserve a share, as well?"

Dylan's reaction was immediate. "God, no. It hasn't been theirs in twenty years. Why now?" He frowned. "I wouldn't want to cash it all out. It should be left intact, most of it, like my grandparents wanted it to be. My grandfather didn't leave any of it to Conway when he died, so there must have been a reason, don't you think? I'd be going against his last wishes if I did otherwise."

"Yet, selling off enough to give Merry a share is fine?"

"What do you want me to do?" Dylan growled back. "I said I'd keep most of it intact, didn't I? Merry and I were kids when my grandfather died. He wouldn't have thought to give us access to that money. My uncle was a grown man, though. I'm sure my grandfather considered giving him a share and rejected the idea out of hand. I'm not changing that now."

They let silence grow for an uncomfortable minute. "And your brother, Awstin?" Mehta kept his voice soft.

Dylan's face flushed. "Dad never wanted anything to do with him, or his mother either. He's not a part of our family."

Mehta nodded and glanced at Will.

Will took a step closer to Dylan, his pen in his hand. "Do you know that your father had been seeing Awstin for the past year or so? He'd been going to his rugby matches and taking him out for meals, forming a relationship with him."

Dylan stared at him, his face flushing with anger. "Who told you that? I suppose Jenna did. She's a liar. Dad never wanted to see Awstin."

"Would he have told you, if he did?"

"We'd have known." Dylan slid off the truck and stood facing them, his hands in fists at his side. "He'd have bragged about it, thrown it in Mum's face." He grimaced. "Mine, too, when he was mad at me."

Will could see that. Mentioning another son during an argument would be a powerful way of saying that Dylan didn't matter as much as he thought he did. Evan might even have used Awstin as a tool for keeping Dylan in line, if he'd wanted to. *Time to back away from that line of questioning.*

"I heard you ran into Bronwyn in the woods yesterday. She said you thought you'd look for evidence that someone might have come onto your property from theirs on Monday. I'm a little puzzled. What evidence exactly did you think you'd find?"

"Well…I don't know exactly what to tell you, Inspector. I wasn't looking for anything specific. I just thought that we hadn't seen anyone drive up our lane to get there, so maybe whoever it was came from their side. I thought tire tracks, or maybe he'd dropped something."

Will let it go. He'd circle back to what he really wanted to say later. "Did you notice anything unusual in the past few weeks or so, Dylan? Maybe see someone who didn't belong here, or maybe your dad was acting differently?"

Dylan blinked at the sudden change of topics. It was clear that he had been ready to lose his temper on them. He took a breath. "I told you, there was nothing. My dad was unpredictable at times, and he'd been fighting with us over the housing estate plan, so that had him huffing off alone more than usual. He was secretive, but a new affair

209

would do that, wouldn't it? He was great at sneaking around, my dad was."

They were going to get nothing more at the moment. "Who do you think killed your dad, Dylan?" Will asked in conclusion. He watched Dylan's eyes.

Dylan broke the eye contact, glancing off to the side where a huddle of sheep cropped the grass. "I wish I knew. It wasn't me, and it wasn't Mum or Merry. Other than that, it could have been anyone." He brightened with a thought. "Maybe it was Awstin. Or Jenna. Maybe they thought it's time they got their due."

"How would that work out for them?" Will wondered, trying not to look amused. "Killing your dad wouldn't bring them anything but trouble."

"Maybe it was revenge for him ignoring them all these years. Maybe Awstin didn't like that and, now he's grown, he decided it was time to make Dad pay."

Will had investigated a case eerily similar to that not long ago. Sometimes, illegitimate children let festering resentment grow into a desire for revenge. Awstin seemed a solid kid, intelligent and goal-oriented. But you never really knew what lay beneath the exterior.

It was time to circle back. "Listen," he said, straightening. He wanted to look intimidating. "I don't want you over in the Bagley's part of the forest, not now or ever. Just stay away from them."

Dylan's eyes narrowed, and then a slow smile curved his lips. "I'm not my dad, but I'm flattered that you think your fiancée might be interested."

Will took a step toward him, fists clenching at his sides. "That's not what worries me, and you know it. Just stay away."

"It's not yours to say whether I wander over there or not. There are laws: the right to roam?"

"That's as may be, but I'm warning you off. I don't want you anywhere near Bronwyn or the rest of her family."

"You think I murdered my dad, and I'll be after them next." Dylan's smile was unnerving, almost threatening. "I told you. I didn't do it."

"Just in case, humour me for now, will you? You're not going to like me focusing on you more than I already am." He could feel Mehta beside him, amused but trying not to show it.

Dylan waved him away. "Okay, okay, I'll stay well away from their land. I'm telling you, though, you'll do better to look elsewhere for whoever did for my dad and leave me well out of it."

That night, Will and Mehta sat with their glasses of Famous Grouse, while Bronwyn had a glass of wine, relaxing. They'd decided to call it a day after Dylan's interview. They'd gone back to the cottage and updated their wall, and then they'd placed a conference call with Bowers, detailing everything on their wall bit by bit, in order not to miss anything.

Bowers had been busy coordinating a major incident just up the coast from Caernarfon on Anglesey. A man had walked into a small shop and shot three people, two of them employees and the third a customer. He'd fled, and they were going all-out to try to identify and arrest him. "We're still short a man," he told them, not pointing out that the shortage was due to Will's actions the previous spring, "and it's taking all our resources to cover this. I nearly called you back, Jay."

Thankfully, that hadn't happened. "I thought we were getting a couple of new detectives in," he commented.

"Next week, if we're lucky," Bowers clarified. "There was a holdup with that, as well, but now with two major crimes on opposite sides of our territory, they've gotten the message that our need is critical."

Will and Mehta took turns going through their list of suspects and what evidence they had available, which wasn't as much as they'd like. "Bottom line," Will said in conclusion, "is that we have a victim who won't be much mourned and a pile of suspects with nothing to point to one of them more than the others."

"What's your gut feeling say?" Bowers wanted to know.

Will looked at Mehta, who spoke up. "Dylan Bennett has the most to gain from Evan's death since he'll inherit everything, but we can't reject the idea of the angry husband until we know more."

"It's hard to want to pin it on someone because we both like the idea that Evan finally got what was coming to him, justice, and all that," Will elaborated.

"No tips this time to point you in the right direction?"

"No, sir," Will assured him, "no tips, not yet anyway." He smiled at Bronwyn, sitting on the couch out of sight of the call.

"Well, tell her to get busy." Bowers sounded like he was joking, but Will was never sure with him. "It's time to wrap this one up. You have a wedding you'll need to attend before you know it."

"We're trying, sir, we're trying." Will smiled into the phone.

"If you find a day with nothing to do, why don't you come back and get some of the reports written up? You need to check in here once in a while. At the rate you're going, Jay will have to buy a house there, too."

"We'll see what we can manage, sir. The memorial service is on Saturday, so we'll have to be here for that."

"Maybe on the Sunday, then," Bowers suggested. It wasn't a bad idea, Will told himself. Bronwyn would be busy with the tea party at his mother's. He'd feel a little less guilty about that if he had to work at the office that day.

They rang off.

"You know," Mehta said, "a tip would be most welcome right now." He gave Bronwyn a meaningful grin.

"Get off it, mate," Will raised his glass in a salute. "Drink up. It's time you were away from here so we can have some cuddle time." He drained his glass and checked. Both Bronwyn and Mehta were blushing.

Chapter Sixteen

With a full day ahead, Will and Mehta left early the next morning for Shrewsbury. They intended to visit with Carys Bennett again with new questions that had come up, and then they'd stop in Welshpool on the way back to talk to Cassadee Richards and – they hoped – her husband Steffan. With a lot of luck, one or another of them would say something that would clarify a motive for them and focus the investigation.

Will kissed Bronwyn goodbye and saw her into the Land Rover, and then he climbed into the driver's seat of his little MGF. It was a fine morning, and despite that it was Mehta's turn to drive, he liked the thought of putting the convertible roof down and cruising from town to town on their route. Lunch out in Shrewsbury after the interview with Carys Bennett would be the icing on the cake, he thought, as Mehta bent down into the passenger seat beside him.

"We'll want to push her about the money," Mehta commented, looking out the side window at the countryside passing by. They drove up a steep hillside, winding around and around the edge, until they emerged at the top onto flat empty countryside. "We know more now, and I'd like to know what her thoughts are about whether to give Meredith a share or not. Is that even Dylan's decision to make?"

"We'll find out," Will promised him. "Do you want to lead this one, or should I?"

"I did it before. I thought it went okay."

"It did. You definitely have a way with women, even those old enough to be your grandmother. How about you start, and I'll pop in with questions when I see you've skipped over something?"

"As if you'd notice." Mehta grinned. "Your mind isn't really on this case, is it? Not with your wedding just a few days away."

"Get off it, mate. My mind is perfectly focused." He said it, but it wasn't exactly true. Pre-wedding jitters had him glad that there was a case to distract him. The thought of committing to someone for life still scared him silly if he let it. The trick was not to think about it at all, if he could help it.

They knocked at Carys Bennett's door just before nine a.m., hoping she'd be dressed and ready for the day.

She answered the door wearing a dressing gown, and Will's heart sank. She had every right to refuse them entry and she well might do just that, if they'd disrupted her morning routine.

She peered at them, looking startled, and then she backed away to let them into the room. "I thought you'd be the server with my breakfast," she said. "I didn't make it downstairs in time to eat today, so they'll send it up on a tray." She stood at the junction between the small sitting room and the hallway that led to her bedroom. "I'll just slip on some clothes," she said, "and I'll be right back. If someone knocks, just get my tray for me, will you?" Without waiting for an answer, she hobbled down the hallway pushing her zimmer frame and shut the bedroom door.

Will looked a question at Mehta, and they both took the opportunity to wander around the little flat, looking at family pictures scattered here and there. A folded newspaper lay on the coffee table beside an empty cup, but otherwise, the flat was just as neat and ordered as it had been the last time they'd been there. A faint scent of liniment competed with the aroma of good coffee that came from the tiny kitchenette.

Will sat down on the sofa, and Mehta took his seat on one of the recliners. The fussy Staffordshire figurines kept a watch on them as they waited, not talking, but listening to the quiet. An occasional rustle came from the bedroom, but evidently the walls were well-insulated because they heard nothing from the neighboring flats.

Finally, Carys emerged from the bedroom and thumped into the sitting room, settling into the empty recliner with a sigh. "They're slow with my breakfast," she complained. "I'm hungry now."

"Can I get you something?" Mehta offered. He glanced toward the little kitchen area. "Biscuits?"

She gave him a knowing look. "Would you like some? Young man like you, I bet you're always a bit peckish."

Mehta shook his head, but he smiled, and Will thought he was trying to charm her. He was a good-looking kid, still boyish with the short beard and longer hair. As often as not, he got a suspect talking when Will was floundering hopelessly.

Carys smiled back at him. "What can I do for you boys today? Did you think up more questions for me?"

"We did." Will let Mehta continue to speak for them. As he had the first time they'd come, he was connecting well with her, so Will was happy to play the subordinate role. "We're wondering if you could just describe your sons' families for us. Seeing them from your perspective might help us see the relationships more clearly."

She frowned at him. "Surely you don't think that Conway murdered his brother." She blinked, her eyes suddenly filling with tears. It was a moment before she continued. "There were only the two of them, you know. They were out there on the farm, and there weren't many friends around for them to be with. They were close when they were young."

"I understand that." Mehta's voice was soft. He'd seen that he'd need to be gentle if he was going to get the answers they needed. "Did they stay close as they got older?"

A knock on the door disrupted the conversation. *Bad timing*, Will thought. Now they'd have to guide her back to a topic she wasn't happy with. He got up and went to the door, opening it to see a boy in his late teens, holding a tray he'd taken from a small cart. "Breakfast for Mrs. Carys," he announced, holding the tray toward Will's outstretched hands.

"Thanks," Will said shortly, taking the tray and shutting the door. He was trying to hear the conversation behind him. Mehta hadn't abandoned his efforts, after all.

Carys glanced up at him when he took the few steps back into the room. "Just set it down here." She indicated a table beside her chair. She reached over and unwrapped the meal: a small pile of scrambled eggs, a piece of bacon, toast and jam, mixed fruit that looked like it had come out of a can. She picked up the toast and shook it at them. "As I was saying, Evan and Gwniera were never a good match. I thought he was making a mistake right from the start, but what could you do? She was pregnant, and we liked to see him take responsibility. We helped out where we could, and I'm afraid that Dylan was a little spoiled in the end. But he turned out well, didn't he?" She looked at Mehta. "He's a good lad, a good family man."

"He seems very devoted," Mehta assured her. He watched her take a bite of the toast. "Let's think about Conway now, okay? Can you tell me about him?"

She reflected while she chewed. "It was sad for him, losing his first wife to cancer so young. He really struggled for a while, and I felt sorry for him. But then he met Mabyn, and they've been happy together. Terrywn was a surprise, but a gift. That lad loves his dad more than any boy ought to."

"We met him."

She waited, obviously hoping for more, and then her lips twisted. "I suppose Evan could have done better by Gwniera. There was another child out of wedlock, you know."

"Yes, we are aware of that. Awstin." Mehta kept his voice gentle, encouraging. "How did you feel about that?"

"Well, I wasn't happy, but there was nothing to be done."

No, Will thought, *by then Lloyd was already dead, and Evan had inherited the lot.* He wondered if she'd regretted it then, if she'd wished they'd gone the other way and chosen Conway to inherit the land. He could think of no way to ask without offending her.

"Tell us more about Conway," Mehta encouraged her.

She had finished the toast and turned to poke at the bacon. "The eggs will be cold," she announced. She picked up the bacon in her fingers and nibbled it. "Conway was always a good boy. He was one of those who always tried to do the right thing." She sighed, and suddenly, she looked older, every bit of her eighty-plus years. "I know Conway struggled, and not just because he lost Rhosyn. It wasn't easy for him to make a decent living with what he had. We thought if he didn't get the land when Lloyd died, he'd go on to find another career, something that didn't involve farming. Like I said before, there wasn't enough land to divide up and make a good living for the both of them, so we made a choice we thought was right. We'd have paid for his education, if that's what he decided to do. But he didn't do what we expected. Instead, he took out loans and bought what he could and leased more." She looked from Mehta to Will and back to Mehta. "If Lloyd had lived longer, maybe we'd have done it differently. It wasn't easy for me, all those years, watching him work hard for every penny while Evan had all he needed and more."

"There's no question of giving him some of the land now?" Will broke in.

She shook her head. "The land went entirely to Evan, and from him to Dylan. There is no taking it back at this point."

"And the investment money? You told us before that you still had some control over what happens to that."

"You'll think I'm a terrible mother." She seemed to have forgotten the rest of her breakfast. "I tried to go against Evan's wishes, Inspector. I told him that, if he was determined to sell off the rest of the investment portfolio, that he had to give some of the money to Conway. That was our agreement."

"Fifty-fifty?" Will wanted to know.

"No, less than that. I had to save some to live on, and Evan's project was expensive. I thought, in the end, he might share the profits from that with Conway, although I never got a chance to talk to him about it."

"You were on board with the housing estate idea?"

"I trusted Evan to make good financial decisions."

Yet, he didn't make good personal decisions, did he? "You know that Dylan is thinking of giving a portion of the money to his sister?"

She nodded. "He mentioned it to me."

Will wondered when she'd last seen Dylan and decided to ask. "When did you talk about that?" They hadn't even had Evan's memorial service yet.

"He came to see me on Saturday. He brought Lisa and the baby with him. It cheered me up to see them."

"What do you think about him sharing the money with Meredith?"

"The world has changed in the years since Lloyd passed, Inspector. Back then, I agreed with him that Evan and Dylan should have the farm when we were gone, and we had to put someone in charge of the investment money. It wasn't so much in those days. We didn't want to divide it up, and the two boys together might not agree on things." She shook her head reflectively. "Maybe it was the wrong thing to do, but it was what we did. It's too late to change things now. Evan made the decisions, and now Dylan will have that responsibility." She looked at Will. "I did suggest to Dylan that he should give an equal share to Conway and to each of his children."

They took that in, exchanging looks. "How did Dylan react to that idea?" Mehta ventured.

"He agreed to think about it." She sighed again. "But he won't. He has no intention of sharing it out that much. It took years to grow into the amount we have now, and Dylan wouldn't like to see that diminished. He thought a bit to Merry would be okay, but he'd like to keep the bulk of it to spend on Lisa and to leave to his little Aeron. You can't blame him. He's just taking care of his own." She looked at them gravely. "Lisa was a city girl, you know. I have the impression that she's not very happy isolated out in the country like she is. Dylan tries to make up for that by buying her nice things, taking her to the city for dinners, going on fancy holidays, things like that. It all adds up. I think he'd like to use some of the money to supplement what he makes on the farm. He'll still have his mother to support, too, even if she and Evan never really got along. Even in a bad marriage, the wife is entitled to something."

"Have you talked to Conway about any of this?"

"No, I wouldn't want him to think badly of Dylan. Conway does fine, Inspector. In many ways, he was better off than Evan was because he got the happy family, and Evan didn't. Conway's children are devoted to him. They come home for holidays and birthdays, and

Terrwyn is right there beside him, working hard." She looked toward the family pictures on the wall. "Those kids love their dad. I can't say the same for Evan."

Will looked at Mehta, wondering what else they'd forgotten.

"Do you remember a gun Lloyd would have had from his father? A Lee-Enfield Mark 4, from the Second World War?" Mehta asked her.

Her head drooped forward. "I remember it. It wasn't from Lloyd's father. It was from mine. He had it during the war and gave it to Lloyd when we married. Was that the gun that killed him?"

"We believe that it was," Will told her. "Do you know who got it after Lloyd died?"

She took her time. "I didn't pay much attention through the years. When I moved, I divided up the remaining guns for the boys, but I don't think that was one of them. Perhaps one of them took it earlier, wanting to keep it safe, or maybe to give it to their own sons as a remembrance of their grandfather. The boys did that: borrowed a gun now and then and failed to return them. It didn't matter. I had no use for them."

They let that go. It was possible that she really didn't remember.

"How about Awstin, Carys?" Mehta asked then, addressing the topic they found most difficult with her. "He was Evan's son, too. Does he deserve a share of the inheritance?"

"That boy would have no right to expect anything," she said adamantly. "Evan had no contact with him. His mother didn't want it."

Will waited, wondering if Mehta would venture further into that relationship with her.

He did. "Would it surprise you to know that Evan had been seeing Awstin the past year or so?"

She reacted the same way Dylan had. "I don't know who told you that, Inspector, but it's not true. Evan would never have done that. And, even if he had, Evan wouldn't have given our money into that woman's purse."

"Call me soft-hearted, if you want to," Mehta said as they ate pasties out on a bench in the sunshine, "but I feel sorry for Awstin. He's family, and not a single one of them would even give him the time of day, let alone get to know him."

"He seems like a great kid," Will agreed. "He's got to be smart if he's headed off to study microbiology at uni, and he was pretty put-together when we talked to him. If they'd just give him a chance, they might find out he's someone they'd like having around."

"Maybe he's our murderer," Mehta suggested. He took a bite of his pasty and chewed it before continuing. "Do you think he resented his dad enough to kill him?"

"I've seen it before," Will told him. "That time the kid got it wrong; the man he thought was his dad, wasn't. Still, it ate at him through the years, thinking his dad had another family he loved and didn't care an iota about him or his mother, and it drove him to murder."

"I don't like to think Awstin would do it. He seems a nice kid, so focused and even mature for his age. I just can't see him giving his whole life up for a bit of revenge." Mehta thought for a moment. "He wouldn't have had that gun."

"We can't rule him out until we know for sure. Evan could have given it to him. The thing is, he's a smart lad, and maybe he'd have been able to carry out a murder without leaving us any evidence to convict him with." Will picked up his garbage and grabbed Mehta's, as well. "Let's bin this and head back to Welshpool. It's time to investigate another possible motive."

They decided that there was no purpose to accosting Steffan Richards at his place of work until they'd talked to Cassadee again first. "We don't even know for sure there was an affair," Will pointed out.

"Will she admit it if there was?"

"Maybe not," Will said. "I don't know how to go at her. The way she acted before, I thought for sure we had it."

"I think we just ask," Mehta suggested. "If she says no, then we go at it again another way."

They parked on the street, lucky this time to get a space nearer to the bank. Before they went inside, they sat in the car and called Quigley to check if he'd gotten any results from the investment statements.

He put them on hold for several minutes, giving them an opportunity to plan several alternative ways to conduct the upcoming interview with Cassadee Richards while they waited, and then he came back on the line. "Magnus says it looks okay to him. He hasn't gotten into it as much as he wants to, though, so it's still early and something may still turn up."

That didn't let Phylip Thomas off the hook, either, then. If they didn't start eliminating suspects soon, they'd never figure it out. "Okay, thanks," Will said, cutting the call off. He looked at Mehta. "Let's see what we can manage here."

They were left sitting in the waiting area again, this time for nearly half an hour before, finally, Cassadee Richards summoned them into her office. Today, she was wearing a neat pinstriped pantsuit, with a crisp white blouse that clashed a bit with her creamy complexion. She'd pulled the red-blonde hair back into a bun at her neckline. She looked at them primly, a little put out, if Will was reading her correctly.

"What can I do for you today, Inspectors?"

"We just have a few more questions for you." It was Will's turn to speak. "Something else has come up in our investigation that points us back here to you."

She blinked at that statement, her blue eyes going wide. "You found something off in the financial paperwork?"

"No, they're still analyzing that," he said, watching her closely. He didn't need Mehta's psychology degree to see if someone was lying to him.

She seemed puzzled, but Will was sure that it was a show, put on to distract them from the real issue. "I don't know what else I can help you with," she said.

"Cassadee, how well did you know Evan Bennett?"

Her face turned more peach-colored than cream. "You asked me that before. I told you..."

"I'm asking you again," he interrupted her, suddenly impatient with the game she was playing. "This time I want the truth."

She wasn't ready to go that far. "I've worked with him ever since I've been here. My predecessor handled his account before that."

221

"Were you and Evan having an affair?" Sometimes, the only thing you could do was to blurt it right out.

She caught her breath, no longer pretending to be confused. "What a thing to accuse someone of," she stammered, trying to look indignant. "Why would you even think something like that?"

"We're pretty sure it's true," Will told her. "If we have to, we'll find the evidence to prove it."

"What difference would it make? I didn't kill Evan. I was here at work until five."

Which didn't prove anything. It was only a half-hour's drive to Llangynog from Welshpool. The timing would have been tight, but it wasn't an impossibility. "Did your husband know about the affair?"

She stared at him. "I don't want Steffan involved."

"You didn't answer my question."

"I think you should leave," she blustered. "I don't have to put up with harassment at my place of work."

"Fine, we'll leave," Will told her. "We'll go straight to your husband and ask him what he knows, and then we'll get the local constables to arrest you on suspicion and take you in for questioning at the station." Beside him, he heard Mehta stirring and he put out a hand to quell him. "Maybe you're telling us the truth, Cassadee. Maybe there wasn't an affair at all. If so, that's all fine. But if you're lying to us, we will find out and, when we do, we'll charge you with obstruction and impeding a police investigation and anything else we can find." It might not work exactly like that, but he wanted her scared now, scared enough to tell the truth.

She stared at him, her cheeks brilliant spots of red, as she turned it over in her head. He could almost see her thinking it through, turning over the possibilities and, finally, coming to a conclusion. "Okay, you're right. We were having an affair. But I was ending it."

"How long had it been going on?"

She considered, her face a mask of embarrassment. "I'd say about a year and a half."

They waited, hoping she would elaborate.

She did. "I know it wasn't professional, but I didn't plan it. Evan was charming, like I said before, and I guess I was craving excitement

222

or something. I never meant for it to continue as long as it did, but it was easy, with Steffan working nights and the house all to myself. Evan never stayed the night, but that was fine. That would have made me nervous anyway."

"You said you were ending it?"

"I was. After a while, I just knew it was wrong, and it wasn't going to develop into anything more, was it? Both of us were married, and even though all Evan did was complain about Gwniera, it was obvious that he wasn't going to divorce her."

She'd seen the account balance and given it her best effort, Will realized. If she wasn't going to snare Evan into marriage, the money would lose its appeal, and with it, the affair, too. Will felt a surge of intense dislike for the woman, but he tried to keep it from his voice. "We'll have to talk to your husband. Did he know about the affair?"

Her face flushed again, this time with a flare of temper. "Of course not. He worked nights. He didn't know anything."

"You're sure?" They'd lose the jealous husband angle if what she said was true. But they'd have to ask him anyway, just in case. Even if she thought he didn't know, it wasn't impossible that he did. "We'll still have to talk to him. Do you want to tell him first, or should we just spring it on him ourselves?" He knew he sounded cruel and didn't really care.

"I....I don't think I can," she stammered. Suddenly, tears streaked down her cheeks. "Oh, God, I wish I had never met Evan. What a mess."

"Yes, well, we'll just go over to your house now, then," Will told her. He refused to allow the tears to sway his determination. "We'll have a chat with him now, and you can talk to him later."

They left, and Mehta gave Will a look.

"What?" he growled.

"You were pretty hard on her."

"I didn't like her. She only saw Evan as a get-rich-quick scheme. She strung him along until she realized he wasn't going to divorce Gwniera, and then she was done. There was no real attraction there. It was all about the money."

"I agree. I'm not arguing."

Will let his temper settle. He shouldn't have snapped at Mehta, who probably didn't like Cassadee Richards any more than he did. "Do you think she called Steffan?"

"She should tell him in person, if he really doesn't already know, but doing it by phone, or maybe a text, would fit with her profile."

Will smiled at that. "Well, we'll know soon enough."

They knocked at the door of the brick cottage that matched the address they had on file for the Richards. No one answered, so Mehta pounded on the door harder. "I hear someone inside," he said, and he pounded again, yelling out, "Steffan Richards, police! Open the door."

The door swung open to reveal a man of medium height and build with a shaved head and a sparce goatee on his chin. He was wearing a tee shirt featuring a band Will had never heard of and was zipping his jeans up. "What?" he barked.

"Can we come in?" Will asked, while Mehta hung back a bit. The kid sometimes did that when he felt a little threatened, a habit he'd have to break.

The man stepped back and let them pass by him into a living room disarrayed with a clutter of books, empty food wrappers, cups, and other debris. The room was dark, the shades pulled. The only real light came from a small table lamp. A large television was dark, but Will could hear television noise coming from the back of the house.

He stood in the centre of the room and faced Steffan Richards. "Did your wife call and warn you we'd be on our way?"

Richards stood still, his shoulders lifting with his heavy breathing, and then he nodded. "She says she's been having an affair," he spat bitterly. Will couldn't tell if it was news to him or if he'd already known, or at least suspected. Maybe Mehta would have a clearer read on it.

It'd be better to face this one head-on. "Yeah, she admitted that to us a few minutes ago. The man she was involved with is dead."

"She said." He glanced toward a hallway.

Will followed the glance. "You were going somewhere?" An athletic bag sat in the hallway, just at the entrance. A jacket was tossed over it, but didn't disguise what it was.

224

Richards followed Will's gaze. His eyes wandered as he thought. "Yeah, well, when you get news like that, you just want to get away."

"Where were you going?"

He shrugged. "I don't know. Anywhere but here. I need to get off by myself and think what to do."

What to do about the affair, or what to do about them catching him out? If he'd killed Evan, he probably hadn't expected them to figure it out, at least not so quickly. *If he did it,* Will reminded himself. "When did you learn about the affair?"

Richards frowned. "Just now, when she called."

"You had no suspicions earlier?"

"I work nights. What do you think?"

"There are no children in the house?" Will wondered about the television noise.

"We never had any together. My ex-wife has custody of mine."

"They visit here, though?" Will demanded. He wanted to know if they'd been witnesses to the affair. If so, they might have told their dad about it.

"Yeah, they visit weekends sometimes. What's it matter? Cassadee was on her own overnight a lot of the time. That's what matters."

"What's your schedule, Mr. Richards?"

"My work schedule? It varies. Most of the time I work the eight to six shift, overnight. Sometimes it's day work. Most weekends I'm off."

"What shift did you work on the Monday before last, sir?" Will was trying to be polite. He didn't like this man much more than he'd liked his wife. *Likes attract?*

"I've been on nights for the last six weeks," Richards said. "We work overnight so as not to disrupt traffic during the daytime."

That wouldn't give him an alibi for the time Evan was killed. "Were you at home that afternoon?"

"How could I remember that?" Richards grumbled. "I suppose you think I killed that man? Truth is, I didn't know there was an affair going on a week ago Monday. I'd never met the man. Can I give you an alibi? Not for the afternoon, no. I was here, getting ready to go to work. But you'll not find any evidence I did it, because I didn't."

225

That was clear enough. "Do you own any firearms?" Will wasn't ready to give up.

The frown on the man's face deepened. "I used to have a little rifle that I used for target shooting, but I sold it a year or so ago."

"Twenty-two caliber?"

"Yeah, for what it's worth. Why? Is that what killed him?"

Will ignored the question. He held out a card. "Would you call us when you settle in somewhere and let us know where you're staying in case we need to contact you again? If we don't hear from you in the next twenty-four hours, we will issue a warrant for your arrest."

"My...arrest?" he sputtered. He gathered himself, fighting for control. "This has been quite a day, all around."

Yes, it had been quite a day, Will and Mehta agreed as they drove back to Llangynog. The narrow lane had Will driving slowly and watching for stray sheep on the roadway. Once, they had to pull into a lay-by to let an oncoming car pass them.

"He's a definite possibility," Mehta commented. "He was going away, whether to flee from us or from his wife, who knows?"

"It's suspicious," Will agreed. "It was only luck we found her and she admitted it."

"That was down to you. Good police work."

"I thought she was one I could push without my conscience bothering me after. She didn't deserve a softer approach."

"We still have the immediate family to think about," Mehta reminded him. "Carys gave us a lot more information today. I could see how Awstin might resent his dad, maybe even enough to kill him over his neglect."

"Or Dylan could have done it. He obviously wants that money if he resisted his grandmother's suggestion that he share it out with his cousins, as well as his sister. It sounds like he needs it to keep his wife happy. Maybe he just couldn't tolerate his dad's squandering it away on that housing estate scheme."

"We're no closer to figuring it out, are we?" Mehta looked out the passenger window as they drove through Llangynog. "Time's getting short. It'll be your wedding day before you know it."

"Well, if that happens, you'll be working this one on your own. You'll get the credit for the solve, all of it."

"But you're the one who gets the tips. That's what we need."

"Sometimes," Will reminded him. "Just sometimes." He was really starting to hope, though, that this would be one of those times.

Janet Newton

Chapter Seventeen

Bronwyn left for work early, anticipating a hectic day. She had a small group of four men from Welshpool booked into the conference room for both the Thursday and the Friday, overnighting at the New Inn B&B. That was easy enough. They'd get booked in and meet her at the centre, and she'd see them settled in for their morning session.

What would keep her busy was the fact that the four men had invited their wives along, and the wives had wondered if Bronwyn could show them some of the local hiking trails while their husbands were working. They'd offered to pay extra for her expertise, and she'd not wanted to refuse them, so after running the idea past both Janice and the Reverend Wycliff, she'd agreed. That meant that she'd settle the men into their meeting and then drive back to the village to meet the ladies at the New Inn. She planned to take them on her usual four-mile hike from Llangynog to Pennant Melangell that morning, which would give her a chance to assess their abilities. If they were decent hikers and not daunted by the climb or the bogs, she'd get them to the centre in time to enjoy lunch with their husbands. On Friday, she thought she could take them to the waterfall, Pistyll y Gyfyng, which was a difficult hike, if they wanted to see the falls properly. She'd know after today if that was going to be an option.

The men arrived on time, a seemingly boisterous bunch who looked fit themselves, so she hoped the wives would match them in that way. They joked and teased her as she escorted them into the conference room

228

and made sure the equipment worked for them, assuring her that they'd be fine on their own and that they were perfectly capable of re-setting the internet connection or troubleshooting the laptop they were using.

She left them feeling that they'd manage just fine on their own. Calling to Daisy, she got into her Land Rover and drove back into the village. This was the first time she'd done something like this. What if it could be another option for people who booked the conference room? She wouldn't mind hiking with groups, if they were willing to pay extra for it and the centre directors approved the idea.

The four women were sitting outside at the green picnic tables, watching for her to arrive. They were dressed appropriately for their hike, in jeans, tee shirts, and sturdy hiking boots, which was a good omen.

Bronwyn introduced herself, and they did the same. Donna was the oldest of the group, probably early forties, with glossy dark hair worn long and brown eyes fringed with long lashes. Glenda was younger, in her mid-thirties, with short curly reddish hair and a fair complexion. Heledd, the youngest of the group in her late twenties, also had dark brown hair, but with green eyes that stood out against a face freckled atop a tan. Lona was about the same age as Glenda, and it was obvious the two of them were close friends, chatting easily together as they set out on the walk.

They all greeted Daisy as if she were their own dog, and then they set out on the trail. Bronwyn kept an eye on them as she set the pace, making sure it was comfortable for them. The first part of the walk was a rough track that led uphill through old quarry workings. No one lagged behind, and no one complained about going too fast, so she finally settled into the hike and let her mind wander as she reveled in the fading summer.

As they went, she stopped them occasionally to point out the landmarks: Cwm Pennant, Craig Rhiwarth, the stunning view down Cwm Dwygo, the prehistoric burial chamber, and another breath-taking view down into Cwm Llech. It was a beautiful hike, and one she forgot to appreciate sometimes since she'd done it all her life and she often had other things on her mind to distract her.

When they passed by the first forested area, she told them to take a break, and then she led them through a shortened version of her nature meditation exercise. She urged them to listen, and was delighted when they heard not only Daisy's snuffling through the undergrowth, but also the scream of a peregrine falcon in the distance. They assured her that they could smell the late-summer warm scent of baking grasses and also the fir needles as they crushed them in their hands. They felt the sharpness of the needles, the roughness of the bark, and the sun on their faces, closing their eyes against the red glare on their eyelids. When they opened their eyes to see, she urged them not just to notice the larger landscape, but the tiniest details, and they took about twenty minutes to do just that, setting them behind schedule a little. Bronwyn thought the exchange was worth it.

After lunch, though, she found that she'd grown tired of their chatter. As nice as they were, she longed to be alone for a while. The upcoming wedding lingered at the back of her mind; she felt overwhelmed by both it and the upcoming tea with Will's mother, and she longed for the freedom to sit and contemplate the whole thing in a few minutes of solitude. She understood that the women were stuck at the centre until their husbands finished for the day, but that didn't keep her from wishing that she didn't feel such an obligation to entertain them. She tried not to resent them, she smiled at their banter and answered their questions, but she just hoped they couldn't see through her false cheeriness.

Complicating her longing for solitude was the fact that she had no time to herself at home, either. She liked Jay, and she loved that Will was working this case, at least, from home, but that, too, left her constantly in someone's company. She felt she couldn't escape, not even for a moment.

In the end, she took the ladies into the church. Alwena was there, dusting the window sills when they walked in, and Bronwyn gestured to her to join them. She should know the church's features, too, in case of pilgrims dropping by when she was there, cleaning.

She showed her small group the church's most prominent features, telling them the tale of St. Melangell and explaining how she incorporated the tradition of the saint into her own purpose at the centre.

She could tell they were impressed, and that lifted her spirits a little. Days like this one did make her feel that she was fulfilling her role as the current guardian in a way that honored the saint and also pleased her otherworldly contacts. She usually enjoyed that feeling. She just wasn't herself today.

Speaking of which, she thought to herself, *I have another reason for getting off by myself at some point.* What if the Twlwyth Teg had a message for her that would solve Will's case? If they did, she'd need some solitude to hear what they wanted to reveal.

She smiled for real as she bade the group goodbye mid-afternoon. Clouds had moved in, threatening another thunderstorm, but after she watched the last car drive away down the narrow lane, she walked into the churchyard and sat on the bench against the stone wall.

In just over a week, she'd be Will's wife. She'd no longer be Bronwyn Bagley, but Bronwyn Cooper. Perhaps it wasn't fair that the wife had to relinquish her old identity to take on her husband's name, she mused. The thought left her unsettled, as if she was giving up who she was in order to marry Will, although she knew in her heart that was an exaggeration. She'd still be the same person. That little girl who chased fairies in her childhood would never disappear. The young woman who felt so homesick when she went off to university wouldn't go away, either. Neither would the woman who sought clues that helped Will solve some of his most complex cases. She'd still be herself, Bronwyn, the same as she'd been before.

She and Will had been living together for almost eight months. That wouldn't change, either. They'd gotten used to each other's habits and had come to love evenings when they'd both come home from work and sit and talk about their days. They were comfortable together, and she felt as if they'd become true partners, in every sense of the word.

When she felt panicked after meeting Will's parents, he'd been there to help her put things in perspective. If he had nightmares about nearly being killed that last spring, and she suspected that he still did, she was there to help him back to peace. When it came to parenting Lark in the future, she knew they'd work together on that, too. Their lives had already become intertwined. She couldn't imagine him not being in her future.

The church door opened with a squeal, and Alwena walked out.

Bronwyn sighed. She'd managed a few minutes to think, but that was obviously all she was going to get. She called out to Alwena and gestured her over. "All done for the day?" she asked.

Alwena walked up to her and stopped, facing the bench. "I still need to clean the counselling centre."

"I'm glad you had a chance to hear about the church's features."

Alwena nodded. "I enjoyed listening to you. You're lucky to have found your calling."

"You don't always have to be a cleaner, you know, but if you keep working here, you'll have chances to help people from time to time, like I do. It's not our official job, but if someone needs a listening ear, we can ignore our other work and do what we can to help."

Alwena smiled softly. "I like that idea." She looked down for a moment and then back at Bronwyn. "I trained as a teacher, but I'm not sure I could do it now."

"Why not?"

"I don't think I'd be any good at it. I'm not as sure of myself as you are."

Bronwyn laughed. "This is the new me. Before, I was about as insecure as anyone could possibly be."

"What changed?"

"Meeting Will, and realizing that I can help people here at St. Melangell's, I guess. Or maybe I just matured into myself." A distant boom of thunder called her from her thoughts. She'd better get on the road back to Llangynog, or she'd be caught in the storm. "I've got to go, Alwena, but I really enjoyed our chat." She waved at the sky. "It's going to rain on me if I stay any longer." She felt better now, for having sat in solitude for even a few minutes in that peaceful churchyard, and even for having a few minutes to connect with Alwena. The solitude had given her a chance to assure herself that marrying Will wouldn't change who she was except in a good way. She loved him, and that was all that mattered.

She had to walk back to the village, having left her Land Rover in the car park beside the New Inn. Janice had offered her a ride, but she'd declined, despite the threat of a storm, wanting to give the Twlwyth Teg a chance to speak to her, if they were so inclined.

She walked fast, to beat the threatening storm. The black clouds raced on a wind that had whipped up with strength, darkening the day to a dusky gloom. The ever-present pheasants must have taken shelter because none of them lurched down the lane in front of her. Even the sheep in the pastures along the way huddled beneath trees, ready for what they sensed was coming.

Her mobile vibrated and rang out when she was less than halfway to the village. She stopped to take it from her rucksack, catching it on the fourth ring before the caller could hang up. *Lark.* She must be finished with classes and have free time to chat. Bronwyn felt a thrill of joy. *She called me this time, not Will.*

"Hi, Lark!" she called out, holding the mobile to her ear as she slowed her pace.

"Hi, Bronwyn. Is it okay that I called you?" She sounded a little off, and Bronwyn wondered what was wrong.

"What's going on? Are you okay?"

"I'm good," Lark assured her.

"You had a good day? Do you want to tell me about it?"

"It was fine. We had our classes, and lunch was just sandwiches and crisps. We played hockey for our gym class, and it was fun."

"What are you doing tonight?"

"Aderyn and I are going to play out on the lawns. We're allowed. We can even climb trees, if we want to, but a bunch of us are going to play tag."

Bronwyn relaxed. "That sounds like loads of fun. You're making friends, then?"

"Lots of friends. It's fun, being here." She hesitated, and Bronwyn tensed again. "Can I come home to your house on Friday night?"

"I planned to come for you on Sunday, on my way to the garden tea at your grandmother's."

"I know. But I miss Hobbs, and Aderyn is going home, too."

Bronwyn thought fast. She had the group in during the day. She supposed that, if she left right from work, she'd be there by seven-thirty to get Lark, putting them back in Llangynog by ten. It'd be a late night, but it was possible. She could pack a picnic they could eat in the car. It wouldn't set a good precedent if they said no the very first time she asked, would it? She had to try to be mindful of their obligations and not give Elizabeth Cooper anything to complain about. "I can try to come for you on Friday night. Let me talk to your Uncle Will, and I'll call you later tonight and we'll make a plan."

"Thank you, Bronwyn!" Lark burbled. "I knew you'd say yes."

"We won't be back to Llangynog early enough for you to see Hobbs," she warned her. "I can't come for you until I'm finished with work."

"That's okay. I'll have Daisy."

It might not do to spoil her too much. "I'll call you later, okay? I know you'll be playing outdoors, but if I called at eight, would that be a good time?"

"It's perfect." Lark sounded happy, and despite the fact that it'd mean two trips south this weekend, it made Bronwyn smile, too.

Even better, her hopes of meeting the Twlwyth Teg were not in vain. She'd put her mobile back into the rucksack and continued her journey home as the thunder grew louder and a spatter of rain portended what was to follow when Daisy stopped sniffling in the hedgerows and stood looking at something Bronwyn couldn't, at first, see. The day had grown dark with the heavy clouds, making the shadows beneath the shrubbery inky. She felt a surge of hope as she peered closer.

They emerged from the undergrowth, some creeping out on silent feet, others fluttering out on filmy, transparent wings of vibrant color that glowed even in the fading light. They surrounded and circled her slowly, beautiful and grotesque, ever-youthful, wise, wispy, frail, delicate, yet strong, they were the Twlwyth Teg, come to give her the message she'd been craving.

She stood stock still, not wanting to frighten them off. Daisy had come to sit beside her. She slowly lowered her hand until it rested on the Labrador's head, where she hoped it would hold the dog steady.

"Apanage denied," hissed a harsh voice. She looked down near her feet to see a creature with wildly disarrayed black hair and spiky horns that curved in on themselves. It cocked its head to peer up at her, its grin diabolic. It wasn't one of the pretty, flighty light ones she'd chased as a child.

"Gavelkind desired," squeaked another voice, this from a tiny creature that hopped and bounced in place in the mushroom circle. It wriggled from side to side as she tried to memorize the words it had spoken. She resisted the urge to pull out her mobile and tap it out. She didn't want to frighten them away by doing something unexpected.

She wondered suddenly if she could photograph them. She'd never dared try.

"Primogeniture undeserved," whispered a third voice, so quietly that she almost couldn't hear it as a drizzling rain began to fall, bouncing on the dirt of the roadway and hissing on the leaves of the nearby hedgerows. The fairie fluttered in the air near her face, and she glimpsed a tiny pointed chin, sharp ears, and eyes that were too big and glowed turquoise blue. Its filmy wings changed from palest blue to a darker shade as the rain dampened them, and she hoped it wouldn't fall from the sky as a result.

"Once, twice, thrice!" They shouted the count in a chorus, and then they disappeared, not fleeing back into the hedgerow, but just vanishing as if they had never been there at all.

She grabbed her phone and tapped out their message, spelling it the best she could. "Apanage denied, gavelkind desired, primogeniture undeserved..." She changed the spelling of the words until spell-check recognized them as correct, and then she shoved the phone into her rucksack and thought about what to do.

The rain was still a drizzle, but the crashing of thunder followed the flashes of lightning more quickly, and that drizzle would turn into a downpour at any minute. She wanted to jog back up the lane to the centre and use her computer there to look up the words and figure out what they meant, but if she did that, she might have to walk home in a drenching rain that probably wouldn't stop for hours.

Using her mobile to research them worked, too, but she always felt paranoid using it because it was so easily accessible. Her office computer was more secure and secret. If she wanted Will to continue believing that the clues that she gave him came from visions rather than from words, she didn't like to chance him seeing that she'd looked them up on her phone.

But the rain…

She turned, called to Daisy, and jogged back up the lane to the centre, unlocking the door with wet hands. Rain pinged off the ground, bouncing higher, and she was soaked and suddenly chilled.

Inside, she called out to Alwena so as not to startle her and then she gave Daisy a firm command to stay by the door until her muddy paws dried. She wouldn't want her to make dirty tracks on the floor Alwena had just cleaned. She hurried into her office and changed into her spare set of clothing, dressier than she would wear for walking home, but at least they were dry. She smoothed the trousers and then sat down and woke her computer.

"Apanage," she whispered to herself as she accessed the medieval dictionary she usually used and typed the word. "A lucrative estate, appointment, or income to provide for the younger children of a king, prince or nobleman." She turned the words over in her mind as she murmured them aloud. None of the suspects in Will's case would qualify as kings, princes, or noblemen, but perhaps the Twlwyth Teg didn't mean it literally, or perhaps the definition was too specific. Sometimes, if she went to other compilations of medieval terms, the definition would vary slightly. Still, if she thought of it as a general term, "apanage denied" would mean that someone's younger children were denied a part of an inheritance, and that would apply to several of their suspects, but most particularly, to Conway. He was a younger son who was denied an inheritance that would have made a difference in his life. Going further, Dylan inherited the lot from Evan, so both Merry and Awstin were also denied an inheritance because they were younger children or, in Awstin's case, a bastard child. She mulled that over as she listened to the rain pounding on the roof and slamming against her window. She was glad to be inside.

She scribbled a quick note on a piece of waste paper about "apanage denied," and then typed "gavelkind" into the search bar. "Land can be given to several sons simultaneously, not just to the eldest." Again, the definition would seem to point to Conway, wouldn't it? She thought it out. Of course, he would have liked to have had his share of the land. No one could blame him. But why wait twenty years to do something about it? It hardly made sense, unless there was more that Evan had done that they didn't know about.

A soft tap at her door interrupted her thoughts. She turned quickly and tried to block the computer screen with her body.

"I don't want to disturb you," Alwena said, her voice soft. "I just wondered why you came back, if there was a problem?"

Her heart beat a tattoo against her ribs. "No, it was just the rain," she lied quickly. "I thought if I came back, it would lighten up in a few minutes."

"I'd give you a ride home, but I walked today, too."

"Cas is coming to pick you up, isn't he?"

"No, that was only the first day. He'd have to get Nia ready to go out, and he doesn't like to take time away from work to do that." Alwena smiled, but something made Bronwyn think it was forced. "Even though he works from home, he does need to put in the hours."

"Of course, he does," Bronwyn agreed. "As soon as the rain slows down, I'll take a brollie and walk. I actually enjoy walking in the rain."

"So do I," Alwena said wistfully. "It's okay if we borrow them?"

"That's what they're for."

Alwena glanced back toward the hallway. "I'd better finish my work," she said. "I hope I didn't interrupt."

"No, I'm just entertaining myself while I wait. It's nothing important."

She waited for Alwena to disappear, and then she turned back to the computer. Thinking hard, she typed the final phrase into the search bar: "Primogeniture." "The granting of a complete estate to the firstborn, excluding the other children." The Twlwyth Teg had focused firmly on the inheritance, she thought, wondering how she could use the information to help Will.

At the least, it didn't look like Will and Jay needed to pursue the idea of an angry husband. What she'd been given didn't point to a specific person, but the killer had to be a member of the Bennett family if the inheritance was the motive. "Apanage denied, gavelkind desired, primogeniture undeserved." Someone obviously felt that the inheritance should have been shared, not just given to Evan, who for some reason hadn't deserved it. There was no way to know who that person was, although the obvious candidate was Conway, she supposed. She hated to think it. She'd always liked Conway; he was nicer than Evan and more respected in the community. Her heart sank.

There was no question that she had to tell Will. He might interpret it differently than she did and, in any case, he'd have to know so that he could get that case solved before their wedding. Maybe it wasn't the most specific tip she could have gotten, but she supposed it'd have to suffice.

How to convey the idea of those words in pictures baffled her. She sat and thought as rain pelted against the window of her office. A soft woof from the centre door caught her notice. Daisy would be dry enough now. She called out to her, "Daisy, it's okay now. Come!" and the dog's nails clattered on the wooden floor as she hurried into Bronwyn's office, tail wagging, proud to have been a good dog.

She patted Daisy and told her how good she was, and then she turned back to thoughts of how to tell Will what she'd heard. Sometimes there was no way around it; she just had to tell him what she'd *heard*, not *seen*, and let him wonder how it had come about. She didn't like to do that too often, though, or someday he'd ask about it, and he'd know she was lying to him.

She tried to form a picture of what primogeniture would look like, or apanage or gavelkind. Perhaps a line of people, slowly walking onto a property, looking around or working it, and then fading away, only to let the next person come into the vision? At some point, make it a group of people rather than a single individual, with happy faces?

Yes, she thought, *that might do it*. It would make an elaborate, complicated explanation, though, far vaguer than she wanted and, therefore, open to other interpretations, she supposed. She'd have to practice it mentally before creating it for him so it'd sound smoother than it was. She wondered when she'd have a chance to talk to Will alone, because she surely couldn't do it with Jay there. But how would he explain it to Jay afterwards?

She blew out a breath in frustration. Why did it have to be so complicated? Maybe she could guide Will to the conclusion she knew he needed and then, between the two of them, they could come up with a logical path forward that wouldn't have Jay questioning why she knew what she did. In the end, she'd have to trust Will for that. She had no choice.

Chapter Eighteen

Will watched the countryside go by in a blur as rain drizzled down and the tyres swooshed through standing water on the roadway. The downpour of the night before had abated, but a thick overcast remained, making the day – and Will's mood - gloomy. The headlamps on Mehta's car had come on automatically when they'd left Llangynog at seven, and he didn't think it'd be light enough for them to turn themselves off before they arrived in Caernarfon.

It felt like a wasted day, but Bowers had insisted that they check into the office to catch up on paperwork, to give him a detailed report on their progress, and to make a plan going forward. He didn't like to think it, but the case seemed stalled, as many did at this point in an investigation. Usually, some new evidence turned up, or the perpetrator did something stupid that revealed who he was. They needed a break.

What Bronwyn had given him the night before had tweaked his interest, but it didn't really narrow things down as much as they needed it to. She'd waited until Mehta had left, and then she'd quietly described what she'd seen, giving him so much detail that he could almost see it himself.

He hadn't decided yet how to tell Mehta what she'd said. Maybe he could just steer the investigation toward the family members rather than Jenna Thomas or the Richards, and that would be enough. Bowers would undoubtedly want them to talk to them all again, though, and he didn't know how he'd manage to avoid it without revealing Bronwyn's involvement. In the end, he'd probably have to ignore what he knew and go through the motions just to keep her out of it.

Thinking of Bronwyn made him feel guilty. He felt as if he was dumping everything on her shoulders, pushing his own burdens off on her. Their wedding was only a week away, and here she was, spending the entire weekend either working or shuffling Lark back and forth, not to mention his mother's wonderful garden tea on Sunday, which he knew would be torture for her. Of course, she hadn't been thrilled at the idea of driving all the way to Chepstow to fetch Lark on Friday night, either. That hadn't been their plan at all. He suspected that Lark was just trying her boundaries, checking to see if they really would be available if she needed them. Things were bound to settle down with her, but at the moment, she was needy just when Bronwyn needed time to do things like huddle with her mum over the flowers for the church and try on her wedding gown one last time to make sure it fit properly. And when was her friend Margred coming in from Ireland? He didn't even remember, although he was sure that Bronwyn had mentioned it.

He felt terrible about it all.

"You're looking like you could bite my head off this morning if I say the wrong thing," Mehta commented, glancing over at him. "Drink your coffee. Maybe it'll help." They'd stopped at a shop in Bala for drinks to keep them awake.

"I've had to push everything onto Bronwyn," Will mumbled, "and now she has to go get Lark tonight after she gets off work, in addition to everything else. It's not fair to her."

"Better she knows now what she's getting into than after she's said her vows." Mehta grinned.

"Maybe it's better if she just backs out now, while she's got the chance," Will growled back.

Mehta's grin faded. "She won't back out on you. She fancies you something terrible. Anyone can see that."

Will slumped in the seat. His fingers found the seatbelt across his chest, and he pulled it looser. "I feel like I'm asking a lot, making her take on Lark, along with me and my family issues."

"She has family issues, too," Mehta retorted, "just different from yours."

241

"Her family does overwhelm me some of the time, even if I do like them."

"What are you going to do with Lark when you're both at work?"

"You mean, like tomorrow?" Will couldn't keep the sarcasm out of his voice. "Bronwyn works most Saturdays, and so do I, when we have a case."

"We could postpone Cardiff until Sunday," Mehta suggested. They'd planned to make the trip to interview Eriana Bennett on the Saturday. She was the last family member on their list, and they'd called ahead to make sure they'd catch her at home. "I could tackle some local stuff in the morning, maybe talk to Jenna Thomas again or Conway and his bunch on my own while you're busy. We could drop Lark off at the centre in the afternoon, when Bronwyn's nearly done with her group for the day."

Will thought about it. What choice did they have, really? Bronwyn's parents would keep an eye on Lark if they asked them to, but depending on them wasn't fulfilling their promise to parent Lark on the weekends. He didn't like to take advantage of Mehta, either, though. Pushing his responsibilities off onto his partner was no better than pushing them off onto Bronwyn. "We'll see how it goes in Caernarfon, and then I'll figure it out."

They drove in silence for a few miles, and then Mehta risked a peek at Will. "I'm not being pushy, but what is our plan going forward? I mean, other than talking to Eriana Bennett, what more can we do to figure this case out?"

Will slowly shook his head. "I'm as much at a standstill as you are, Jay. I think we should concentrate on the family members." Maybe he wouldn't have to tell Mehta why, if he could figure out a way to naturally steer them in that direction. "I don't know what more we can get from Cassidee and Steffan Richards."

"He was packed up and ready to leave," Mehta pointed out. "She called him, maybe warned him, and he decided to do a runner rather than face us questioning him. It was only luck we got there fast enough. Another five minutes, and he'd have been in the wind."

"That's true," Will conceded, "and we have only his word that he was leaving because of Cassadee's affair, not because he was a suspect in a murder. If he killed Evan, though, why would she warn him we were coming? Why not let us arrest him?"

Mehta drove in silence, the sound of the tyres loud inside the car. "Maybe she thought he'd look guiltier if he was on the run." He waited, but Will didn't say anything. "Maybe she didn't want to lose the account, so she killed Evan herself and didn't want Steffan blamed. If Evan cashed out most of his portfolio to finance his housing estate idea, she'd probably lose a commission and look like she wasn't doing her job well. I'm sure her bosses put pressure on her to keep the clients happy."

"She apparently did keep him happy, at least for a while," Will commented wryly. "You might be right, but can you really see the two of them conspiring to kill Cassadee's lover in order to keep his accounts intact? That seems like a flimsy reason to kill someone. And she'd already given up on Evan ever being serious enough about her to marry her, so that was a dead end. She was better off staying with Steffan."

"Okay, back to Steffan again, then. Jealousy is a powerful motive. We know that. We can't assume that he didn't find out and kill Evan in a rage."

Will sighed. "I don't know, Jay." He wanted Mehta to decide to abandon the Richards, and his attempts to guide him toward that conclusion just weren't working as well as he hoped they might. He couldn't just keep having 'feelings' that this person was or wasn't guilty. That might have worked before, but he'd done it too often now.

Mehta signaled and passed a lorry, his wipers going full-force on the windscreen as the lorry's tyres threw up rivers of water. "Okay, we'll go with your gut feelings for now. I know you have a lot of experience, far more than I do. We'll look into the family members more for now." He looked over at Will and then back through the windscreen as the car hit a stream of water and tried to slew sideways. Will thought he probably suspected that he had information he wasn't sharing, but he'd let it go for now.

They'd planned to go straight into Bower's office, but Quigley caught them before they had the chance. "Come here," he said. "I want to show you something."

243

They went to his desk and bent to look at his computer. "This," he said, with a nod toward the screen, "is a list of the guns registered to Lloyd Bennett."

"Okay," Will said. The list filled the page.

"Lloyd Bennett was something of a collector," Mehta went on, "but apparently no one bothered to transfer the registrations after his death." He glanced back over his shoulder to make sure they were watching and changed the screen. "This is a list of the guns confiscated from both Evan and Conway Bennett's homes after Evan's death. I matched them to the registrations. Most are still registered to Lloyd, with just a few exceptions."

"I'm guessing none of those are a match to our murder weapon, though," Will said. "Right?"

"Right." Quigley picked up a pen and used it to point to the screen. "There are a couple of guns that had been registered to Lloyd Bennett that weren't among the guns collected after Evan's death." He swiveled his chair to look up at them. "One of them is a Lee-Enfield Mark 4."

Will felt suddenly dizzy. "Then we have proof that gun belonged to the family, at least. That's a huge step forward. But where is it?"

"I'd imagine that one is long gone now, hidden somewhere you'll never find it."

"Beneath a pile of rocks in the woods," Mehta suggested, "or thrown into a particularly thick section of hedgerow somewhere in a remote area of North Wales."

Quigley nodded. "Find the gun, and you find the murderer."

That pointed back to the family, Will thought with relief. He'd won that battle and could stop trying to subtly direct Mehta's attention toward them. He wished Bronwyn's tip had been less vague and more timely, but what Quigley had come up with supported her information, at least. There was no longer any doubt that their perpetrator was a member of Evan's own family.

Bowers welcomed them with the twist of his lips that passed for a smile when they knocked on his office door. "Is that Will Cooper?" he queried, peering at Will as he took a seat on one of the comfortable chairs that were only to be found inside Bowers' office. "I'd almost forgotten what you look like, it's been that long."

"Sorry, sir. I didn't mean for a neighbor to be murdered, right in front of my eyes, more or less."

"That little village certainly has its share of shady characters." Bowers nodded at Mehta. "All right, Jay? Will's not abandoning you to do all the investigating while he entertains his fiancée, is he?"

"No, sir," Mehta sat down. "He's right by my side through it all."

"A fact that he regrets, I'm sure." Bowers picked up a pen and tapped it on his desk. "Do we need a board?"

"Only if you want, sir," Will told him. "We have one back in Llangynog that we've made, and we can re-create it here for you." They'd spent an hour the night before sketching it out on a sheet of paper, which he now pushed across the desk for Bower's perusal. "That's our victim, Evan Bennett, in the centre."

Bowers followed along for more than an hour as they went through each suspect, detailing family relationships, possible motives, and the absence of alibis. He stopped to ask questions from time to time, jotting his own notes on the paper they had given him. They referred to their own handwritten notes as they moved along, relying on their memories when he asked specific questions they hadn't answered in writing.

"You're not considering this Cassadee Richards or her husband serious suspects at this time?" Bowers frowned as they hinted at dismissing them from the list.

"We've just gotten some new evidence," Mehta said, "that points to one of the family members as our villain." He explained about the gun.

"You're assuming that particular gun is the murder weapon? As I recall, there were quite a few of those floating around after the war."

"It'd be quite a coincidence if there were two of them possessed by our suspects," Will pointed out. He'd let Mehta do most of the verbal report. It was good for Bowers to see what an asset the kid was.

"You can't dismiss the idea entirely." Bowers was adamant.

"No, of course not, but since we know there should be one in the Bennetts' inventory, and it's missing, that would seem to merit more focus right now."

Bowers nodded. "Tell me what you think of the surviving family members? Any impressions you can share?"

Will looked at Mehta, who nodded. "We like them, sir. Dylan, Evan's son, seems to be a good, solid man, for the most part. He admits to arguing with his dad about the family money just before he was killed, and he also admits that he often disapproved of his dad's extramarital activities. He seemed honest when we talked to him. I never got a sense that he'd murdered his dad, no matter what issues they disagreed on. He seems devoted to his wife and his son, and also to his mother, and he says he intends to give his sister a share of the investment money, if his grandmother agrees to that."

"You got the same impression?" Bowers looked at Mehta.

"I might add just a couple of things. We've heard that he has a bit of a temper, and we've seen a little of that when we've been with him. It might be a factor. Then there's the money. It seems to be the central issue in this case, sir, and Dylan wants it. He might give his sister a share, but there's no question in his mind of giving some to anyone else, no matter what his grandmother says."

"Interesting points," Bowers muttered. "He wouldn't have inherited that missing gun?"

"He could have," Mehta admitted. "They were, all of them, hobby shooters, so any of them could have ended up with that gun."

"How about the brother, then? Tell me about him."

"Conway struck us both as a strong family man. He obviously disapproved of his brother's life choices, and we're sure he would have appreciated inheriting some of the family farm, at least, but why would he wait twenty years to murder Evan? It doesn't make sense. He seems very close to his wife and the son who still lives locally and helps on the farm. We've only met the older daughter, but she was clear that she's close to her parents, as well. They seem a very happy, close family, in contrast to Evan's family."

"Evan's wife stayed with him," Bowers observed.

"Yes, she says she stayed because of the lifestyle she had there. She has horses. I have the impression, though, that Evan wasn't close to her or to any of his kids, including the illegitimate one, at least not until recently."

"But Conway struggled financially?" Bowers was frowning over the paper.

"Yes, it was a struggle for him to make a living on the farm. We understand that he leased more farmland eventually, but he struggles to make the payments on it."

"Did he say that, or did it come from someone else?"

Now Mehta stopped and thought. "He didn't mention it, but his children did, and his mother admitted it, as well. I did sense that the two children we interviewed weren't happy that their father had to struggle, when their uncle obviously had it easier, especially since their uncle wasn't much of an admirable man. I'm sure both of them would see it as unfair that Evan inherited so much and their own father so little. They might resent that. It was obvious when we talked to them that they loved their father very much."

"What would a child who felt like that do for a father they watched struggle throughout their lives?" Bowers wondered.

It was a good point.

"Staff meeting at four," Bowers informed them when they finished. "That's why I wanted you in today and not tomorrow. We're meeting the new detectives, and I want the whole team here. You can leave right afterwards. I know you're headed back to Llangynog tonight."

"We're off to Cardiff tomorrow morning early to interview Eriana Bennett, and then we'll be back for Evan's memorial service at three in the afternoon," Will said, feeling defensive. "The drive to Cardiff is an hour shorter from Llangynog than from here."

Bowers' lips twisted. "I'm aware, Cooper. You couldn't have done that interview earlier?"

"She's a flight attendant. She's been out of country, so this was our first opportunity. We called her to make sure it wouldn't be a wasted trip. She isn't coming to the memorial service, so going there is our only option if we want to talk to her. She's leaving again on Sunday."

They spent most of the rest of the day filling out paperwork, the part of the job that Will dreaded. It all had to be done precisely and carefully so that when a case went to trial, all the facts were documented and correct. He sat at his desk, trying to concentrate on hand-written notes and recorded interviews, while his mind drifted off to Bronwyn, the mess of a weekend she was facing, and the upcoming wedding. He didn't like to wish any of his time on earth away, but he longed for the next weeks to be behind them, the hassle of the wedding over, Lark settled into her school routine, and life peaceful again. At the moment, time couldn't pass fast enough for him.

At four, they stood up beside their desks, the low murmur of speculation that had undercut the day quieter now that the event was upon them. Beth Holway and her partner of the day Ian O'Flynn had come in a half-hour earlier, called back from a case they were working. Beth had bent over Will's desk, whispering, "I hear it's a middle-aged man who's easy to work with and a younger woman who isn't." It was now time to see if she was right.

Bowers walked from his office to the door of the staff entrance, and a moment later he returned with a middle-aged man and a younger woman in tow. Will smiled to himself. Beth had gotten that much right. He wondered what else she knew and whether she'd share more gossip when they had the time.

Bowers lined the two new detectives up, one on his left and the other on his right, and looked out into the open-concept room, his gaze catching eyes as they all fell silent. "I'd like to introduce you to the newest members of the North Wales Major Crimes division," he began, "Rufus Pew and Mina MacDonnell."

There was a murmur and Will scrambled for a pen and a scrap of paper so he could jot down the names before he forgot them. "Rufus and Mina, "he repeated under his breath. "Rufus and Mina."

Bowers interrupted the undercurrent of chatter. "Rufus comes to us via Bristol. He grew up on Anglesey and has been in Bristol for eleven years. He requested a transfer here in order to be nearer to his extended family, and the powers that be saw fit to grant his request. We're happy to welcome him back to an area he's very familiar with." There was a polite applause, and Rufus beamed at his new co-workers. Will guessed his age to be early forties from the gray streaks in his thinning light brown hair. His portly frame strained the blue shirt he wore, but it was obvious he'd taken some care with his appearance, with gray trousers neatly pressed, a bright red and blue striped tie, and polished leather brogues. From his appearance, Will thought he'd be easy-going, nice to partner with if he wasn't expected to squeeze himself into Will's little MGF.

Bowers turned to his right, nodding at the young woman who stood there. "I'd also like to introduce Mina MacDonnell. Mina started as a constable in Edinburgh, and then she transferred to Cardiff, where she was promoted to detective inspector a year ago." Mina looked to be in her early-thirties, somewhere between Will and Mehta in age. She was tall, rail-thin, and dark, with a rounded nose, a wide mouth, and lazy eyes that tried to look sultry. She wore a pantsuit, navy with a white blouse, and her dark hair fell loose to her shoulders. Will couldn't help speculating about the multiple transfers. Unless there was a problem or a better opportunity somewhere else, police officers tended to stay in the same jurisdiction where they started. His transfer from Cardiff was a case in point. He hadn't wanted that transfer; it was forced on him after his sister Julia died from an overdose, compromising his ability to work drugs and alcohol without prejudice. He wondered what had prompted Mina's transfers both from Edinburgh and from Cardiff.

The desk sergeant who worked at the employees' entrance came in then bearing boxes full of pastries from a local shop. She set them on an empty desk, opening a bag of paper plates beside the box.

Everyone stood still at their desks for a minute, no one wanting to be the first to speak to the new officers or to take a pastry, hoping someone else would start the process so they could rush up behind them. Finally, Beth snorted and strode up to the desk, grabbing a plate and putting a pastry on it. She turned and cast a triumphant grin at the rest of them, and then she walked over to Mina MacDonnell and introduced herself.

Will joined the queue then, with Mehta behind him. He waited patiently until he could choose a cream horn, and then he stood away from the table and ate it slowly, savoring the sweetness and postponing the moment when he'd have to greet the new people. Why two of them? He caught a glimpse of Ian O'Flynn chatting across the room with one of the tech people, and wondered if Ian was thinking of retirement sooner rather than later. He had to be getting close.

When he could postpone it no longer, he threw his paper plate in a bin and strode up to Rufus Pew, who was busy chatting with Quigley. "Hello," he greeted them both, "I see you've already met the best tech whiz in the country." He smiled at Quigley, and turned his gaze to Rufus. "I'm Will Cooper, one of the DCIs here."

Rufus reached out a hand to shake Will's and looked him over. "I've heard of you," he commented.

That didn't surprise Will. After the debacle last spring, he supposed most police officers in the country would recognize his name. "I hope you give me a chance to redeem myself, then."

Rufus laughed, a genuine laugh that made Will smile. "You grew up on Anglesey?" he asked.

"Yes, my wife and I were both from Newboraugh. We knew each other as children and re-connected at Uni in Cardiff."

"I don't suppose there's much opportunity for police work in Newboraugh." Will waved at Quigley, who had nodded his goodbyes and was moving away.

"None at all." Rufus smiled. "I hear you spent time in Cardiff, too, working drugs and alcohol."

Everyone seemed to know Will's history, a fact that embarrassed him. "That's all in the past," he said firmly, taking charge out of habit. "So, you're married? Your wife wanted to come back here?"

"My wife always wanted to come back. She wanted the children to know their grandparents before they'd totally grown up. And there's just something about home...do you know the Welsh word, 'hiraeth'?"

Will shook his head, amused.

"It doesn't really have an English equivalent, but it means a longing for home, not just homesickness, but a nostalgia for the land and the people."

Bronwyn would like that word. He'd have to ask her if she knew it.

"We both grew up in Welsh-speaking families," Rufus went on, "and we missed it all after being away for so long. We had a big family celebration when my transfer came through."

"How old are your children?" Will thought it polite to ask.

"My oldest Gruffydd is thirteen, then there's Bedwyr, who's eleven. My only daughter, Anwen, is nine, and the baby is Jac. He's six."

"That's quite a family," Will said, astounded that anyone could have four children and manage a career as a detective, too. "Does your wife work?"

"She's a nurse," Rufus said, "and she was able to take a transfer here. It's only part-time. That's what she did in Cardiff, too. Someone's got to be home with the kids most of the time. Are you married?"

"I will be next weekend."

"Congratulations, then. What's her name?" Rufus' smile now included Marcus Robb, head of their forensics department, who had come up to join them.

"Bronwyn."

"A good Welsh name. She grew up here in Caernarfon?"

"In Llangynog. It's over between Bala and Oswestry. I commute."

Rufus' eyebrows went up. "She must be something special if you're willing to take that on."

"She is." He introduced Rufus to Marcus then, and wandered away toward Mina MacDonnell, who looked lonely at the moment.

"I'm Will Cooper," he introduced himself, reaching out a hand.

She shook it, her grip firm. "I've heard of you, and now I've finally gotten to meet you. You're famous, you know."

"Take everything you've heard with a grain of salt. I'm sure it's all exaggerated."

"We'll see," she said, her wide lips pouting. "What's it like here?"

"I'm not sure what you mean," Will told her. "It's a good crew, everyone works hard, and we all celebrate our solved cases."

"And Bowers?" She said it nonchalantly, but Will caught a hint of concern.

"He's always been fair to me."

She lifted heavy eyebrows. "That's saying a lot, knowing what I do of your reputation." She gave him a slow smile, studying him with lazy, mocking eyes. "Actually, I'm a little surprised to see you here."

He didn't return the smile. "Why's that?"

"I understand that Will Cooper does what he wants, and that he doesn't just come running when his boss gives a shout. Aren't you working a case on the other side of the district?"

"I am, but that doesn't mean we don't check in occasionally." He narrowed his eyes. "And I do come in when Bowers asks me to, if I can."

"Then maybe your reputation has been exaggerated in the telling," she concluded, again with the mocking smile. He hoped that he wouldn't be assigned to work with her until someone else, maybe Beth, put her in her place a bit. He'd barely met her and already she put him off.

"What did you think?" Mehta asked as he negotiated the turn just past the town gates.

"Well, I can't say I'd rather work with either of them over you, but Rufus seemed nice enough. He's very Welsh."

"I liked him, too. He's got a lot of experience, and he asked for the transfer so that means he wasn't a problem that Cardiff needed to be rid of. But Mina?" Mehta encouraged him. "What about her?"

Will didn't like to speak ill of someone he barely knew, but he knew that he'd taken an instant dislike to her, for what reason, he couldn't figure out. She'd seemed arrogant, somehow, a little too sure of herself, a little too mocking. "Once we've partnered with them, we'll have a better idea of them," he said at last.

Mehta gave him a knowing look. "I thought she might be trouble, too. She's a little too exotic for our corner of the country, maybe."

Exotic? Coming from East Indian Mehta? "There has to be a reason she's been transferred twice."

"Beth will find out," Mehta suggested. "You're aware that she digs up all the secrets that people prefer that we not know."

Will laughed. "You're right. Beth will get to the truth of it."

"Do you think Ian's going to retire?" Mehta voiced Will's earlier speculation.

"That's the only reason I can see for them sending us two detectives to replace Notley."

"Notley was experienced. He had a good solve rate, as I understand it. I only knew him for a short time, though."

"Rufus seems experienced, too. He's a DCI?" Will asked.

252

"He is. He got his promotion eight years ago. Mina is a DI like me."

"She'll be after a promotion," Will guessed.

Mehta shrugged. "So am I," he pointed out.

Chapter Nineteen

Bronwyn and Lark had arrived home late the night before, so Will tried to get up quietly the next morning so as not to disturb them as he dressed. To his dismay, though, Bronwyn sat up in bed before he could sneak out the door.

"It was Daisy's tail flopping against the wall that did it, wasn't it?" he groaned. "I did try to let you sleep."

"I know," she blew him a kiss, "and I appreciate it. But I've got to get ready for work, and Mum and Dad said Lark could hang out with them this morning, so I've got to get her ready, too."

"I'm so sorry to put all of this on you." From the corner of his eye, he saw Mehta pulling up in his Subaru. Six a.m., sharp. The kid was nothing if not punctual. "Was it a bad drive to Chepstow?"

"We'll be getting used to it," she replied with a little pout that he thought – or hoped, at least – was faked. "Anyway, Lark is good company, so that's a positive."

"She didn't just play her video game?"

"I didn't bring it. She chattered to me all the way home. I now know every detail of her first week at school."

"She likes it?"

"I'd say she does."

Will edged toward the door. "Jay'll be sounding his horn if I'm not outside in twenty seconds. The neighbors will complain."

She slipped out of bed, padded over, and kissed him. "Bedtime mouth," she warned him. "I'll see you this afternoon."

He slipped out the door, blocking Daisy, who intended to dash out with him.

There was little traffic at six in the morning on a Saturday, so they cruised at speed once they emerged off the little B4391 and onto the A483 at Welshpool. Early clouds had given way to a clearing sky, with a brilliant sunrise off to the east.

As they traveled, they ate muffins and fruit from the breakfast bag Mehta's B&B had prepared for his early departure and drank Will's coffee from the flask he'd filled in the kitchen before they left. It seemed a long way to drive for an interview they didn't expect to produce anything, but procedures had to be followed, he supposed, and at least it promised to be a nice day.

They arrived in Cardiff at a quarter to nine and found Eriana Bennett's flat easily. They sat in the car for the extra few minutes until their appointment at nine and discussed a strategy.

"We have to ask about the gun." Mehta stated the obvious. "Someone knows who had it after Lloyd died."

"That'd be either Evan or Conway, unless he gave it to Dylan."

Mehta considered that, stroking the soft beard that curved around his chin. "Carys might have kept it. She had a sentimental attachment to it."

Mehta had better conduct this interview, Will thought, looking at him. Eriana would almost certainly be charmed. "That's possible, but I can't see her having it in her new place. Maybe it was just left at the old house. We need to ask Carys about that again, push her more."

"Eriana was almost definitely not involved," Mehta said, "but she might know who was. She can give us a feel for the other family members, at least."

"She'll have an attitude about the money."

"I guess we'll find out." Mehta reached over and pulled his door handle. "Let's get it over with and get back. I could use a bit of a rest before that memorial service this afternoon."

Eriana Bennett had inherited her father's curls, although hers were much darker than his. She wasn't beautiful in any normal sense of the word, but she exuded a self-confidence that, combined with a genuine smile, made her attractive, Will thought as she greeted them at the door and invited them inside.

She'd prepared for their visit with pots of tea and coffee and a plate of bakery-bought scones with a jar of fig jam. She set a tray on the coffee table in front of the sofa, poured for the three of them, and settled herself into a wingback chair across from them.

"I was never close to my uncle," she began. "I was only a baby when the big feud started, so I've only ever known Evan as the family villain." She sipped her tea, watching their reaction. "Oh, but that's a terrible thing to say, isn't it? You're going to be thinking I'm guilty of his murder with such a cavalier attitude as that."

Will glanced at Mehta and gave a slight nod, indicating that he should begin.

"You called Evan the family villain just now," Mehta said. "What does that mean exactly? What did you disapprove of?"

She seemed taken aback by the question. "I didn't mean to sound flippant," she said after a moment's reflection. "You must know by now that Evan wasn't a very savory character. He had a reputation. He was enabled by the fact that he inherited most of my grandfather's estate, which made him financially secure. He thought he could get away with anything, and no one could interfere."

"And your branch of the family resented that?"

"Of course, we did." She looked from Mehta to Will, who was eating a scone and enjoying every bite. "It wasn't easy watching my father struggle for every penny through the years. We, my siblings and I, always felt that he was cheated of his share in what should have belonged to all of us, not just to Evan and Dylan. Dad was a good man, a lot better man than Evan was. It wasn't fair."

"Did you know that Evan was planning to sell off the investments and to spend the money on a housing estate in the wooded part of the farm?"

"We all knew that. Dylan was frantic to stop him squandering the money, so he talked to Grandmum, who talked to us. There was nothing we could do to stop him, though. Evan had the right, according to the trust, to do what he wanted with that money, as long as there was some left to support Grandmum in her old age."

"Your grandmother didn't have a voice in how the money was used?"

"She did, but she'd have gone along with what Evan wanted. She wouldn't have wanted to argue with him over it." She picked up her tea cup and sipped. "I know I'm making it sound like Dad killed Evan after all these years of watching him waste money that rightfully should have been shared between them. But he wouldn't have done it. Dad is a really good man. He never complained about Evan inheriting it all, not once." She looked at them earnestly. "He really is a good man. We all love him to bits."

"And your stepmum? How do you get on with her?" Mehta's voice was gentle.

"I call her my mum. I was only four when my mother died of cancer. I don't remember her much, other than her being sick all the time and having no hair." She glanced up at Mehta. "That's a terrible thing, isn't it? That my main memory of my mum, who I know loved me, is of her having a bald head and lying in bed, too sick to get up."

"You were very young. Maybe your dad talks about her sometimes? I'd think he might like you to have other pictures of her in your mind."

"Yes, he did that for a while and still does sometimes." She went quiet, thinking, not as bright as earlier, but serious now. "I was six when Dad married Mabyn, and then my grandfather died soon after that. Evie and I liked Mabyn from the start, and when Terrwyn was born, we both adored our little brother. Mabyn made Dad happy, and as we got older, we wanted that for him. Like I said, we knew he struggled to make a living, but he took joy in us, his family. We'd do almost anything for him."

Interesting statement, that. Will wrote it down.

"You were on a flight on the Monday when Evan was killed, is that right?" Mehta asked.

"Yes, Aer Lingus, Cardiff to New York. The flight left at ten in the morning, and I didn't return until two days later, when I was scheduled for another flight back."

Mehta softened his voice. "May I ask, do you have a boyfriend, Eriana? Someone serious?"

She straightened and held out her hand, showing off a glittering small diamond ring. "I have a fiancée. We're getting married at Christmas."

"He lives here in Cardiff?"

"He lives here with me." She smiled.

Will was startled. He'd seen no sign of a male occupant in the little flat.

"Does he have a job?" Mehta pressed for details.

"Mark works for Aer Lingus, too, in baggage. It works out well for us because we both get free flights when we want to travel."

"Oh, yes, that's very nice," Mehta encouraged her. "I suppose that Mark has a last name we could have?"

She giggled. "Mark Keefer." She spelled it for him. "He was on shift Monday until four. You can check if you need to."

Will wrote that down, too, but he doubted they'd bother to check. She wouldn't have given them such a specific alibi if it wouldn't be verified when they followed up.

Mehta looked a question at Will, and he took over. "You know that Evan was shot, Eriana. Do you or Mark shoot guns? Maybe as a hobby, target-shooting or hunting?"

She shot him a derisive look. "We have alibis, Inspector," she pointed out.

"I know that, but it's something we have to ask. Procedure." He smiled.

"You'll probably already know this, but pretty much everyone in my family likes to shoot. My grandfather was an avid hunter, and he made sure to pass that interest on to his sons. They don't hunt any longer, but they still like to target shoot and shoot trap. I am the exception to the rule. I never liked guns, and I never joined in when they had a family day out shooting pheasant or whatever other game was available."

"And Dylan? Is he a shooter, too?"

"I don't know about Dylan." Again, she took time to think before answering. "I remember when we played together as children, before my grandfather died, there were toy guns involved sometimes."

"We understand that your grandfather had quite a collection of guns registered to him. Most of the registrations are still in his name, although he's been gone for twenty years. Would you have any idea who has those guns now?"

"I think my grandmother kept them for a while after he died, but I won't swear to that. I'm guessing that she had them, and then through the years Evan or my dad would borrow one or two, or maybe she gave them away, and eventually they both would have had some of them." Her nose wrinkled. "You'd have to ask Gwniera and Conway, or Dylan. Since she's moved out, I wouldn't think any are left in the old house. Someone would steal them."

Will glanced at Mehta. "I think that's all we need right now, Eriana. Thank you for speaking so candidly to us. We really appreciate the insights you've given us."

"I hope I haven't implicated my dad in the murder," she told them as they prepared to leave. "He's a good man." She hesitated. "We are all of us good people."

"Thoughts?" Will asked as Mehta negotiated through the traffic and back onto the A470 North toward Llangynog. They'd arrive back in the village early in the afternoon, plenty early for Evan Bennett's three p.m. memorial service. He'd be able to take Lark off Bronwyn's parents' hands for a couple of hours before farming her out again to a friend of Mai's, who had volunteered to watch Maegan and Griffyn during the memorial service. Parenting was a juggling act, he'd discovered very quickly, but with luck – and occasional outside help – it could be managed. He hoped.

"We can cross her and her fiancée off our list." Mehta merged onto the fast lane and sped up. "She's a lot like her cousin Merry. I liked both of them a lot. Nice girls. Nice family, or at least Conway's side is."

"I didn't get the impression that she struggles financially as much as the rest of the family does."

"No, but she's not happy watching her dad work hard and have little to show for it."

"Maybe it's a conspiracy. Someone kills Evan to keep him from squandering the family money, and then they get Carys to give them each a share."

"Finally, after all these years, they would benefit from Lloyd's estate," Mehta summarized. "But Dylan only wants to share with his sister, so killing Evan probably wouldn't help Conway and the others anyway."

"It might depend on how much influence Carys has."

"Either Dylan or Conway got that Lee-Enfield, and Dylan has the greater motive in the killing."

"He also has the opportunity," Will mentioned. "He was right there on the property that day. His mother and his wife would both provide alibis for him. They'd be benefitting, too."

"But can we prove it?"

"That's the big question, isn't it?"

Lark was excited to see Will when they stopped by the farm to pick her up. She'd been riding Hobbs earlier, but was trailing around after Bronwyn's dad when the collies chased them up the driveway.

She hugged him around the waist, embarrassing him in front of Mehta, who stood aside, grinning. "I rode Hobbs for almost two hours, Uncle Will, and then I brushed him and braided his mane."

"I'm glad you had fun," he told her, reaching out to ruffle her reddish curls. "Are you ready to go back to the cottage? Are you hungry?"

"Grandmum made me a sausage and chips for lunch."

When did she start calling Bronwyn's mother 'Grandmum'? "Well, Jay and I are hungry, and I bet we can find something sweet for you while we eat our sandwiches."

"Can I have ice cream?" she wondered, bouncing from foot to foot.

"We'll check to see what we have." He looked over at Bronwyn's dad, who was watching, a smile on his face. "We'll see you at the memorial service. Thanks for keeping an eye on this little rascal this morning. She was dying to ride Hobbs, and we wouldn't have managed it without you."

"It's no problem," Bronwyn's dad assured him. "We're enjoying her, Gwawr and I. She reminds us of Bronwyn when she was young."

Of course, they were enjoying her. Her own grandparents had never tried to develop much of a relationship with her, even though she was living in their house. He felt a surge of gratitude toward Bronwyn's family. They'd taken Lark in as if she was one of their own.

They arrived early at St. Cynog's church in the village centre. Will and Jay wanted to stand outside and watch the attendees as they arrived, looking for clues in body language or interactions among them that might point to a killer.

Bronwyn left them to it. Will accompanied her as she walked inside and marked out two of the narrow pews for the family. It was a small church, and she'd said that she didn't know how many people would come to pay respects to Evan, so she thought it best to be prepared. A building of local stone, the walls inside were whitewashed and plain, with oak beams and a black ceiling. It was a simple place, in many ways less decorative than St. Melangell's, with few ornaments other than two pots of flowers on either side of the altar and a photo of Evan propped atop the casket, which had already been placed in the front of the church.

Once Bronwyn was seated, he left her and emerged back into the sunlight outside. The quiet streets had become clogged with slow-moving vehicles, everyone searching for a parking space. The little car park across the street was already full; now, people were parking alongside the street, blocking one lane of the already-narrow roadway and forcing other cars to wait a turn to get through.

He and Mehta stepped up into the churchyard and sat on a wooden bench beneath a gothic-arched window. They could hear the mourners walking alongside the stone retaining wall below and saw them lumbering up the steps to the church. Some of the arrivals cast curious glances their way, no doubt wondering why the two strangers were watching them from beside the old graves. Sitting there was awkward, but the only other alternative was to stand in the street, which wouldn't give them as much opportunity to see what they wanted to see.

Dylan, Gwniera, Lisa, and Meredith stood at the church door, greeting people as they arrived. Gwniera looked pale and tired, but Dylan seemed hardy as he cast out firm handshakes and welcoming words. Lisa stood beside Meredith, holding their little son in her arms. Of the four of them, she was the only one who looked truly shaken, and Will wondered why.

He didn't know many of the people who arrived, but he recognized a few of the local farmers he'd talked to during the spring, when he'd been investigating another local death. He couldn't recall their names. Their presence didn't surprise him; he learned that farmers supported each other through the hard times in these little communities. They'd want to pay their respects, no matter what they'd thought of Evan.

He hadn't expected Conway or any of his family to attend, but to his surprise, Conway and Mabyn appeared on the steps, Mabyn carrying Carys' zimmer frame and Conway nearly carrying his mother as she labored up the steep staircase, holding onto the metal handrail. He watched them as Carys hugged Dylan, Gwniera, and Meredith hard, then stepped back to coo at her great-grandson, Aeron, shy in his mother's arms. Conway and Mabyn watched from behind Carys, detached, but polite. When Carys had grabbed onto her zimmer and moved into the church, they greeted Dylan, Meredith, and Gwniera briefly, and then followed Carys inside.

Will and Mehta had abandoned their post and gone inside the church when the final mourners arrived. Rather than sit with Bronwyn and her family, they took seats at the back of the church where they could watch the service and, more importantly, the attendees. The officiant was preparing to begin the service when, from the corner of his eye, Will saw Jenna and Awstin Thomas pad quietly through the open door and take a seat at the back, near them. He nudged Mehta, who turned slightly to look.

The service lasted about an hour. Will fidgeted through it, uncomfortable on the hard pew and impatient with the formality of a service that focused little on Evan Bennett and more on a set program that had to be gotten through. He tried not to let his impatience show. As far as he could see, there were few tears shed. If the killer was there, he or she took care not to look so grief-stricken as to attract attention.

In the end, they decided it had been a wasted day all around, first the long trip to Cardiff, which had resulted in no new information, and then the service, which alerted them to no one they didn't already suspect. They'd gone through the expected motions, but the pace had slowed, and if something new didn't come up soon, they'd struggle to solve this case, maybe forever.

Chapter Twenty

Bronwyn slept restlessly, nightmares about the garden tea making her sleep shallow and fitful. When she heard a voice through the door, she thought it was part of a dream until Will slid out of bed. "Go back to sleep," he whispered. "You don't need to be up yet. I'll take care of Lark."

She dozed for a while, half-asleep but unable to still the restless thoughts racing in her mind. Finally, she threw back the sheet and rolled onto her feet beside the bed. She could smell bacon from the kitchen, and she heard Daisy's nails clicking on the wood floor as she paced outside the bedroom door.

Will looked up from the stove as she padded into the kitchen. "Did you get some more sleep?" he asked.

"I did," she lied. "What's all this?"

He held up a spatula. "I thought you deserved some spoiling today. I feel I've been taking advantage lately, dumping all my responsibilities on you, so I'm hoping to regain some of my standing by making you a beautiful breakfast and then driving you to Gloustershire."

She gaped at him. "You're driving us?"

He grinned, looking pleased with himself. "There's nothing Jay and I can do today that can't be done as easily tomorrow. I told Jay to take the day off. He's coming around for breakfast, and then he'll be off to Caernarfon to sleep in his own bed for the night."

"What will Bowers say?"

"I already called him. He gave us his blessing. Sometimes, with a case like this one where you have lots of suspects, stepping away for a day makes things come clearer."

"You didn't need to do this, Will." But, secretly, she was thrilled.

"I know I didn't. I wanted to. Lark is my responsibility, and you drove all the way to Chepstow after work to fetch her because I couldn't. My mother is my burden, and you're headed off to a tea party you're dreading, just to keep her on our sweet side. I owe you." He gave her a look, a half-smile curving his lips. "Come here. I need a kiss."

She hurried over to him, stretched up, and kissed him quickly. A second kiss lasted longer. "Where's Lark?"

He grinned at her knowingly, and then he set the spatula down on a plate and reached out to wrap her in his arms, nuzzling his face in her hair. "I sent her out to the field to give Daisy a little romp."

"You're brilliant," she told him, wriggling free and looking up at him. She loved him even more when he went out of his way to spoil her. "When was this? Will she be gone long?"

"Unfortunately, no. She went out about five minutes ago. I imagine she'll be back in another ten."

"Oh, too bad," she teased, pulling away. "I thought we might get a few minutes to ourselves."

"Jay will be here any minute, as well." He frowned in mock disappointment. "But I have plans for tonight."

She looked at him, her eyebrows raised. "You're burning the bacon," she pointed out.

He grabbed the spatula and flipped the bacon onto a plate, turning the gas down on the burner. "You deserve a date night," he informed her. He turned back and grinned at her. "My plan is to get out of Gloustershire as fast as we can manage it. We'll drop Lark at school, and then I'll drive like the devil. We'll drop your mum home, and we'll still have plenty of time after that for an evening to ourselves, just the two of us. I have plans I think you'll like."

"I think that sounds perfect," she said, as a shiver of anticipation ran through her. She kissed him again. He was trying so hard to make up for what she anticipated to be a difficult day.

He grinned through the kiss and pushed her away. "Go get dressed. I'm making your omelet now. It'll be ready in ten minutes."

They left at eight, wanting to make sure they had plenty of time for the trip. Lark bounced into the back seat wearing a new yellow sundress, her shoulder-length curls in wild disarray. Bronwyn had tried to style the curls into something more fashionable, but in the end, she'd given up, resolving to ask Mai for some tips for the future.

She was wearing a new dress she'd bought for the occasion, a cream-colored sundress with subtle autumn flowers scattered on it. Will had complimented her when he'd seen her, and she'd seen the honest pride in his eyes. It made her feel more confident going into the day.

Thankfully, the sky was clear, summer having extended itself into September with only occasional rainy days to hint at the autumn to come. Bronwyn chatted with Lark and her mum, watching the countryside go by as the A483 led them south toward the dreaded garden party. She wished she was alone so she could try to calm her raging nerves. All she really wanted was for the day to be over so she could be home again and alone, just her and Will.

They arrived early, a fortunate circumstance. Will's mother, wearing a blue dress shimmering with sequins, greeted them at the door and introduced herself to Bronwyn's mum. It seemed that, in arriving early, they had done one thing right. "I'm so glad you're here already," Mrs. Cooper exclaimed, glowing with anticipation as she touched Bronwyn's arm with a finger. "Now I can introduce you to everyone as they arrive." She turned then and looked at Will. "I didn't know you were coming. You could have sat with your father instead of me hiring someone."

"I found that I was able to get free at the last minute," Will told her.

She waved him off. "Go on into the library, then. Your father's in there with Mark, the respite carer." The smile returned to her face "Now, you ladies come with me out to the garden. Everything's all set. And don't you all look lovely!"

They followed her through the house, Bronwyn exchanging looks with her mum behind the woman's back. Her mum rolled her eyes, then raised her eyebrows in shared commiseration. The expensively-decorated home Will had been raised in contrasted sharply with the old farmhouse they knew. It was a treat to see, but neither of them would have been comfortable living in such pristine conditions.

Tables had been set up in the garden behind the conservatory, each with a blue satin tablecloth and matching covers on the chairs. Crystal and fine white china with cream linen napkins decorated the tables, and classical flute music played quietly in the background from an unknown source. The smooth lawn was bordered by shrubs and featured a rectangular garden pond with floating water lilies, still blooming pink in the September sun. Two women in black and white outfits scurried from table to table, filling water glasses and setting out little bowls of mints and nuts.

"You ladies will be sitting here with me," Mrs. Cooper indicated the table nearest the conservatory doors, "but we'll stand here by the doors to greet our guests first and, of course, you'll want to go around and talk with everyone once they're all here." She turned to Bronwyn's mum again. "Can you pronounce your name again for me? I know I should know it, but the Welsh trips me up."

"It's Gwawr. I know it sounds strange to ears that aren't accustomed to hearing Welsh."

"Yes, well, I suppose we'll get used to it." Mrs. Cooper's attention was drawn by a pair of ladies who'd just emerged from the conservatory's French doors. She waved at them. "It's Elaine Potts-Browne and Alice Buckley," she murmured, as if the names should mean something to them. "Come in, ladies! I want you to meet William's fiancée and her mother."

In the end, twenty women joined them in the garden. The caterers served finger sandwiches, scones, cakes, and fruit, along with pink champagne in gold-edged flutes. Bronwyn did her best to do what was expected, wandering from table to table and stopping to chat with all of the ladies, a fixed smile on her face that she hoped didn't look too fake.

At nearly every table, she was asked for details about 'the venue,' which confused her until she realized that they were asking about the wedding site. She did her best to try to make St. Melangell's sound intimate and charming, and managed to evade specific questions about the reception, which in their case was just a meal at the counselling centre. Although she was proud of their wedding plans, she realized that nothing they were doing would be up to the standards these ladies would expect. In their world, if you didn't spend tens of thousands on a wedding, what was the point of doing it at all?

"Elizabeth mentioned that you are the director of a counselling centre?" one woman asked. She wore a flowered skirt with a black blouse, and a necklace of what Bronwyn suspected were real rubies hung around her wrinkled neck.

"That's nearly right," Bronwyn corrected her. She was slightly insulted that Elizabeth Cooper had embellished the truth a bit, but not surprised. She felt a fleeting sadness that Will's mother had thought it necessary. "I'm actually the coordinator. I manage the office, arrange fund-raisers, things like that."

Another woman settled on Bronwyn's background. "Your family has an estate that's been passed down through the generations, I'm told," she announced with a cheery smile. She was too thin, and her hair was too blonde to be natural.

"It's not as fancy as that," Bronwyn told her, suddenly not caring if Elizabeth Cooper's friends knew the truth. She was tired of the pretense of a more pedigreed background than she possessed. "We have a sheep farm, and we sell organic meat and crops to local restaurants and shops." As soon as she'd said the words, she regretted them. Maybe the women would think they lounged in their estate house and just managed a staff who did the actual work of farming?

When she'd made the rounds of all six tables, she sat down for a few minutes and nibbled at what was left of the lunch while Will's mother invited Bronwyn's mum to join her in her own trip around the garden. Watching them, Bronwyn thought her mum was holding up remarkably well. Despite everything, she was nodding and chatting with the ladies as if they were the villagers she encountered every day. Bronwyn envied her that ease, which she obviously hadn't inherited.

As the women had arrived, the packages they'd carried with them were deposited on a bigger table near the decorative pool. Bronwyn hadn't expected gifts; now, she'd be forced to open them as all the ladies' eyes focused on her, the centre of attention as she pretended excitement over gifts she suspected she'd have no earthly use for.

She wasn't wrong. The first gift she opened, to the murmured admiration of the ladies, was a wine set of antique Swedish crystal. It was lovely, but she couldn't picture it in their rented cottage, always in danger of being swept off a table and broken by Daisy's errant tail or Lark's happy antics. She held up a glass, though, and tried to look delighted despite her reservations, throwing a "thank you" in the direction of the giver, an elderly lady in a pink suit with a flowered hat who beamed at the praise.

There were other impractical gifts: an expresso machine, a silver tea service, a glass photo cube, matching his and her dressing gowns, and a silver cake knife engraved with their names. She supposed most of it could be donated to Oxfam, although she was sure these ladies had spent more on their gifts than she and Will were spending on their entire wedding. Perhaps Will would take the expresso machine to the station? And she might use the photo cube on her desk at the centre. She kept the smile on her face and exclaimed in delight at every gift, hoping not to embarrass Mrs. Cooper in the company of her friends.

And, after what seemed hours, it was over. The last guests said their goodbyes, and they were left alone again as the caterers scurried around cleaning up.

Mrs. Cooper smiled. "That went over very well, didn't it? Would you like to stay for coffee?"

God, no. Bronwyn just wanted to get into the car and drive away as fast as they could. But she needed to do it politely, for Will's sake. "Thank you, Mrs. Cooper, for everything. This has been amazing," she enthused, "but I know Will must be anxious to get on the road now. We'll have to deliver Lark back at school, and Mum needs to get home to my dad. It's a long drive back to Llangynog. Will has to work in the morning, and he'll need to relax a bit after all the driving today."

"Yes, well, I can see that the two of you have a lot of responsibilities, don't you? I'm glad you are realizing what having a child entails before we make a final decision about Lark." She smiled, but even Bronwyn could see it was more a smile of triumph than of empathy. "Why don't you just come and say hello to Charles before you go, won't you? Gwawr hasn't met him yet." Mrs. Cooper's smile had faded. "William's always in a hurry to get away. Lark doesn't need to get back quite so early, do you?" She turned the frown on Lark.

"I want to get some things from my room to take with me," Lark said. "I won't be coming here much anymore now. I'll either be at school or at Uncle Will's on the weekends."

Mrs. Cooper looked up sharply at that, but didn't comment.

They trailed behind her as she led them into the library, where Will sat with his father and another man, who was introduced as Mark, the carer. Will and Mark had been talking when they entered the room, and Bronwyn hoped they'd found something mutually interesting in common to pass the time. Will's father was dressed in pressed brown trousers, with a tan dress shirt and a blue and brown tie. He sat upright in his chair, looking impatient. "Must I sit here all day?" he asked when he saw them. "I have things to do."

Will stood up. "We'll be leaving now, so you can get back to your usual routine."

His mother shot him a disgusted look. "Your father hasn't met Bronwyn's mother yet, William. Surely, you can spare a few minutes of your time so they can be introduced."

Will blinked. "I'd forgotten," he mumbled. "Father, this is Bronwyn's mother, Gwawr. She's going to be my mother-in-law."

Mr. Cooper glared at her, his eyebrows drawn together tightly, but Bronwyn didn't think it was a look of anger, but rather, of confusion. "I'm glad to meet you," he said formally. "I'm Charles Cooper. I think William is going to be married?" He said the last as a question.

"Yes, our wedding is next weekend," Will told him. "You'll be coming to it, you and mother and Lark."

"I'll look forward to it," Mr. Cooper said politely. "Now you should go. I have things to do at the office."

Will looked at his mother, who sighed. "Come with me, Charles. It's time for a cup of tea." She peered sideways at Will. "I suppose you can show yourselves out? Things aren't really normal here any longer." She directed the last at Bronwyn's mum, an obvious attempt at covering up the difficulties she faced in caring for Will's father.

Bronwyn let out a sign of relief as they drove away from the house. She tried to do it subtly, so as not to draw attention to herself, but Will saw her out of the corner of his eye and grinned, eyes on the road. The hard part of the day was over; now, they just had to get Lark back to school and Bronwyn's mum back home, and then they'd be free. She didn't know what all Will had planned for the evening, but she'd seen the gleam in his eyes that morning and knew whatever it was, it'd help her forget the stress of the past days.

"So, what did you think of my family?" Will glanced back over his shoulder to where Bronwyn's mum sat in the back seat. "We didn't exaggerate about them, did we?"

"Your mother is lovely, very pretty." Of course, Bronwyn's mum would never say anything bad about Will's parents, particularly not in front of their granddaughter, who was sitting beside her listening avidly.

"You didn't find her a bit…what should I call it? Ostentatious?"

"She's used to a different life than ours, is all."

"You're being generous," Will said. "You should hear her when she tries to manipulate me. She makes it very clear that she disapproves of my every life choice." He seemed to realize then what he'd said. "Except for Bronwyn, of course. She wouldn't dare."

"You should try to get along with her. She has a hard road to navigate right now."

"I do try," Will told her. "Bronwyn and I both try hard to keep her happy."

They'd just dropped Lark off at St. John's on the Hill and driven off toward home when Will's mobile rang out from the centre console. He glanced toward Bronwyn, who picked it up and looked. "It's Jay," she told him, hoping it wasn't anything that would disrupt the date night Will had planned.

From the back seat, her mum spoke up. "I hope it's nothing to spoil your evening. I know you're both looking forward to some time alone, without work in the way."

Bronwyn's finger darted toward the green button, but Will put out a hand to stop her, shaking his head. "No speaker," he murmured.

She supposed he couldn't have her mum overhearing whatever it was. He wasn't supposed to share information with her, let alone with her family.

The old Land Rover wasn't equipped with Blue Tooth. She handed the mobile to Will.

"Hi, Jay," Will greeted him, holding the phone with his left hand while he steered with the right. "What's up?"

Bronwyn watched as Will's face drained of colour. "When?" he sputtered. "Just now?"

He listened for a long minute, holding the phone to his ear as he continued to drive one-handed. He'd slowed their speed and moved into the left lane. "He's dead?"

Bronwyn turned to look at her mum in the backseat. Will shouldn't have taken the day off to drive her to Gloustershire. If he'd been working instead, maybe whoever this was wouldn't have been hurt. She sent a silent prayer skyward to anyone who might be listening. *Please, don't let Will be in trouble again.*

Will interrupted her thoughts. "Okay, I'm about an hour out, maybe just a little more. I'll get there as fast as I can. I'll meet you at the site." He listened again for a minute. "Bronwyn can do that. I doubt you'll get a chance to sleep tonight anyway."

He cut off the call, tossed the mobile into the centre console, signaled and moved into the right lane, picking up speed. "Dylan's been shot," he said tightly, staring straight ahead through the windscreen. The afternoon sun came in on the driver's side, lighting his face and beaming across the seat. "I had him down as my major suspect."

Bronwyn's mind spun. "He's...dead?"

"Yes. Gwniera found him. He'd been working out there by the forest land, near where Evan was shot. She heard the shot and drove up there to check on him."

"It was like before," Bronwyn murmured. "Someone hid behind a tree and shot him."

"Only this time, there was no thunderstorm to cover up the sound," Will observed. "The shooter would have been in a hurry to get away from there. He had no time to hide the body."

Bronwyn hesitated, not wanting to say it aloud, but she had to know. "Will you be in trouble over this?" She said it carefully, hoping it didn't sound accusatory.

He glanced at her, then turned his eyes back to the road ahead. "We had no reason to suspect that anyone other than Evan was a target. It should be okay." He sounded uncertain, though.

"Did Gwniera see anyone when she drove up there?" Bronwyn's mum spoke from the back seat. "The shooter must still be out there if she didn't pass him on the road."

"He could walk away," Will said. "Go across country until he gets to a road."

"There aren't many roads out that way. The hillside is steep beside the forestland. He'd have had to go toward the road to Gwniera's house or through the woods to ours."

"There are constables on scene now. They'll be looking. They'll call in the dogs. Maybe, with luck, they'll find him."

"Someone has a grudge against the Bennetts," Bronwyn's mum observed, "and not just Evan, but his family, too. Poor Gwniera."

"It's not a grudge against them," Bronwyn argued, thinking of the Twlwyth Teg's words. "It's to do with the inheritance, with Evan getting all the land and then passing it to Dylan. Someone thinks it should have been shared. Now that Dylan is out of the way, it probably will be."

Chapter Twenty-One

Will dropped Bronwyn's mum at home and then took Bronwyn to the cottage. He parked the Land Rover on the side of the driveway; he'd drive his own car to the crime scene so she'd have hers.

He walked her to the door, took a quick look around inside, and admonished her to stay home and keep the doors locked. "We have a killer, and he's someone local. Until we figure it out, I don't want you out on your own."

"I have to take Daisy out for her walks," she warned him. "I'll be careful. I won't go out to the woods, I promise." She let Daisy brush past her out into the front garden again, where she circled the Land Rover, smelling its tyres. "Can I bring you something to eat later?"

"You won't be able to come all the way to the site, but I'll tell the constables on duty down on the road to watch for you. They'll let me know when you get there, and I'll come to you."

"I'll bring something for Jay, too."

He stood in the doorway, knowing he needed to go, but feeling like a failure again. "I owe you a date night. A real one, not like this."

She laughed and kissed him quickly. "Just hurry home, okay?"

As if that was a possibility. This murder would keep him out all night again, almost certainly. He'd be lucky if he found time by morning for a shower. He knew there were local constables on site, but he wondered if the crime scene techs had arrived yet and where Jay was.

He folded himself into the little convertible, leaving the top up since it'd soon be night, and drove through the village and onto the now-familiar lane that led past the homes of the Bennett brothers, who shared a road but nothing else, thanks to a feud now lasting twenty years. He mused over that as he drove. He and his brother George were never close, but he couldn't imagine not wishing him the best in life, even if George had deserted the family after Julia's death and moved to Canada. Why couldn't Evan have shared the inheritance, no matter what their father's trust said? He felt sure that Carys would have supported and even encouraged that idea. It couldn't have been easy for her to watch one son struggle for every penny while the other lived extravagantly, at least for a farmer.

Another thought nagged at him, but he couldn't quite grasp it with all the other ideas running rampant in his mind. He dismissed it. If it was important, he'd think of it again later.

The constable blocking cars from the little farm lane recognized him and waved him through. Will stopped beside him. "My girlfriend will be coming by later with some dinner for me. If you could just text me when she arrives, I'll come meet her here."

The man grinned. "I remember her from before, sir. Pretty girl, and local, too, if I remember right. Give me your number, and I'll let you know."

Will watched as he tapped the mobile number into his own, thanked him and drove on to where he could see a mess of emergency vehicles clogging the lane and spilling out onto the pasture. He parked his car a distance behind a waiting ambulance, locked it, and walked toward the blue tarp that covered the body of Dylan Bennett, lying on the ground not too far from Carys' old farmhouse. A truck sat parked at the edge of the lane where the old driveway abutted the roadway. It'd be Dylan's, he remembered, noting the black colour.

He joined the mixed crowd, finding Jay already there and squatting beside the body. He joined him. "Another gunshot?"

275

Jay glanced up. "You're here, thank goodness. I don't much fancy doing this alone."

"No medical examiner?"

"Frances Ruark should be here any time now. He got the call right after I did, I'm guessing." Jay pointed. "Two shots; both of them hit the target this time. Until Frances does his work or they find a shell casing, we won't know for sure, but the wounds look like Evan's did, so I think it's the same weapon."

Will squatted down beside him. Dylan was lying face down in the pasture grass, sprawled forward, face and body turned slightly to the side in the dirt. He pulled on gloves and poked at the hole in Dylan's left back beneath the shoulder. "Heart shot," he commented. He turned his attention to the second hole, to the right of the first. "He fired once, saw that the shot had missed the heart, and fired the second shot to kill him," he speculated.

"Evan had two shots, too. One of them missed."

"If it's the Lee-Enfield, it's an older weapon. It might be harder to get the aim right unless he's shot it a lot. The first shot is to fix the aim on target, and the second is the kill shot."

"They'd come fast, one after another," Mehta said. "Otherwise, the victim would duck away or run."

Will stood up and looked at the site. "If the shooter was standing in the woods behind a tree, Dylan might have been running away when he was killed. He's twisted to the side a little, but he kept moving. The second shot took him down."

Mehta nodded. "That sounds right." He stood up. "Gwniera told the constables that Dylan had come to do the weekly check on the house. They took turns," he reminded Will. "One week it was Conway, and the next was Evan's turn, or Dylan's now."

"Sir?"

They turned to see Lew Griffiths, the constable who lived in Llangynog, standing nearby. "I thought you should be aware," he said.

"Of what?"

"I was first on the scene, sir." He addressed Will, but his gaze included both of them. "I live here," he reminded them. "I was off-duty, it being a Sunday, but when the call came in, I heard about it and responded."

Will nodded. "It was good of you to come in on your day off."

"Well, as it was someone I knew, I couldn't just turn away." Griffiths grinned, obviously pleased with the praise. "Gwniera was in a state, sir. I couldn't calm her. She was screaming like a banshee, a real mess, and I could hardly drag her away from the body."

Dylan was her only son, her firstborn. Of course, she'd be hysterical. "Did she say anything that made sense?"

"She was mostly just making noise, but I made out a few words here and there. I gathered that she thought it was a kid who'd done it. She repeated it a few times. 'That bloody kid.'"

A shout interrupted him. Will and Jay turned in unison to see one of the techs waving from the edge of the nearby woods. "I've got a casing," he called out. "You'll want to come have a look."

Will turned back to Griffiths. "What was she doing when you arrived? Was she near the body?"

"She was sitting there next to him, crying and mumbling to herself."

"About the bloody kid?"

"Yes, and other stuff. How sorry she was. That she loved him."

Awe, Christ, it was hard. "Someone is with her now?"

"We sent Dilys. She'll manage her fine."

"And Dylan's wife? Lisa?"

"They sent someone to her, too. I don't know who." He looked around, as if to tally who might be missing.

"That's okay. As long as someone's there, we don't need to know who. Thanks, Lew. You did great."

He beamed as they started toward the man who'd called out, but the tech held out a hand. "You can't come over here until you put a suit on." No one, least of all the techs, wanted the crime scene contaminated.

They knew better. They turned back to head toward the van where they'd be kitted up when they saw Frances Ruark striding across the field, his own white suit making him look like something just beamed down from the future.

"You take the casing," Will decided, "and I'll get started with Ruark." He liked working with the forensic pathologist, and he wanted to be there for the initial examination so as not to miss any details. Mehta wouldn't mind.

He went to the van and hurried to pull on a suit, hopping from one foot to the other as he yanked it up over his clothes. At least it was still warm out. In winter, it was nearly impossible to pull one up over a heavy coat. He zipped it up, flipped the hood over his head, and pulled on a fresh pair of gloves as he hurried over to where Ruark was kneeling beside the body.

In the end, he didn't learn anything he didn't already know. Dylan had died from a gunshot to the heart; death wouldn't have been instant, but very quick. Time of death wasn't dependent on Ruark because they had Gwniera's statement to rely on. As long as Ruark didn't see a discrepancy once he'd done his exam, they'd consider it accurate.

Mehta came up to stand beside Will as they watched Ruark finish with his initial examination. "It's too bad, this," he commented. "He was greedy about the money, but he didn't seem a bad sort otherwise."

"If he'd agreed to share it with the extended family, maybe he'd still be alive," Will speculated. He sighed. "I had him down as my major suspect."

"So did I," Mehta agreed. "He had the most to gain from Evan's death, and they obviously disagreed on a lot of things."

"The casing is from the Lee-Enfield .303?"

"Same gun," Mehta confirmed. "Now, who used it?"

Will shrugged. "I have no idea. We'll have to check alibis again, see who looks suspicious. I'd like to check them all for gun residue, but I suppose they have rights that'd keep that from happening." He looked out toward the woods. "I'd like to find that gun."

"You think someone else is in danger?"

Will thought about it. "I think that depends on which of them inherits everything now." He didn't want to assume the others would be safe, though. This was the first investigation he'd run pretty much without direction from Bowers, the first he'd been primarily responsible for. So far, he hadn't heard any fallout from his failure to protect Dylan, but there'd be no more relaxing until they figured out who their perpetrator was. One death after the fact, Bowers might overlook. More than that, though, and there'd be trouble. If he wanted to continue working in Llangynog, he'd have to make sure he did everything he could to both protect the Bennet family and to solve the case.

The sun hung low in the sky when Will got the call that Bronwyn had arrived with their supper. He called to Mehta, and the two of them squeezed into Will's car and drove back up the lane to where Bronwyn was chatting with the two constables on duty.

They all watched as Will and Mehta drove up and got out. Bronwyn walked over and gave Will a quick kiss. He was aware of the constables watching with some amusement. He ignored them.

They sat on the tailgate of the Land Rover and ate the simple meal of cheeses, meats, and bread she had brought. She poured lemonade for them.

"Lemonade?" Will looked askance.

"You can't have beer or wine when you're working," she told him primly.

He laughed and reached for a cube of Irish white cheddar. "Who did it?" he asked. "Who killed them?"

"We have to eliminate Cassadee and Steffan Richards," Mehta said, chewing. "They had a motive for Evan, but not for Dylan."

"They never really looked good for it anyway," Will conceded. "We can check their alibis just to be thorough and cross them off the list."

"A family member, then," Bronwyn said. "I hate to think of it. I like Conway and his family. They're good people."

"Salt of the earth," Will mumbled. He looked at Mehta. "I hate to say it, but Conway is our most likely suspect at this point, don't you think? With both Evan and Dylan out of the way, he might have a chance again at the family farm."

"Dylan would have left everything to Lisa and Aeron," Bronwyn argued.

"Unless he had no will. He was young and probably thought he had plenty of time for something like that. Until he inherited the land from Evan, he really had no need for a will. And Lisa can't very well farm the land, can she?"

"The land will still go to his wife," Mehta argued. "Community property."

"But maybe not the investments." Will looked toward the sunset, where a brilliant crimson sky was edged in charcoal clouds. "We'll get Quigley onto checking that trust. We'll have enough for a warrant now, I'd think, with two deaths. We need to talk to Carys, too."

"Sooner rather than later." Mehta scooped chopped fruit into a bowl. Apples, pears, and raspberries, chopped into a salad. He nodded as Bronwyn handed him a spoon. "We need to get to Gwniera and Lisa, go through Dylan's house, tonight or tomorrow morning. We might have time to get to Carys, too, depending on how that goes."

Will's mobile rang. He looked at it. "Bugger. It's Bowers." He hit the green button. "Cooper," he answered the call.

"Put me on speaker," Bowers demanded. He did not sound happy.

Will tapped his phone. "We're both here, sir."

"You've got another murder, and on a day you took off. That's not acceptable. I thought you two were on top of this one, near to an arrest."

Will looked at Mehta, whose eyes had grown wary. It had been his request to take the day off; his responsibility now. "I'm sorry, sir." Bronwyn was watching him. He wished she weren't there for the upbraiding he knew was coming. "We thought we were getting close."

"So why not finish it and then take a day off?"

"Because, sir, the man we thought was responsible for the first murder is our new victim."

There was silence. "You got it wrong." A statement, not a question.

"Everything we had to go on led us that way, sir. We went over it with you. The problem is that we have no physical evidence. Everyone had a motive. No one had an alibi. If we'd had another day or two..."

"Yet you chose to take a day off," Bowers interrupted, his voice betraying his anger. "We'll look like fools to the press and the public. They'll be all over us for this one."

Will had nothing. Bowers knew the details of the case. He'd approved the day off. But he was obviously tired of taking the fall for Will's mistakes. "Blame it on me, sir. I made the call, not Mehta. This second death is on me." Even if they'd been working, though, he couldn't see how the second death would have been prevented. They'd have had no idea. He glanced at Bronwyn, who avoided his eyes.

"You will get this mess figured out now."

"Yes, sir. We're working here through the night." He felt a sharp pain behind his eyes, a headache coming on. Too much stress, between his mother and the case. Then there was the wedding, as well.

"Details," Bowers demanded.

"The victim died of a gunshot wound to the heart. His mother heard the shot and found him a few minutes later. We have a shell casing that says it's the same gun as before."

"Your plan?"

"We'll be here as long as there's new information coming in from the scene. Then we'll interview the victim's mother and his wife, look through the house, do the usual. I have some things for Quigley to do for us, mainly checking to see who inherits the estate now, both the land and the money. And we'll talk to the victim's grandmother, whose name is on the trust. We really think it's about the money and what happens to it now."

"You need physical evidence," Bowers pointed out impatiently.

"We know that. We're looking."

"Don't just look. Find it." Bowers snapped.

Back at the murder site, they watched the technicians comb over the field and Dylan's truck. Dylan's mobile phone and wallet were confiscated and bagged. Frances Ruark finished his work, and the body was loaded into the ambulance to be taken to Caernarfon for the post-mortem.

It was near eleven at night with a half-moon competing with the stars when a thin young man with close-cropped dark hair and black-rimmed glasses called to them from the old farmhouse. "Sirs! I've found something you need to see."

They jogged to the house, the weedy pathway now trampled by foot traffic from the technicians. "Come inside," the young man urged them. "I'm Henry Riggens, by the way."

"Will Cooper and Jay Mehta," Will responded automatically. They climbed onto the front stoop and stopped to put fresh booties on their feet. "Were you here the last time?"

"I was. We did inside the house then, too. This is something new."

They followed him inside, through a living room with a stone fireplace and into a bedroom. Carys had left many of the furnishings in the house, and this room featured a double bed, unmade, but with a mattress still lying on it and, beside it, a dressing table. Will remembered them from before, slightly dusty, but he'd thought at the time that they should be donated if they weren't going to be used. *Better than letting them rot.*

He noticed it right away, something new in the room that hadn't been there before. The rifle lay on its side on the dressing table, age-darkened wood with dark metal fixtures. Its position had it pointing toward the bed, for no reason that Will could immediately grasp. His heart raced. "My God," he murmured. "Lee-Enfield Mark 4?"

"Yes, it is," Riggens said. "It wasn't here before."

"No, it definitely wasn't. No one's touched it?"

"Not yet. We're waiting for a kit. We'll check it for fingerprints, DNA, anything that can identify who had their hands on this gun last. We'll do a preliminary here and then take it to the lab."

Will looked down at it. Their murderer had abandoned the rifle now, so he or she must be finished with it. Why leave it in Carys' abandoned house? Because it was convenient, or because it sent some sort of message?" He couldn't figure it out.

Beside him, Mehta leaned down toward the gun. "On the stock, Will. There's something there."

Both Riggens and Will bent closer. The rifle would be nearly eighty years old. It had seen use in a war. It would naturally be weathered, scratched, well-used. But Jay was right. Among the other scratches and dings, he could see letters scratched purposefully on the dark wood of the stock.

Riggens shone a light on it, and suddenly he realized. "SORRY."

They stayed at the site until after midnight, but by then, they decided that all the major discoveries had been made. Anything else the techs found could be relayed to them the following morning.

They debated and then determined that it was too late to interview either Gwniera or Lisa. They would have been given something to help them sleep, and the constables on duty with them would keep an eye on them, making sure they didn't remove anything from their homes or talk to anyone they shouldn't. They'd already been informed of the death. Questioning them could wait for the morning.

Mehta had not checked into the B&B and Will had forgotten his intention to have Bronwyn make him a reservation, so Will brought him back to the cottage with him. Mehta would have to sleep in Lark's room. Bronwyn would not have had time to wash the sheets on the bed, but he supposed the kid would survive. They were both dead tired. He gave Mehta an extra toothbrush they kept on hand, rumbled in the cupboard for a towel, and then pointed him in the direction of Lark's room.

Daisy had heard him. She'd met them at the door and then gone back to her doggy bed in the corner of the bedroom. As he slipped into the bedroom, she watched him, but made no sound, her tail thumping only once on the bed before she settled onto her side and went back to sleep.

He pulled off his jeans and unbuttoned his shirt, then slid into bed beside Bronwyn.

She roused a little, turning sleepily to face him. "Will?" she mumbled.

"Yes, it's me. It's after midnight. Go back to sleep."

She sighed and wriggled a little, getting comfortable. "How did it go?"

"We found the gun."

She opened her eyes. "In the woods?"

"No, it was in Carys' old house. The shooter left it there after." He considered it for a moment. "We won't find any prints on it."

"I don't want any of them to be guilty," she murmured. "They're good people."

"I know, love." He waited, but she'd already fallen back to sleep, snoring softly beside him.

Chapter Twenty-Two

Morning came too early. Bronwyn didn't have to go to work that day, but Will and Mehta had a full agenda to accomplish if they were going to place themselves back in Bowers' good graces.

They ate a quick breakfast while Bronwyn bustled around in the kitchen making sandwiches for their lunch, and then they drove off in the little MGF, intending to go first to Gwniera's house, and then to Lisa's.

Gwniera was outside, tossing feed to the ewes in the pens. She was dressed in jeans, a tee shirt, and rubber boots. Two horses whickered to her as she shredded out the hay into the feeder and, when she turned back, she saw Will and Mehta.

She approached them slowly, every movement seeming to tax her strength. Her face was pale and drawn, her eyes empty hollows. She looked at them with what seemed like dread, and Will wondered why.

"Let's go inside," Mehta suggested, watching her.

"I can't. I have to feed the animals. There's no one else to do it." She looked ready to collapse.

"I'll get one of the neighbors to come over," Will offered. He knew that Bronwyn's dad and her brother would come in a heartbeat if he called. He was almost surprised that they hadn't already turned up. He paused to text a message to Maddock and then caught up easily to Mehta and Gwniera, who were ambling slowly toward the house.

They went inside. The house looked neat and clean, with no discarded cups on the tables or paperback novels lying on the arm of the sofa. The constable who'd spent the night with Gwniera frowned and whispered behind Gwniera's back. "I couldn't stop her going out. She was worried about the livestock."

"We've got someone coming over," Will whispered back. "Can you make her some tea? Maybe some toast?"

"She said that she didn't want anything earlier, but I'll just pop into the kitchen and do it anyway. Maybe once it's on the table in front of her, it'll sound better." The woman, middle-aged and well-filled out, shook her head sadly. "The husband she'd get over sooner or later, but it's never easy to lose a child." She hesitated. "I think she knows who did it, but she isn't saying."

They sat with Gwniera at the dining room table. Her shoulders slumped and she rocked back and forth slowly, eyes opening and shutting in rhythm with the rocking.

"I know it's a difficult time, Gwniera," Will said gently, "but can you tell us about yesterday? The sooner we talk to you, the faster we can try to solve this crime. That's what you want, isn't it?"

"No one else should die," Gwniera muttered, surprising them. Will hadn't expected to get much from the interview. "That's what comes of greed." She jerked her face up to look at Will, and her voice was suddenly shrill in the quiet kitchen. "Evan was selfish. He should have shared it instead of wasting it on his fancy women all those years. He was too full of himself. He always was, even in the beginning."

Will waited, not knowing whether to prompt her and not wanting to interrupt her stream of revelation.

After a moment's silence, she went on more quietly. "I told Dylan that he needed to help the others, but he didn't want to give any of it up, either." She glared at Will and then at Mehta. "You men, you all want to be rich. Makes you feel important, does it? Money's not the answer to happiness, believe me." She took a breath, letting the flare of anger subside. "Why didn't he listen to me?" She sighed again harshly, and

285

then suddenly she let out a cry, a wailing of grief that echoed through the empty house.

Will rolled his eyes toward Mehta, giving a little shake of his head. Gwniera might not be able to give them any information at the moment, at least nothing helpful.

Mehta reached across the table and took her hand in his. "Gwniera, what were you doing yesterday when you heard the gunshot?" he asked softly.

She stared at their entwined hands. "I was unsaddling Commander, my horse. I'd gotten his tack off, and I was brushing him."

"Had Dylan been here at the house earlier?"

She nodded slowly, still staring at their hands. "He came to take care of the animals, around three o'clock. I don't know what he was doing earlier. There are plenty of chores to keep him busy. He did his work, and then I reminded him that it was our week to check on the old house." She looked up at Mehta. "Carys had the house for sale, so we had to keep it up. We didn't do much, just tidy it a little inside and check to make sure no one had broken in. I don't know why we bothered. No one came to look at it."

"You didn't go with him?"

"I was just finishing my ride when he left. Why would I have gone with him anyway? He was a grown man, capable of doing whatever needed doing." She drifted off, lost in thought. "I'd been clearing out Evan's things all day, putting his clothes and things in bin bags to take to charity. It was difficult, sorting through everything." She paused again, and then gave Mehta a little smile. "Our marriage wasn't a good one. You know that. We led separate lives, for the most part. I wanted to stay here in the country, and Evan didn't want to give me my share of the farm or of the investment money, so we stayed together. But I cared for him, at least a little. In my own way, I did care." A tear rolled down her cheek.

Mehta nodded, encouraging her. "You were putting your horse away when you heard the gun," he reminded her. "Did you hear one shot or two?"

"Two. They were one right after the other. I knew right away that someone had shot at Dylan." Now the tears were flowing in earnest. She

286

sniffed and brushed at her nose. "I got my key and drove up there as fast as I could."

Mehta waited.

After a moment, she went on. "I saw Dylan right away, lying there near the old house. I sat down beside him and stroked his face." She freed her hand from Mehta's and wiped at her nose. "He was already gone, but I just sat there with him. After a bit, I called 999."

"How long was it between when you found him and when you called it in?"

She thought it over. "Time stands still when something like that happens. It felt long, but it was probably only a few minutes, less than five."

"Did you turn him over? He was on his stomach when we found him."

"I rolled him to the side a bit so I could touch his face."

"Did you notice anything else? Another vehicle? Maybe you heard one? Or a door open and shut?"

He's thinking of that gun, left in the old farmhouse. Had there been time to do that before Gwniera arrived at the scene? The drive would have taken her maybe ten minutes. That wasn't much time for someone to get in and out of the house without being seen. Still, if someone were quiet enough, he could probably creep out the door without Gwniera noticing, if she was occupied with Dylan as she claimed to be.

She drooped, shoulders sagging. Mehta reached across the table and pushed the plate of toast toward her. "You need to eat a little bit, Gwniera. Please."

She stared at the plate, and she took a slice of toast and raised it to her mouth. She nibbled at it, and then took a bigger bite. "I didn't see anything else." Her eyes darted from one to the other of them. "I didn't see anyone."

Will thought she was lying. *Why?* "You're sure? Only, the first man on scene said you were talking about a 'bloody kid,' to use his words. Do you remember saying that?"

"I don't remember." She said it, but weakly. "If I did say it, I was talking about Dylan. He just wouldn't listen to me. I begged him to share out that money, but he wouldn't listen."

Will let that sink in, hoping for more, but not getting it. "And you don't know what guns Evan might have inherited from his dad?"

"Just what you took. They'd all be there."

"We're looking particularly for a Lee-Enfield Mark 4. It wasn't among the guns we took from your house."

"Then Evan didn't have it."

"You're sure, Gwniera? You know guns. It'd be from the Second World War, passed down in the family. Could Dylan have had it?"

"Evan and Conway divided the guns when Carys moved out, the ones that were left. Conway must have gotten that one because I don't remember it, and I think I would." Her lips twisted. "It's time everything was sorted, Inspector." She took another bite of toast and swallowed it, then she looked across the table at Will. "I'm going to leave here now. Lisa won't stay, not without Dylan to hold her here. She was always more of a city girl. I'll want to be near Aeron, my grandson, and perhaps Merry, as well."

They waited, watching her think it out.

"The farm will have to go, but it should stay in the family. That was always important to them all, especially Lloyd and Carys. I'm going to talk to Lisa. I suppose she and little Aeron will inherit the land, but if she's financially sound, I think I can talk her around to selling the land to Conway for a price he can afford. He should have it, and now he has Terrwyn to farm it after he's done. There'd be no one else."

Will tried not to let his shock show. She needn't make big decisions when she was emotionally compromised. "You haven't had much time to think this out, Gwniera."

She shot him an angry look. "This isn't new. I've been thinking about it for years. It was never right, Evan having it all and Conway nothing. You won't know about this, but Mabyn and I were friends. We used to meet when the men were working, just to chat mostly. I like her and, because of what she tells me, I like Conway, too. He's a better man than Evan was." She shook her head, frustrated. "I tried to raise Dylan right. He understood about his dad, how wrong it was for him to embarrass me time and again with his women. But the money...that he didn't understand. He wanted nice things, too, for himself and for Lisa. He wanted to send Aeron to the best private schools. I had him talked into giving his sister a share of the investment money, but I couldn't get him to think beyond that." She paused. "That damn investment money. I wish it had never existed."

Lisa Bennett was still in bed when they arrived. They waited while the family liaison officer, a pretty brunette about Will's age, checked on her. She'd been playing with Dylan's son, a game involving superhero figurines and Duplo blocks.

"She wants to talk to you," she reported a few minutes later. "She'll be out in a few minutes." She left them in the living room and took Aeron with her to the kitchen to make tea.

When Lisa came out ten minutes later, she was dressed in jeans and a tee shirt, and her hair was combed back into a pony tail. She sat down on the sofa and pulled Aeron onto her lap. Her eyes were puffy and red, but otherwise, she looked very put-together for a woman who'd just lost her husband.

"Can you tell us about the day yesterday, Lisa?" Will began. It'd be his turn to at least make a start.

She didn't hesitate. "It was an ordinary day, after a week of stress. Having the memorial service over was a relief to us both. We could put the whole thing behind us once that was over and get on with our lives. Dylan went out to see what needed to be done on the farm. He came back for lunch, and then he went out again. There'd be a lot of work if he was to do it all himself now." It almost sounded as if she'd rehearsed the words and was now just happy to get it all out.

"Do you know where he was working? What he was doing?"

She shook her head. "I didn't know the details would be important at the time." Her voice broke, and she took a moment to regain control before going on. "Farming is just routine. I don't ask what he's doing every minute of every day." She stumbled over the words. "I *didn't* ask," she corrected herself, emphasizing the past tense. "I do know that he went over to his mother's place in the afternoon. That's where the main farm buildings are, so he's there more often than anyplace else."

"Did you know he intended to go to the old farmhouse, to do the weekly check on it?"

She shook her head again. "Things were confused with Evan gone so suddenly. We weren't involved in that rotation before. It was Evan and Conway who took it in turns to keep the old place up. If it'd been me, I'd have skipped it a week or two until we caught up with other things. The place wasn't going to fall apart in a week's time." She sounded resentful, as if the old place should be someone else's responsibility.

"Did Dylan seem worried about anything?"

Aeron wriggled on her lap, and she helped him down. "Go play with your action figures," she told him, with a little pat. She frowned at them. "He wondered how he was going to keep up with the farming by himself. He and his dad had expanded through the years, and they probably should have hired help before now. But if you're asking if he was afraid for his life, then no, not that I noticed. He did seem angry one day last week when he came home, but not afraid."

"Which day?"

"I don't remember now. He was short with me, and I didn't like it. I asked him what was wrong, but he said he didn't want to talk about it."

Will let that sit for a moment, but he couldn't think what more to ask. It was probably too late now to find out what had happened. "How did he feel about inheriting the farm?"

"He was excited about it, I think. He wanted to use some of the investment money to hire help, to expand even more." She nodded at Will. "He knew your new in-laws were going into organic farming, big time, and he thought it was the right way for us to go, too. He said it was the future."

"He hadn't talked that over with his dad?"

"His dad was all about his housing estate. That's all he talked about. He wouldn't have wanted to try to compete with the neighbors for business." She closed her eyes and sighed. "Evan did have some scruples."

"But that wouldn't have bothered Dylan?"

She shrugged, giving Will an embarrassed look. "We had more land. We'd have been a bigger operation. It sounds selfish now, but Dylan intended to go ahead with it."

Did that implicate the Bagley men in his murder? God, forbid.
"How did Dylan feel about his extended family? His uncle and cousins?"

"I don't think he thought of them much at all. He was young when his grandfather died. They'd been estranged since then."

"We've heard that his grandmother wanted him to share the investment money with his cousins, as well as his sister. Do you know anything about that?"

"Dylan mentioned it. He didn't want to do it, and Carys couldn't do it without his consent. That was in the terms of the trust."

They needed to get a look at that trust, to see all of its stipulations so they could understand how it was set up. Doing that might point them toward another suspect. "And you don't know if Dylan inherited any guns from his grandfather? A rifle?"

"If he did, I don't know about it. I told you before, I asked him not to keep them in the house once Aeron was born, and he agreed not to. If he wanted to do some shooting, he got a gun from his mother's house."

There didn't seem to be anything more they could ask. Will glanced at Mehta, who shrugged. "Can we have a look around your house, Lisa? We always do that when someone's been murdered, to see if there's anything that points to who did it."

"Knock yourselves out," she told them. She looked at the family liaison officer. "Will you watch Aeron for me again? I need to make some phone calls." She glanced at Will. "My parents need to know about Dylan. I didn't call them last night." She seemed resigned, not as devastated as Gwniera had been, but holding herself together with effort. Perhaps, Will thought, it was easier to lose a husband than it was a son.

Leaving her to make her calls, Will and Mehta pulled on gloves and took their time walking around the house. Not as large as Evan and Gwniera's house, it was comfortable and welcoming, more what Will would expect for a country home. Toys were scattered in nearly every room, books lay on side tables, and expensive electronic equipment filled shelves beneath a large flatscreen television. In the main bedroom, dirty clothes overflowed a hamper in the corner, and the unmade bed was rumpled, but underneath it all, the floors and tabletops were clean, if cluttered. Confirming what Lisa had told them, they found no evidence of guns in the house. They bagged and left a laptop computer for the techs that would arrive after them to confiscate. Nothing else caught their interest.

"What do you want to do?" Mehta asked Will as they jolted back down the rutted farm lane. Will hated to think what it was doing to the suspension on his little car.

He pulled to the side where the lane met the B4391, which wasn't much wider, and put the little car into park. "It's not quite noon. We could go into Shrewsbury for a chat with Carys and then stop in Welshpool to get alibis from Cassadee and Steffan Richards so we can cross them off our list, or we could go to Bala and see what Jenna and Aswtin were up to yesterday afternoon. And Jenna's boyfriend, what was his name?"

"Phylip Thomas," Mehta reminded him.

"Or we could talk to Conway again. Terrwyn, too. He's a kid. We know that Gwniera was screaming about a kid when Lew Griffiths got there."

"Terrwyn or Awstin," Mehta concluded. "She didn't want to tell us about that. She said she was talking about Dylan, but I don't think it was the truth."

"No, I thought she was making it up as she went." He thought it over, drumming his fingers on the steering wheel. "I think she might know who the murderer is, but she doesn't want to say. She probably saw him yesterday. A kid. Right then, she couldn't stop herself screaming it, but after she got home, she got control of herself. Maybe she thought it out and decided it was time to stop the feud, or time to start recognizing that Awstin is family, too, if it was him, no matter the circumstances."

"It'd be Terrwyn." Mehta stared out the windscreen. A hawk wheeled in circles in the field across from the road. "He'd have the gun. It'd have been passed down through the family."

"If Evan had been visiting Awstin, maybe he'd have given it to him," Will argued, his headache growing stronger. He didn't want it to be Awstin, not with the bright future the kid had waiting for him. But nor did he want it to be Terrwyn. "It's not impossible that Evan gave him that gun. He might have wanted to pass something on to him that made him feel a part of the family, at last."

"A bequest," Mehta murmured. "If it was a kid at all. Gwniera might honestly have been referring to Dylan when she said it. He was her own 'bloody kid.'"

Will gave him a dirty look. "Rather graphic, that, isn't it? She meant it literally? Of course, Dylan was bloody, right then. He'd been shot."

"Gwniera was frustrated with Dylan's selfishness. She'd tried to talk him into sharing the money with the rest of the family, an extended family that she'd reached out to and ended up liking. It sounds like Carys was onboard with that, too, but Dylan refused to consider sharing it with anyone other than his sister. Maybe Gwniera really was calling Dylan a 'bloody kid,' not literally, but because he might not have died if only he'd listened to her."

"Damn. I thought 'bloody kid' would get us somewhere. Now, I don't know." Will put the car in gear. "I say we talk to Conway now and maybe Jenna and Awstin afterwards. We can do them both and still be home in time to check you into the B&B for the night. We'll save Welshpool for tomorrow."

"We know Carys didn't kill them, and Steffan Richards would have no grudge against Dylan, so that seems reasonable to me. Let's get our main suspects interviewed first."

Chapter Twenty-Three

They found Conway in the sheep pens, coddling a half-grown lamb that looked sickly. Mabyn was bent over it with him, the two of them huddling together in a manner that looked almost intimate.

They looked surprised when they saw Will and Mehta. Conway straightened first, holding out a hand to his wife, who joined him. "We didn't hear your car," Conway commented. That wasn't surprising. The ewes and other lambs in the pens were bleating with concern, making a racket that made Will want to flee. The noise was worse than a crowded city street or a screaming rock concert.

"We just have a few more questions for you," Will told him. He kept a distance from the sheep, wanting to keep his shoes clean if he could. "Is Terrwyn here?"

They stiffened, both of them in unison. They tried to hide it. "He's at work in Llanfyllin now. He'll be back in an hour or so," Conway mumbled.

"We'll catch him later, then," Will said easily. He'd rather talk to Terrwyn alone, if he could, away from their protection. If they hurried this interview, maybe they could catch Terrwyn in Llanfyllin as he got off work.

"Would you like to come inside for a cup of tea?" Mabyn offered.

"This won't take long," Will told her. "I'd hate for you to have to interrupt what you're doing out here. Sick lamb?"

"She's lethargic and doesn't want to eat. We were just trying to decide if the cost of a vet was worth it."

Will nodded, wanting to put them at ease. "You'll have heard that Dylan was shot yesterday afternoon, too?"

Conway's mouth twisted in a grimace of sympathy. "I just talked to Gwniera. She'll be needing help with the livestock until she hires someone to do it. I've offered my help, and Terrwyn's, too."

"That was kind of you, especially considering the history between you." Will watched him carefully.

"Gwniera was never a part of that," Conway admitted. "She tried afterward to keep in touch, especially before Rhosyn died. The two of them were close, living all the way out here as we do. She reached out to Mabyn, too, when she and I married. Evan didn't know."

"So, the problems were only between you and Evan?"

Conway stood a minute, thinking. "The problem was mine, Inspector. Most of it, anyway. I was angry that Evan just took the land and didn't give me a minute's thought. He knew how I felt, and I think he felt guilty about it. Maybe he imagined more animosity on my part than was really there. I don't know. I accepted long ago that I would have to work hard just to get by, all the while watching my brother flaunt his money." He hesitated. "There was more to it than just the land, though. I couldn't approve of the way Evan treated Gwniera, either, as if she was just there to take care of the house and her feelings didn't matter. He treated her like a live-in maid, not a wife."

Will let that settle for a moment, hoping for more. "Who do you think killed Evan?"

"Someone's angry husband? That was our first thought."

"And now?"

"It's hardly likely to be an angry husband now that Dylan's been killed, too." He looked at Mabyn, again with shared intimacy. "We've talked about it. We really have no idea who it could be."

"Where were the two of you yesterday around six in the afternoon?"

"We were in Shrewsbury, Inspector. We'd brought my mother back here for the memorial service, and we kept her here with us overnight." His shoulders slumped and he looked at them with empty eyes. "She'd lost a son, inspectors. Her firstborn. No matter that Evan had faults, and he had many, he was always the love of her life." He sounded wistful. "She stayed with us until mid-afternoon, and then she asked to go home, so we drove her to Shrewsbury. We stopped for a dinner at a restaurant before we took her back to her retirement centre. Her treat, to thank us for fetching her. The centre can verify what time she checked back in with them. They do keep track of things like that."

He shouldn't have, but Will felt a surge of relief. If they could cross Conway and Mabyn off the list, along with Cassadee and Steffan Richards, that would narrow their suspect list considerably. Now he'd have to tread lightly, though. "And Terrwyn? He didn't go with you?"

Mabyn answered him. "Terrwyn is a grown-up, Inspector. He has his own life now, even if he does still live here with us. I'm sure that he was eager to go hang out with his friends after being with his family all day on Saturday, but we didn't ask. We don't want him thinking that we're checking up on him."

"No, of course not." His mobile vibrated in his pocket and he pulled it out nodding to Mehta. Caller ID showed Marcus Robb, the head of forensics. *He must have results on the gun.* That was fast. He'd call him back as soon as they finished with Conway and Mabyn.

Mehta had taken over while he was distracted. "Your daughters didn't come for the memorial service on Saturday? Evan was their uncle, after all."

"No, Eriana was on a flight to New York, and Evie had a photography gig that day, another wedding. I'm not sure they'd have come anyway, but they were both busy so there was no question about it."

He let that go. "Can we ask again about the guns, Conway? We understand that your father had quite a few guns, and the registrations were never transferred to anyone else after his death."

"An oversight, I'm sure," Conway said. "My mother kept most of them in the old house until she moved. We just never thought to change the registrations."

"When she left, you divided them with Evan?"

"Mother went through them and decided who would get the more valuable ones. Once that was done, she let us choose from the ones that remained, first me, and then Evan, each week, until they were gone."

"Who got the Lee-Enfield Mark 4? That would have been a sort of family heirloom, a gun your grandfather would have used in the Second World War."

"Is that the gun that killed Evan and Dylan?" Mabyn interrupted, her eyes suddenly sharply focused.

"Yes, we believe so." No need to tell her they knew it for sure, nor that they had the gun in their possession now. Mehta addressed Conway again. "Did you get that one, or did Evan?"

But Conway evaded the question. "I'm not sure. It must have been Evan. If I had it, you'd have found it when you took my other guns away."

"You don't know if you were given it?" Will butted in. He wanted to sound incredulous, to make Conway re-think his easy evasion. "I'd think you'd know which guns you got and which you didn't, especially one that would be considered a family heirloom."

"There were quite a few guns, Inspector, and several of them had been in the family for years. I couldn't be expected to remember every one of them." His eyes slid to the side, toward the sickly lamb.

Will was sure that he was lying, but, of course, he couldn't prove it. "Okay, we'll let you get back to your lamb. We'll catch Terrwyn in Llanfyllin." He tried not to make it sound like a threat. He suspected they'd call and warn Terrwyn as soon as he and Mehta drove away, but there was nothing he could do about that.

He called Robb back as soon as they'd settled back into the car. "You must have results on the gun already. That was fast."

"Yes, well, you caught us at a good time, and it wasn't difficult. The gun was wiped clean, not a trace of a fingerprint of any kind. It would have taken some time to clean it that well, so my guess is that it was cleaned ahead of time and then your shooter wore gloves when he handled it afterward."

"No DNA?"

"You couldn't be that lucky. The message was scratched on with a blade, probably just a pocketknife. Sorry I couldn't be more help."

297

"No, that's what we expected. I wish he'd left us something definite, but you can't always get lucky."

"It was definitely the murder weapon for both murders," Robb told him. "That's the only good news I have. Rifling in the barrel matched the bullets retrieved from the two bodies. There were no prints on the bullets, either."

"We figured that, but it's good to have confirmation. Thanks, Marcus." He cut the call and looked at Mehta. "No joy."

They decided not to return to the cottage for lunch, keeping in mind that Llanfyllin and Bala were in opposite directions and would take them the rest of the afternoon. They were tired from the late night and the early morning, and they agreed that an early evening would be more welcome than a mid-day stop. Will liked working with Mehta. More often than not, it felt as if they were in synch with each other. He never had to argue his case with Mehta like he had to with Beth or Ian. Notley, of course, had been a nightmare, opposing everything Will said as a matter of course. He'd always feel guilty about his role in Notley's early retirement, but it was still a relief not to have to struggle through cases with the man.

The drive to Llanfyllin took twenty minutes, giving them time to stop by a bakery for a sweet bun to eat in the car as they waited for Terrwyn to get off shift at the auto repair shop. They spotted his motorbike parked at the edge of the customer lot and settled in to watch for him to come out of the garage.

He emerged fifteen minutes later, striding quickly toward his motorbike.

Will stuffed the last of his pastry into his mouth and grabbed the door handle. "Let's go."

They caught up with him as he was fastening his helmet. He stopped when he saw them and took it back off. "I was expecting you."

"Want a late lunch?" Will offered. The sweet buns wouldn't stave off starvation until dinner that night, after all, and he doubted that Terrwyn had the extra money to treat himself to a meal out very often.

Terrwyn thought it over before answering, suspicious of their motives, but allowing the lure of a meal to win in the end. "Okay. There's a café just up the street."

They bought hamburgers and chips, with beers all around. Terrwyn relaxed as he sipped his drink, wiping foam from his upper lip where a mustache had begun to shadow the skin. He turned curious eyes toward Mehta. "You'll want to know if I have an alibi for yesterday afternoon."

Mehta nodded. "That's part of it anyway. We need to know where everyone was when Dylan was shot. Standard procedure."

"You seem to catch me without every time." Terrwyn took another long gulp of beer. "I went over early to help with the chores. After lunch with my grandmother, I stayed home and hung out by myself. Mum and Dad had gone to take her home, and there were no other chores pressing that couldn't wait until Dad came back. I listened to some music and then I played some video games. I went for a ride on my bike later in the afternoon, nowhere special, but just cruising on the backroads and in the fields. You know how it is? Wind in my hair and not a care in the world."

"Would anyone have seen you?" Mehta wanted to know. "Maybe a neighbor or a friend?"

"I don't think so. Not that I was aware of, anyway. I'll admit that I rode along the back side of the farm by the cliffs. It's fun, that. A little challenge. And I can do it now that Evan's not there to object."

"You rode back where we found Evan's body?"

"No, not that far. I'm not supposed to ride in the forestland. My aunt rides her horses there, and I'd startle them if I came upon them unexpectedly. She's asked me not to, and I'm happy to comply."

"You speak to your aunt, then?"

"My mum does mostly, but I see her once in a while. When I first got my bike, I took it out there and she saw me and that's when she asked me not to ride there. She was nice about it." He glanced up as the barmaid dropped the plates on the table. He looked at his burger greedily and reached for a chip, plopping it into his mouth.

"What time was it that you were riding your bike, then?" Mehta asked carefully. Will could tell that he was trying to keep it casual, to connect with the boy. "Did you see anyone else out there?"

299

"You mean the murderer?" Terrwyn picked up his burger and looked it over. Will thought he was tempted to lie, maybe to describe a fictional person in order to divert their attention away from himself. He saw Will watching and made his decision. "Nah, I didn't see anyone else. I wasn't really looking. That doesn't mean no one was there, though. I was just watching the path so I wouldn't crash my bike."

"Did you like Dylan, Terrwyn?" Mehta's voice was soft.

Terrwyn chewed the bite of hamburger he had in his mouth. He swallowed hard. "I didn't know him very well."

"How would you describe him?" Mehta urged him. "Like, if we didn't know him, what would you say about him?"

Terrwyn thought about that as he took another large bite of his hamburger and chewed. "He was taller than me, and his hair was darker. He was older, too. He liked flash things."

"Like what?"

"Like his truck. It was nearly new, but I heard he was looking to buy something even nicer." He shrugged. "My mates from the garage told me. His clothes were nice, when he wasn't out working, and he hired work done on the barns and his house, rather than doing it himself. He and Lisa went out a lot, into town for movies and for nice dinners."

"Were you jealous of him?"

Terrwyn snorted. "Why? Because he had stuff?"

"Because he had stuff your father probably couldn't afford." Mehta was choosing his words carefully.

"It wasn't right," Terrwyn shot back. His mouth clamped shut. He struggled to control himself and failed. "My dad deserved more than he got. Maybe now he'll get his share."

"What do you mean by that?"

"Who else is going to keep that farm going? Aeron? He's just a baby."

It wasn't untrue. "When did you see Dylan last, Terrwyn?"

Again, the boy hesitated, as if tempted to lie. His eyes wandered before he admitted, "I talked to him a few days ago."

"Where was that?"

"On the road. He was passing by our house, and I flagged him down."

"Why?"

He bit at his lip. "I asked him about the investment money, okay?"

"You wanted a share?"

"We all did, but I didn't tell him that. I just asked if he'd share it with my dad now. I know Grandmother was in favor of that, so I thought I could talk him around, make him see it'd be the fair thing to do after all these years."

"What did he say?"

"He said no, that if our grandfather had wanted Dad to have some of the money, he'd have written the trust differently."

"And that made you mad," Mehta concluded quietly.

"Yeah, it did. But it didn't make me murder him." Terrwyn glared at him defiantly.

Mehta nodded. He took a moment to eat a couple bites of his own hamburger, allowing Terrwyn to calm down. "I know you shoot for sport, Terrwyn," he said finally. "Do you remember a gun your grandfather owned, a Lee-Enfield Mark 4?"

"No, I don't," Terrwyn said, too quickly, Will thought. "Is that the gun that killed them?"

"We believe so." Mehta stuck with their official line. "It was registered to your grandfather, but it wasn't among the guns we confiscated after your uncle's murder."

"Maybe my grandmother sold it," he suggested. "Or someone gave it away."

It was possible, Will thought, as they finished their meals. He doubted it was sold, but perhaps it had been given as a gift to an illegitimate son who had finally connected with his father.

It took them another forty minutes to drive to Bala, with a quick stop at the cottage to say hi to Bronwyn and use the toilet. They booked a room for Mehta at the New Inn B&B, and they arrived in Bala by mid-afternoon, in plenty of time to catch Jenna when she got off her shift at Spar.

No one answered the door, so they waited in the car, hoping that she was working the same shift as before and that she hadn't made plans for when she finished it. For all they knew, she had a date with Phyllip Thomas that afternoon. They hadn't checked, but they assumed he'd be working, too.

They were just debating whether to go to the bank and tackle Thomas first when Awstin walked up the street. He turned into the front garden and unlocked the cottage door.

Will looked at Mehta, who nodded. "Even better," he said, and they slipped out of the car and hurried to the cottage. Mehta pounded on the door.

Awstin opened it almost immediately. He was wearing jeans and a black tee shirt, and he held a packet of crisps in his hand. He straightened when he recognized them. "Inspectors Cooper and uh…"

"Mehta," Jay supplied. "Could we come in and ask a few more questions?"

"Is this about my dad? Or my half-brother?" Awstin stood back and waved them inside, glancing out the door before he shut it. "I know Dylan was killed yesterday, too."

"It's about both of them," Will told him.

Awstin sat in a chair, leaving the sofa for Will and Mehta to share. He watched them with alert, wary eyes. Why? They had so many questions to sort out.

"We know you'd been seeing your dad recently. How was that going, really? I mean, after all those years of him ignoring you, I wonder how it'd feel when you finally got to spend time with him?" Mehta's voice was reasonable, inviting confidences.

Awstin responded as they hoped he would. "It was awkward at first. I know my mum said he asked to meet me, but I was the one who reached out to him, not the other way around. I wanted to try to get to know him before I went off to university. My mum told me about him when I was growing up, and she never made him sound like a bad person. I figured that he might want to meet me, too, but maybe he didn't know how to make that happen." The boy was well-spoken for someone his age.

"What did you think of him once you started spending time together? Was he what you expected?"

Awstin gave that some thought before answering. Obviously, he didn't want to implicate himself in the murders by expressing a dislike for his father. "I liked him, for the most part. He was better-looking than I expected, and I could see why my mum was attracted to him. He was interested in me. He asked lots of questions and I thought he really wanted to know what I was like."

"What didn't you like about him?"

Awstin wasn't fooled. He'd said he liked his dad, *for the most part*. Now he'd have to come up with an explanation. "He didn't want me to know his family. I asked if we could get together with Dylan, too, and he made excuses. It was as if he wanted to keep me separate from them." He looked at Mehta earnestly. "I didn't mind. I understood why he felt that way."

"Would you have liked to meet Dylan, then?" Mehta said quietly.

"I wanted to. I had a brother and a sister, and I didn't know anything about them. Wouldn't you be curious, if you were me?"

Will tried to put himself in Awstin's place. He'd taken his own siblings for granted; they had never been close. Would he have wanted to meet them, though, if they'd lived apart? *Probably*, he admitted to himself.

"Did your dad ever give you gifts, Awstin?" Mehta pushed on. "Maybe a family heirloom, to make you feel a part of things?"

"He gave me things sometimes. Nice things that Mum couldn't have afforded – a TV, two game systems, some games. He went with me to Oxford, to look at the campus there. I think he was proud of me and hoped I'd make it into one of the great schools."

"I was thinking more of something that'd been passed down through the family," Mehta prompted him.

Awstin shook his head. "Nothing like that." His bright, intelligent eyes darted from Mehta to Will. "Is something missing?"

"No, nothing that we know of." Mehta chose not to explain the question for him. "Do you have any pictures of the two of you together?"

Awstin reached for his mobile, lying on a side table. He nudged it on and scrolled, then held it out. "We took these a couple of weeks ago, just before he was killed."

"Would you mind copying those to my phone?" Will asked, holding his own out.

They waited while Awstin accomplished his task and returned Will's mobile.

"Can we ask where you were on Monday afternoon?"

"I had class until about half three, and then I spent some time in the library studying. I have to do well on my exams this year. Mum was out with Phylip, so I came home around six and scrounged around in the fridge for something to eat. She'd left me some casserole from Sunday." He swallowed. "We went to Dad's memorial, you know, Mum and I. It hit us both hard, that."

"We saw you there," Will informed him. "Do you know where your mother and Phylip went on Sunday afternoon?" They'd might as well get alibis from the whole family.

He shrugged. "They usually go out to dinner and then over to his place to watch the telly or play cards." *No joy there.*

"Can anyone verify what time you were in the library, Awstin?"

"I doubt it. I was studying alone, and you know how it is. They don't have time to keep track of everyone who's in there unless they check out a book, and I didn't."

"Anyone see you come home?"

He shook his head. "I wish I could say yes, but I can't."

Chapter Twenty-Four

Mehta had joined them for dinner at the cottage, and they'd stayed up late, looking at their wall and debating the truth of each suspect's statements.

"We have to eliminate Conway and Mabyn from our list," Mehta pointed out, setting his small glass of Famous Grouse on the side table. They'd been going through a lot of it. Will would have to stock up next time he was near an off-license. "They have rock-solid alibis for Dylan's murder, at least. I think we have to assume that the same person killed both of them."

"The same gun did, at least," Will agreed. He tipped some more whiskey into his glass. "Unless it was a conspiracy, it follows that the same person killed them both."

"I could have seen Gwniera killing Evan, but I can't see her shooting her own son."

"She was strange when we talked to her, though, wasn't she?" Will frowned. "All that about wishing the money had never existed and moving away now, after all the years of putting up with Evan. Maybe it's the shock of the deaths, but didn't she seem a little erratic to you this time?"

Mehta took a meditative sip of whiskey. "I'd say she finally reached her breaking point. She was too stubborn to leave Evan before. I'd guess that the horses were just an excuse to stay and make him pay for all his affairs through the years. Think about it. She wanted to punish him for his philandering, right? He couldn't get rid of her without having to pay her off, so she stayed to be a thorn in his side. It probably got to be an obsession; her life's purpose became a crusade to make Evan miserable."

"I can see that," Will agreed. "But losing her son wasn't what she'd bargained for, was it?"

"I think she tried to take Dylan away from Evan as best she could. She made sure that Dylan knew she was hurt by Evan's affairs, tried to create him in her image, rather than his dad's. I'm sure she was there urging Dylan to oppose Evan's housing estate, whispering in his ear behind the scenes. And that's why she denied that Evan and Awstin were developing a relationship. She saw creating a wedge between Dylan and Evan as another way of punishing him for the hurt she'd suffered through the years, and she didn't want to think that Evan would just turn to his other son as a replacement for the one she was taking away."

Mehta's psychology degree paid off in cases like this. What he said made sense. "She claims not to have remembered the gun being in Evan's possession, or Dylan's. Was she lying?"

"She might have been. I think she lied about something, but I'm not sure what. It's like she said. She wants the feud over and peace in the family. She likes Conway and Mabyn. She might protect the killer to make that happen."

"Would she protect Terrwyn?" Will ventured. "He admits having been on the property that afternoon. He has no alibi."

"That 'bloody kid'? She might. If she was close to Mabyn like she says she is, maybe she's generous enough to let her keep her son, despite it all." Mehta thought about it. "She wrecked her own life, so maybe she sees it as an atonement to give Mabyn the life she never got to have. A faithful, loving husband, devoted kids…I could see it, an unselfish act to clear her conscience."

"Terrwyn would have done it for the money?"

"Terrwyn would have done it for his father, not for himself. He made it obvious that he loves his dad and hated seeing him struggle. It might be motive enough."

"Awstin doesn't have much of an alibi, either, but I can't see any of the girls doing it. They live too far away, for one thing. I suppose we should check, though."

"Meredith was here for the memorial service. She might have stayed over. She had something to gain from the two deaths, too."

"We'll check. And then we need to talk to Carys. She can tell us about the trust, who gets the money now."

Will's mobile rang just after they'd seen Mehta out the door that evening. He'd turned after closing the door and pulled Bronwyn to him, kissing her hard and nudging her toward the bedroom when, unexpectedly, it had vibrated on the table and started singing out the Harry Potter theme. He tried to ignore it, but Bronwyn's giggle broke the kiss, and he released her, shaking his head.

"I'm letting it go. It can't be that important."

"It might be Lark," Bronwyn said, pushing him away with both hands. "Just check. She'll have to be in bed soon and there won't be time to call her back."

He rolled his eyes and scowled. Walking over to the table, he grabbed the mobile and activated the screen. "My mother," he grumbled. "What does she want now?"

"Call her back," Bronwyn suggested, "and then you'll know."

"I can call her later. Tomorrow," he amended. Bronwyn was disheveled from sitting around all evening, looking sexy, and all he wanted now was to continue what they'd started a few minutes earlier.

"It'll only take a few minutes," Bronwyn pointed out.

"And it'll totally ruin the mood," he grumbled back. "You know how it is with her."

"Take Daisy out for her evening stroll while you call her back." She tossed him a grin. "I'll be waiting for you."

Still grumbling under his breath, he opened the door and followed Daisy out into the back garden. He could see the overgrown grasses in the field across the ditch, blowing in the breeze. Clouds scuttled across the sky, moving fast, and he wondered whether the wind meant a change in seasons coming sooner rather than later.

He watched Daisy cross the ditch and emerge into the field. He liked Bronwyn's new self-confidence, and he felt he could take at least some of the credit for it. Sure, he knew that she felt valued at her job, that she was proud of carrying on St. Melangell's mission, as she put it, but he was glad that she now trusted him with her emotions, that she knew him well enough that she could flirt with him without feeling the self-consciousness she'd had early in their relationship.

He lit his phone and touched the call icon beside his mother's name.

"Hello, William," she said when she answered. "I thought it was late enough that I'd get you if I called." She sounded imperious, and he wondered if she'd been drinking. "I'm glad you called back."

"I was working when you called," he lied. "We're done for the night now. What is it you need?"

"I thought we should make arrangements for Lark."

He frowned, but he couldn't ignore the sudden hope that surged through his mind. "What arrangements?"

"For the wedding," she said, crushing the thoughts that had sprung up with her previous words. "I know you think we can stop by the school and bring her with us, but that just isn't convenient with your father being the way he is."

What? They'd be driving right by. *How hard could it be?* "It's my wedding day, mother. We have the rehearsal in the morning. There's no time for me to go fetch her from school. Can't you help me out, just this one last time?"

"It won't be just one last time, will it? I know how it'll be," she snapped. "I'll be driving back and forth to Chepstow every weekend because you have a case to work and no time for a child."

"It's my wedding day," Will repeated slowly, trying for patience. He could feel his temper ready to explode, and he fought to contain it. "How about if I book you a room in Chepstow? You can go on Friday night and spend the night, then drive up from there the next morning. That'll make it an easier trip. I'll book a room for you here, too, maybe a B&B in Llanfyllin or Welshpool." He wondered if there were any.

"That way you'll have a place to go and relax, and I'll be here to help with father once you arrive." He thought fast. "I know it must feel overwhelming to you, trying to travel with Father, but I know you can manage it. You've always been very capable."

"So, you aren't willing to help out," she spat back. "We may have to skip the event entirely, then."

The phone went silent. Will held it out and looked. The call had been cut.

He fought the urge to throw the phone down into the ditch, choosing instead to kick at a rubber toy Daisy had left in the lawn, sending it flying toward the field. He clenched his teeth. *Why does she always have to make demands? Can't she just give me some peace for my wedding?* Now, he supposed, he'd have to somehow get to Chepstow and get Lark on the Friday night, the night he'd planned his stag party in Caernarfon with his friends. He couldn't ask Bronwyn to go get her again; this time, she'd have Margred here, celebrating her own final night as a single girl. Maybe Lark could skip the last day of school, and Bronwyn could drive down earlier in the day and bring her back? But that'd be putting it all on Bronwyn again, and he couldn't keep doing that.

He'd put off trying to resolve the problem. Maybe his mother had been drinking, and if he ignored her, maybe she'd come to her senses the next morning and try to be more cooperative. He could only hope.

Will refused to think about it as he and Mehta drove to Shrewsbury the next morning, a windy autumn day that portended rain to come. Will hoped it would come and go before the wedding, but time was getting short. The forecast said a chance of rain on Saturday. They'd just have to make the best of things, no matter the weather. *Their wedding day.* He still got the jitters when he allowed himself to think of it.

Carys Bennett opened her door to them and offered tea, in the porcelain cups, with milk, sugar, and a packet of biscuits, set on a decorative plate. She seemed happy to see them, perhaps lonely for company in her lovely flat.

They expressed their sympathy for the loss of her son and her grandson and watched tears streak her papery cheeks as she dabbed at them with a tissue.

"We'd like to ask you more about the trust," Will began, as Mehta pulled out his pad of paper and pen to take notes. "You told us before that it was a complicated set-up. Can you tell us who inherits what now that both Evan and Dylan are gone?"

"Gwniera tells me that the money is the cause of everything that's happened," she quavered, "and I don't disagree. When Lloyd decided to give our land to Evan, that started it all." She peered at them through watery blue eyes. "It hurt me to see Conway struggle for money. I'll admit that now."

It probably hurt more to see Evan and Dylan murdered. "I'm sure that wasn't what you had in mind when the trust was written up," he said.

"No, of course not." She settled back into her rocker, getting comfortable. "Evan was the spoiled one, though. I can see it, looking back. He was good at getting whatever he wanted, and he always wanted the best of everything. We gave it to him, too. Clothes, cars, money. He'd make demands, and we denied him very little. We were proud of him. He was a good-looking boy, full of charm. I guess he charmed us, too." She bit off the words with some bitterness now. "Conway was a quieter boy. He was gentle, undemanding. He did what we expected, and we never quite noticed him the way we did Evan."

It was a sad confession, a mother trying to explain why she favored one son over another. *Really, there's no excuse,* Will told himself. Neither he nor George had been favored in his family, growing up. No one had. Maybe that hadn't been a bad thing, after all.

"When we wrote the trust, the boys were still quite young. Evan had made it clear that he wanted to farm, and Conway leaned that way, too. We knew they would both struggle if we split the land in half, so we felt the only option was to give it to one of them and hope that the other would find a different career path. Evan was the logical choice because he had a son who could farm it after him." She looked at Will, her pale eyes far away. "We didn't mean to leave Conway out. When it became clear that he wanted to farm, too, we took money out for him to buy an

310

abandoned property that adjoined our land. It wasn't much, but it gave him a house of his own and a few acres of land."

"Evan got an equal amount? The money to build his house?"

"Well, yes. All of that happened before Lloyd passed. We were still farming our land then. It wasn't Evan's yet. We assumed we'd go on farming it for years to come, with Evan's help and maybe Conway's, too."

"Why didn't you compensate Conway for his share of the land out of the investment money?" That would seem logical to Will.

Carys shook her head. "We'd set it up so that Evan and whichever of us survived the other would manage that money. It wasn't meant to be spent. Lloyd felt that too many voices would only lead to quarrels."

"And whose voice controls it now?"

"Mine," Carys told them. "I am the sole survivor of the three of us, so now I get to decide what's to be done. Lisa and Aeron will inherit the land. There's nothing to be done about that; they are Dylan's heirs. But I will manage the investment money from now on."

"What do you intend to do, if I may ask?" Will encouraged her softly. He was sure that she'd thought it through already.

"I'll keep enough to maintain my home here for the remainder of my life. The rest I will sell off. Gwniera is right when she says the money was the cause of all the trouble, the feud and the deaths, too. It's time it was gone from our lives. I intend to give Conway half of the money, which will enable him to buy more land if he wants to. Gwniera says that Lisa will sell him the family farm if he wants it, and I would like to encourage that to happen. The other half will be divided among my grandchildren."

"Does that include Awstin?"

She looked at him sharply. "I told you before that Evan never had a relationship with that boy."

"But he did," Will contradicted her. He pulled his mobile from his pocket. "Look. I have pictures." He held the phone out so that she could see.

She reached out and took it in her withered hands, staring at the pictures as the silence stretched. "He's a handsome boy," she said at last. She returned the phone to Will. "I'm glad he got to know Evan."

And perhaps she was. "Thank you, Carys," Will said as they gathered their things. "For what it's worth, I think you're doing the right thing by your son and your grandchildren."

"I hope so, Inspector. I'm just tired now, and I can't keep worrying over it."

"I hope she finds the peace she's looking for," Will commented as they drove away afterwards.

"I'm sure that she will. She loves her family. It'll be nice now for her to see those who are left prospering. The guilt she was feeling for all those years will be behind her now."

"We're no closer to arresting someone, are we?"

Mehta stared out the windscreen, straight ahead. Will suspected he was seeing nothing. "We may never make an arrest in this case," he said slowly. "Maybe it'd be for the best if we never did."

Will's head jerked around to stare at him. He found himself without words.

"Watch the road," Mehta admonished him.

Traffic clogged the main streets of Welshpool that day, but they found parking only a short distance from the bank. Will maneuvered the MGF into the tight space, thankful that he wasn't driving Bronwyn's Land Rover.

They requested time with Cassadee Richards and waited twenty minutes before she appeared, looking none too happy to see them again. They followed her back into her office, and she shut the door.

"I told you my affair with Evan ended before he was murdered," she spat at them almost before they were seated. "Now Steffan is gone. You've ruined my life, and for no reason."

Will didn't think it prudent to point out that she'd ruined her own marriage; they'd only brought her transgressions out into the open. "We won't keep you long, Ms. Richards. Can you tell us what you were doing on Sunday afternoon, around five to six o'clock in the evening?"

"What? Was Evan murdered a second time?"

"Evan's son Dylan was murdered."

There was a moment of silence, and when she spoke, her voice was quieter. "I'm sorry to hear it, but it's nothing to do with me. I didn't even know the lad."

The 'lad' was near to her own age, but again, Will didn't think it necessary to say so. "We just need to cross you off our list, if we can."

"I was at home, clearing out the rest of Steffan's stuff. He's gone off on his own; I don't know where."

"You were on your own?"

"Sorry, I've no one to verify my alibi, Inspector." She frowned. "Wait. You said around five?"

He nodded.

"Steffan stopped by and picked up the stuff I bagged up for him," she said triumphantly. "The neighbor saw him. I remember it because we were fighting, yelling some, and she came out and grabbed her little boy away from the door."

"Can we get her name and number?"

"I don't have a number for her, but her first name is Stella. I don't know more than that. She lives next door. You can find her."

They did find her. She opened her door and looked at their warrant cards, and then she began. "I very nearly called you to come and stop them. The way they were yelling obscenities at each other, one after another, I was sure one of them would end up in hospital, or worse." She looked hopefully at them. "Did one of them do something? Only, I could see either of them getting themselves arrested, the way they were carrying on."

At the end of the day, they called both Gwniera and Meredith. Both of them insisted that Meredith had left for Bangor on Sunday morning. No one had reported seeing her in the area that day and, considering that it was a long drive, they concluded that both were telling the truth. They marked Meredith off their suspect list, too.

Chapter Twenty-five

That evening, they started taking down their murder wall, intending to move it to Caernarfon the next day. The case had stalled, so they were taking it to the station, where Bowers would go over it minutely, asking questions they probably hadn't anticipated, and then it'd probably be classified as unsolved unless new evidence showed up.

Will didn't like the thought of leaving it that way, but nothing they could think to do was moving them ahead, and truthfully, he liked all the suspects who remained and didn't like to think that any of them might have done it. He already knew that Mehta felt the same. He just hoped that the likeability of their suspects wasn't why they weren't finding the evidence they needed to convict one of them. Bowers wouldn't be pleased that the first case Will had handled from Llangynog hadn't resulted in an arrest.

He'd have liked to have left the wall for a few more days, but he was well-aware that Bronwyn would like her living room back to normal before Margred came to visit, and in the off-chance that his parents came to see the cottage, they'd send Lark off to Canada immediately if they saw the living room wall decorated with murder suspects rather than fine art. He wondered if he'd ever escape his mother's threats. *Probably not until Lark was grown and able to make her own decisions*, he decided, discouraged. He'd tried so hard to sway his mother around to letting him have her, but still her criticism of him persisted and marrying Bronwyn hadn't seemed to help as much as he'd hoped it might.

Mehta stood by the wall, removing the sticky notes, photos, and string, and placing it all on the coffee table in piles: victims, people eliminated from suspicion, and active suspects. They discussed it as they worked.

"The three young women all go in the eliminated pile," Will said firmly. "None of them were here for either murder, if their alibis are to be believed. We didn't check up on them this last time, but I just don't feel like any of them were ever serious suspects. What did they have to gain?"

"Money," Mehta reminded him. "Meredith would probably have gotten some anyway, so she had no motive for murdering her brother. But the other two, they could have hoped for a share if both Evan and Dylan were eliminated. We know their grandmother wants to split it among them all now. She probably told them she was in favor of selling off most of the investments and dividing that money up, but that Dylan was opposed."

"Or like Terrwyn, they were tired of seeing their dad struggle," Bronwyn put in. She usually just watched, but she didn't want them putting the girls in a different light from their half-brother. She'd miss these nightly sessions after Will and Mehta left. It had been fun watching the case develop.

"I still think we eliminate them," Will argued. "They may have had motive, but none of them were here in the area at the time of the murders."

"We should have Quigley check their alibis," Mehta suggested, and that eliminated the need for more discussion. They left them on the active suspect list, at least temporarily.

"Conway and Mabyn didn't have an alibi for Evan, but they did for Dylan. Are we assuming the same person killed both of them?"

"Same gun; likely the same killer," Mehta said. He thought it over for a minute, stooping to pick up his glass of whiskey. "We can probably eliminate them," he said finally, "unless we get more evidence that points their way."

"There's the issue of who owned that gun," Will pointed out. "It would have been either Evan or Conway that got it from Carys, unless she gave it to one of her grandchildren for some reason. I think she was lying about not knowing who got it, but I can't see Evan or Dylan having it. They certainly didn't kill themselves. If Evan was going to pass it down to a son, Dylan would have been a more obvious choice than Awstin. He, at least, probably knew his maternal grandfather and would have heard the war stories through the years."

"You're saying that Conway inherited it, then?"

"He must have done." He thought, reaching out for Bronwyn's hand, squeezing it and letting go. "Carys admits that as years went by, she realized that Conway was cheated out of a fair share of the inheritance when Lloyd died. I think she ended up favoring Conway in other, smaller, ways, trying to make up for it. I could see her giving him that gun. It would have had sentimental value to her, at least, and probably to him, as well. It follows that Conway had to know what happened with that gun, so he's either protecting himself or he's protecting one of his kids. If we're eliminating the two girls, that leaves Terrwyn."

"Are we ready to talk about Terrwyn?" Mehta reached for the photo on the wall.

"He has no alibi for either murder. He admits to being nearby on the afternoon that Dylan was shot. He has a motive."

"I was surprised that he told us he'd ridden his bike out there that day," Mehta confessed. "He must have thought someone had seen him."

"He also admitted to arguing with Dylan about the money," Will pointed out. "He was very open about it all, volunteering details that he had to know would make him look suspicious."

"Maybe he's playing with us, taunting us. He knows we probably don't have any evidence, and without something definite, we can't arrest him."

"He's young enough to be arrogant," Will agreed. "That alone makes me hope we do find something to pin him down, if it's him." He hesitated. "Maybe it's not arrogance, though. I didn't see it that way when we talked to him. Maybe he's just afraid someone did see him, someone like Gwniera maybe, so he's admitting to being there rather than being caught in a lie."

"He definitely goes in our 'active suspect' pile," Mehta concluded. "I like the kid, though, and if he did it, he did it for love of his father, not for selfishness on his part."

"A young man's motive," Bronwyn murmured.

They looked at her. "What did you say?" Will asked.

"Young people are more likely to justify their actions by seeing them from just one perspective rather than the whole picture. From what he's said, it's obvious that Terrwyn is angry that his dad's had to struggle through life. If that anger has festered enough to become an obsession, that would have been a good enough motive for him. What I want to say, though, is that he wouldn't have thought it all through before he acted, if he did it. He wouldn't think about the consequences that'd follow later. If Terrwyn ends up in prison, that'll destroy Conway. You know it will." She focused on Will, pleading with her eyes. "But even if Terrwyn gets away with the crimes, if he actually did it, they know because of the gun, and that will destroy them, too."

"Conway and Mabyn would protect him," Will mentioned. "They'd pretend to know nothing about the gun if they thought Terrwyn had done it. Without them admitting he had access to that gun, we can't prove anything."

"But that'll make no difference to them. They'll know."

Mehta was nodding. "I like him for it, but, as you say, we have no evidence to prove it, at least not now. In the end, maybe his parents' knowing what he did will be punishment enough." He waited, but when no one said anything, he moved toward the other side of their wall. "Let's go on with this side and see what we come up with."

"We're eliminating the Richards," Will said. "Unless the motive was to keep them from cashing in the investments, they had no reason to kill Dylan once Evan was gone. I suppose they couldn't know that Dylan also intended to cash them in, but I doubt they'd kill two people just to make her look good to her bosses."

"I agree," said Mehta, dumping their notes onto the discard pile. "Now, let's take the easy one. Meredith?"

"She'd benefit more if she'd let Dylan live. He was going to share the investment money equally with her, after Carys' portion was taken out. Now it'll be shared at least seven ways."

"Conway, Evie, Eriana, Terrwyn, Lisa, Carys, and Meredith. That's seven. We agree that she's a non-suspect then?" Mehta added her photo to the pile. "Lisa?"

"She had no motive," Will said. "Dylan was worth more to her alive than dead, and by all accounts, they had a happy marriage."

Mehta nodded. "And Gwniera?" He pulled her picture down and held it in his hand. "She was first on scene both times. She could have shot Dylan and put the gun inside the old house before she called us." He looked at Will earnestly. "She'd have had a good chance of seeing someone else, and she says she didn't. That makes her look guilty."

"I could see her killing Evan, but would she kill her own son?"

"She might. She was screaming about that 'bloody boy,' and that could easily have referred to Dylan. Maybe he was cheating on Lisa, and Gwniera knew about it. Maybe she saw him as being just like his father, who we know she disliked, and decided to take him out. She endured Evan all those years, but maybe thinking that Dylan was following in his footsteps was the final straw."

"She could have had that gun if Evan inherited it. She shoots; she'd know how to fire it. She was there both times, near to the crime scene." Will set his empty glass on the table. "Could she have dug that cairn?" He looked at Bronwyn.

"She spent a lot of time out in the woods riding," Bronwyn said slowly. "She may have worked at it for quite some time. No one would have noticed."

Mehta dropped her picture onto the pile atop Terrwyn's. "The only negative I can see for her is that Conway would have known that, if he didn't inherit that gun, Evan did. He could have said."

"Unless he was reluctant to point the finger at Gwniera. She kept in touch with that side of the family, befriended Mabyn after they married. Maybe he realized that she did it at least partially to benefit him and his kids."

"You're right," Mehta agreed. "She stays." He looked at the wall where only the two victims' pictures and those of Jenna and Awstin remained. "I don't think Jenna killed Evan and Dylan, but what about Awstin?"

"The abandoned, illegitimate child who resented both his father and his estranged brother? Why do it now, when he and Evan had finally formed a relationship?"

"Maybe he finally saw Evan for who he really was," Mehta speculated. "Maybe he'd built up a picture of a man who was larger than life. He said his mother had never criticized his father. Then, when he got to know him, he realized that his father was all flash and no substance, that he'd never wanted to know Awstin, that he'd abandoned Jenna through all those years of affairs with other women."

"And he saw Dylan as being the same, with his tendency to throw money around," Will agreed. "Evan had left him the gun, a family heirloom, and maybe he saw it as divine retribution to kill them with it. A sort of symbolic act, on his part."

"Awstin is a smart kid. We know that. He wouldn't have killed them for the money, but he may have done it because of what they represented. I don't think we can count him out. He had no good alibi either time."

"But if Gwniera saw him that day?"

"Maybe she mistook him for Terrwyn. Or maybe she thought he wasn't to blame for his anger. Maybe she saw it as right for Evan to be killed by the product of his own philandering. There could be all sorts of reasons why she'd lie about it." Mehta dropped Awstin's picture onto the pile of active suspects.

Will looked at the piles on the table. "So, it's one of those three," he concluded, "Gwniera, Terrwyn, or Awstin. But we have no evidence to point to which one." He tried not to glance at Bronwyn. He knew she'd be feeling guilty at not having gotten the right clue this time. "Which one do you favor?" He addressed his question at Mehta.

But Mehta shook his head. "It'd just be a guess at this point, a gut feeling that may well be wrong. I won't say."

They stayed the night in Llangynog, Will cherishing his last night with Bronwyn before their wedding. They sat up late, talking in the conservatory, and then they went outside to look at the stars while Daisy romped in the garden. He held her hand, content just to have her at his side.

"Do you know the word, 'hiraeth'?" he asked suddenly, thinking of the conversation with the new detective, Rufus Pew. "It's a Welsh word."

"Where did you hear it?" she answered, turning to look at him. "I do know it, but it's a hard concept to explain to non-Welsh people. There's no real English equivalent for it. Do you know what it means?"

"I think it describes what holds you to this place," he said, "why you want to stay here. It means a longing for a place, not like homesickness, but a reflection of how it's a part of your very soul. It means a belonging, how you'd leave part of yourself behind and never get it back if you were to leave."

"Wow," she breathed, "you've been thinking that one out, haven't you?"

"The new detective, Pew, mentioned it, and I thought then that it described how you feel about Llangynog, and about Pennant Melangell. I think I understand now why you couldn't just follow me to Caernarfon and get a job there."

She was quiet, holding his hand. He wondered if he'd gotten it right. Finally, she snuggled up closer to him and said, "Let's go in, Will."

"You didn't say. Is it 'hiraeth' keeping you here?" He couldn't help asking. He needed to understand, to know that it wasn't that she didn't love him enough, but something more elemental that explained her determination to stay in this isolated little village.

"I'd never thought about it," she said softly, "but yes, that word describes what I feel perfectly. I wouldn't be complete anywhere else; it would change who I am." She met his eyes. "But I wouldn't feel complete without you either, now, so thank you for not making me choose, for all you've done to make *us* work. I do love you, so much it amazes me."

He nodded. "I love you, too, sweetheart." He knew it was true.

Inside, the peace of that moment was disrupted again when he saw that he'd had another missed call from his mother. He hoped she'd had a change of heart, that she'd called to apologize and to let him know that she'd take care of getting Lark to the wedding. If not, he'd try to deal with it somehow or other. He'd have to try to appease her, or she'd threaten him again with sending Lark to George in Canada.

He let Bronwyn go to bed without him before calling her back. It was late, but if that inconvenienced her, so be it. He let it ring until it went to voicemail, and then, with some relief, he left a message saying he'd call her back in the morning.

He went into the bedroom and pushed Daisy off the bed. "We don't need you here right now," he told her, and then he sat down, caressing Bronwyn's hair off her cheek. "I'll just be a minute," he whispered. He let his hand linger for a moment longer, and then he got up and went to brush his teeth. The next time they slept in that bed, they'd be husband and wife. He pushed the thought away.

Afterwards, he lay in the bed and thought about the case. He was reluctant to report back to Bowers without a conclusion. Had he done something wrong, ignored some procedure or overlooked a bit of evidence? He didn't think so, but he still had the nagging thought that, somehow, he'd failed. He couldn't let his liking for the villagers cloud his investigations, or he'd be back in Caernarfon full-time before he could blink.

He and Mehta arrived in Caernarfon well before noon, driving separately but meeting up at the station after they'd both taken some time to stop at their homes first. Will looked around the flat, trying to see it through Maddock's eyes. He'd invited Maddock to his stag party, and Mehta, too. Edward was probably already in town, ready to fulfill his duties as best man. He guessed that Maddock had accepted the invitation just to keep an eye on him, but that was okay; he didn't plan to overdo it anyway. He'd actually prefer to be at his best on his wedding day, for Bronwyn, not to impress his parents or anyone else.

He took a minute to phone his mother, having dreaded the conversation during the drive that morning and now eager to get it over with so he could think about other things. He wanted to call when he was alone, and not in the car, in case she inspired another tantrum. He had a little time before his friends arrived.

"William," she said when she answered. "It took you long enough to call me back. I suppose you're working again."

"I'm always working, mother, unless I'm spending time with my bride-to-be. I do have a life of my own. And we just talked, remember?" He regretted his words as soon as he spoke them.

"Yes, well, we didn't solve anything, did we? It's a problem, isn't it? I don't know how you think you can parent a child with the schedule you keep. It isn't fair to Bronwyn, you know, to push it all off on her, or to me, when you expect me to step up every time you're busy."

He didn't respond to her goading. It'd do no good. "What did you need now? I told you I'd book you rooms so you can make the trip in small stages and not push Father too much."

"I need more help than that, William. I don't know how I'm expected to drive to Chepstow and get Lark, and then drive to the backwoods of Wales for the wedding. I don't even know how to get there."

He tried to put patience into his voice again, suppressing the urge to yell or, worse, swear at her. "You're making it harder than you need to, Mother. I told you that you can go on Friday night to get Lark and spend the night in Chepstow. From there, it's only a couple of hours' drive to Llangynog on Saturday. You'll be here in plenty of time for the wedding. I'll make your reservations in Welshpool for Saturday night, for the three of you, after the wedding. You'll have all day Sunday to drive back home." It seemed simple to him; yet to her, it'd never be simple enough.

There was silence for a minute. "You can't go get Lark yourself? Only, your father will have his routine upset with all these nights away, and that will make him difficult."

"I told you, I can't. I'm sorry. I just don't see how I can make it work. I have to be in Caernarfon on Friday, and then there's the rehearsal on Saturday morning before the wedding. When could I possibly get Lark? Please, try to manage this for me, just this one last time? I don't ask you for much, but this is my wedding, and I really need to have that time free."

"I'll just send her off to George, then, shall I?" she snapped, and the call ended as abruptly as her previous one had.

He tried to still the turmoil in his head and, this time, kept himself under enough control not to kick or punch anything. He knew she was unhappy, her life disrupted by his father's illness. When she was miserable, she wanted everyone else to be, as well. He'd have to try to figure something out, but he didn't have a clue how.

At the station, they checked in and re-created their murder wall on the whiteboard in one of the rooms before calling Bowers in to update him on the case.

Bowers frowned and asked questions, obviously not pleased that they hadn't made an arrest, but in the end, he agreed that, without further evidence, no one could be singled out and charged, a conclusion that surprised Will and filled him with relief. "It might well be someone you haven't even thought of," Bowers said.

Was he casting doubt on their investigation methods? "Sir, it was a family gun that killed those two men. We have to conclude that it was a family member who did it."

He nodded. "That sounds right," he conceded, "and you have it down to one of three, but without someone stepping up with information about the gun, that's as close as you're likely to get, isn't it? When is the memorial service for Dylan Bennett?"

"It's on Friday," Will told him, hiding crossed fingers in his lap. He knew they should attend, but that was the night of his stag party.

Bowers studied him, seeming to guess what he was thinking. He was a pretty decent boss, in the end. "We won't close the case just yet. You may still stumble across something that solves it for you." He gave Will a stern look. "I take it there was no pillow talk this time?"

Will glanced at Mehta, who was trying to keep a straight face. "No, sir, there wasn't."

"Maybe there should have been." Bowers' lips twisted in his half-smile. "You'll be on the rota for the next two days, and then you'll be on leave for your wedding. I hope you don't catch a big case meantime."

"No, sir, I hope that, as well."

Bowers addressed Mehta. "You're entitled to a couple of free days. Do you want them now, or are you saving them for the weekend?"

"If you don't mind, sir, I'd like to work the next two days and then have the weekend off, as well. I'm planning to go to the wedding." He didn't mention the stag night. No reason to.

"We all intend to go," Bowers told him, "but I suppose you're involved in the stag night, too, so in any case, you'd need the Friday night off."

"Yes, sir," Mehta agreed, grinning. "I hope there aren't any major cases before then."

"If there are, Ian and Beth can take them, with the two new people."

"They're doing well?" Will wanted to know.

Bowers gave him a look that told him asking was beyond his pay grade. "Well enough."

They emerged from the room into the large, open space where their desks mingled with those of all the other detectives, constables, tech workers, and everyone else except for Bowers, who had his own office.

"Your case is going unsolved, I hear," his sometime partner Beth commiserated as he brushed past her desk.

"For now," he mumbled, trying to avoid more detail. It wasn't something he was proud of. He was aware of more eyes on him, the new people checking him out as he walked to his desk. They probably marveled at how he got away with so much time out of the station and were wondering how they could manage something similar.

He ignored them. He sat at his desk and busied himself with paperwork, typing out transcripts of interviews, dates and times, and any details he thought pertinent to the case. He tried to concentrate on getting it done, pushing aside thoughts of murdering his own mother and of fleeing the wedding – it still wasn't too late. But he didn't really want to do either of those things, so he sat at his computer and typed.

Mid-afternoon brought a report from Quigley. "I've verified some things for you," he said. "Evie and Hugh Lewis were, as reported, working as photographers at a wedding during the time of Dylan Benentt's murder. Eriana Bennett was on an Aer Lingus flight to New York that departed Cardiff at two that afternoon. She returned on another flight the following day."

"Okay, thanks," Will said, tossing a smile at the tech. "Good work." He turned to Mehta as Quigley walked away. "They're off the list, for sure, now."

As he saw it, they were right to keep just the three suspects on their list: Gwniera Bennett, Awstin Thomas, or Terrwyn Bennett. He wondered what more they could do to pin down which of them had murdered the two men. Which did he favor? He mused about that for a few minutes. He liked them all personally and would hate to have to arrest any one of them.

When Will's mobile vibrated and rang as he was washing up after a microwave dinner, he picked it up, expecting Bronwyn or Edward. Instead, it was his brother, George, calling from Canada.

"This is a surprise," Will said. He hadn't expected George to attend the wedding, and a phone call was almost as unexpected. They hadn't talked in a couple of years. "What's up?"

"I couldn't let you get married without calling with my best wishes," George said.

Will thought he heard a hint of affection in George's voice. Could it be? "It's great to hear from you. How is everything over there?"

"We love it. We bought a nice house, the kids love their school, and we're flourishing here," George boasted. "Tell me about your bride. I have to say that I was surprised. I never figured you for the settling down type."

"I never figured me for the settling down type, either," Will laughed, "and then I met Bronwyn." He tried to capture her in his description, but as always, he knew he fell far short of explaining why he found her so alluring. "She makes me feel peaceful at the end of the day," he concluded, knowing it wasn't enough.

"You two need to come visit us," George said. "You know you're always welcome here."

"Thank you," Will responded, thinking that they just might take George up on that one day. He thought Bronwyn might like Canada, at least the more rugged parts of it. "We'd like that."

"Hey," George went on, his voice light, "we didn't send a wedding gift yet. We didn't know what you'd like, and I'm sure Mother provided you with lots of stuff you didn't want already. The last thing you need is more garbage to send off to charity. Do you have any suggestions?"

And suddenly, the thought that had nagged at the back of Will's mind came into focus. "Actually, there is something you could give me, and it wouldn't cost you a cent."

"What's that?"

"I want you to tell Mother than you won't take Lark off her hands."

Silence. "You don't want me to take her?"

"Bronwyn and I want her to live with us when she's not at school, and right now we're doing a trial run on that. Mother is making it as hard as she can on us. She constantly makes demands that we have to fulfill in order to stay on her good side. If we balk at something she asks, she threatens to send Lark off to you. I'm just tired of her games. I know she's struggling with Father, but we are totally willing to help with Lark, to take that stress away from her, if she'll just let us. I want full custody, and I'll never get that as long as you're her backup plan."

"Well," George laughed, "that's an easy enough gift to give. We were never wild about the idea of taking on another kid we'd never even met anyway. I'll just let Mother know we've changed our minds and, while I'm at it, I'll suggest that she let you have custody. I'll call her now, shall I? I'm sure she's had a trying day between Father's needs and her frustration with you and your wedding plans. I'll just hit her with more unwelcome news, and maybe she'll give in and let you have your way."

"God, George, you're awful, you know that?" Will was amused. George's relationship with their mother must be much the same as his. "But you don't know what you've just done for me. I don't know why I didn't think of it before. Thank you."

"I'm glad I could help. Listen, you have a great wedding day, and really, do come visit one of these days. I can't see us getting back there anytime soon, and we'd love to meet Bronwyn."

As he set his mobile back on the kitchen counter afterwards, Will felt like a giant weight had been lifted from him. Things were going his way, for sure. He had a career he loved, a beautiful wife-to-be, and now he had a way of ending his mother's mind games. Life couldn't get any better.

He waited for a half hour, timing it on his mobile. While he waited, he searched for lodgings he could book for his mother, calling and making the arrangements easily in the short time. *She could have done this*, he thought angrily. It wasn't hard. When the half hour had passed, he scrolled to her number and touched the call button before he could think it through further. It was time to stand up to her, and he wanted that confrontation over and done with, now that he had George's support.

It rang several times before she answered. "Hello, William. I hope you're calling with a plan for Friday."

"My plan hasn't changed," he informed her. "I'll text you the details of the lodgings I've booked for the three of you, and I'll see you all on Saturday."

"That's not acceptable." Frustration made her voice abrupt.

"Acceptable or not, that's the way it has to be. I have no way of picking Lark up from school on Friday, and you'll be driving right by. You are her grandmother. I won't ask you to help with her much from now on, but occasionally you will have to step up. You are her legal guardian."

"Don't try to manipulate me," she snapped.

Like you manipulated me these past two years? He let the silence stretch.

"I know you've talked to George. You convinced him that taking Lark was a bad idea." Her voice had turned bitter.

"I did no such thing. We did talk, and I told him that I really want custody of Lark, that I'm willing to take her on full-time. He agreed that it was in Lark's best interest for that to happen."

"Maybe we'll just skip the wedding. I think it's too difficult for us to attend."

"That's your choice." He had the upper hand, and he knew it. He couldn't give in now, or he'd be giving up any ground he'd gained. If she really did refuse to come, he'd figure something out for Lark, maybe beg Bronwyn's parents to go get her. They'd do it. He knew they would. "I'll call you on Friday morning, and you can let me know what your

327

decision is. I'll still be able to cancel the reservations I made you then."
He ended the call before she could say more.

He was sitting in his chair, drinking his Famous Grouse and trying
to listen to the voices outside his opened window when a knock on his
door interrupted his thoughts. He got to his feet and wandered over to
open it, finding Edward standing outside, grinning.

"Hey, mate, glad to find you home," Edward greeted him as he
slipped past Will into the flat. He looked around. "It smells better in
here than it did before."

"It took some doing to get the stink out," Will told him. "I'm glad
you came a couple of days early for the stag party. It's good to see you."

Edward shrugged. His curly blonde hair was tousled, and he was
wearing faded jeans with the hems in tatters. "Not much else on my
agenda these days."

Will knew that a second trial that summer had upheld Edward's one-
year suspension from the force. He'd made choices that last spring when
they'd gone rogue in order to catch Edward's superior officers'
involvement in a drugs importing business that had serious consequences
for his future in the force. "You do still intend to go back to the force
when your suspension's up?"

Edward flopped into Will's favorite chair. "The new bosses have
made it clear that they'll welcome me back when they can. Meanwhile,
I live off the dole."

"You do not." Will pulled a chair away from the small kitchen table
and sat near to Edward. "You had savings to draw on."

"That doesn't go as far as you'd like to think," Edward grumbled.
"I'm staying here with you for a few days."

Will's eyes drifted to the double bed tucked into a nook in the corner
of the room. "You're not sharing my bed."

Edward's eyes followed Will's. "I'll sleep on the floor, then. I don't
care as long as it's not outside on the curb under a pile of cardboard."

Will laughed. "You can use the lilo I keep here for when Lark
visits."

"That'll do." Edward looked around, and his eyes fastened on the
tiny kitchen. "I don't suppose you have anything to eat here?"

"I've eaten, a microwave meal. I have another one in the freezer, curry, I think. That okay?"

"Sounds great." Edward got up and went to the fridge, opening the freezer compartment. He pulled out the parcel, unboxed it, and put it in the microwave. "I'm assuming you have another glass of that." He looked pointedly at Will's whiskey.

"I do," Will told him, and he got up and poured a glass for Edward and a second one for himself. *If Mehta and Edward don't stop drinking with me, I'll be in AA before I know it.*

When they'd settled in again, Will told Edward about the Bennett case, going over it in as much detail as he could remember. He liked Mehta, and he did well with Beth, but Edward would always be his favorite partner of all time. He just somehow knew the right questions to ask.

"So, it's down to those three?" Edward asked when Will had told him everything he could remember. "The wife, Gwniera, and the two boys, Awstin and Terrwyn?"

"That's it."

"You know which one of them did it." Edward's look was direct.

Will hesitated, and then he nodded. "I'm ninety percent sure."

"But there's no evidence." It was a statement again, not a question. Will answered it anyway. "Not a shred."

"If you confronted him, he wouldn't confess?" Edward had said, 'him'; he knew who it was, too.

"I could say there were fingerprints on the gun, but he'd just agree because, after all, it belonged to his family so, of course, he'd have shot it. They'd all say that they'd forgotten they had it among all the others in their collection. That's the story so far, and I can't think why they wouldn't stick with it in the future. I could say he'd been seen in the area at the time of the murders, and he'd agree because, after all, that property adjoins his family's property and he'd already said he was there, at least on the afternoon of Dylan's murder. I could point out that he had a motive, but every one of them had one, so that puts us no further ahead.

No matter how I spin it, I can't pin it on him without some solid evidence, and that's in short supply."

"Do you really want to?" Edward's voice was soft. "He sounds like a good kid, and his motive was altruistic, not selfish. He'll never murder anyone again because, for one thing, he's gotten what he wanted, and for another, he'll mature and realize there are other ways to achieve his goals."

"It might mess with his head as time goes by," Will pointed out.

Edward shrugged. "Would he be able to live with it better later on if he did time for the murders? Or would that make it even worse?"

Will gave it some thought. "I think Terrwyn has enough of a conscience that he'll struggle with it all his life, but I also think that he'll try to ease his conscience by making that family farm more prosperous than it might have been with Evan or Dylan in charge. He'll be motivated to try harder, to work himself into an early grave over it. That's the way he'll atone for what he did."

"Then let it go unsolved," Edward suggested. "Quit looking for clues and just let it go."

"I can't," Will told him. "It's my first case to work from the eastern side of the district." He ducked his head, embarrassed. "My first case without Bowers directing it. I need to be successful, to prove that I can handle being in charge so that I can keep doing it." He cast Edward his most pitiful look. "I'm desperate to quit making that commute, and I really want to live in the cottage more full-time."

Edward grinned. "Then we either find some evidence, or we find a way to push him into a confession."

Chapter Twenty-six

Bronwyn woke to the sounds of someone in her kitchen and the smell of raspberries and something baking. She rolled over onto her back and closed her eyes. *It's my wedding day*, she told herself. Will had called late the night before, waking her up from sleep. His voice soft with affection and, she suspected, too much alcohol, he'd declared his undying love so vividly that she had to stifle giggles. He'd meant to amuse her, she knew, and he'd been a roaring success.

Daisy padded into the bedroom and leapt onto the bed, curling herself against Bronwyn's side with a sigh. She'd been outside; Bronwyn could feel moisture on her fur. She hoped the rain would clear by afternoon.

Despite feeling lazy, she wriggled to the other side of the bed and got up. She pulled on a dressing gown and wandered out into the kitchen, barefoot.

Margred was clattering bowls as she washed the dishes she'd used. "Good morning, beautiful bride," she said. "I hope I wasn't too loud." She turned from her task and ladled batter onto a cast iron pan.

"No, whatever you've made smells wonderful," Bronwyn told her. "You're spoiling me." Margred had spent the night, a last childhood fling before Bronwyn was married, too. They'd sat in the living room the night before in their pyjamas, giggling over memories and sharing dreams for the future like two teenagers rather than two women grown.

"I've made pancakes with raspberries and blueberries," Margred announced, "so you'll have the energy you'll need for the day ahead of you."

"Now that the day's arrived, I'm not nervous anymore," Bronwyn told her. "I think I'm actually looking forward to it."

"You should. It only happens once in a lifetime." Margred flipped the first pancakes, and then she set the spatula down and stirred a bowl of berries. "Go sit in the conservatory and relax. I'll bring our plates as soon as they're ready."

Bronwyn did as she was told. A vase of fall asters and mums had appeared on the little table as if by magic, and Bronwyn wondered where Margred had hidden them the night before. The table was set with lacy placemats that she also had never seen before, silverware set on linen napkins.

Margred appeared first with a small pitcher of orange juice, and then minutes later with their plates of pancakes, topped with icing sugar and berries. She sat across from Bronwyn, obviously proud of her efforts.

"It's beautiful," Bronwyn told her as she picked up her fork. "I'm so happy right now."

"I hope you enjoy it." Margred picked up her own fork and tried a mouthful of pancake. "Mmmm. I think I got it right."

"It's perfect," Bronwyn assured her, "a perfect morning."

"Just so you know, I'm going to have to dash over to Mum's in a few minutes and rescue her." Margred's eyebrows lifted and she sighed. "Much as I've enjoyed re-living our childhood, I'm sure Mum is ready for a break from Cara. She can be a handful, and she's not used to my being gone overnight. I'll have to make sure she's fed and bathed and dressed, and Michael is useless that way. I'll be to St. Melangell's for the rehearsal by eleven, if that's okay."

"It'll be great. Afterward, Mum and Mai will be excited to get busy. We'll be going to my parents' place to get ready, and Will has the cottage with Edward and probably Jay. I wish Lark could be here with us ladies, but she'll be coming later with Will's parents. I hate for her to miss out on the fun." Will had told her about the confrontation with his mother. In the end, she'd given in to *his* demands. He was triumphant. The tables had turned, thanks to the conspiracy he'd managed to arrange with George. She suspected the brothers' relationship would grow stronger as a result of them tackling their mother as a united front.

"Have you heard from Will this morning?"

"Not yet. I suspect he's still sleeping off the stag party. He'll call later." She didn't want Margred to know, but she was glad that she'd have some time to herself before things got busy. She needed to be alone for a bit, to think about the day and wander in nature to settle her nerves. If she was honest, she also wanted to give Pysgotwr or the Twlwyth Teg the chance to show up, perhaps to acknowledge her marriage or, even, to give her a clue for Will's case. Better late than never. If they had nothing for her, the case would go unsolved, and she knew that Will didn't want that, not with it being the first case he'd tackled from Llangynog.

Once Margred had left, she walked with Daisy further up the lane from the cottage and onto the footpath that led to Pennant Melangell. The drizzle of the night before had disappeared, and the sun tried to push through the clouds that remained, a bright spot behind a mist of gray. The ground was damp, puddles abundant both on the roadway and on the trail, but she side-stepped around them, while Daisy splashed through them, and neither of them minded.

She wouldn't have time to walk the entire path, but even a part of it would be the best bet for the solitude she sought that morning. She'd chosen to avoid going to her pool in the woods behind her parents' house and also the village itself, where she might run into someone who wanted to chat. She wanted to be alone with her thoughts on this, her wedding morning.

Daisy ran ahead of her, happy to be free to explore. A buzzard soared overhead as they climbed uphill through the old quarry workings, and she finally arrived at the stile that led past a cottage and toward the views she was seeking.

She paused to admire Cym Pennant and Craig Rhiwarth, and then she decided that she'd gone far enough. It was time to sit and relax and take in what the day had to offer. She looked around and found a

333

reasonably flat rock to perch on, low to the ground, but sufficient to keep most of the wet from soaking her jeans.

Once seated, she raised her face toward the sky and closed her eyes. She could feel the moistness of the air on her cheeks, with a coolness that hinted at fall's fast approach. She took a breath. The air smelled of wet grasses, along with the slightly metallic scent of wet rocks. Faintly, she could smell sheep from the pens further up the trail, but perhaps she imagined that scent since she knew they were there. She could hear Daisy rustling through the grass, trying to smell out a bird or mouse to chase. It was never quiet when Daisy was around. She smiled and, suddenly, the light behind her closed eyes brightened.

She opened her eyes to see the panorama opening up across the way. This morning a lingering mist draped itself over the mountains, obscuring the top slopes. Shadows moved across the hillsides as clouds drifted away and allowed the sun to stream through. Nearby, a flock of finches twittered in a thick fir tree. She could see none of them, but they made a loud ruckus in the quiet of the morning and she supposed they were fighting over rights to the food the fir would provide.

Her mobile vibrated and she picked it up just as it began to ring. *Will.* "Hello!" she called as she pushed the green button. "I wondered when you'd be up and about. Did you have fun last night?"

"I had a great time," he admitted. "Edward, Maddock, and Jay took me out on the town. We didn't get in until after midnight, too late to call you."

"You're on your way here?" He still had plenty of time to get there for the rehearsal, which they'd had to schedule on the morning of the wedding because of all the out-of-town participants.

"I'll be there soon, sweetheart. I'm actually going to Welshpool to rescue Lark from my parents. I'll bring her to you so she can help decorate the church. You're not at the cottage, are you?"

"No, I took Daisy out for a walk partway up the footpath. We didn't go far. I'm just sitting on a rock, looking out at the view at the moment."

"You haven't managed to see anything in a puddle of water, have you?" His voice was mocking. "Only, I'm nearly positive that I know who our murderer is, but I have no evidence to prove it."

"Even if I saw something, it might not give you what you need."

"It'd give me confirmation that I'm right, and that'd be enough for me to go on. I know I could push a confession from him, but I have to be sure. I don't want him to be confessing to something he didn't do, just because of how I went about it."

"Him? So not Gwniera? Jay agrees with you?"

"Yeah, and so does Edward. I presented the case to him on Wednesday night, and he was right with me on it."

"Are you going to tell me who it is?"

"I think you know, too."

She thought for a minute. She did know, or she thought she did. If Terrwyn had done it, he was no threat to her or her family in the future, but the same would be true for Awstin. "I don't like to accuse someone unless I know for sure," she said, once she'd thought it out. "If I see something, I'll tell you."

"I know." His voice had grown husky. "I love you, sweetheart. I'll see you in a little while."

Movement caught her eye as she ended the call, and she looked at the huge sky. Below her lay the Tanat Valley and in the far distance, the mountains, but in the sky almost on her eye level flew a peregrine falcon, floating on the updraft. It tilted toward the sun, and then it cruised back toward her, closer and closer, until it landed on the fir tree just behind her. She turned and craned her neck upwards to see it, perched on the very tip of the tree.

They came to her moments later, silent in the quiet of the morning. Daisy alerted, ears up, listening, and then she trotted back to Bronwyn and sat, leaning against Bronwyn's knee, staring at the rocks and grasses that surrounded Bronwyn's rocky perch.

They formed a circle around her, wizened little creatures of indeterminate age, and she wondered suddenly if the fairies made families, if they fell in love and committed to each other and had children. If so, how would it work? Some were miniature beings, while others were more substantial. Some had wings, others horns, and many of them wore circlets of flowers or leaves or even crowns made of tiny antlers. The flowers, leaves, nuts and seeds of the forest provided materials for their clothing. Some were indescribably beautiful, while

Janet Newton

others were so ugly as to be the stuff of nightmares. How could such disparate beings belong together as life partners?

Her thoughts faded as they circled her, the mushrooms that sprang up beneath their feet vivid in oranges, yellows, browns, and creams: the colours of autumn. She watched them, familiar and unthreatened, waiting for their message. She wondered if it would be one of congratulations or one of revelation.

"Not the ribibe," announced a taller creature as he paced the circle across from her.

"Ribibe, ribibe," she repeated under her breath. It was a strange word, completely unknown to her. *Ribibe, Ribibe.*

"Not the mamzer," called a second voice, melodious and almost songlike as it took its turn to stroll the circle across from her. She strained to see it. Tiny, with wings that gleamed metallic copper in the sunshine.

"Ribibe, mamzer, ribibe, mamzer," she muttered. *How can I spell those right, if I ever manage to remember them? Ribibe, mamzer.*

"Filial piety twice overcame inwil. It is done," pronounced a third voice, and she turned her head to the side where a gnome-like being walked between two beautiful, butterfly fairies, fluttering just above the ground. She caught her breath, watching them.

Usually, they would be done after three messages and disappear as quickly as they'd appeared, but this time they continued to circle her, the mushrooms growing thick where their feet trod the ground.

She watched them, suspicious, holding onto Daisy. She wished they would hurry before she forgot their words. *Ribibe, mamzer, inwil.*

"The singlewoman weds before eventide," intoned a deep voice, but she didn't have a chance to see which creature it belonged to.

"Efenblissung!" It was a chorus of voices, some rasping, some melodious, some squeaking, some musical, all blending into one. Then, "once, twice, thrice," they called together, and this time they did disappear.

She pulled her mobile out and typed the words as fast as she could manage, spelling them as best she could. *Ribibe, mamzer, inwil, filial*

336

piety. She didn't need to type out the final message. It was obvious that she was the singlewoman who would be wed before eventide, and the way they had shouted "Efenblissung" made it obvious that they were giving her either their blessing or their congratulations. Either way, she'd take it.

She turned so that her mobile was in shadow where she could see the screen better. There was no time to go to the centre to use her computer, so she'd have to look up the words on her phone. Hopefully, Will would never look at her searches. Visions she could claim came from the pool of water, and sometimes they did. But words? She had no good way to explain them to him.

"Ribibe," she mumbled the word as she typed it in the search box once she'd found a dictionary of Old English. She spelled it as it sounded, and it came up. "A worn old woman, once youthful and attractive." That would be Gwniera, then. The fairie had said, "Not the ribibe," so Gwniera wasn't the murderer. She paused, reflecting. She wouldn't have blamed Gwniera for wanting rid of Evan. Perhaps she hadn't fired the fatal shot, but Bronwyn would bet that she'd been almost grateful to whoever had. There was little chance, though, that she would have killed Dylan, her own son, no matter what he'd done to possibly disappoint her. She'd never thought Gwniera guilty, but it was good to have confirmation to settle the last, tiny doubt. If it was confirmation. She reflected on it again and couldn't see any way she'd gotten it wrong.

She scrolled back to the search box and typed, "mamzer." Again, she spelled it as it sounded, and it came up immediately. "Bastard." It was so easy, once they gave her the words, wasn't it? "Not the mamzer" meant, "Not Awstin Thomas." She knew that Will and Jay had believed Awstin when he said he was happy that he'd gotten to spend time with Evan. He'd never gotten to meet Dylan, though he'd wanted to. Maybe now, he could meet Merry and have a relationship with his sister, the last of the Bennetts related to him. She was glad he hadn't killed his father, not when he'd just started knowing him.

That left only one suspect.

"Filial piety" gave her the definition of "loyalty and love a child feels for his parent." She already knew "inwil," from a previous case. It meant "conscience." Terrwyn's love for his dad was stronger than his conscience, then. It must have been hard for him, watching his uncle flaunt his wealth while his own dad struggled, through no fault of his own. It had obviously eaten at him until he felt compelled to do something to change the circumstances. What had Lloyd been thinking when he'd willed all of his own land to one son, instead of dividing it between them? Yes, there was Dylan, a son to carry on farming after, a way to keep the land in the family. If Lloyd had lived long enough to see Terrwyn born, would he have changed his will? They'd never know. It made her sad.

She thought about calling Will back. Her mobile signal was strong there on the open hillside. If she did, would he feel obligated to race off and arrest Terrwyn on their wedding day, despite the lack of evidence? She knew the answer to that question.

She slid off the rock and called to Daisy, who was confused when they turned back toward home rather than continue on the footpath.

Chapter Twenty-seven

Will buzzed into the car park beside the church and threw the door open. He was only a few minutes late, not bad considering that he'd had to drive all the way from Caernarfon to Welshpool, with a stop in Llangynog to drop Edward off, and then back to Pennant Melangell. A wave of gratitude swept through him. Maddock's presence at his stag night had quelled any impulse he might have felt to celebrate harder so at least he'd avoided the dreaded wedding day hangover that many men suffered.

Lark slipped out of the passenger seat and skipped ahead of him toward the church. "Hey," he called out. "Come get your dress. I'm not going to fetch and carry for you today."

She turned back, grinning. "I could get it later."

"Nope," he smiled back, "I don't want to take a chance on forgetting it. Grab it now, please. I've got too much on my mind today to think of your obligations, too." He hadn't planned to see Lark until just before the ceremony, but celebrating with his friends the night before had put him in a generous mood so he'd called his mother after the first couple rounds of drinks and told her he'd meet her in Welshpool the next morning to take Lark off her hands. She'd sounded both harried and grateful, a mood which appeared to carry over to that morning when he showed up at the B&B and she'd actually thanked him with what sounded like a truly sincere tone in her voice.

He handed Lark the dress bag and followed her through the lych gate and into the church.

Bronwyn had been watching the door, her face lighting when she saw him enter. She held out her arms for Lark, but even as she hugged her, her smile focused on him.

He walked up the aisle to where the group was gathered, conscious of the eyes on him. *That's what I get for being late*, he chided himself. Edward had made his way to the church on his own, and the Reverend Wicklyff looked relieved, as if he'd feared that Will's tardiness meant he wasn't going to show up at all.

He hugged Bronwyn, giving her a quick kiss. He wasn't sure what custom allowed. He knew he wasn't meant to see her on their wedding day until the ceremony, but needs must; they had no other option for when they could do a rehearsal.

Everyone seemed in a jolly mood, laughing and teasing each other as they walked through the practice ceremony. Everyone but Bronwyn. He watched her go through the motions, but she seemed preoccupied to him, as if something was weighing on her mind. She smiled and followed the reverend's directions happily enough, but somehow it all looked perfunctory, as if her thoughts were elsewhere. Was it last-minute wedding jitters, or something else?

Watching her, thinking about it, his suspicions focused. *She knows,* he thought. *She's seen who it is.* Excitement fought with hesitancy as his mind raced. If she told him, would he have time to interview Terrwyn before the wedding?

He wanted this arrest. He wanted it badly and, if he was sure of his suspect, he knew how to make a confession happen, even without solid evidence. Sure, Jay could handle it on his own if he had to. There was no question of that. But he didn't want to leave it to Jay. This solve would support Bowers' impulse to let him work from Llangynog; he knew it would. There was no question. He had to get it done, either before the wedding or after, and he didn't want to interrupt their wedding night with work. He knew what he had to do.

"It's at this point that I'll say, 'You may kiss the bride,'" Reverend Wicklyff informed them when they'd finished.

Will bent to kiss Bronwyn, whispering into the kiss, "Terrwyn or Awstin?"

She pulled away and looked up at him, a question curving her lips. Then she reached up and pulled him down to whisper in his ear. "It was Terrwyn."

The reverend was watching them, amusement tugging his mouth into a wry smile. "You two can save that for later," he suggested, to the open laughter of their small audience.

Will glanced around. He wanted to get Bronwyn alone, to talk to her before he raced off to make the arrest, and the sooner that happened, the better. But there was her matron of honor, Margred, pulling at her arm and teasing her and Edward slinging his arm around Will's shoulders; everyone was lingering, in no hurry to rush away.

"I know I'm not supposed to see my bride until the ceremony," he announced, "but I'd really love a moment alone with her, here in the church, before we all scatter off to do what needs doing."

They all laughed and Edward had a slightly off-colour remark to cast his way, but they all wandered down the aisle toward the back of the church, leaving him standing at the altar with Bronwyn.

He took her hand and steered her toward the front pew, sitting down beside her. "You saw him? You're positive it was him?"

She nodded, silent. He didn't miss the apprehensive look on her face.

"I'll be as fast as I can," he promised her.

"Don't do it, Will," she protested. "Not now."

"When would you like me to do it? After the ceremony, on our wedding night? Or tomorrow, when we should be heading off on our honeymoon?" He felt an unreasonable frustration with her. Now was not the time for her to hold him back, not when Bowers might let him work from the cottage if he proved he could handle it.

Tears glistened in her eyes. "It'll ruin that family, Will. Can't you let it go this time? He's not going to kill anyone else."

He shook his head and glanced around. The others had gone outside. There was no one to observe their discussion. "That family is already ruined, love. Conway knows that gun was given to him. Mabyn knows it, too. Since neither of them used it, they have to know it was Terrwyn who did. Carys probably knows, too, and I'm sure Gwniera saw Terrwyn when she went to find Dylan. He was the 'bloody boy' she was

341

screaming about." He reached out with his thumb to catch a tear streaking down Bronwyn's cheek. "They are good people, sweetheart. They wouldn't be able to live with the guilt." He sighed. "I need to do it now, love. It'd be irresponsible to ignore what I know. God forbid, but what if someone else died because I'd put my wedding before my responsibilities?"

"You don't have any evidence," she whispered desperately.

"I don't need it if I can get a confession."

"Why would he confess now? He hasn't before."

"Because of his motive," Will told her. "I can use his motive against him, and he'll say whatever he needs to. I didn't want to do it before, just in case he was innocent. Once I make it clear to him that it's his parents who'll suffer if he stays silent about it now, he'll tell me everything. You know that, too. I just had to be certain before I pushed him into it. Now, I am, thanks to you." She probably wished now she'd not told him.

"Jay?" she blurted then. "Tell him you know it's Terrwyn and let him make the arrest."

"Sweetheart," he murmured, trying to organize his thoughts. He took a breath. "I'll just take him to Llanfyllin and question him there. It won't take me long to get him talking. After that, I'll leave it to Jay to get him to Caernarfon and to start the paperwork." He looked down at her and took her hand in his. "I need this arrest, love. Bowers needs to know that I can handle the cases that come up here so he'll let me work from home. I promise I'll be back in time. It shouldn't take long."

She nibbled at her bottom lip and then squeezed her eyes shut tight. "I'll stall them if I need to."

"You shouldn't need to stall for long. If I go now, my part in this case will all be over before the ceremony. I'll have no more obligations to fulfill for the next couple of weeks, and we'll be free to enjoy ourselves with nothing else to worry about. Okay?" He peered at her.

She nodded. "I wish it had turned out differently, is all."

"I know. I feel the same way. But Terrwyn made choices that have consequences, whether we like it or not. I can't just look the other way, knowing he killed two men."

She squeezed his hand. "Your job is hard sometimes."

"That, it is," he agreed. "It'll be faster if I take the Land Rover. That way, I can arrest him and be on the road to Llanfyllin without having to wait for backup."

"Lark and I can manage without it." She stood up and pulled her key from her pocket, handing it to him. Her eyes were red, but the tears had stopped. The others would wonder what had caused her distress. He hadn't wanted to give her anything but happiness on her wedding day, and he didn't know how he'd ever make that up to her.

Worried about her, but relieved to have that discussion behind him, he walked with her up the aisle and out the church door, emerging into the sunlit graveyard. Edward gave him a speculative look, which he answered with a subtle nod.

He turned to Bronwyn. "You ladies have fun getting everything ready. I'll see you this afternoon." He held her gaze until she relaxed, and then he strode away.

Edward caught him at the car. "I need a ride," he told Will. "And an explanation."

Will turned the key and slammed the car into gear, backing out of his parking space fast. "It's Terrwyn," he said. "I'm dropping you at the cottage, and then I'm off to make an arrest."

"I could be backup," Edward offered.

"No, you couldn't," Will retorted. "You're suspended, remember? I need to do everything by the book. The last thing I need is some breach of protocol to mess things up when this goes to trial."

"She's sure?"

"Yes, she's sure." He didn't know if Edward believed in Bronwyn's visions, but he'd never found her to be wrong. He pulled over into a lay-by and braked. "I've got to call Jay. He'll need to meet me at the station in Llanfyllin."

He waited at the intersection where the little B4391 met the farm lane that led to the Bennetts' farms. He'd called for backup, and as it happened, the local constable who lived in Llangynog, Lew Griffiths, had been lounging at home when the call came and offered to come to Will's aid on his day off. Griffiths was proving to be useful, Will thought, and his being local gave Will a better understanding of why Bowers wanted a detective in the eastern part of the district. Griffiths arrived within a few minutes, wearing his uniform, and Will filled him in on their mission as they sat with windows rolled down on their vehicles. They'd need to drive separately if Will were to accomplish what he intended to do.

Griffiths followed him up the rough lane, both vehicles jolting slowly over ruts in the road. They turned into the driveway that led to Conway's farmhouse and parked one in front of the other. Will thought it must be obvious to Conway and Mabyn what they'd come for.

Will stepped out of the Land Rover. It still featured some dents from the beating it had taken in the spring; they had never followed up on getting it repaired beyond replacing the windscreen and the driver's door, both of which were damaged too badly to ignore. He shook his head. He hadn't lived up to his responsibilities very well. He needed to do better.

Other vehicles were parked nearer the house, but Terrwyn's motorbike wasn't among them. That might be a complication, but it could be handled. Will steeled himself for what was to come and walked up to the front door, Griffiths at his side. He knocked.

Mabyn opened the door, looked at them, and swayed on her feet.

Will stepped up and took her arm. "Where's Conway?" he asked, steadying her.

"Just out in the barn," she mumbled, and then she looked up at him defiantly. "Why are you here again? Are you harassing us? Just because Conway and Evan didn't get along, it doesn't mean we had anything to do with his death. Or with Dylan's, either."

Will steeled himself. "Mabyn Bennett, I'm arresting you on suspicion of aiding in the death of Dylan Bennett and as an accessory after the fact in the death of Evan Bennett," he told her, ignoring the terrified tears that streamed from her eyes.

He nodded at Griffiths, who reached out to turn Mabyn away from them and pulled her arms back to cuff her wrists. "You don't have to say anything, but it may harm your defense if you do not mention when questioned something you rely on in court. Anything you do say may be given in evidence." He turned her gently back to face them when he finished, a sympathetic look on his face. "I'm sorry, Mabyn."

She looked as if she wanted to scream at him, but she clamped her mouth shut tight and stood silently, waiting.

Will nodded toward the cars. "Let's put her in your Cherokee and go find Conway."

"Wait!" she mumbled. "Just what is it you think we did?"

But Will shook his head. "You'll find out soon enough," he told her.

He waited for Griffiths to accomplish his task, and then the two of them started around the house. They'd just rounded the corner of it when they saw Conway come out of the barn.

He waved at them, and Will's heart sank. Why did he have to be so friendly? Still, he knew his son was a murderer, and he had to also know that they couldn't ignore that fact.

The concern on his face contradicted his friendly wave as he got nearer. "Where's Mabyn?" he demanded, his face contorted with fear. "I heard you drive up. I had to finish up what I was doing."

"She's been arrested," Will informed him.

"She didn't kill anyone," Conway said, his voice tight with control.

"Well, one of you did it," Will insisted. "I have the evidence now." He didn't elaborate. Let the man think his wife had been arrested for murder, not just as an accessory.

"It wasn't Maybn." Conway's eyes flickered as he tried to find a way around it. After a moment that was agonizing to watch, he surrendered, his face caving into resignation. "It was me. I did it."

Will waited, watching him squirm.

"Mabyn had nothing to do with it," Conway insisted after a moment. "She didn't even know I had that gun. It was all me. I did it alone, and no one knew but me."

Will took a breath. A tiny lie wouldn't hurt, would it? "We have a witness who says it was Terrwyn. You were out of town when Dylan was murdered, after all."

He watched Conway's face crumble. All the bluster seemed to have fled and, suddenly, he looked older than his fifty-something years. He'd might as well get it over with. "Conway Bennett, I am arresting you on

345

suspicion of being an accessory in the death of Dylan Bennett and of withholding crucial evidence and being an accessory after the fact in the death of Evan Bennett."

"No," Conway protested. "Who's the witness? She was wrong. It was me, not Terrwyn." His voice faded. "Not Terrwyn."

"Where is Terrwyn, Conway?" Will asked softly. "We will find him, and we need to question him. It's time to let it go and get it over with."

Conway struggled with the thought for a moment, and then he clamped his mouth shut tight and shook his head.

They put Conway in Griffiths' Cherokee with Mabyn, despite their reservations. They might try to flee, and they certainly would talk and try to plan a strategy, but they had no other options until reinforcements arrived from Llanfyllin.

They left them there and took the Land Rover further up the lane, keeping a watch on the fields for the motorbike. Terrwyn wouldn't be working at the shop on a Saturday, so he must be nearby. Will glanced at the time on his phone. Three hours until the wedding.

Where the overgrown driveway led to the old farmhouse that had belonged to Carys and her husband Lloyd, and to their parents before them, they found Terrwyn's motorbike leaning against the front stoop, forlorn against the weeds that had taken over the neglected flower beds that once brightened the house.

They walked up to the front door and Will knocked, shouting out, "Police, Terrwyn! Are you in there?"

A voice came from behind them. "No, I'm here, Inspector."

They turned in unison to see Terrwyn standing beside the motorbike, his hair disheveled and his eyes bright with defiance.

Will saw no reason to draw it out. "We're here to arrest you on suspicion of the murders of Evan Bennett and Dylan Bennett, Terrwyn."

He listened as Griffiths repeated the right to silence warning, turning so that his hands could be cuffed. "I didn't do it," he told them when the warning was finished. "You have no evidence against me."

"We'll see," Will told him. "We'll see."

They split up after that, driving the two vehicles to Llanfyllin, where their suspects were taken to separate interview rooms. The station was small, so in the end Mabyn was placed in the chief constable's office, the two men occupying the only two other available rooms.

Will left them sitting alone in the rooms. Mehta had texted to say he would be there shortly, and Will wanted to wait for him. While Lew Griffiths seemed reliable and capable, Will would rather have his partner beside him for the end, especially since he hoped that Mehta would take charge of getting Terrwyn to Caernarfon later that night and of writing up the reports that had to accompany him. As he waited for Mehta, he watched the clock ticking by the minutes. Everything seemed to take longer than it should. He did have hopes, after all was said and done, of making it to his own wedding on time. Bronwyn would give up on him for sure if he missed it entirely.

When Mehta arrived, Will took another few minutes to explain what he intended, and then the two of them walked into the interview room.

Terrwyn sat at a table, his hands now cuffed in front of him. He glared at them. "We've been through this, Inspectors. I don't have alibis for the times of either murder, but I didn't kill them. I've been totally open and honest about that. I know you have no evidence, or you'd have said. Just being near the scene of a crime doesn't make me guilty of it."

Mehta took a chair across from him, and Will joined him, facing Terrwyn. "I'm going to record this interview, Terrwyn." He flipped the switch and checked that the video was working. He nodded at Mehta.

Mehta made the introductions for the benefit of the recording.

"I want a solicitor," Terrwyn protested as Mehta finished. "This is harassment, at the least. Just because our families didn't get along, you think you can pin these murders on me, but you can't. You have no evidence and no witnesses." He stumbled on the last word.

Will nodded, not arguing. *Let him think we have a witness. He'll be worried about Gwniera.* "As it happens, we have a solicitor waiting for our call. We suspected you'd ask for one. Is that okay, or do you have a private solicitor you'd like instead?" Will held his breath, hoping. Every minute was precious, and he didn't have the time to wait for someone to arrive from Welshpool or Shrewsbury or somewhere else in the remote reaches of northeastern Wales.

"That's okay," Terrwyn agreed reluctantly. "If it's someone you called, I don't have to pay, right?" His eyes darted around the room. "After I give my statement, can I go home?"

"We'll see," Will said noncommittally. Terrwyn wouldn't be going anywhere if this went the way he hoped it would.

They waited in uncomfortable silence for the solicitor's arrival. Finally, Will got up and went into the hallway in search of a vending machine. He found a coffee machine in the break room instead, and filled three cups, suspecting they'd be awful. It wasn't what he wanted, but he'd been too restless to just sit there and wait.

Back in the interview room, he handed one cup to Mehta and offered one to Terrwyn, who shook his head. He sipped his own while he watched the hands on the old-fashioned clock on the wall slowly tick by.

There was a light tap at the door, and a man poked his head inside. "I hear I'm wanted?" he asked. The solicitor was an older man with thinning gray hair combed across a mostly-bare scalp. His gray suit was impeccable, the white shirt gleaming clean. He looked like a kindly grandfather, which he probably was.

Will nodded and waited for him to introduce himself to Terrwyn and to sit down beside him. He murmured quietly to him for a moment, and then he looked up expectantly.

"Let's get started, then," Will said. He started the recording again, stated the time, and addressed Terrwyn, "Where were you on the evening of Monday, August twenty-ninth?" He led Terrwyn through the same questions they'd asked him before, hoping for discrepancies, but noticing nothing blatant.

Terrwyn freely admitted to not having alibis for the times of either murder, repeating the same information he'd given to them in his earlier interviews. When Will pointed out that he'd been in the vicinity of both murders at the time they'd been committed, he lifted his chin defiantly. "Why would I tell you I was there if I was worried about it? I didn't think it was a problem."

When asked about his relationship with the two victims, he denied seeing either of them regularly, but again, he admitted to having had an

348

argument with Dylan Bennett over the inheritance money shortly before his death. "But it doesn't mean I killed him," Terrwyn pointed out. "Lots of people have arguments. I didn't like Dylan. But our disagreement didn't mean anything."

Time was passing too quickly, Will noted, keeping an eye on the clock. He wanted to get to the meat of it, to force the confession he knew would come, but failing to follow procedure wouldn't get him any accolades and might lead to a failed court case. He knew he'd have to conduct the interview carefully, step by step, before guiding Terrwyn to the final, inevitable, conclusion. "Why ride your bike up near where Evan died, Terrwyn? Why go there?"

"I like riding in the rough. I didn't know Dylan was going to be murdered, did I? I wouldn't have been there if I'd known what was going to happen."

"Were you aware that Dylan was up there, checking on the old house, that evening? Did you know that Evan was in the forested area the day he died, planning his estate?"

"How could I know that?"

"You live nearby. You'd hear their vehicles."

"They drove up and down all day long. I didn't notice where they were headed."

"And you were alone on both occasions, not working with your dad?" Will pushed him.

"He'd gone to take my grandmother home, so I was alone," Terrwyn pointed out.

"And when Evan was killed?"

Terrwyn shook his head. "We didn't work side by side every minute of every day. No one does. If I'd known they were going to be murdered, I'd have worked harder at alibis."

Will let that settle. "Tell me about your dad, Terrwyn. How did he feel about his brother inheriting the land from their parents?"

"You know how I felt about it," Terrwyn grumbled. "I already told you. My dad never complained, but it wasn't right that he had to struggle and my uncle didn't. My dad was the better man. If only one of them had to inherit it all, it should have been him."

"You dad did inherit a few things, though, didn't he?"

Terrwyn looked confused. "My uncle got the land and control of the inheritance money. He got them both. That was everything."

"But your grandmother divided up some of the family heirlooms between them, didn't she?" Will clarified. "She told us that she did."

"I guess so," Terrwyn conceded. "None of that was worth much, not like the farm and the investment money."

"One of those heirlooms was a gun, a Lee-Enfield Mark 4, wasn't it?"

Terrwyn stiffened. "Evan must have gotten that one. My dad told you, he didn't have it."

Will nodded. "But that was a lie, wasn't it, Terrwyn? We know that your dad did inherit that gun, the gun that was used to kill both your uncle and your cousin."

Terrwyn shook his head. "No, that's not true. If Gwniera said otherwise, then she lied about it, not my dad. Why aren't you looking harder at her? She had plenty of reasons to kill Evan."

Mehta leaned toward Will. "You need to go," he murmured. "I'll finish up here."

Will shook his head. He'd have liked to go more slowly, to lead Terrwyn through more incriminating questions, but it was nearly three o'clock. He was out of time. "As soon as we asked about it, your dad and your mum knew that you were the one who murdered Evan. I could see it in their body language. They both knew the gun had been in their collection, and they knew that, if neither of them had done it, then you had to have. So, they lied to protect you, Terrwyn. But they knew. They've known all along."

Terrwyn bit at his lip. "It's not true, I'm telling you. You have it wrong. It had to be Gwniera."

"I don't think so," Will insisted. "In fact, I'm sure of it. Your parents' lies make them accessories after the fact to Evan's murder, you know. They'll be guilty of obstruction, as well. And then, their lies kept us from arresting you before Dylan was shot. That makes them accessories in his murder, as well. They'll be charged and sent to prison. Is that what you want, Terrwyn? Was that your goal?"

Terrwyn blinked away tears. "I didn't shoot them, so my parents couldn't be accessories. It's not true."

Will suppressed a niggle of doubt. "When we confronted him, your dad confessed to the murders, Terrwyn. He told us that he did it."

Terrwyn leapt out of his chair, knocking it to the ground behind him. "My dad didn't kill them!"

"He confessed, Terrwyn. We have no choice but to charge him. He'll go to prison for the rest of his life."

"He was gone to Shrewsbury when Dylan was murdered," Terrwyn insisted desperately. "He couldn't have done it."

"But he confessed, nevertheless," Will pointed out. He waited then, letting the silence grow.

The solicitor reached out to take Terrwyn's arm and tried to urge him toward the chair again.

Terrwyn shook him off. "He loves me," he choked, and then he collapsed into the chair and started to sob. "My dad loves me."

"And you love him," Will told him softly. "That's why you murdered Evan and Dylan, because you love him so much, you'd do anything for him. It hurt to see him struggle through life, didn't it, Terrwyn?"

Terrwyn didn't respond. He slumped in the chair, stifling sobs that shook his shoulders.

Will glanced at the clock. If he left right then, he'd be at Pennant Melangell in time to dash upstairs to the loft at the back of the church and throw on his suit. "Your dad wouldn't confess to protect Gwniera, Terrwyn. He'd only be that desperate if he was protecting you. You know that."

"He didn't lie." His head jerked toward the solicitor as he realized what he'd said. "I meant, about the gun. He and my mum aren't guilty of anything."

"But you are, aren't you, Terrwyn?" Will struggled to keep his voice reasonable. *Come on*, he thought. *Give it up. I'm out of time.*

Terrwyn sat in silence, seemingly unaware of the tears that now streaked his face.

"You love your dad so much. He's a good man, a lot better man than your uncle was." Will forced himself to speak softly. Compassion would elicit more at this point than would the desperate force that wanted to explode from his mouth. "You'd hate to see him in prison, probably

351

for the rest of his life. And there's your mum, too. If we accept his confession, we'll have to charge her. She'd have been an accomplice if they figured out a way to murder Dylan while giving themselves the rock-solid alibi they had. Is that what you want, Terrwyn? Are you willing to let them pay for what you did?"

Terrwyn sniffled, and his solicitor handed him a wad of tissues. He looked at Will resentfully. "Why did you have to involve my parents? They wouldn't kill anyone. They're good people. The best people."

"Yes, they're good people. They never complained about the lack of money or about the hardships of farming land they struggled to pay the rents on. They created a good childhood for you and your sisters. They hoped that love would compensate you for the lack of material things, the things they couldn't afford to give you." He paused, thinking. "You returned their love, Terrwyn. You loved them more than life itself. And that's why you're going to confess to these murders. Because you love them, and you can't let them suffer for choices you made. You did it to make their lives easier, not harder. Am I right?" He held his breath. It was his last card, all he could put on the table.

Terrwyn drew a shaky breath, but didn't speak.

Will glanced at the clock again. If he finished this in the next five minutes, he'd only be a little late. Bronwyn wouldn't give up on him. God, he loved her so much.

Terrwyn noticed this time, and realization brought hope to his face. "You need to go now, don't you? If you don't leave now, you'll be late to the wedding."

Will was out of time. "Okay, Terrwyn, this is how I see it. One, your dad goes away for murder, probably for life, and your mum will go down as an accessory. You get off free, but you'll live your life knowing that your crimes took their freedom away. Two, you confess to the crime and we'll take your word that they didn't know about the gun. You'll go to prison for a long time, but probably not for life. Three, I keep investigating until I find something to prove what I know. You still go to prison, but your parents go, too, because they've helped you. When we take it to court, they'll be charged with perjury if they lie on the stand. So will your aunt Gwniera, because I know she saw you that day Dylan was killed. She'll be our witness, even if she doesn't want to tell us what she saw. We can get it out of her; you know we can." He paused, then leaned close to Terrwyn across the table. "Which do you choose? One, two, or three? There's no fourth choice."

Terrwyn stared at Will, and then he looked down at the table, at his hands. He hesitated. "I didn't kill them," he repeated stubbornly.

Will let out his breath in a huff. He hadn't realized he was holding it, waiting for what he hoped would be a confession. "You're right, Terrwyn. I do have to go. But my partner can stay here and keep talking with you all night if he needs to. One way or another, you'll have to make a choice. One, two, or three."

Terrwyn swallowed hard, glancing at Mehta.

Will pushed back from the table and stood up. "Out of time, Terrwyn," he growled. He looked up at the constables by the door. "Book them all and take them on to Caernarfon. We'll just hold them there until Terrwyn manages to make his choice known."

"You won't charge them as accessories? For...for obstructing?" Terrwyn cried out.

Will sat down again. "They knew the gun should have been in their collection."

"They didn't know I had it." Terrwyn lifted his chin. "If I did."

Will nodded. "Okay, we can go along with that, I guess."

Terrwyn eyed him, glancing at Mehta, and then his shoulders drooped and he lowered his eyes in surrender. "I did it, then. All alone, with no one's help."

Beside him, his solicitor stirred.

Terrwyn noticed. "No," he said, his voice stronger, "I can't let my parents take the fall for what I did. I shot Evan from behind the tree. I poked a hole in the quad's gas tank, and then I waited for him and I shot him. I'd already dug the hole to bury him in. I didn't think you'd find him so fast."

Will wanted to be out the door, but he had to finish what he'd started. The case had to be solid. "You'd obviously planned ahead. When did you decide to murder Evan?"

Terrwyn drew a shaky breath. "When he started talking about selling off the investments to build the housing estate. My parents were talking about it, how it'd be like throwing the money away, how there'd be nothing left." He looked up at Will. "Not that it was our money anyway, but Grandmother Carys was talking like she wanted to give my dad a share, after all, and she did have some control over that money."

"You thought she might do it after Evan was gone," Will suggested.

"Yeah, but when I tried to talk to Dylan about it, he wouldn't listen, and I knew it had all been for nothing. My dad would still be poor, and Dylan would have nice things that he didn't even have to work for." He took a breath. "It wasn't right."

"It wasn't right," Will agreed, "but neither was murdering two men, was it?" He waited, but Terrwyn seemed to have said his piece. "You're a good kid, Terrwyn. You just loved your family more than you should have."

His face crumpled into hopelessness. "You promise you won't charge my parents with anything?"

"It's not up to me to decide that, but I'll do my best to keep them out of it." They'd suffer anyway, knowing that their son had killed two men for them. "Why did you choose that gun to use?"

Terrwyn shrugged, fighting the tears. "I liked it. It was the one thing my dad inherited, so I thought it was the right one to use. Plus, there was ammo for it in the gun cabinet, and I'd fired it before, so I knew how to use it. I hoped they'd just think they'd misplaced it somewhere." His voice had grown shaky again. "I didn't want them to know I'd killed Evan."

Will stood up. "Thanks for this, Terrwyn. I've got to go now." He shot a grin at Mehta. "I've got a wedding to get to. My own," he added, when the solicitor reacted. "We'll be leaving you here, Terrwyn, and later tonight someone will drive you to Caernarfon to finish booking you."

"Not him?" Terrwyn wondered, looking at Mehta.

"No, he's coming with me to the wedding," Will said. "I'll make sure your parents are released before we leave the station."

"Thank you," Terrwyn said, relief suffusing his face.

"You'll have to write down your confession before you leave here," Will told him. "Details are important. Remember, you can't use something later during the trial that you don't say now."

"Okay." Terrwyn seemed subdued, almost relieved. Perpetrators often were, once they'd been caught and it was all over.

Chapter Twenty-eight

Bronwyn tried not to let it ruin her wedding day. Although she was determined not to resent Will's job and the times it took him away from her, today should be different, shouldn't it? Disappointment bit at her. Not only did she abhor the thought of what Terrwyn's arrest would do to neighbors she liked and respected, but she hated even more the idea that he'd put the job even before their wedding. *He could have let Jay make the arrest*, she thought, angry despite her resolve, *or if he really felt he had to prove something to Bowers, he could have waited a day or two to do it himself.*

Maddock and Edward stayed at the church after the rehearsal to help decorate it with the carload of flowers her parents had brought. Her mum and Margred directed them, with Lark skipping around the churchyard, happily playing with Griffyn and Maegan. Alwena was there, too, helping to carry the buckets of flowers and then standing back to watch, nodding in approval. She'd brought her little daughter with her, a pretty little girl with straight dark hair and startling blue eyes.

"I hope the flowers stay fresh enough," Bronwyn worried, watching Maddock on a ladder, putting an arch of flowers over the doorway.

"You'll look gorgeous coming through that door and into the church," Margred told her firmly. She'd gathered enough from the little Edward and Bronwyn had said to know that Will had rushed off to finish working a case, and that Bronwyn wasn't happy about it. "This is the perfect setting for you," she went on, "almost like Saint Melangell herself has returned."

Bronwyn looked at her and then laughed, despite her mood. "Saint Melangell came here to flee a wedding, not to have one," she pointed out.

"Well," Margred defended herself, "if she'd wanted a wedding, this is the place she'd have chosen for it."

"It's gorgeous," Alwena joined in. "You couldn't have a more beautiful place for a wedding."

It did look beautiful, Bronwyn told herself, looking around. The simple little Norman church with its friezes and flagstone floor reflected the peace and simplicity she sought in her own life, the life she wanted to create with Will, and the fall-colored flowers stood out brightly against the creamy stucco walls, giving it the exact, subtly festive, atmosphere she wanted for the day. She sighed. Will would make sure to be back in time. He wouldn't let her down on her wedding day.

She caught Maddock as he headed to his truck after they'd finished. "What?" he asked, turning back.

She walked to him and hugged him, hard. "Thank you for being the interfering big brother you are."

He laughed, hugging her back. "Then you realize now that you and Will would never had made it this far without my meddling?"

"We probably wouldn't have," she admitted. "You always wanted it to work for us, didn't you?"

He snorted. "Don't tell Will, but I saw some kind of potential in him right from the start. I just had to encourage it a little." He smiled at her. "I'm happy for you, Bron. He's a good man."

"Thank you," she said, "for everything." She tapped his arm with her hand. "You can leave us alone now, though. We can manage our own lives from here."

He laughed again, and she felt encouraged.

They dressed in the counselling centre, she and Margred and Lark, with her mum and Mai and Maegan helping. Her mum cast her worried glances when she thought Bronwyn wasn't looking, and she tried not to

357

let her concern show. Will hadn't returned yet, and time was getting short. He and Edward were to get ready upstairs in the loft at the back of the church. Soon, their guests would arrive, and it wasn't right that they'd have to mingle with them in their street clothes. She'd seen Edward take their suits into the church, but she hadn't seen Will's car come back, although she'd made excuses every few minutes to look out the window toward the car park.

"He'll be here soon," her mum said, coming up behind her.

She turned to look at her. "I know." She wished she was as sure of Will as she pretended to be.

"You look beautiful," her mum told her then. She looked a bit wistful. "I always dreamed of this day, of my daughter's wedding day."

"I'm so happy," Bronwyn said. And it would be true, if only Will got back soon.

Their guests began to arrive, cars pulling into the little car park one after another. She saw the reverend get out of his car and watched him stand in the churchyard near the lych gate, greeting people. She wondered if he knew that Will wasn't there yet and supposed that he did. Edward would consider it his responsibility to watch out for Will and to keep the reverend informed. Her co-worker Janice arrived, holding hands with her partner Catherine, and she saw Maddock walk up with Griffyn. Edward came back out of the church and stood with Maddock, letting him introduce him to the other guests. Will's co-workers arrived all together in a Ford Taurus: his boss Chief Superintendent Bowers, his partners Beth and Ian, and another younger man she didn't know but assumed to be the famous Quigley, the tech whiz who helped them along with their cases.

Mai and her mother left, both of them giving Bronwyn tight hugs before emerging from the counselling centre and joining the guests chatting in the churchyard. Her parents would stall things as long as they could, Bronwyn knew, thankful that neither of them had criticized Will for not being there on time.

She saw Will's parents arrive then, his mother Elizabeth and his father Charles. She thought she should go out and greet them in Will's absence, but she knew she couldn't, not in her wedding gown. She watched her mother and father approach them and knew they would do their best to make them welcome.

"He's still not here?" Margred asked from behind her.

"Not yet." Bronwyn strained to look up the lane. "He'll be here."

"Of course, he will," Margred assured her.

And he was. Fifteen minutes after the ceremony had been scheduled to begin, the little MGF raced up the lane and pulled into the space reserved for it in the car park. Will and Mehta scrambled out, Will glancing toward the counselling centre. He'd know she'd be watching out for him, even though he couldn't see her.

Relief made her legs weak.

They waited for the guests to go into the church. The morning's drizzle had settled into sunshine for the afternoon, brightening the churchyard and turning the gray stone of the church into silver. They'd have to walk the path through the ancient gravestones to get to the church door, and Bronwyn felt the tug of the past, of all the women who'd come there for sanctuary in the past thirteen hundred years. Their spirits gave her courage.

Her dad came for her a few minutes later. "Ready?" he asked, his eyes shining with love. He'd protected her, taught her, encouraged her through her childhood, she thought, and now he was giving her to Will in the belief that he would do the same. It must be poignant, a father giving his daughter away at her wedding. She hoped that her father saw in Will a man who he'd trust, through all life brought, to do the right things, the honorable things.

As she walked up the aisle behind Margred, she saw friends smiling and giving her little waves: Janice and Catherine, the two of them holding hands and no doubt thinking about whether they should make the same commitment; Daryn Reese and old Clarence Randall, volunteers at the centre she'd grown close to; Will's co-workers, come to see him married. She was glad his boss had seen fit to come despite his misgivings about the wisdom of their relationship early on. Will's parents sat in the front row, on the right side, his mother's stiff posture speaking of disapproval, although hopefully she'd not express it today.

On the other side, her own mum sat with Maddock and Mai. Most importantly, in the front of the church at the altar waited Will, wearing the formal suit she'd told him wasn't necessary, but looking great in it, nevertheless. His eyes shown with pride when he saw her, and he gave a little nod of encouragement. Edward stood beside him, his unruly curls and impish grin not diminished by his current lack of employment, and beside him waited Griffyn, looking down at the rings he'd draped on his own fingers until they were needed. Across from them, Margred and Lark smiled in their bridesmaid dresses, and Maegan hopped up and down, wearing the fairie wings she'd insisted on with her flower girl dress.

She reached the front of the church, and her dad unhooked the hand she had wrapped around his arm and kissed her on the cheek. "We will always love you, sweetheart," he murmured, and then she was standing there, facing Will, as the reverend began.

Will leaned close to her. "All right?" he whispered into her hair.

She put her arms around his neck and squeezed. 'Now, I am."

It was done in a flash, she thought later, the ceremony, their rush down the aisle as newlyweds, and then pictures in the churchyard and the sensory garden while the catering company set up the reception in the counselling centre. The clouds lingering from the morning drifted lazily across the sky while they turned this way and that to a background sound of Lark giggling with Maegan and Griffyn, their guests chattering amongst themselves, and one loud dove that kept calling from the peak of the church roof. No one seemed in a hurry to go inside, instead lingering in the garden to enjoy the early fall sunshine. Maddock disappeared for a time and then reappeared with Daisy in tow, only to disappear again, this time to do some mischief with Edward and Mehta.

Will's mother interrupted their photos, marching up as they posed in the shadow of the lych gate. She was holding her husband's arm, pulling him along behind her. "We'll have to leave now," she announced, her lips twisted in a frown. "Your father is restless, and I think I need to get him home, back to a familiar setting."

"But Lark…" Will started to say.

She interrupted him. "Lark has to come along with us, unless you want to drive her back to Chepstow tonight yourself."

"She's having fun," Will managed. "She's a bridesmaid. She'll want to stay for the reception."

She tossed a contemptuous look toward the counselling centre. "I doubt she'll miss much."

"What do you mean by that?" Bronwyn sputtered. She couldn't believe Elizabeth Cooper would be so rude as to denigrate their wedding venue to their faces.

Mrs. Cooper turned her gaze to Bronwyn. "I didn't mean to insult you," she said. "It's just hard to manage Charles when he's out of his usual element. I'm sure you understand."

This, on top of everything else that had happened that day, was a step too far. "I *don't* understand. I don't understand at all. I know Will's father is confused, but surely you could put a little more effort into helping him enjoy his son's wedding, if not for him, then for us." She looked at him. "He seems fine to me."

Will stepped forward. "Don't make a scene, Mother, please. Give us just another hour."

"If you'd been to your own wedding on time, I wouldn't need to give you another hour," she snapped back. "He's getting tired, and when he gets tired, he gets agitated."

Bronwyn reached out and put her hand on Mrs. Cooper's arm. Her parents would help out with Lark, or Maddock would. She could stay with Maegan and Griffyn tonight and one or the other of them would take her back to school the next day. "It's okay, Elizabeth." She kept her voice quiet, but wanted to sound strong. "You can leave if you need to. We'll take care of getting Lark back to school. It's no problem."

"You say that now, but knowing Wlliam, he'll have a case again by tomorrow."

"He's finished with the case he was working on, and he's on holiday now for two weeks. Really, Elizabeth, we're fine with Lark if you need to leave."

"Well," Mrs. Cooper huffed, "I suppose we can stay a little while longer, as it is a special occasion. You won't want a child interrupting your honeymoon."

"Thank you, Mother," Will mumbled, a smile tugging at his lips. He watched her lead his father toward the counselling centre and leaned close to kiss Bronwyn. "Well done, love. Well done. You handle her far better than I've ever done."

Twenty minutes later, the photographer had finished with the formal pictures. Bronwyn and Will walked hand-in-hand, wandering slowly toward the counselling centre, greeting their guests as they strolled past the small groups that had formed. The sensory garden bloomed with sunflowers, goldenrod, and fall asters whose bright purple contrasted with the golden yellow of the other flowers. The little fountain gurgled as a background to the quiet chatter. Bronwyn felt the day had gone beautifully.

Will's co-workers stood together, chatting and unaware. Will looked toward them and led Bronwyn their direction.

"The most beautiful of brides," Bowers pronounced as Will re-introduced them all to her. He was gazing at Bronwyn curiously, probably wondering how she got the tips that helped with Will's cases. As if reminded, he turned to shake Will's hand. "I hear you've made an arrest in your case. It's a triumphant day all-around, isn't it?"

Will slung his arm around Bronwyn's shoulders and pulled her closer. "Yes, sir. Everything came together in the end, the case and our wedding, all at once. Things were a bit tight this afternoon, but now it's done. I think we can relax and enjoy our honeymoon, after all."

Beth Holway stepped forward to offer her congratulations, admiring Bronwyn's dress and gesturing toward the old church. "What a beautiful wedding," she said, smiling at Bronwyn. "It's perfect for you." Her smile didn't quite reach her eyes, but she managed to sound sincere when she said it.

She'd always been a little possessive of Will, Bronwyn thought. Will had mentioned it, too. "I work here," Bronwyn told her, "so there wasn't really any other choice, when it came to it. But we like how simple it is here, how peaceful and personal."

"It's been a perfect day," Ian O'Flynn assured her.

Margred found her then and lured her away from Will and his co-workers. "It's time to throw your bouquet!"

She stood beneath the lych gate, hoping the bouquet would make its way to Janice. Fate decided otherwise, though, as happy shrieks alerted her even before she turned to see Lark waving the bouquet above her head while Margred's daughter Carys and Maegan danced around her.

"He confessed?" she asked as they drove away at last, aluminum cans rattling behind the car. Will ducked his head lower to see past the words painted on the windscreen. Their mischief-makers had obviously concluded that, if they decorated the side windows of the little MGF, Will would only put them down. He'd put window cleaner in the boot and would stop and clean the windscreen as soon as they were safely out of sight.

"He did."

"Why? He could have gotten away with it."

Will shook his head. "No, he couldn't have. Like I said, I used his motive against him. He loved his dad and wanted the best in life for him. That's why he killed them, Evan and Dylan. I knew that, if I threatened to arrest Terrwyn's dad, and his mother, too, that Terrwyn would break."

She sighed. "I suppose there was no choice, but I'm still sorry it ended that way."

"So am I," Will told her, "but Bowers is more than pleased with me, so at least some good came from it."

"When did you tell him?"

"I didn't have a chance. Everyone was already seated and waiting when I got to the church, so I just sneaked in the back. Edward had my suit waiting upstairs in the gift shop, thank goodness." He grinned. "Jay told Bowers about it while they were waiting for the ceremony to start."

"You think Gwniera knew it was Terrwyn?" she asked.

"I do. I think she saw him when Dylan was killed, coming out of the old farmhouse or walking across the field after. She decided to let it go."

"Accusing him wouldn't have brought Dylan back," Bronwyn pointed out. "Maybe she just decided that no one else needed to suffer."

"Because of the bloody money." Will pulled into a lay-by and stopped. "Her words, not mine."

"And now Conway will be able to buy the land from Lisa."

"Lisa wants to move into a city; I don't know which one. Gwniera intends to follow her, so that she can be near to her grandson."

"Gwniera will miss her horses." Bronwyn watched as Will sprayed the windscreen and started rubbing at the words with a wad of kitchen roll, smearing them.

"I think the horses were just a means to an end, more than anything." Will got a fresh sheet of kitchen roll and rubbed at the mess. "She used them as an excuse to refuse to leave Evan, and she used them as a way to get to where she could meet Mabyn in secret. That's all behind her now. I think she'll want to leave the bad memories behind and make a new life in a place where no one knows her past and pities her."

"Do you think Conway and Mabyn will stay and farm the family land?"

"There'll be no happy ending for them," Will said. "I don't know if they'll stay, knowing what Terrwyn did. The memories will haunt them, probably for the rest of their lives. They thought they'd lived their life well, creating a happy family. Look how it turned out."

"It'd be hard to start over at their age."

"We'll see." He threw the dirty kitchen roll into the boot and slammed it down.

"It's not right, the way it turned out, but I suppose it's not wrong, either. Terrwyn had to pay for what he did." Bronwyn caught a glimpse of black and white at the edge of the field, where it joined to some forestland. She looked away, fast. So Pysgotwr had attended her wedding, too. She smiled. "Do you have to go to Caernarfon now to write up your reports?"

"I'll get to it eventually. Jay can get it started." He pulled back onto the dirt roadway. "The case is the furthest thing from my mind right now, sweetheart. It's our wedding night. I don't want to think about murder anymore, not today."

"Something else on your mind, then?" she teased.

"Definitely," he answered, grinning.

364

What Lies Beneath the Cairn

Janet Newton

Printed in Great Britain
by Amazon